THE DJED

THE 2012 TRILOGY II

Published by:
P.T. William Publishing Company, Buckhannon, WV

www.PTWilliam.com

The Djed is a work of fiction. All names, characters, places and incidents either are the culmination of the author's imagination or are used fictitiously. Any resemblance to actual events, places or people, living or dead, is purely coincidental.

ISBN: 978-0-9825129-4-4
978-0-9825129-1-3 (Hardcover)

Text set in Times New Roman

This book is printed on acid-free paper.

Printed in the United States of America

FICTION BY PETER GALARNEAU JR.:

The Edge of Hell (1994, 2010)
The Worms Within Us (1994, 2010)
Blood Barters (1996, 2010)
Muldoon's Nursery (1997)

The Cubit: The 2012 Trilogy I (2008, 2009)
The Djed: The 2012 Trilogy II (2009, 2010)

In memory of
Arah Edgel Galarneau Cox Maloney

Part

One

666

1945

"This war—*Your War*—will cost this planet over seventy million lives!" Alax's voice stumbled over the words. He felt nervous but absolute. Another mortar blast crumbled brick thirty feet above them.

Eva spoke up, something she rarely did, but she was a newlywed and her husband was being wrongly accused. "What do you know? Your information is as much a lie as all of meine ehemann's generals. And see what they've done to him." She grabbed her husband's arm and gently massaged it.

The bunker, now full of billowing concrete dust, reminded Alax that time was running out. The dust pulsed dull crimson and was enlivened by the red light that beamed from a crate on which Eva's husband sat. Alax had never seen anyone touch his boss with such compassion. "He is not the one," Alax said to Eva. "Look at him. How can *that* last another sixty-seven years? He is premature. His life is premature. This war is premature."

Alax's dialect was slowly transforming from consolatory German-Slavic to one which Eva had never heard before. "Imposter!" she grumbled and raised the Walther P38 loaded with a single bullet that had been meant for her. "Who are you? What have you done to meine ehemann? What have you done to Deutsches Reich?"

The red light from the Cubit and the thickening concrete dust filled the bunker with a crimson iridescence that danced in the short distance between Alax and Eva. As more explosions ripped the ground above them and more dust rippled into the room, the curtain of wispy red became so thick that the occupants could barely see each other. Eva's gun wavered, the hand holding it, indecisive. She looked between her husband's legs at the glowing crate then at his face which was twisted in a frozen expression of despair. His eyes suddenly popped wide open and he glared at Alax. For some reason, he couldn't talk but Eva knew what he wanted her to do. Still, it wasn't until the red light began emanating from Alax's waist that Eva pulled the trigger.

Alax was too fast—even for a bullet. He'd unsheathed the dagger and was beside Eva before the curling red dust could identify his speed. "He cannot be allowed to live," he whispered in her ear as the locked, steel bunker door shook from the fists outside that beat against it. "WE cannot allow such Evil to exist. It was a mistake to believe otherwise."

The Cubit hummed quietly as Eva jammed the pistol into Alax's ribs and repeatedly pulled the trigger on empty rounds. Her husband moaned, stirred. Dust flew from the bunker door as German feet, fists and exclamations demanded entry. The star in the dagger's haft and the one at the top edge of the Cubit blazed with such intensity that the entire room floated in a wavy sea of crimson.

"I'm sorry for you, Eva," Alax said, still whispering as if consoling and apologizing and asking for forgiveness all at the same time. "Innocence is Evil's greatest victory." He smacked Eva in the back of the head with the haft of the dagger and she fell forward onto the floor, kicking up a red cloud of dust when she landed. When he looked up from her body, Alax flinched. Hitler was standing there, suddenly not so weak, suddenly not so vulnerable, suddenly determined that it was not his time to go, that another sixty-seven years of life was not only possible but was his destiny. He kicked Alax in the throat with the point of his boot, then turned to the Cubit which now opened. Alax flailed backward, red dust clouds encircling his unbalanced withdrawal.

The top of the Cubit lifted on its hingeless edge and deepened the crimson that enveloped the bunker. The bunker's door dented inward as heavy objects assaulted it. Hitler planted one leg into the open Cubit. "I'll be back," he said, the opening sucking at his appendage.

Alax raced forward, aimed the dagger's point, and jammed it into the back of Hitler's neck.

"NOOO!" the cubited fuehrer screamed, clutching at the hole in the base of his skull. "I am da one! I am da…"

The Cubit slammed shut, amputating Hitler's right leg below the knee before the rest of his body dissolved to bone. The bunker door bent further inward. Another explosion rocked the room from above. Alax sat on the Cubit, and gazed up at the shaking, dust swirls above him.

"Take us back, great Spirit," he said to the ceiling. "We are its keeper and none shall gaze eyes upon it until the time of reckoning, until the Raising of the Djed. Take us back and forgive me for my transgressions."

Alax lifted the Creation Dagger above his head then thrust it downward in a swooping arc that buried the blade into the star in the Cubit.

One of Hitler's generals broke into the bunker just as the last visage of Alax and the Cubit disappeared.

Part

Two

"That's great,
it starts with
an earthquake,
birds and snakes…"
—R.E.M.

Sedona, Arizona, is a story about rocks, great monoliths jutting from ancient seabeds, ragged-edged spires shaped by the hand of God, majestic and magical to the mortals who have gazed upon them, who have felt the red rock vibrations resonate within their very souls.

Sedona is also a story about hope and heaven and those who would take advantage of such naiveté. Leylines and vortices, shamans and sages, crystals and dreamcatchers and incantations—all waiting for those who believe, want to believe or, like Billy Jo Presser and Marcy Ruminski, have come in search of the truth.

But revelations of truth are rare: sometimes it takes an act of God—a flood, a firestorm, a hurricane—to make mortals understand. The earth must open up at the very heels of those in denial…tempting fate. Tempting finality.

Such was the case on the first day after Thanksgiving at five past ten o'clock in the evening. The tremor that shook the red rock monoliths and left Billy and Marcy grasping at the city park bench served as a reminder to all of Oak Creek Canyon: something higher than man existed.

Billy and Marcy had been in Sedona for more than five months looking for answers and had, as yet, found nothing. Billy was beginning to believe there was nothing to find. Billy was beginning to lose all faith and had, increasingly, started doubting everything that had led them here in the first place. Nothing new had been added to the mystery and nothing old had been subtracted, since he'd almost killed the crazy woman in Las Cruces on the drive out. Wasted time and wasted money all because of a promise.

Marcy had just begun talking about her exhilarating day when the tremors shook her face, chattering her teeth. She grabbed the wooden bench boards, her long, red fingernails digging for support. The shallow Oak Creek, flowing under the city lampposts just a few dozen feet away, seemed to freeze as if in panic that the fault line underneath would suddenly open and swallow its timid flow of precious water. Car alarms blared from the direction of "The Y," a central hotspot where the city's two main roads intersected. Screams resounded as glass shattered in the distance.

The quake lasted less than ten seconds, causing Billy to release a tiny belch filled with the flavors of the milk and Fruit Loops he'd had for dinner. He gazed over the horizon, more to ensure himself that the sculpted Coffee Pot Rock was still there, that, indeed, God had not kissed it and Sedona goodbye by swallowing the majesty only He could have created. Billy placed a hand over Marcy's. Nightfall had dropped the temperature ten degrees to a comfortable seventy-five but, still, her skin was cold to the touch; apparently, her hands had been clamped so hard to the bench that the blood had raced away from her fingers.

"It's done," he said, gently patting her flesh. A thin, red dusty haze enveloped the numerous lampposts along the L'Auberge Resort front road and had clogged one of Billy's nostrils. He sniffed.

Marcy gazed toward the west, toward The Y, ignoring the dust and the quake to return to her revelations. "I found this woman who knows about the Cubit."

Billy released her hand and turned toward her, ignoring the sudden rush of emergency vehicle sirens that quickly grew from fade to furious as they approached the center of town behind them. "I don't want to hear it. I said, it's done." Marcy's long black hair glistened with specks of red silica. The dark, cosmetic applications to her eyebrows, and the ruby red lipstick reinforced her similarity to Cher. As she licked her lips, the match was indelible. "Look. We've been through this before. These damned spiritualists around here will say anything to make a buck. How many times, now, has someone told us they knew this or that about Cubits and daggers and death only to be found out as frauds?"

"Yeah. But Cooper seems legit."

Billy shook his head. "No. I'm tired of it. I just want to go home." A shrill memory echoed once again from his mind's deepest hiding places. Paranoia leaked into his rationality, causing beads of sweat to emerge precariously close to his brown eyes.

"You're doing it again," Marcy said, wiping away one salty runner on his forehead with her thumb, leaving behind a red rock streak of moistened mud. "You're thinking about that woman in New Mexico, aren't you?"

He nodded quickly, his chin rising and falling a fraction of an inch, his shoulder-length blonde hair slapping his cheeks.

"She was just some crazy ol' vieja pumped up on pills." Marcy said, trying to comfort him.

Up the creek, toward the exclusive L'Auberge Resort, a pack of vacationers ran along the asphalt access road away from the resort. "You are the end...the end!" one woman seemed to scream as she approached. She wore a collection of rich accoutrements that dangled and jangled around a much-too-tight black halter top that was just wrong, especially since the woman was a good thirty pounds beyond what her body was meant to carry. Designer flip-flops struggled with the weight and the speed of her descent down the uneven slope of paving. She tripped twice—the first time, she almost fell flat on her round face; the second time, she lost one of the flip-flops and shrieked when the asphalt touched her bare heel. After recovering the flip-flop, she jogged the remaining distance to where Billy and Marcy sat.

You are the end...

Billy shook his head. She really wasn't saying that was she? Of course not. None of it had been real. None of it! But Billy's denial was no match for the shock that had never really gone away. The drive from Port Aransas and through Las Cruces and the memory of lost friends had embalmed his neurons with cautious uncertainty that tiptoed on fragile rationality. He would never get the blood-washed vision of Stephanie Drake out of subconscious...or the bodiless head of Mitchell Bone… or poor Janine as she'd turned to face him just before blowing apart. No matter how hard he tried, he would never forget Las Cruces, either, or the woman whom he'd nearly hit with the car. She'd screamed, just like the woman running toward him was doing right now. Damn, he wished she'd shut up. Damn the earthquake. If not for these things, Billy's decision to leave, this time, would have been irreversible.

"The end," the woman panted. "We have to get to the labyrinth and pray for salvation before the end." Her eyes spun aimlessly. When she stopped beside the bench, her sweaty hand grabbed the backrest behind Marcy.

"It's just a little tremor, hon," Marcy offered. "I'm fine. You're fine. Here, sit down."

A man who might have been her husband passed the bench. He was much thinner and a whole lot lighter on his feet. Six other resort guests ran with him. All stopped when he did. "Lana," he said. "We have to keep going. The labyrinth will only hold so many."

"Sit here," Marcy repeated. "No one is going to go anywhere. Besides, that tremor was only a warning shot meant to remind us of how fragile we all are." She scooted closer to Billy, placed her small, cloth handbag on her lap, and patted the empty bench space with her hand. "Labyrinths are meant to show us the path, hon, but not necessarily its outcome." Lana looked confused by the statement but Marcy's words seemed to calm her for a few moments. Lana sat and Marcy placed a hand on her shoulder. "See. No more rumble. We're all fine."

More sirens bellowed in the darkness from multiple directions as emergency crews descended on The Y. Billy saw a ladder fire truck race toward town along Highway 89 and wondered why a ladder would be needed for any of the small buildings in Sedona. The accumulative sirens and scant mixture of car and theft alarms reignited Lana's tension. She quickly rose and ran to the man, hobbling on the one heel that had touched the asphalt. On her face was an expression of what Billy could only describe as compliance.

"Yes," the woman said to her husband. "To the labyrinth. He told us this would happen just before the end. Did you call the kids?"

The man hugged his wife which drew the other resort guests closer. "I left a message on their cells," he whispered to Lana. "We'll meet them there." The husband glared protectively at the pack and snuggled Lana closer. Husband and wife quickly scuttled, clasped together, down L'Auberge Lane to its intersection with Highway 89, stopped, turned and looked in both directions as if lost, turned back toward Billy and Marcy and the pack, then headed right, toward Uptown Sedona.

The rest of the resort guests dispersed as fine red mists of dust settled across the shallow waters of Oak Creek. The lampposts, spaced a hundred feet apart, cast a fluorescent sheen on the water, turning the small shards of silica dust into red-tinted sparkles of light. The creek water snatched the starry points and churned them into its current, creating a long, wavy snake that twinkled and slithered in and out of shadow toward the center of town.

"Wiped clean by the hand of God," Marcy said as if in chant. She waved her hand out across the creek and giggled like a child. Billy perked up and turned, not realizing Marcy was still quite close to him. One red fingernail pressed against red lipstick. Fat sunglasses sat askew atop her head, and black hair at her temples looped around the arms. "Sorry. It's just so silly. I mean, those people. This isn't the end and you're not the end. We both know that the end doesn't come for four more years." She stood. "That's why we're here: to find out how."

Billy crossed his leg, drawing his cargo shorts pant leg up and above his knee. "Any of your new knowledge make reference to earthquakes?"

"Come on, Billy. We all know earthquakes are precursors of bad-things-to-come.”

"I'm glad you can make so much light out of this."

"Just trying to cheer you up and get you out of this funk you're in. We've got a job to do. Remember?"

Billy had known Marcy in only coincidental ways while living in Port Aransas. She'd been to town hall meetings often and had been a go-between friend for the poor fisherman Joel Canton, but other than that, her personality and added idiosyncrasies had been a mystery. In the past five months, though, he'd gotten to know her better. Marcy seemed to be the consummate optimist and she had used this sanguinity (along with innocent giggles) to help remedy his anguish. Today was not the first time he'd thought about giving up and today wasn't the first time she'd tried to cheer him up. It just seemed that each time, it was getting harder and harder to convince him that Sedona was where he should be.

"So, are you going to take me out for coffee like you promised?" Billy asked, trying as hard as he could not to smile.

"Only if Charleys is still standing." Marcy strolled off in the direction of The Y, toward the sirens that had decreased in number and in volume, her small plaid handbag bouncing against one hip. Billy sat for only a moment as the remnants of defeat faded, then quickly joined her at the end of the road.

When they arrived at the Y-intersection of Highways 89 and 179 just ten minutes later, cars stood still in all three directions. A new lamppost that had been anchored in place just a week before, had fallen and now blocked all passage as it lay across Highway 89 like a long, broken, railroad crossing arm. The shattered array of lamps at the top of the metal post were scattered across the far side of the road and the adjoining sidewalk. Charley had dodged losing his coffee shop by about twelve feet. Billy now understood the need for the ladder truck he'd seen earlier. The firefighters were using the boom of the ladder to raise the lamppost. They had just finished hooking everything up when Billy and Marcy stopped among dozens of other pedestrians who were curious as to the success of the emergency crews. Billy pointed at Charleys.

"It's still standing," he offered. "You think they're serving?"

Billy and Marcy pushed through the crowd and into the street, circling around a perimeter set up by the police. Most of the cars sat unoccupied, the drivers now a part of the gawking mass of pedestrians. A few parked rows of cars away from the intersection sat a VW Bus, late 60s model. With a different paint job and less chrome it could have doubled for the one Billy had owned in Port A. He'd loved that vehicle, but it had been swept away in the hurricane just like so much else.

"Come on." Marcy grabbed his elbow.

As they neared the coffee shop, the top side of the lamppost was winched in the air six feet. A police officer's hand suddenly jutted forth, pressing back against Marcy's chest. Marcy looked at his hand then at his face.

"Sorry ma'am," the officer said with a tepid, southern drawl. "Please stand back." He removed his hand though, to Billy, it seemed to have remained there an uncomfortable few too many seconds.

The truck ladder swung the lamppost toward the opposite sidewalk and crews quickly lowered it onto an area where pedestrians were slow to move out of its way. Cleanup crews assembled around Billy and Marcy and a street sweeper rolled across the broken glass in the street. In a few minutes, traffic began crawling through The Y while police directed the flow.

Billy and Marcy crushed shards of glass underfoot as both entered Charleys. Not only was the place serving, it seemed that Charleys was *the* place to be with standing room only. Chatter was overwhelming, no doubt centered on eyewitness accounts of the lamppost and the earthquake that had toppled it. The counter where coffee was ordered and where pastries were few behind the counter's glass enclosure was inundated with people drinking, eating and ordering.

"I thought the damn thing was going to drop right down on top of my head," said a lady who looked a lot like the Lana from the resort. "The glass flew like shrapnel. Got me here." The lady pointed at the back of one of her legs. Her flip-flop hung from the heel. A small, red line that looked more like a paper cut than shrapnel marked the skin above her Achilles tendon. Another woman who was listening to the story, gasped, covering her mouth with both of her hands.

"Starbucks is close enough for a walk," Billy suggested to Marcy. "Injuries are probably not so life-threatening over there." The wounded lady looked at him, started to say something, but instead turned to her friend, took her hand, and nudged further into the human mass.

West Sedona was pockmarked by alternating chunks of small retail shops, larger strip malls, ranch-style residential homes and essential city buildings. On one street corner sat a lot filled with all of the big national businesses whose signage challenged peaceful spirituality with monikers glowing in Walmart blue, Subway yellow and Home Depot orange. On the next street corner, an elementary school sat in recess for the Thanksgiving break, its playground filled with motionless swings, merry-go-rounds and basketball nets. For blocks of sidewalk further along, there was nothing but mom and pop shops carrying the essential experience of impulse buying. Everything under the Arizona sun could be purchased for those who thought, for just one instance, that this Native American Indian curio or that bottle of holistic remedy was perfect for themselves or for someone they loved. Sporadically thrown into the mix sat modern homes built of masonry and spackled with stucco, with roofs cascading red and brown Spanish tile, and landscaping akin to scaled-down versions of desert botanical gardens.

Because it was Black Friday (or perhaps because an earthquake had just awakened the curiosity of residents and visitors), West Sedona seemed overly active. It was closing in on eleven o'clock when Billy and Marcy reached the intersection of Airport Road where a bench for the city shuttle, Roadrunner, was full of shoppers. On the far side of the crosswalk, the neon glow of Starbucks green infiltrated the night. Most of the rustic stores they'd passed in the last block and a half had remained open to scattered foot traffic and slow moving vehicles, inviting, what Billy thought, were dozens of women just like Lana and the "shrapnel maimed" lady from Charleys. These were women who looked less like each other than they were psychologically connected: women who were more so predisposed to the same beliefs and controls only a "Lana" could understand, women whose massed knowledge (which by their own admittance was way too much) had been created by a recipe of big city pressure accelerated by dead economics. The Lanas that walked the sidewalks and sampled the wares of Sedona's small retailers wore flip-flops, shorts and tops that bared too much skin and were one size too small, and they all complained about the simplest of life's challenges.

While Billy and Marcy waited to cross the street, a Lana who had just emerged from Vor-Tech's Glass Menagerie ran haphazardly into Marcy. She held a green glass sculpture of what looked like a winged dog with two heads. One of the wings was broken. She held the body of the dog creature in one hand and shook the sharp edge of the wing at Marcy.

"Dammit," she growled. "Look what you made me do!" Marcy tried to ignore her, looking instead at the traffic light which had just turned yellow. "Hey," the Lana continued. "I spent good money for this and you just broke it."

In Vor-Tech's storefront window, Billy noticed that several glass sculptures were toppled over and broken. The hand of one of the store owners was busy setting many of the pieces upright. Another hand on the opposite side of the storefront propped a sign in the window that read:

EARTHQUAKE SALE.
50% to 70% OFF

The man who had placed the sign looked up at the commotion between Marcy and the Lana. He shook his head at Billy and pointed at the sign, then walked around his wife who continued to rework the storefront presentation. When he appeared at his shop's front door, Marcy turned to the Lana and said, "You clumsy duck. Get off my back or I'll break *your* wing."

For a moment, Billy thought that Marcy would really do it…break the Lana's arm. The act would have gone against everything Billy had come to understand about the fortuneteller. She had shown streaks of aggression but nothing that had ever neared physical violence. Marcy, from what he knew, would have broken the Lana with an intelligent array of metaphor and simile, anchoring on the psychology and spirituality of the person and not the skin and bones.

"Ma'am," the store owner said. "That piece was broken by the earthquake. If you'd like to return it, I'll give you a refund but don't go blaming others for what Mother Earth did."

The Lana turned, huffed, glared once more over her shoulder at Marcy who had not shifted her stance by a single inch, then flip-flopped off down the sidewalk.

"Sorry," the store owner said. His wife now stood beside him. "We get 'em every now and again. I guess you just can't please everyone."

Marcy relaxed and stepped closer to Billy. She grabbed his hand which sent a slivered happy chill into Billy's body. "You're a good person," she said to the store owner. "Thank you."

"No. Thank *you*." The store owner snatched his wife's hand in much the same way that Billy held Marcy's. "I just didn't want to watch you belt her, though the woman certainly deserved it. She gave my wife quite a fit. That's a five hundred dollar piece she got for fifty bucks. Even broken, it's worth twice that to the insurance company." He looked at his wife and grinned. "But I guess anyone like that is easier to deal with than the insurance company. Either of you interested in some great, glass shop, post-earthquake bargains? I was about to close up but if…"

Billy absently looked into Vor-Tech's storefront. "No thanks. We were just heading over…" And then he stopped mid-sentence. Words floated in saliva that had suddenly become too thick for his tongue to work with efficiently. Lying on a fabric-wrapped curio display was—what Billy swore was—what couldn't be. "What's that?" he said to the owner.

The man followed his pointing finger as his wife took the cue to grab the object from the display and bring it to Billy. "Lots of people look at it but no one has ever shelled out the cash for it," he said. "It will protect you from evil, or so the myth goes."

The owner's wife handed Billy a glass replica of a Creation Dagger, one very similar to the real thing which Billy had carried hidden in a sheath under his shirt since leaving Port Aransas, since killing his best friend. The very thin tip of its seven-inch, curved blade was broken off but the handle and the red star in the handle's haft was etched to near perfection. Except for the red star, the glass was clear and used the neon green glow of the Starbucks' sign to cast dancing sparkles of emerald onto Billy's face.

"That's why we call it the Glass Menagerie," the owner said, pointing at his shop's entry door nameplate. "All of our pieces tend to do that. It's usually the prism effect that gets to most peoples' wallets. Should I wrap it up for you?"

Billy's fascination must have been transparent. "How much?" he asked.

"I'll tell you what." The store owner smiled. "You hold onto it. If you like it, we'll talk price tomorrow. Besides, I have this strange feeling you might need it tonight." Billy looked up, the emerald reflections dancing into his open, gasped, mouth. "You know…to ward off evil. Like that woman." The man thumbed in the direction that the Lana had gone.

"But you don't know me from Adam," Billy said, his lips kissing the green sparkles.

"But I do." The owner snatched the glass dagger from Billy's open hand and gave it to his wife who disappeared into the soft light of the store's interior. "You are a gentle soul on a perilous journey that needs a little trust to help you along…to help you believe."

"You must be a fortuneteller," Marcy said, squeezing Billy's hand, encouraging him.

"Yes," the owner said. "I'll see you tomorrow."

His wife reappeared and gave Billy the dagger, which was now wrapped in a soft, purple velvet cloth. And then she did something that took all three of them by surprise by craning her head forward and up about six inches to kiss Billy on the cheek. "You'll know what to do when the time comes."

"You mean pay for the dagger?" Billy whispered not knowing why he did so.

"Yes, of course." The store owner's wife backed up to stand beside her husband. "Take care of her."

Billy quickly looked directly at Marcy's red lips then down at the wrapped glass dagger.

The Vor-Tech's Glass Menagerie proprietors waved farewell as Billy and Marcy crossed the street. Before entering Starbucks, Billy turned back to find that the store's interior was dark and the owner and his wife were gone.

Billy could not stop staring at the purple cloth that rested in the center of the circular tabletop.

"It really is beautiful," Marcy said. "How close is it to the real thing?"

"Spot on." He sipped from his glass of iced coffee and considered the real dagger sheathed near his heart under his shirt. "Except of course for the broken tip. And the star."

"The star?"

"The one in the handle. It is completely red." He pointed at the cloth. "The real thing has a star that is red in only one of the star's points."

"Is that significant?" Marcy sipped mocha latte and stroked the soft velvet with an index finger.

"Of course not. This isn't the real thing."

"I wish I'd been able to see one…to hold one. All I know is from what is drawn on the back of your book."

In the five months that they'd been in Sedona, Billy had never told Marcy the complete story. How could he? The memories were too insanely complex and upsetting. Foremost, he'd not told Marcy about the Creation Dagger he'd kept hidden from her because he was certain that to do so would endanger himself, Marcy and anyone else that knew of its existence. Trust wasn't an issue. Marcy had proven herself time and again and, if truth be told, had really helped save them all. She'd rescued Joel Canton from the mass of cubited Port Aransas residents and Joel had saved Janine Bender who had then killed the real antagonist, Albert Stine. He trusted Marcy but the Creation Dagger was much more important than trust. As far as he knew, it was the last of its kind, the other four having been swept away by Hurricane Antiago. And, since the Creation Dagger was the only thing he knew of that could kill a cubit, and, since he remained paranoid that any one individual he came across could be a cubit, the dagger remained close to him. He slept with it, showered with it and had even swum with it a month ago when he'd finally visited Slide Rock Park, a local recreational swimming spot.

Most everything else he'd explained, particularly those parts that were necessary for her to help him find out about Professor Cower, the man who had seemingly started this whole mess by carting the Cubit, one of the Creation Daggers, and the Book of the Djed halfway across the country en route to Sedona.

Marcy unwrapped the velvet cloth and the glass menagerie immediately began: tiny prisms of rainbow colors bounced in every direction. "There were five of them, right?" She tapped the dagger with her index finger, the red nail adding singular dissimilitude to the multi-colored sparkles.

Billy chewed an ice cube and spit a chunk back into his glass. "There were five but they're gone now." His attention momentarily shifted to the jingle of the front entry door as two men entered and sat two tables away. The Caucasian man wore a John Deere ball cap that nearly matched the color of the Starbuck's sign mounted on the wall behind him. The darker skinned man wore a straw hat with a brim wide enough to cover most all of his face.

"Well then," Marcy said. "I don't know how we're gonna save the world without them. Didn't you say some time ago that we needed all of them?"

Billy's mind pondered and prodded and picked. It was something about the two men who, instead of ordering from the waitress, began a discussion that caused the white man to glance over at Billy. Billy looked away, deciding that he was enthralled by the glass menagerie. "I did, but I just don't know anymore," he said.

Marcy stopped tapping the velvet cloth and slipped the finger through the handle of her coffee cup but did not drink. "Strange."

"What's that?" Billy traced condensation on his glass, unknowingly writing something similar to the letters that spelled out C-u-b-i-t.

"How we met. I mean it's been months and we haven't really uncovered much info. And just by accident, I found Cooper." Marcy giggled more out of perplexity than out of humor. It momentarily diverted Billy's growing paranoia of the two men.

"By accident?"

"Her van hit a huge pothole and she scraped the guardrail up on Boynton Pass Road. She popped a tire and her whole tour group was stranded there on the side of the road. I was actually right behind them and saw the whole thing."

"So you rescued them?" Billy smiled.

"Not really. I hit the same pothole. I was too busy watching her crash. That's why I'm without the rental now. I took out…what did Les say?…I took out the tie rod bar."

"Les?"

"The mechanic. Lester is his real name, but he markets his business with the slogan: *You get more with Les*." Marcy absently stroked the broken point of the glass dagger blade. "So we were both stranded. Fortunately, I've built a good relationship with Les who I met a few months back. He's a great storyteller, especially when it comes to Sedona mythology. Anyway, he brought his wrecker out in record time. I think Les has a shine for me."

That someone had a "shine" for her was not surprising to Billy. That Marcy felt the need to tell him so was. "You'll have to lay some of those myths on me some time," he said, dryly, then added, "Tell me about this woman."

"Les called for a ride to come pick us all up and on the way back into town we just started a bunch of small talk…you know, like where are you from?…what do you do for a living?…that kind of stuff. When I told her that I was currently unemployed and in search of answers to some of life's perplexing questions she said that she'd heard it all before."

The waitress again approached the two strange men but they waved her away. Billy now noticed that the man in the John Deere hat was mostly bald except for a thin flip of blonde-white hair that peeked down across his forehead from under the brim.

Marcy continued, "…and when I told her I was looking for stories about the Cubit and….well, you should have seen the look on her face."

Billy stopped listening to her altogether. The man with the Deere hat—now Billy realized where he'd seen him before. Billy interrupted. "Turn slowly like you're looking for the waitress and check out the guys that came in a few minutes ago. That's them. Those are the guys from Las Cruces. I'm sure of it. But that was five months ago."

Marcy's face twisted into an expression of distraught. "I thought we already went over all of that. Besides, if they had followed us here, we would have seen them before now."

"Please. Just humor me. At least tell me that Deere-hat man over there isn't the same guy from that Las Cruces restaurant. He's got that same bald head and wavy flip of hair. It has to be him. Who else looks like that?"

Marcy rolled her eyes and slowly turned and as she did so, Billy relived the entire experience, his brain's memorization engine flipping through static images that flashed quickly, like frames in a movie. It had been the day after the "Hurricane of the Century" had swept away the cubited population of Port Aransas and what remained of his life. They had fled toward Sedona in search of answers and had made a stop in Las Cruces, New Mexico. In Las Cruces, the crazy Hispanic woman whom he'd almost killed had attacked the bald man with the thin flip of blonde-white hair while screaming: *You are the End! You are the End!*

In Las Cruces, the hunters had shown themselves.

They'd needed gas and Marcy had been complaining about hunger, though how she could have had an appetite after living through such a massacre had been beyond Billy. He'd been nauseous for the entire ten-hour trek that Interstate 10 ran through Texas. He'd felt that he might puke at any moment. And there'd been that constant feeling that he was being watched…followed…chased, a feeling that he supposed would never go away. Stephanie's SpongeBob Squarepants toy, which sat in silent, smiling humility in the middle of the dashboard, had only served to increase his body's malign attacks but he'd been unwilling to move it, thinking that the toy also represented one final link to a somewhat sane world.

Though he wasn't hungry, he wanted to explore what living arrangements might be found in Sedona. They'd left in such a hurry, considerations for living had entailed nothing more than the acquisition of cash from two teller machines and a brief overview of credit lines and available balances. When he exited the interstate near New Mexico State University, he asked Marcy to be on the lookout for some sort of Internet café. From the exit ramp, a right turn onto University Avenue had them driving near the heart of the campus within minutes.

The transposition was numbing at first. On the right side of the four-lane road, the glass and brick majesty of college life pulled him like a magnet, refilled him with a passion that only those in pursuit of knowledge—those meant to pursue knowledge—could understand. On the left side of University Avenue there was poverty, some seemingly too extreme to have been erected just across the street from such academic dissimilitude. It reminded him of a couple of years back while he was still at MIT, when he'd visited Yale in New Haven for a lecture on nanotechnology. There'd been that grandiose aura of social importance on the east end of town and the entirely opposite state of welfare a block away. He'd remembered that when leaving his motel, to turn right meant textbooks and importance and safety, and to turn left meant illiteracy, self-loathing and danger. Complete opposites and a complete care-less attitude. Those who had so much to gain cared the least about those who had little to lose.

On the north end of the Las Cruces campus they entered an increasingly broken-down part of the neighborhood…a stereotyped area of the city where the unemployed reigned, where the lost hopes of immigrants were stenciled into the landscape as broken cars, tiny stucco homes, dirt yards, and many, many sad faces. Immigrants sat on porches that skewed to one side, some wearing broken straw hats, some chewing on the ragged brown reeds of grass that grew in scattered clumps between the cracks in the porch floorboards. But it was the children that really drew Billy's attention. They didn't run and jump and play. They didn't laugh with the delight of learning new things. There was nothing new for them to laugh about. And the sun—it beat down upon their tiny heads, browning further their Hispanic skin tones, a relentless heat that was already pushing ninety degrees at noon.

And Billy thought that he was in another country. He had to be. How could the land of the free and the home of the brave treat its people with such antipathy? Billy's country was made up of immigrants, wasn't it? It was the immigrants who had been given the opportunity to become the masters of the universe which now denied the hopes of these people… and their children. How could they? Had the powerful forgotten their past? Was materialism that strong a force? Had all hope and goodness been wrested from their souls? Had they become…

One of the children he'd been staring at suddenly jumped up and pointed straight at him. At that same moment Marcy yelled, "There's one." And then she screamed, "Look out!"

Someone was in front of the car and Billy mashed the brake pedal. He'd been driving just under the 35 mph speed limit but the Cavalier still took an agonizing two seconds to stop. The pedestrian stumbled backward and fell to the pavement. As the pedestrian disappeared beyond and below the car's hood, SpongeBob tumbled from the dashboard and onto Marcy's lap. The Book of the Djed, which he'd stashed under the seat, slid into view across the floorboard.

"Oh my God!" Billy moaned, his fists locked tight to the steering wheel. "Did I hit her?" He craned his neck forward.

Marcy sat motionless, neither a smile nor frown revealing how she felt, with SpongeBob's face planted between her knees. She absently swiped the toy to the floor and matched Billy's forward-leaning gaze.

Suddenly, the pedestrian popped up in front of the car. She was Hispanic, middle-aged, and Billy could see no blood on her. She was clothed in the same scant wardrobe as the residents on the left side of University Avenue: a torn, sweaty blouse, and ratty, off-brand blue jeans that had been cut off to make shorts. She was not wearing anything on her feet and Billy wondered how she could walk the asphalt's temperature without shoes—he wondered, for that matter, how she was even alive.

He grasped the car door handle with the intention of getting out and helping her but before he opened the door, the woman continued across the road, paying no attention to him, the Cavalier, or the delivery box truck that screeched to a halt before hitting her. The woman staggered between cars parked along the curb then tripped onto the sidewalk, supporting herself with the metal pole of a street sign that read *One-Hour Parking*. Nobody came to her aid. Nobody asked if she was hurt. The half-dozen bystanders that *had* stopped to gawk continued in the directions of their midday destinations.

"That was close," Marcy said, turning from the stumbling woman to Billy.

"I think I hit her." One of Billy's hands still death-gripped the steering wheel. His foot seemed cemented to the brake pedal.

"No," Marcy said, "but it was damned close." She grabbed his clenched wrist. "That's what the sun can do to you—daze and confuse." Billy was uncertain if the comment was meant for him or the woman. A horn blared behind them. "Come on. I saw a restaurant with an Internet sign in the window back there just before…" She smiled, comfortingly. "Head around the block. I'll show you."

The side streets around University Avenue were filled with just about every kind of store a typical college student could want, from used textbook dealers to small outdoor pubs to shops selling New Mexico State University Aggies mascot paraphernalia. Billy turned back onto University Avenue and parked behind the delivery truck that had almost hit the stumbling woman. When he stepped from the Cavalier he couldn't help looking back toward the center of the road, hoping that another woman would not be there sprawled over the asphalt under the baking sun, wondering how many others on the poverty side of University Avenue had failed to cross over to the land of plenty, wondering if anyone had ever been killed, wondering if anyone had ever really cared.

The food in the restaurant was exceptionally tasty and inexpensive; at least, that's what Marcy told him. Beans and rice and tortillas were the perfect ingredients for a multitude of recipes and, with his fork, Billy prodded several on the "Taste of Mexico" platter he'd ordered. He was a restaurateur, a sampler of all things edible, but for some reason, none of what he smelled or tasted was very appetizing. Marcy, on the other hand, wolfed down her chimichanga then proceeded to help Billy with his order.

While he waited for one of the three computer kiosks to become available, Billy watched the Saturday midday news on one of the two wall-mounted flat screen televisions. News anchors reviewed local stuff, mostly. Much of it was bad news as all TV news seemed to be anymore. More deaths at the Mexican border. More drug busts in homes not so dissimilar from those across University Avenue. He looked in that direction through the restaurant's storefront window. They were there, all huddled on their busted wooden porch looking at him. An entire family. Three complete generations. They looked at him and pointed, their mouths working on words that could not be heard. Then, one by one, they stood and walked into the traffic. One by one, their bodies were crushed by bumpers, grills and wheels. They didn't scream. The cars that hit them didn't stop. The bodies simply disappeared from his view beyond the frame of the storefront window. The oldest went first. The smallest girl was last. A BMW doing fifty missed her by a foot. A speeding 4-Runner missed her by an inch. She walked directly into the window and squashed her face up against it, her six-year-old incisors biting at the glass, squeaking out the garbled words: *You are the end...*

Squeaky...squeaky.

Her brown eyes bulging and her brown face bloating as it pressed harder into the glass. Breath and tongue and teeth.

Squeaky...squeaky.

And a tear.

Squeaky...squeaky.

"The end," a voice that was not the little girl's said. "The one at the end is open."

Squeaky...squeaky.

"Billy!"

He turned from the window when Marcy grabbed his forearm.

"The computer on the end is free. You Okay?"

Billy's breath and heart skipped in unison. When he looked back toward the window the little girl was gone. Across the street was an open field occupied by a single utility pole. "I...eh...yeah...Okay."

"You sure you don't want some food? At least drink some water." She pushed his tall plastic glass across the table until it touched his clenched fingers and followed his gaze. "I'm sure she's all right. You didn't hit her."

Billy forced a smile, then rose with the water in hand and turned toward the computer kiosk. "Let's see what Sedona has to offer," he said. Marcy followed him.

It took his mind a moment to adjust, to force out the squeaky teeth and moaning cries, to understand that what it had just logged was not real. He chugged half the glass of water then let his fingers fall atop the keyboard to tap haphazardly while his mind still wandered.

"That's not how you spell Sedona," Marcy said. Billy had inadvertently entered "the end" in the Google search box and the results listing was inundated with references to prophecy and the year 2012. "Here." Marcy pulled the keyboard away from Billy's hands. "You drink some more water."

Billy sipped as Marcy searched for rentals in Sedona. The water did have a calming effect and by the time he'd emptied the plastic glass, the daydream of the little girl and the squeaky window had moved sufficiently into subconscious that he could concentrate on the choices Marcy had saved.

"Most of them are six- to twelve-month leases," she said, scrolling. "How long are we going to be there?" Marcy shifted the sunglasses that sat atop her head so that they would act as an anchor against the long bangs of black hair that kept falling in front of her face. She quickly looked from Billy's blank stare back to the computer screen. "Don't know, do we? I'll revise to see if there's any places with monthly terms." A few minutes later, she found two units, though not in the same complex, that accepted monthly arrangements. One was an efficiency apartment; the other was a one bedroom house located across the street from the efficiency's street address. "Six hundred for the efficiency and nine hundred for the house," she said.

"We'll split the costs." Billy pointed at the computer monitor. "We're in this together after all."

Marcy smiled but did not look at him and Billy was struck, again, by her beauty, her tan cheeks, her long, jet black hair, her manicured fingernails on the keyboard. He thought for a fraction of time that, perhaps, they should room together. Logic said that it would be cheaper that way. Lust said that it would provide opportunity. But he wasn't brave enough to make her the offer. She was at least ten years his senior. She had children. She was a fortuneteller for Christ's sake. How could his science and her mysticism live in unison, rest in the same house—sleep in the same bed.

"I'll take the efficiency," he offered. "I'm used to tight living arrangements. Besides, a small place will force me to be outside, exploring, trying to find out why in hell we went to Sedona in the first place." He pulled out his wallet and gave her his credit card.

While Marcy made the reservations, Billy's attention wandered again to the television. The midday news had just ended and a commercial

was telling him about flat abs and the breakthrough nutritional supplement
that would guarantee them.

> With a great body and healthy nutrition...
> You, too, can be a star with Popstar.
> The only nutritional supplement you'll ever need.
> Brought to you by BETH Pharmaceuticals,
> **Bringing Everyone Total Health.**

"Lies! Lies!"

Billy jerked around to the front of the restaurant.

"Hijo de putas! Hijo de putas!"

It was the woman he'd almost killed. She picked up a salt shaker
from the nearest table and threw it at the TV. The shaker broke against the
wall beside the flat screen.

"This is what it does to you. This is what they'll all do to you,"
she continued, enraged. Then she locked her attention on two men who
sat near the television. "You...You!" She pointed. "Killers! Murderers!
It's all your fault!" She stepped toward then men then suddenly rushed
forward, her bare feet slapping the ceramic tiling. "You are the end!"

The man sitting on the left, stood. His funky-looking flip of blonde-
white hair that tried to cover increasing baldness flopped down between
his eyes.

"You are the end of us all!" the woman bellowed, and when she
was within arm's reach, the man shoved forcefully with both hands. The
sudden, halting impact snapped the woman's head forward then backward
as she fell against the edge of one diner's table. Beans and rice and red
sauce flew against the wall above the computers. A basket of tortilla chips
and the squat cup of salsa next to it jumped across the toppling table and
dropped on top of the woman as she fell. The thud of her head against
ceramic tiling mixed almost seamlessly with the crackling of broken
tortilla chips. The woman's body went limp.

"What the hell!" The man grumbled at the manager who came
running from behind the service counter. "Is getting attacked a part of
today's special?"

"Lo siento," the manager said; he was young enough to be a student
at the university. "They sometimes do that." He paid no attention to the
injured poor woman as he turned his complete customer service training

on the old Mexican diner whose food had just taken flight. "Por favor, señor. Déjame ayudarte."

Billy didn't know how long his mouth had been open but he now closed it. Marcy snatched both credit cards from the kiosk then took Billy's hand. "Come on. We've got what we came for."

"But the woman…"

"No sense in getting involved."

Marcy pulled him from the stool but he paused as he stepped around the woman on the floor. The woman clenched a prescription bottle that had opened upon impact with the ceramic tile. Several of the pills had rolled out and now soaked into the Mexican salsa pooled between her fingers. The pills looked exactly like the ones in the commercial: the Popstar pills.

And the man she'd been screaming at, the one who was apparently the end of us all, the one whose bald head and flip of blonde-white hair that had not been covered by a John Deere hat, was the same guy who now sat two tables away from Billy in a Starbucks that was five months and five hundred miles away from that day in Las Cruces.

"No," Marcy insisted. "Please, Billy. It's not good to live with such paranoia."

"But it is!" His voice raised one octave too high. Deere-hat man and his buddy both peered more intently at them. How much had they already overheard? Billy wondered. These *were* the same men, paranoia be damned. He lowered his voice. "Let's get out of here." He shoved the glass dagger toward her. "You take this."

"Why? So I can ward off evil? So I can protect myself from your paranoia? I'm a fortuneteller not a mystic." It was evident that Marcy had momentarily lost her optimism but she took the dagger anyway and slipped it into her cloth handbag. "The things I put up with. And I thought scientists were stronger than this."

The waitress asked Billy if he wanted another iced coffee before they closed at midnight. Instead of answering, Billy quickly stood without acknowledging the two men and exited.

Marcy said to the waitress, "Sorry, hon. Looks like we're leaving. Is

Roadrunner still making the rounds toward Cottonwood tonight?"

"Yeah. I think so." The waitress snatched the empty glass and cup and set them both on her tray. "For Black Friday, I think the shuttle is running an extended schedule. Earthquake might have messed that up though."

Marcy dropped two dollars on the table before leaving. She looked back at the two men and, simultaneously, both tipped the brims of their hats. The flip of blonde-white hair fell farther down the forehead of Deere-hat man and for a moment, Marcy stopped and stared. When Deere-hat man smiled at her, she quickly left.

Outside, Billy had already crossed the street and was, again, standing in front of Vor-Tech's Glass Menagerie. The store was closed. The display stand in the storefront window that had promoted Billy's new glass dagger now featured a glass replica of the Mayan calendar round; the top edge was chipped.

"Maybe," Marcy said, coming up from behind him. Billy didn't turn.

Vehicle traffic remained robust with late night shoppers traveling in search of the perfect Christmas bargain. Pedestrian traffic, however, was sparse in this part of West Sedona; most of the three or four adjacent street blocks were lined with mom and pop shops that had extended their businesses two hours past the usual nine o'clock closing time but had closed almost an hour ago. Other than Starbucks, only bars and nightclubs remained open.

"Maybe what?" Billy continued staring at the round glass calendar, wondering if what Marcy had told him really was true. Paranoia had taken root so completely that he was now seeing things and connecting things and fearing things that weren't really there. He considered how unscientific it all was. He considered how much he really had changed. He hated to admit how powerful suggestion was, how coincidence was more believable than fact, how myth and magic were mightier than Mensa. He absolutely hated to admit it.

"Maybe we are being followed or watched or…whatever you want to call it." Marcy grabbed his shoulder. "I got to admit that the one fella did look a lot like the man from Las Cruces."

"Please don't patronize. It's bad enough as it is. I didn't ask for any of this shit. I'm really thinking of going back to Port A, the surf, the serenity. I gotta get back to the restaurant. Kale can't manage it alone.

Damn it all!"

Marcy placed her second hand on his other shoulder. "Do you really think going back there without finding what you came for is such a good idea? I thought you said you were given a duty—a mission to accomplish. Didn't you tell me you were supposed to save the world?"

Billy spun around so quickly that Marcy's hands remained on his shoulders. Her face was full of shadows that illuminated then darkened as cars and trucks rolled past. Flecks of white headlights and red taillights flickered against her eyes. "You said what? You said what? That's crazy!"

Marcy shook him, lightly. "You saw all of those people…all of the people who were your friends…all of those people who you cared about—dead. You might not want to believe it now but it's true. They came back to life and Janine and Alixel killed them—just like you said. How do you explain…"

"I don't. I can't. I won't. We have found nothing here to substantiate anything. Nothing!"

"There's Cooper."

"You mean the woman who was saved by a mythological storyteller who doubles as a mechanic. Woo-hoo!" Billy threw his arms in the air and Marcy's hands fell from his shoulders. "*I've* got a story—you wanna hear it? It's about two people who traveled a thousand miles to spend all of their money and time looking for ghosts. Punch me now and wake me up and I'll tell you how this story ends."

"Ghosts." Marcy said just as the Roadrunner shuttle stopped beside them. Its double doors opened and the driver asked if they were going to get on. "It's funny you should say that. Cooper told me she knew Professor Cower."

Billy's mouth hung open in disbelief. "But he's not real."

"Yes, he is. I've been trying to tell you all night." She grabbed his hand. "Come on. I'll explain everything."

Sedona's Roadrunner shuttle service was an easy and convenient method for getting around most of the town and its sister cities of Cottonwood and the Village of Oak Creek. Billy had used it almost exclusively since arriving, mostly because of its convenience but also because Stephanie Drake's Cavalier was just too full of too many memories. Every time he sat in the damn thing he remembered Steph being yanked inside and her neck snapping against the roof, how the driver's seat had been splattered with Steph's blood and how hard it had been to clean before they'd left Port A, how Steph's cubit had mewled at him, taunting him closer with those damned eyes roiling with red and silver sparkles of insanity. Whenever he did get the courage to drive the car, he'd always make sure Steph's SpongeBob was with him, the square, yellow character sitting happily on the dashboard as if the toy was some kind of guardian angel. And he'd always cry—not a slobbering waterfall of tears, but the kind where the eyes moisten for a fraction of time before the mind pulls them back in denial.

The shuttle was understandably busy this Friday-after-Thanksgiving evening. Shoppers and intoxicated bar crawlers flowed on and off as the shuttle slowly made its way toward the city limits. Billy and Marcy had rented a couple of places just south of Boynton Canyon—the shuttle would drop them about a mile or so away.

Throughout the entire trip through West Sedona, Billy silenced each attempt Marcy made to explain what Cooper had told her about Professor Cower. He just didn't trust any of the shadowy people that filtered through the aisle and shuffled in their seats, especially the guy wearing a John Deere cap that had boarded three blocks from Starbucks; he'd sat right in front of them. And when he'd started to turn in his seat, Billy thought about the Vor-Tech store owner's wife.

You'll know what to do when the time comes, she'd said.

Take care of her, she'd said.

The real Creation Dagger snuggled against his left breast had seemingly warmed up, as if it had known that the man who'd turned to ask for directions *was* Deere-hat man from Starbucks. And when Billy had asked the shuttle rider to remove his cap, just to see that no blonde-white flip of hair was present, the man whose hair was dark and curly turned abruptly away before moving to another seat.

The Creation Dagger had remained warm all the way through West Sedona to the point that it caused his breast to itch. His baggy shirt was actually sweat-stained from the casual heat. He had decided that the dagger's warming was a warning not to speak of such things like Cooper and Cower and Cubit in public…that such information could be used by the Evil that the dagger knew was present even if Billy saw nothing and no one that caused him alarm. Until…

They were a block away from their shuttle stop when Billy first noticed the red eyes. They peered from the very last row where a bench seat spread across the breadth of the shuttle's interior. They didn't glow as much as they reflected—a color of red that matched Sedona's red rocks.

Glaring circles of rust.

The shadowy figure behind the eyes did not move as Billy and Marcy rose to exit the shuttle, but when they stepped onto the sidewalk at the corner of Dry Creek Road and the shuttle drove off, he saw the eyes looking at them in the rear window. He told Marcy to look, quickly, to reassure him that they really weren't eyes at all but just simple window glass reflections, but by the time she looked up, the shuttle was too far away to really see anything inside except for the dim glow of one overhead reading lamp. The farther the shuttle receded into the distant darkness, the more Billy's dagger cooled until, finally, it was only as warm as his heart.

The walk wasn't long—at least it wasn't anymore. In five months, he'd traversed Dry Creek Road dozens of times. He knew that the words "Sam is an anus" was finger-stenciled into the concrete sidewalk at the corner of Thunder Mountain Road. He knew that after that intersection, there was only scantly paved sidewalk and that the remainder of the journey would be dusty underfoot and a bit too close to the road for anyone walking near midnight. The light of the moon often helped the sparse streetlights in illuminating what flora or fauna hugged the shallow berm, but tonight, the moonlight was missing—only a fingernail sliver dodged in and out of sparse clouds. Cacti and the creatures that lived near them were scattered mere feet from them.

"Cower came here a year ago," Marcy said after ten minutes of silence. Soft Arizona sand crunched as they walked.

Billy didn't respond but instead looked up from the dirt he'd been staring at and out across the landscape. Even this far from Highway 89, a few acres of dry earth had been cultivated into square lots of Spanish style homes. On another acre or two resided small businesses: a dentist's office, a touring agency, a spiritualist shop. It was because of the vortices. It was because of the shamans. It was because of the marketing hype that Billy believed anyone in their right mind would spend so much to build such extravagance in the heart of such wasteland. And the farther Dry Creek Road stretched toward Boynton Canyon, the sparser the landscape became and the fewer more extravagant homes had been built. This place, this manmade oasis in the middle of scorched hope, really was the perfect setting for blasphemous artifacts such as the Cubit. If Professor Cower had found it anywhere, Billy thought, Sedona was it.

A car approached from behind, its headlights bouncing against red rock silica which projected sparkles of rust from the ground into Billy's face. When he finally turned to acknowledge Marcy's statement, the car was a dozen feet behind them and its lights snapped from high beam to low. In that instant, whatever reflections that had taken hold of Marcy's silhouette dimmed. For a split second, her forehead, cheeks and nose had glowed with an aura of rust; her eyes had been saturated with the color. She was looking right at him when the car passed and her eyes reminded Billy of the shuttle passenger in the rear seat—*its* eyes…rust red reflections…full of memories…of Steph…of death…of massacre.

The car tooted its horn and Marcy blinked as did Billy. Marcy said, "Your eyes. They looked just like…"

"I know. Yours too. Sedona red. Just like…" Billy pushed the bad memories back. He shook his head, grabbed it, stood near a tall saguaro cactus, the faint street light glow dropping the cactus' meager shadow of a sombrero at his feet. Marcy took the single sidestep that was necessary to stand beside him, grabbed his shoulder and gently massaged it. The grip felt firm, almost manly strong, but reassuring and pleasant.

"Okay," she said. "Enough about the Cubit. Let's just enjoy the walk."

Within thirty minutes they reached Gringo Road, a T-intersection which did not cross Dry Creek Road. To the right, Gringo Road skittered and curled into the shadowed distance. A small, twelve-unit apartment complex stood on one corner; Billy's efficiency was among them. A single-level, one-bedroom home occupied a sparse lot of land across from the complex in a space where Gringo Road would have continued had developers found the need. Marcy lived there. Both stood at the intersection.

"You feel like talking some more?" Marcy asked. "I could put on a pot of coffee. I think I've got a couple of donuts left over from this morning."

Billy knew that sleep would be impossible anyway and believed that, even though such a discussion might pull him too far back into the recent past, such a verbal release might just be necessary medicine. He'd been keeping it all down for far too long. Five months of repression could not be good for the mental soul. Most professionals by now would have prescribed a couch and psychiatrist—someone who would listen without prejudice. Billy thought that a fortuneteller and a donut might serve as the perfect substitution. Billy thought that—just to be close to her, to listen to her sultry undertones, to be infused by her girlish giggles, her soft tanned skin, the way her red lips undulated and her red fingernails played with whatever she held in her hands—she could, indeed, sooth his torment. He was so tired and susceptible. He could think of no better place to be right now than in her room, within her arms…soothing words and red lips.

"What flavor?" he asked.

Marcy turned; more rusty red reflections bounced from the streetlamp, to the ground and into her eyes. "What?"

"The donuts. What flavor?"

She giggled. "Chocolate frosted and maybe one or two jelly-filled."

Billy grabbed her hand, which was comfortably cool, and together they crossed Dry Creek Road. Before entering Marcy's temporary cottage, Billy glanced back toward his own rental in an apartment complex named The Getaway. Steph's Cavalier sat all by itself near the far corner unit that Billy now called home.

Though the small Spanish cottage (they called them casitas in Sedona) had been furnished, Marcy had added many personal effects, so many in fact that Billy thought she would need a small U-haul trailer to get everything back to Port Aransas when they left.

Port A. He'd had another sudden squirt of homesickness that had shown Marcy a side of himself few would ever see: a man with a lack of control, weak, susceptible to suggestion, and easy to manipulate—a man who mirrored just about every other man on this planet—a man who could be convinced of just about anything as long as a good illusionist was around who knew how to pull just the right magic strings. Men like these were married to the Lanas of the world. Men like these believed that lust was love and that a few clicks across Internet porno screens always found satiation for such misguidedness. Lanas were everywhere and so where men that Billy never wanted to become, men like his father who was not married to a Lana but, instead, had always been married to an office, clients, and money. Men like that meant growing up fatherless and no child deserved a life like that. No one!

"What are you thinking so long and hard about?" Marcy poured two cups of coffee and set them next to a white box on the kitchen's round, glass tabletop. Billy stared out the ceiling-high bay window onto a black night that, in the morning, would reveal the distant Kachina Woman rock formation at the trailhead to Boynton Canyon. Marcy sat and sipped. "Come here. Sit down. Have a donut. You'll feel all sugary better."

Her words made him think about the movie *The Matrix*.

Here, take a cookie. I promise, by the time you're done eating it, you'll feel right as rain.

He really wasn't the same man anymore. He actually felt as if he was inside a computer generated program, one that kept tossing his emotional well-being as easily as the Smith had tossed Neo the first time they met. Cookies nor donuts would ever make him feel right as anything again. He remained standing, his back to her.

"We've been here five months and nothing," he said. "Then all of a sudden the earth shakes and revelations come tumbling out. We've talked to dozens of people and have visited dozens of places only to find what we already knew. Sedona is a spiritual mecca where lost people come to try and hide from reality. That's why Cower came here. That's why anyone comes here."

"I don't think so."

Billy turned abruptly. "No!?" His voice was unintentionally aggravated and loud.

Marcy stared at the donut box; one finger tapped the glass top of the table. "No. I told you. Cooper knows something…really knows something. But, what does it matter now anyway? Seems like you've lost your belief in this whole thing."

Billy turned back toward the window panes. Something moved through the darkness outside. It was low to the ground: a prairie dog perhaps. He followed its rust red eyeball reflections as it scooted past shadowy short desert trees and cacti. "Do *you* still believe?" he asked.

"Of course I do. I've left my kids with my ex for far too long to no longer believe." Marcy stood and stepped beside him. "How can you just throw away all of what has happened? You saw it for yourself. You experienced it. You killed for it."

Billy couldn't face her because she was right. He did, however, find a distant comfort in seeing her reflection in the window. Another prairie dog's rusty eyes moved across the blackness in front of her image.

Marcy continued. "I know you have a hard time believing in fate, that events aren't merely coincidence. Even when the cosmic tumblers turn square up in your face you deny it. Now that takes guts." Billy wanted her to touch him but she didn't. He wanted to touch her but he couldn't…he just couldn't. "Think of it this way. What about all of those believers out there? What happens when you, the scientist, try to explain away what they feel is true in their souls. No matter how many facts and figures you give them, they don't listen—do they?"

Billy's head shook involuntarily.

"These people—these faith seekers will deny every piece of evidence you place in front of them no matter how convincing because, like you, they are so rooted and without an open mind that science does not connect for them just as faith doesn't seem to connect for you."

The memories started resurfacing and Billy, again, tried to seal them.

"You saw Steph as a cubit. You saw what Evil was within her. You saw the manifestation of her darkest half. You know this is what the Cubit does to people. Are you so blind as to disregard these accounts? Your own eye-witnessed facts?"

"No!" Billy turned away from the window and quickly walked to the adjoining living room. He sat on the couch which Marcy had dressed up with frilly pillows and a black comforter. He grabbed the sides of his head with both hands and stared at the hardwood floor. "Is that how you do it? Is that how fortunetellers and mystics and all of the John Edwards of the world do it? Grab a person's emotions, ask a few questions, spin answers into confusion, rearrange emotions and continue until a person starts believing?"

Marcy remained in the kitchen but she wouldn't back down. "You…saw…her. And *you* killed Bottlenose. And the sand pile blew up to the heavens. And Alixel…you told me she was some kind of God or something."

"No. No! I was wrong. It didn't happen. People don't eat people."

"And the Cubit isn't real even though you said you saw it in the bank's vault."

"I never saw anything but a wooden crate."

"And the Book of the Djed isn't real either. You never saw it write anything all by itself."

"Yes. Of course the Book is real. But I never saw…"

"And the daggers? You used one to kill Bottlenose. It burned a mark in your hand for Christ's sake."

That's where the argument ended since, as soon as she said it, Billy lowered his right hand from the side of his head. The pentagram that occupied the haft of the Creation of the End dagger scared his palm. Most of the fleshy pink star points were still easily distinguishable, especially the point in the lower right quadrant—the point in which a red jade had blazed brilliantly at the moment he'd driven the dagger into the back of Bottlenose's skull. He dropped his right hand to his heart where the Creation of the End dagger rested in a sheath under his shirt.

And then he cried. This time the tears came as an endless waterfall. He fell back onto the couch and grabbed a frilly pillow to cover his embarrassment.

Marcy came to him then. She pushed the pillow aside and covered his forehead with her lips. "I'm sorry," she said. "Why don't you stay here tonight? Being alone might not be such a great idea."

As if her permission had been the enabler, Billy felt himself suddenly falling asleep. He blinked twice, the tears rolling down both cheeks, and the last thing he remembered was her blurred, red lips and the cold touch of a red fingernail.

The second time that Cooper Reyes would actually see the walking dead was on Black Friday, the night of the earthquake. The eerie similarities between the two incidents—the one last fall and the one that was about to happen, would have her questioning her very sanity.

An anonymous email earlier that morning had directed her to The Y. She was to sit in this exact chair at this exact table under the outdoor terrace of the Café Aus at two in the morning, or "shortly after the bars close" as the email had demanded.

"Hey Coop."

The voice from behind startled her. It was Luke, an Australian, and the restaurant's manager.

"We're shuttin' down. You want one more before I turn the key?"

Her sweaty glass of iced tea sat half full in front of folded arms. A lick of strawberry-blonde curl fell over one eye. "Got what I need," she said. "And, hey." She turned at the waist toward him. "Thanks for letting me hang out past closing."

"No worries. Your fella stood you up, did he?"

Cooper grinned. "Who says I'm waiting for a fella?"

"Good luck." Luke waved. "And be careful."

Cooper habitually waved in reply though her arm stopped halfway through the second wave.

Be careful, she thought. This was certainly a time to be careful. The anonymous email had implied danger and irrationality.

Situated just west of The Y, the Café Aus provided the perfect roost for anyone interested in people watching. Tonight was no exception. There were lovers and transients and professionals (with a few professional transients thrown in for good measure). The display of vehicles still cruising under the Friday night lamplights were just as varied: clunker to classic to cavalier, including a flower-painted VW Bus that spewed blue smoke, and more than one Hummer floating on lift kits that were as tall as their tires were wide.

People watching had always been one of Cooper's favorite habits. She loved leading tours into Red Rock Country as much for the quirky habits and personalities of her tour groups as she did for the enjoyment of teaching them about this part of Arizona. The habit had been ingrained by her Psych 404 professor at Arizona State University nearly eight years ago. Dr. Doer had enjoyed giving her students assignments she'd called "people peeking" (her creative term for people watching), assignments that had helped her own research more often than it had helped student learning. But Dr. Doer had been an easy A as long as you fulfilled her survey requirements and mastered her four, thirty-page reports, most of which had been a permanent part of the Greek cheat filing system for some time. "People peeking," the doctor had said, "is an inherent gratification activity meant to ratify the abnormality of an abnormal life." Under that definition, everyone was abnormal and you couldn't walk a step without running into someone needing therapy, including yourself.

Cooper remained at the table for another thirty minutes before she began to feel uneasy. People peeking had all but dried up. Most of the pedestrian crowd had abruptly disappeared, as if some Morlock bellow had suddenly filled the evening with the threat of Eloi casualty. At around 2:45, she saw (and naturally started to analyze) a man who could not find his center of gravity. The guy was in his twenties and seemed to be a happy drunk. When he tripped into the iron railing that marked the café porch's perimeter and pushed off of the railing before stumbling momentarily into the street, Cooper almost stood.

"Naw," the man slurred. "Ya'll go on ahead. Ol' Digger'll be jess fine."

Cooper didn't know if the man was talking to her or an imaginary character, one that often springs forth from the intoxicated mind. She'd learned all about that psychosis from her substance abuse class. Drunks often made friends out of inanimate objects and people that just weren't there.

The man stumbled onward for another half a block, partially on the brick paver sidewalk and partially on the concrete road, before staggering into an alley between Charleys coffee shop and a branch of the First Arizona Bank where an ATM machine's blue signage traced the man's silhouette into the darkness.

Cooper had to laugh. She was nervous and, admittedly, even a little frightened. The comic tickle that teased the back of her throat relieved the tension when it finally surfaced. She raked short fingers through her short, strawberry-blonde hair and dropped the hand to her knee.

Not going to happen, she thought. *It's not going to happen because no one knows where it is.*

It was the reason why she was sitting here. *It* was the location of the Great Hall of the Anasazi, the place where the Cubit had been kept. The anonymous emailer had said that she could obtain a map here, tonight, at the Café Aus, after the bars closed. Apparently, it was just a ruse—just another jokester who was now happy to have pulled one over on Cooper Reyes, Sedona's answer for those who wished to find spirits within the red rocks.

She stood with the intention of leaving but, instead, sat back down when her bare knee rubbed against something that wasn't the table. She reached under the wrought iron top and yanked it free. Because it was wrapped within a plastic bag that read *Sedona Red Rock News*, Cooper thought that it was a newspaper. The clear tape that had fastened the bag to the table snatched three of her fingers and she struggled to pull the stickiness free. She untwisted the wire bag tie, unfolded the closure and looked inside—gently, carefully—as if something might jump out and bite her.

And that's when she heard the scream; it came from the direction that the stumbling drunk had gone. She thought that the man had finally fallen onto, into or through something. When the second scream echoed from the same direction, she decided that he might have hurt himself to a degree that necessitated some help.

She retied the newspaper bag, moved from the table and hopped the fencing, her short, athletic frame easily managing the iron railing's hip height.

Traffic was very light. She passed one old man walking in the opposite direction and wondered why he, too, was not investigating the screams. He didn't look at her; his eyes were locked on his feet.

She walked into the alley unalarmed for her own safety, her mind recounting every volume of first aid knowledge (which was necessarily broad for a guide who escorted ignorants through rattlesnake country) that might be needed to save a poor drunken man from himself. Only two dim halogens interrupted the vast shadows that filled the length of the alley. She had walked its one hundred yards in bright daylight on many occasions but never at night. It wasn't like there was anything to be afraid of—she wasn't in New York City for crying out loud—she was in Sedona, Arizona. The alley wasn't constructed of tall brick buildings and fire escapes and large smelly trash bins housing cats and rats and robbers. A Sedona alley was more like one you'd find in an old western movie, a shortcut for townspeople to get from one end of the town to the other. Cooper knew that at the end of this particular alley a person could turn left and walk a narrow passage en route to a small desert botanical garden one local resident had made from the land he owned.

She quickly moved to the end of the alley but stopped before stepping into the passage when she heard the argument.

"I won't let you," one voice threatened—and to Cooper it sounded like a threat: masculine, bold, forceful.

A second voice, female, retaliated. "You. Won't let? What can you do without the dagger?"

It was at that point when Cooper, again, remembered the first time she'd seen the living dead. Professor Cower had killed it with a dagger.

"The earthquake has done its job," the woman's voice screeched with an echo that reverberated within the passage. "The location of the Great Hall has been revealed. It's all just one more step toward the inevitable."

"Your death?" The male voice.

"Without the dagger? Without the Cubit?" The female voice.

"That no longer matters." The male.

"Liar. Are you now so lost as to wallow in a pit of denial?" The female.

"You know as well as I that Cower stole it. You don't have it either." Male.

"Oh, but we do." Female.

"We?"

And then the passageway lit up in what Cooper thought was a blaze of fire. She slowly stepped toward the passage, her back scratching against swirls of stucco wall, suddenly wondering if either of the two combatants in the passageway had anything to do with the anonymous email she'd received. When she reached the corner that, with one more step, would entwine her into the scuffle, she peeked forward; her cheek felt as if it were glowing.

Each combatant was dressed in costume, the kind ancient Mesoamerican warriors wore, complete with ceremonial headdress and mask. The one on the left had a face that resembled a wild, spotted cat, perhaps a jaguar. The one on the right wore a mask that resembled the sun embossed by the face of a featureless man. The sun face glowed with a brilliance that Cooper assumed was the source of the heat.

"You can't kill me," the jaguar said in its female voice.

"And nor can I die," replied the manly sun. "But I can sure make you remember what pain feels like."

When the sun stabbed the jaguar in the heart with a long, broadsword, Cooper covered her mouth to prevent the escape of an audible gasp. When the broadsword struck the second time, cleanly severing the head from the jaguar, she squeaked and quickly dodged back around the passageway corner. She pulled the iPhone from the pocket of her jeans and was greeted by the anonymous email that had brought her here. She wiped the message away with a forefinger and dialed 911. A second later, she hung up. The cops couldn't get involved. They'd confiscate what she'd found under the table and then where would she be? Back to zero.

Again, slowly, with a single eyeball, she braved the corner. The jaguar stood headless, leaning against the back wall of Charleys coffee shop. The sun warrior lifted its broadsword for a second strike and kicked the jaguar's head toward Cooper, a thick black-red blood oozing from the neck and splattering the brick paving in blotches of gooeyness as it wobbled to a stop a few feet from her. The sun warrior slashed downward but the woman jaguar, without her head, quickly dodged the blade and drew from her waist what looked to Cooper like…

A dagger! But not a dagger at the same time…at least not the same kind of dagger that she saw Cower use to kill the walking dead a year ago.

The headless jaguar thrust the glittering blade into the chest of the man in the sun mask. And Cooper squeaked again, her hand rising too slowly to squelch the sound this time. Both combatants turned simultaneously, the jaguar without a head, the sun with a dagger near the heart.

"Ma'am?"

The voice came from behind. Cooper shrieked and dropped the newspaper bag. When she turned, the police officer's flashlight beam hit her square in the face.

"Ma'am. What's going on here? Who's with you in the alley?"

"I don't know who they are but they have weapons."

The officer's free hand dropped to his holster, releasing the gun strap. He grabbed the mic dangling from one shoulder and called for backup as he drew his weapon. "Stay here," he said.

But Cooper didn't stay. She'd seen enough. She snatched up the newspaper bag and ran back the way she'd entered. Behind her, three quick cracks of gunfire riddled the acoustics of the alley. And then a scream.

Cooper escaped the police backup by running into the tree line that paralleled Oak Creek. Her jeep was parked several blocks away. She could get there undetected but she'd have to follow the creek, atop uneven ground, between patches of city lamplight and complete darkness. She gripped her new treasure, believing that, if she tripped and fell or dropped the newspaper bag into the water, the Great Hall would be lost forever.

Slowly, she crept along the creek bank, slipping on the first rock her shoe touched.

The Daykeeper

Billy's Saturday morning filled him with such panic that he immediately reached for his heart. As his eyes struggled to unglue themselves from the dried and crusty remnants of last night's sorrow, he saw Marcy with his Creation Dagger. She was washing it in the kitchen sink. When she noticed that he had awakened, she said, "Looks beautiful all shined up." Billy traced the outline of the real dagger under his shirt as Marcy continued. "Even if the point is broken, it's still quite a find."

Billy expelled one long, gasping breath then daintily swung his legs from couch to floor. He rubbed his eyes.

Marcy turned off the kitchen faucet and wrapped a hand towel around the glass curio they'd gotten from Vor-Tech's Glass Menagerie. She walked to the fireplace within the wall opposite the couch and held the dagger above the mantle where a collection of other Sedona novelties and collectibles had already found a home. Her lips and fingernails were still red but her long robe was jet black. It did not have frills; it did not have lace. The robe was light and airy—almost see-through. Imagining what was underneath the soft, thin cloth was easy to do since it clung to Marcy's body at the hips and hugged each breast with cuddly care.

"What do you think?" she said, never taking her eyes off of Billy as her arm remained stretched out to the side and above the mantle, the dagger resting in the palm of that hand.

Billy, in his early morning grogginess, thought about many possible responses, not the least of them was one that might have had Marcy forgetting all about the dagger with interests more tuned to showing Billy how accurate his X-ray vision really was. He also thought that a proper response might have had something to do with how the dagger in no way fit with the Native American worship motif she'd chosen to display above and around the fireplace. Twinkling glass menageries didn't seem to have a place among hand-carved peace pipes, feathered headdresses, symbols of ancient animal and planetary gods and one dreamcatcher. But what he actually said was, "Who needs a fireplace in Sedona, Arizona?"

Marcy set the dagger on top of a black wad of silk cloth right next to what looked to Billy like (and just might have been, knowing Marcy) a pair of buffalo testicles. She giggled. The dagger's broken point touched the balls atop the oval nibs as if it had been the dagger that had performed the castration. "It'll get chilly enough for it in another couple of months. Besides, fireplaces at any time of the year are so romantic. Don't you think?" She didn't wait for an answer. "What would you like for breakfast?" She strolled back to the kitchen, her robe taking its time to catch up with the back of her legs. Billy stood from the couch and pressed what wrinkles he could from his shirt and shorts, then walked to the fireplace. Somehow, the balls that looked like testicles turned his stomach when Marcy added, "How about a couple of boiled eggs?"

"Nothing for me, thank you. I've got some energy bars that need my attention across the street."

Marcy cracked and peeled two boiled eggs. Billy refused to watch her; the eggs' smell added an additional churning attachment to the testicles.

"How much do you think it's worth?" Marcy asked, a shaker of salt in one hand and a fresh bite of egg in her mouth. "If you don't want it, I'll be glad to take it off of your hands. If I can't have the real thing, might as well."

"Not sure. Without the broken tip, I imagine it might have gone for a pretty penny. At least that's what the store owner seemed to imply."

"It is curious why he just gave it to us." Marcy finished one egg and sprinkled salt on the second while walking over to stand next to Billy. The boiled egg smell was overpowering and melted away what visions of nakedness Billy had recorded. He turned away and walked to the bay window where, last night, prairie dog eyes had glared in at him. The box of donuts still sat on the kitchen table and he almost grabbed one, but then he saw Marcy. He'd never imagined what Cher eating a boiled egg might look like but now it was all too easy. White and yellow mush peeked through red lips as she chewed. "You might get him down to a hundred bucks," he said. "Perhaps offer him a barter if he's into the tarot card, crystal ball thing."

Marcy returned to the kitchen to wash her hands and pour a cup of coffee from the space saver coffee maker under one cabinet. "Hey. That's not a bad idea. Are you sure you want to give it up? I know how much those things mean to you."

She swished the egg from her teeth with coffee and Billy was, again, able to look at her without grimacing. "No, really. Go ahead. I think it was probably meant for you anyway."

"What do you mean?"

Billy glanced over at the glass dagger. It had captured a beam of sunlight that had found its way through a separation between the Venetian blinds that covered the window beside the front door. A rainbow band of colors bathed the rest of her collection with an aura that seemed almost protective, almost sacred. Even the balls that looked like testicles appeared angelic. "It fits perfectly there on the mantle, don't you think?"

Marcy nodded. "You sure you don't want something to eat?"

"Naa. I gotta get going. Today's shopping day; time to restock my own cabinets. You know me, always the consummate health food nut." He slipped on his sandals. "Thanks for letting me crash here last night and thanks for listening with a critical ear. Everyone needs a little hard love every now and then."

"I hope I wasn't too harsh." Marcy leaned backward at the hips across the kitchen countertop, her breasts pointing north of her chest.

"Like I said…" Billy went to the front door. "Slapdowns are a necessary part of any relationship." He opened the door. Marcy's voice followed him outside.

"We should do this more often."

Billy nodded. "I'll get a hold of you later. Maybe we can talk some more about Cooper."

He tried not to look at her as he closed the door.

When Cooper had finally gotten home last night, she'd anxiously opened the newspaper bag and had gently unrolled a current edition of the *Sedona Red Rock News* to find, buried within its pages, a sheet of brown parchment paper. She was certain that she would find a map; that's what the anonymous emailer had promised. But what was written on only one side of the parchment certainly was no map, at least not any kind of map that she had envisioned. Maps had arrows and Xs and recognizable geography that the treasure hunter was supposed to stitch and knit and decipher.

So she'd stuck the parchment to her bedroom wall with masking tape, had taken off her clothes, and had sat there in her underwear, staring at the three Mayan glyphs and ten scattered dots, trying to find some meaning to them by mentally connecting the dots in a dozen different patterns, trying to understand why two of the three glyphs looked so much like the sun and jaguar she'd seen in the alley behind Charleys. She'd sat and stared until she'd fallen asleep. Her subconscious had done the rest.

Her resting mind had connected the dots.

When she awakened Saturday morning, she almost leapt from the bed and ran over to the small desk she used to do all of her business-related paperwork. The bottom drawer of the desk was the one she used to organize folders. From it, she plucked a larger, bulging, manila envelope that was labeled "Vortex," dropped it on top of the desk and pulled out much of its contents. Any time she'd run across information related to energy vortices she'd always stuff it into this envelope. The information didn't necessarily need to be Sedona specific (there were energy vortices all over the world) and that was probably the reason why it was so full. She'd often thought about organizing the contents better, using different envelopes for the different vortex locations, but had never quite gotten around to it.

She shuffled through flyers and pamphlets and pictures and personal experience letters from places like Tibet, the Egyptian pyramids, the Bermuda Triangle, Easter Island and the Incan ruins. She found what she was looking for and yanked it from the stack. A sticky note was attached. On it was written, "The immortality of the stars." Chris Cower had given this to her. Cower had written the note. The very thought of him made her shiver. Goosebumps popped out across the entire surface of her exposed skin. How could she have been such a fool? How could she have given that old son-of-a-bitch her body? He'd lied to her. He'd set her up. She angrily pulled the sticky note from the paper and haphazardly threw it.

The drawing on the sheet of paper was of what Cower had described as Sedona's leylines, patterns of energy that flowed through Red Rock Country. The patterns were in the shapes of two stars, one six-sided and one five-sided. Most of the named rock formations in and around Sedona marked the points of the stars. The two stars came together at a common location: the Airport Mesa, one of Sedona's most popular tourist attractions.

Cooper walked to the parchment paper stuck to her wall and held the drawing out in front of her. The points in the drawing matched the dots on the parchment. She traced the two star patterns with a forefinger. As the pad of the finger touched each of the points, she named several of them: Steamboat Rock, Cathedral Rock, Twin Buttes, Lee Mountain, Airport Mesa.

So the Sedona leylines were actually a map? she thought. And all of this time, she'd had the map to the Great Hall of the Anasazi buried in an

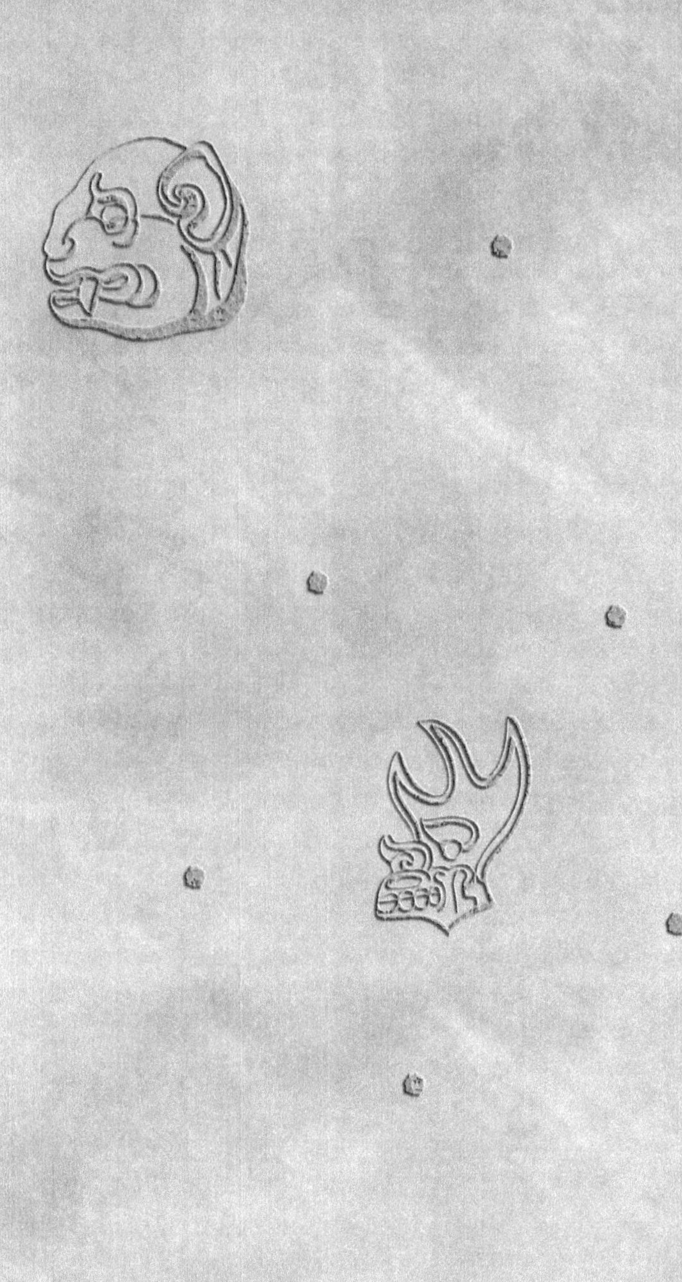

envelope in her desk?

Visualizing the two stars on the parchment, she determined that the Mayan glyph of the jaguar was centered inside the six-point star; the sun glyph was centered in the five-point star. The third glyph, one she had never seen before, was isolated all by itself in the lower right corner of the parchment. She sketched a mental diagonal line that intersected the centers of the two stars and the lonely third glyph, but that really didn't decipher anything. She supposed that the obvious might be the answer: the Great Hall was located at one of the two stars' ten points. But with that kind of reasoning, the intersection of the lines that connected the points could also be locations, or perhaps the center of the stars were locations, or the middle of the crossing lines, or…the number of possibilities could be dozens. Finding it would take forever, even if this was a map, even if this wasn't another diversion, even if this wasn't…

And then she thought of something that set her blood on ice. What if Cower had returned? Could that have been him last night, dressed as the sun? Had he left her the message and the screwed up map? Cower had used her once and he was using her again. Right?

She threw Cower's leyline sketch onto the bed then shook her head more out of shame than from a nonverbal refusal to believe that Chris Cower was even alive. She glanced away from the parchment to her flat belly and to the waistband of her white panties, remembering how he'd taken her, his sixty-year-old body desiring her thirty-year-old youth. She was forbidden fruit, the only kind of fruit that Chris Cower ate. Young lust. Right out there on the back porch where many of her private tour groups had feasted, where the spiritual energies of the masculine and feminine had pulsed through both of them, blinding them, taking them to places they should never have gone.

She walked the four short steps to the mirrored sliding doors of her closet and just stood there, all five-foot-four of her, never looking her own self in the face, the same forefinger that had traced star patterns on the parchment paper now tracing the tight lines on either side of her dark-skinned abdomen, her other hand snatching a firm grip of one hip and strong buttocks. She flipped strawberry-blonde curls from her forehead with one quick jerk of her head and this forced her eyes to lock on her own facial reflection. Her appearance was convincingly Hopi except for the hair which she attributed to her real Puerto Rican ancestry.

"Is he here?" she said to her reflection. "God help me if he is. God prevent me from killing the son-of-a-bitch."

And as if God was actually going to answer at that very moment, her cell phone rang, its vibration causing it to skitter atop the lamp table beside her bed, its sudden shrill echo causing nerves to skitter up her spine.

She stepped quickly to the bed and sat, scooping up the iPhone at the same time. She did not recognize the incoming phone number. "Hello," she said.

"Cooper Reyes?"

The voice was only slightly familiar. "Speaking."

"My name is Marcy Ruminski. Perhaps you remember me from yesterday?"

"Of course. How are you? How's the car?" Cooper was only being polite. She cared much less for the condition of Marcy's vehicle and much more about the conversation they'd had on the way back from the accident, yesterday. She stared at the ten dots and three glyphs on the parchment.

"I suspect Les will get both of our vehicles back to us on Monday. Keep the fingers crossed." After a moment of silence, Marcy continued. "Listen. The reason I called is to ask you what your schedule might be like for the next day or so."

This was the woman who'd asked her about the Cubit. This was the woman who'd talked about Cower. Might she know something about this map? Might she even be involved? Their random meeting on Friday was just too coincidental. "I'm free for the most part," she said.

"My friend and I would love to exchange more info concerning some of the—"

There was a long pause during which Cooper thought about Cower, and Cower's book, and the Great Hall.

Marcy continued. "Well, I promised I'd call."

"Yes," Cooper said. "Why don't you and your friend come over to my house. I'll fix us up a good old-fashioned Sedona fiesta, one that's good for thinking and sharing and, well…understanding."

"Sounds great. Shall we say five-ish?"

"Five it is unless I hear otherwise from you. Need a ride?"

"Actually, we're only a mile from you. We'll walk over."

Cooper hung up, dropped the phone on her bed and just sat there, numb. A complete stranger knew Chris Cower, she thought. A complete stranger wanted to talk to her about a man she loathed. Her fingers drummed lightly against one thigh as she thought about the stranger named Marcy, about how they'd met, about what had been said.

The entry of Marcy into her life had, indeed, been quite convenient. Cooper had been traveling toward the canyon with a group to celebrate what she termed "Red Friday." Cooper had always despised the day after Thanksgiving and the way corporate America had turned it into some kind of shopping spree. So she'd created an alternative. Red Friday was meant for those who realized, as she did, that no day was *meant* for shopping and that every day provided another chance to reconnect with the beauty of the world. Red Friday was their (and her) deliverance from the madness that Madison Avenue had created.

She'd hit the pothole with one rear tire doing forty-five, which had immediately caused it to explode. Marcy had been behind her and had struck the same pothole with the same tire. Until now, Cooper had never really considered how convenient that had been. Who in their right mind would hit the same obstacle they just saw someone else hit? The natural reaction would be to swerve out of the way. It was almost as if the stranger had hit it on purpose.

Also convenient was that Marcy had known someone who could, with just one call on the day after Thanksgiving, send help that would have everything taken care of in less than an hour: Cooper's touring van and Marcy's rental each had their own tow truck; a separate van had been sent to escort the Red Friday tour group back to town; and Les, the mechanic, had driven them home himself.

Sitting in the backseat of Les' 1972 Chevelle (one that he continually had boasted as the best car ever made), Marcy had started asking questions. How long had she lived here? What did she do for a living? Had she ever heard of a Djed or a Cubit? Did she know of a man named Cower? Just like that. Right out the blue. A complete stranger. Had she met Marcy on Saturday instead of Friday, if she would have met her after the anonymous email and the incident in the dark alley, she probably wouldn't have told her a thing.

Why do you ask? Cooper had said.

A friend and I are trying to figure out a mystery that was left on our doorstep, Marcy had replied.

By Cower?

Yes. By Cower.

Because of Cooper's spite for Cower, and because her first assumption was that Marcy was some sort of undercover agent looking to put Cower away for life, she'd told the stranger that she'd known Chris Cower almost a year ago and that she hadn't seen him since.

The short drive from the accident to Cooper's house had not provided enough time for further details, but both had agreed that they should continue the discussion later. Cooper had given Marcy her number and Marcy had said she would call.

But that had been before the map and the earthquake and the headless jaguar. That had been before she'd seen the walking dead for the second time and had remembered how Cower had confronted his own Evil before leaving Sedona for good. That had been before, once again, the world had started turning upside down right on top of her.

One of the few times that Billy did drive Steph's Cavalier was when he needed to restock his kitchen cabinets. He would always purchase enough to last him several weeks so that the necessity to drive remained limited.

As he waited to turn left from Gringo Road onto Dry Creek, he looked past the smiling face of SpongeBob Squarepants to the front door of Marcy's casita where, less than an hour ago, he'd left a beautiful woman dressed in a scant, black robe, standing alone by her kitchen sink. Admittedly, he'd been as close as ever to acting on youthful urges, those that swallow common sense for the chance at fulfilling fantasies associated with younger men and older women. But to succumb would have opened doors that he was too paranoid to walk through. It wasn't so much the idea that Marcy was a friend and that to screw a friend meant forever changing a good relationship as it was the concern that to do so would reveal too much of himself. Too many psychological secrets were always revealed once climax was shared between two people. Moreover, he couldn't succumb because of the tacit pact he'd made with Alixel to never reveal that he possessed the Creation of the End dagger. Of course, he could have simply dropped his drawers and taken her with his shirt still on (a notion he'd already imagined several times), but he was always too paranoid, too shy, too chicken to attempt even that feat. At any time, he could have unclasped the sheath, storing it from sight before revealing himself, but that would mean that the dagger would be out of reach, if only for a moment, and he just couldn't let that happen. He would be unprotected and mentally naked, and this would dull any attempt to fulfill physical fantasies.

Billy's attention to the Cavalier's brake pedal slipped as he pondered, causing the car to creep into the intersection. It was the blast of the tour bus horn that simultaneously slapped his daydreaming and caused the muscles of his right leg to mash his foot forward. The bus swerved into a vacant left lane. Passengers' faces pressed against tinted glass as the bus missed the front of the Cavalier by a foot. Most of their expressions promoted surprise—gaping mouths, bugging eyes, lips drawn downward—but two of the passengers near the back of the bus flipped him off—city dwellers, perhaps, that were used to aberrant drivers that didn't pay attention. **Boynton Canyon Express** was emblazoned on the side of the bus below their faces. **Feel the Vortex**, the slogan read. **Escape the Rudimentary**.

Rudimentary, Billy thought. *Nothing about life will ever be rudimentary again.*

His first stop was Walmart where he always purchased inexpensive necessities for hygiene, house cleaning and cooking. He made quick work of this hated chore, speeding quickly through the aisles, wanting to leave the pack of humanity that was taking far too much advantage of Sam Walton's family heritage that promoted a plethora of Christmas marketing schemes.

The checkout line was long enough that he had the opportunity to (and, really, it was hard not to) gaze at all of the "temptation" items stocked on either side.

2012 Prophets Agree:
It's the End of the World as We Know It.

The bold headline that topped the most recent issue of *National Enquirer* was within arms' reach and he tried not to look at it; he convinced himself *not* to grab it. He *would not* avail himself unto the Walmart clientele that he, too, held enough mystical curiosity to read such nonsense. More so, he didn't want to admit to himself that his mind was full of enough uncertainty to even consider what the tabloid contained. He was not like these people. He didn't believe in such drivel, did he?

But the simple fact was, he really didn't know—not anymore. Even as a scientist he'd always understood that some things just couldn't be explained. As a protective mechanism, these things labeled "unexplained" he'd always stored safely away from consciousness. It was a seldom-accessed mind vault (at least it had been); its content was similar to that found in the X-drawer of the steel cabinet in Fox Mulder's office—unique collections of unique experiences, catalogued and waiting for evidence that could move them out of the unexplained vault and into reason. Education had helped him move a lot of that stuff out. Multiple experiences (also referred to as age and wisdom) had helped to empty it as well. But then there were the intangibles.

Regardless of your smarts or how long you'd lived, a person's degree of malevolence toward science or reticence toward mysticism always directly affected the contents of that "U-File," the mind's vault of stored anomalies. Some people could explain the existence of UFOs just as easily as they could a peanut butter sandwich; their U-File on this subject was empty. Being a doctor or a dropout didn't matter. Either could produce evidence that supported their truth. But for Billy, such evidence based purely on faith and belief were different matters altogether. Faith and Belief always acted as temporary storage containers, as the intangibles, for all of his ideas that never quite made sense, ideas that could not simply be catalogued as real or unexplained. These were the ideas that never really made it into Billy's U-File but, instead, hung around outside like unwanted trash, waiting to be converted into understood knowledge or unexplained ignorance, perhaps never to find a proper home as either.

Marcy had plugged into that concept last night. She might not have realized it, but she had used it against him…or perhaps to help him. Billy had way too much information orbiting the U-File, in a place of suspended animation as it were, where the label was neither "reality" or "unexplained" but was instead being processed by faith and belief.

Someone grumbled behind him and Billy pushed his cart to fill the empty space ahead. He could now see that the lower half of the *Enquirer* contained several mug shots of world figures: Osama Bin Laden, Dick Cheney, Pope Benedict, Hu Jintao, and a man whose name was familiar but not the face: Richard Manson. Below the mug shots was written:

Would the Real AntiChrist Please Stand Up?

"Sick," the old woman behind him said. She hunched over the eggs and bread in an overflowing shopping cart and was staring at the *Enquirer*.

Billy blinked. "I agree. Such drivel."

The woman continued as if he'd not even spoken. "How could they even consider that poor Dick Cheney is the Antichrist when everyone knows it's Obama."

"You mean Osama."

"No. I mean our new president, Obama Bin Laden."

Billy turned away from the woman, knowing full well that one of her belief containers had mistranslated some knowledge into her own reality. To her, the president was the Antichrist and there wasn't a soul on the planet that would ever convince her otherwise.

"Grab it or go," the checkout girl urged since he'd not placed any of his items on the conveyor. The old woman looked at him as if he, too, would soon be entered on her list of Antichrists.

His second stop was the Health Heaven Haven, one of the largest wholesome food store outlets in Arizona. Fresh, non-genetically engineered, organic and natural were words spread out in mass throughout the store—words that had become mantra to Billy since he'd left Massachusetts for island-living in Port Aransas two and a half years ago. His Surf Side Restaurant had been built on the idea of fresh and healthy and this business model had always separated his restaurant from most of the others on the island.

He drove into a crowded parking lot and absently wondered how Kale and the restaurant were doing. The last time they'd talked, about a month ago, Kale had told him that business was pretty much as usual. Kale had said that the restaurant had gone through several chefs since Pedro's "disappearance" but the new guy, also Mexican, seemed to be working out. Immigration was really the only concern.

Billy parked the Cavalier two spaces beyond the deepest row of cars. The lot, as large as it was, reminded him of those used for overflow traffic at ball games and amusement parks. A good portion of Sedona could shop at the "triple H" and still find plenty of parking.

"Let's see what Heaven has to offer us today," Billy said to toy SpongeBob. "Perhaps a Krabby Patty or two?" SpongeBob's eternal, two-toothed smile accepted the notion.

A sudden distant scream caused him to look up from SpongeBob and into the rearview mirror. Just beyond the parking lot's perimeter, he saw two people running around within a cloud of red dust. He quickly exited the car and looked back across the roof. Beyond and above the dust cloud, Sedona's Airport Mesa rose thirty feet to a flat surface where the airport's runway remained hidden from sight. What Billy at first thought was the sound of a distant propeller was actually the object the two people were chasing: a gas-powered, radio-controlled monster truck. It jumped and flipped a few feet off the ground then stopped. A boy picked up the toy and showed it to a man who was, perhaps, his father.

The tiny toy buzzing and the screams of human happiness resumed and resounded across the mass of motionless steel as Billy walked the lot toward Heaven's entrance, a squirt of extreme loneliness suddenly pulsing though him. Again, he thought of Marcy.

Inside of Heaven the crowd was as thick as it had been in Walmart but this crowd, of course, was different. First, there were far fewer children and, therefore, far less skittering, scrambling and screeching. Parents weren't yelling at unruly offspring and soft sounds of desert life were easily heard and enjoyed through the store's speaker system. Wide aisles were crowded but the shoppers in those aisles respected other shoppers by maintaining clear passages. Talk amongst the shoppers was not about bargains for unnecessary Walton emotional purchases but was centered on the information trade of health knowledge—of healthy bodies and healthy minds and how the ingredients of the items they handled could further benefit such perceptions. Just as there was in any crowded shopping venue, at least one disgruntled person could be seen and heard, arguing with a store clerk or their own significant others, but in the triple H, such displays were the exception not the rule.

Billy rolled his cart through familiar aisles, plucking from shelves and bins and refrigerator cabinets items that were easily prepared and mostly free of processed foods and additives. When he was satisfied that his collected goods would last him at least two weeks, he went to check out.

The lines were long but hassle-free. There were no shock-riddled magazine and tabloid covers, and no last minute, useless gimmicks except for a small display that promoted Clif Bars and PowerBars and other "natural" energy products. Billy snatched a few Clif Bars; the display reminded him that he might need a quick bite sometime in the future.

Back out in the parking lot, Billy loaded the Cavalier's trunk and noticed that the man and his boy were still out beyond the lot's perimeter but were no longer running around. The dust had settled. The mechanical buzz of the toy had died.

Curiosity led Billy's drive from the parking space toward them. As he approached, he noticed that the man, kneeling, held the truck chassis in his hands. The body of the toy sat on the dusty ground next to him. His boy stood there, analyzing the toy's guts as his father prodded it with a small screwdriver. They looked up when Billy stopped, the Cavalier idling.

"Need any help?" Billy offered.

The man, who looked to be Native American, turned to him and smiled. "Not unless you know anything about RC toys."

Billy switched off the ignition and stepped from the car. "Looks like you're in luck." He strolled from the parking lot's concrete pavement and onto red earth. Wheel ruts from the monster truck toy twisted crazy patterns underfoot. "I've fiddled around with a few of these in my days. What seems to be the problem?"

"I think we gave it a little more than it could handle," the man said, his accent matching his ancestry. "Jumped it over there but when it landed, the rock would not allow the machine any more rights today." His words were almost respectful and were in no way angered. The boy, who was also Native American, nodded agreement.

The man stood and handed the chassis and screwdriver to Billy who then prodded the plastic and metal components for only a minute. "The flywheel is busted. It needs replaced. You have any spare parts?"

The man shook his head. "They tried to sell us a repair kit with the truck but I thought it was only a pitch, you know, like how salesmen always push add-ins to up the price." Billy handed the chassis to him and the man followed the direction of the screwdriver as Billy pointed. "We should have listened." The man looked at the boy, then offered his free hand to Billy. "They call me Lax. My son is Aaron."

Billy grabbed Lax's right hand and immediately felt its strength as he shook it. "They call me Billy," he said. "Good to meet you." He released Lax's hand then offered his to Aaron. "And you too." Aaron, who looked to be a year or two away from adolescence eagerly accepted.

"He's got a tattoo in his hand," Aaron exclaimed. "I've never seen one there before."

If Billy had been paying more attention to Lax than to his son, he would have seen Lax's astonished expression. Billy did, however, hear the man gasp. "It's not a tattoo," Billy said to Aaron. "It's a…"

"Sign," Lax interjected. "A sign of divine protection."

Divine? Protection? Yes, Billy thought. *That's exactly what the Creation Dagger was.*

"A holy sign," Lax continued. "Where did you get it?"

Billy, for what seemed the hundredth time, traced the pentagram's pink edges, pressing harder as the pad of his forefinger passed over then denser flesh that filled some of the points. "Holy?" he mumbled. "A sign of protection?"

"Yes," Lax reassured. "The pentagram. Used as a seal to protect us from evil." When Billy looked up, Lax was staring directly at his chest. "To protect your soul."

Lax suddenly reached out and Billy stumbled backward, tripping over the body of the RC truck; he landed on soft earth as the truck's body, which had been launched skyward by the toe of his sandal, landed on his chest, an audible thud-click resounding as plastic bounced off of the haft of the sheathed dagger under his shirt. Billy gasped as much from Lax's sudden move as from the name emblazoned across the truck body's green surface: "Gravedigger" it read. The name meant something to him, though he couldn't remember ever having such a toy.

"Oh, please. Please forgive us. You are only trying to help. I didn't mean to…"

Billy waved his hand, the one with the pentagram burnt into the palm, then sat up. The Gravedigger truck body rolled from his chest and onto the dirt where it sat gutless and upright. "Nope," he said. "My bad. My clumsiness." He stood and brushed red dirt from his butt and legs. "You ought to go back to your dealer. I'm sure he'll help you fix it up in no time."

Aaron said, "We are sorry, Billy. Really. Maybe we can treat you to some maize and frijoles?"

"A custom," Lax added. "For disturbing your spirit." He patted his son's head while his eyes pleaded with Billy's. "Besides, you helped us. Maybe we can help you."

An onslaught of embattled thoughts kicked up a storm so strong in Billy's head an immediate response was impossible. *Help him?* How could complete strangers help him? And why had Lax tried to grab him? His heart? His dagger? What the hell did this man know about daggers and pentagrams and the powers of protection they represented?

And then it occurred to him. Something had happened in the past twenty-four hours. Something esoteric…something you couldn't get your hands on or wrap your mind around. It was like a locked door that was now open, a flood of circumstance and coincidence unleashed, a Pandora's Box of illogical continuity. Disparate pieces of some greater spiritual puzzle were suddenly rushing together and the keystone date had been Black Friday, the day after Thanksgiving, a day when an earthquake had shaken Sedona for the first time in over two hundred million years. He'd been in Red Rock Country for five months and had met no reliable sources who knew anything about cubits or djeds or daggers or the living dead…there'd been lots of myth-talk, superstitious mumbo jumbo and pure faith-mongering but nothing that he had found to have been of any use beyond pure entertainment. And now, just by chance, Marcy had met this woman named Cooper, stranded by accident, and Billy had met Lax suffering from a strangely similar predicament: an accident with a radio-controlled monster truck toy. Perhaps Lax could help, but Billy felt overly cautious. It was Lax's grab for his heart that had done it. Could he know what rested underneath his shirt?

"Help?" Billy finally said. "I don't even know you."

Lax looked at Aaron as if he were testing the boy to make a decision and put thoughts into words. Lax wasn't going to answer; he wanted his son to provide reason.

"Then that's where we'll start," Aaron said. "We'll help you know us so we won't be strangers anymore."

Lax smiled, his cheeks bulging dark skin, the corners of his lips rising into them. He clasped one of his son's shoulders with a hearty hand and they stood there on the red earth, the Airport Mesa rising behind them, saguaro cacti dotting the landscape, the sun almost directly overhead, a portrait that could have hung from thousands of walls in thousands of homes whose occupants loved the great Southwest but had never seen it.

"So, you will join us for dinner on the holy day." Lax said as if the decision had already been made. "We will pick you up tomorrow at five and we'll nourish our bodies as the sun touches the horizon. Where do you live?"

Billy was already speculative about having dinner with this man. He certainly didn't want him to know where he was living. "I'll meet you at The Y," he offered instead.

"He does not trust us," Aaron said to his father.

Lax nodded. "Yes. At The Y. Tomorrow at five. Look for my truck." He pointed at a white Ford Ranger that was coated by thin layers of red dust. Lax, again, reached for Billy but this time, he offered his hand to shake. Billy took it. "Forgive me," he said. "We'll talk about it tomorrow."

Billy drove away from the Health Heaven Haven parking lot dazed by expectation. He did not notice the green Cadillac that exited behind him nor the driver who wore a John Deere cap that was of the same green color.

The green Cadillac and Deere-hat man followed the white Cavalier all the way to Getaway Apartments. This wasn't the first time the stalker had followed its prey but it was the first time that Deere-hat man had made it evident that he was doing so. He did not maintain a division of at least two cars between him and the Cavalier. He did not continue on past the apartment complex when Billy pulled in but instead, turned into the driveway of the house directly across the street and just sat there, knowing that, at least, the car would be seen. Once Billy entered his apartment, Deere-hat man and his passenger, whose bald head was covered by the wide brim of a sombrero, exited the Cadillac and walked around to the back of Marcy's casita. They stood, together, in front of the same bay window from which Billy had tracked prairie dogs the night before and waited until Marcy opened the back porch door to let them in.

By far, the best thing about Billy's efficiency apartment was the stacked washer and dryer that sat in the corner of the kitchen. Sure, it reduced the elbow room when it came to cooking but, quite frankly, he'd fixed few full-course meals since arriving in Sedona. He'd simply lost the desire. Two years as a restaurateur had made him a pretty damn good cook but transferring that knowledge to this efficiency just wasn't practical. Perhaps it was the size of the kitchen. It contained a single tub sink, a small refrigerator, and an unusual two-burner stove that included, instead of an oven, a small microwave set into a narrow shelf under the burners.

And, of course, the Whirlpool stacked washer and dryer unit. Being able to do one's own clothes in one's own home was a luxury best appreciated by those who'd struggled through any extended periods of time without the ability to do so, as had been the case for him in Port Aransas. This convenience trumped all other household luxuries by a factor of one hundred...especially on laundry day.

The kitchen countertop was so small that he placed some of the plastic grocery bags in the sink, rustling a couple of bowls, dishes, and a spoon or two as he did so. He'd been able to slip the handles of most of the bags around both arms but there remained one bag of non-perishables from Walmart in the Cavalier. He decided to put off retrieving it until he'd stored the rest of the groceries and sat for a moment. He was quite exhausted. He'd not slept well. But mostly, his brain felt tired, the cognitive muscle overworked, the plentiful new data not stored, unsorted—scattered. It was moments like these that he had to stop forcing himself. Understanding would arrive; all it took was time and rest. Convincing himself of this simple relaxing exercise, however, was never easy.

After he emptied the shopping bags, he sat on the mahogany red sleeper sofa in the adjoining living room and closed his eyes, took a long, deep breath, felt his lungs expand to their fullest, then he slowly exhaled. The surge of oxygen relaxed his brain for a second or two and all of the collapsing memories and thoughts and confusions intertwined into one gray nothingness. He followed the calming exercise with three more before the blast of a car horn outside jerked him out of temporary solitude and reminded him to retrieve the last shopping bag.

When he opened the door and stepped out onto the welcome mat that read "God Loves You" (also furnished with the apartment), he saw a green Cadillac backing out of the driveway to Marcy's casita. From his vantage, only the tail end of the car was identifiable. The tags were from Texas and there were two occupants visible through the rear window. As the car sped away toward town, a flash of sun reflected into Billy's eyes and he raised his hand to shield the glare.

A ball cap, Billy thought. *The driver was wearing a ball cap.* The sun's reflection had somehow stamped the image onto his eyes like a flashbulb onto film. His imagination filled in the remaining pieces including the color of the cap, the insignia sewn into it and the color of the flip of hair that fell from under it. He ran from the front porch to the road, trying to catch a final glimpse of the retreating car before it was too far away for him to confirm what he thought he'd seen, but it was useless. What he did see was Marcy, staring out of her casita's front window. When he waved at her, she shut the blinds though he was uncertain if his wave had been what had caused her to do so.

More deep breaths, he said to himself. *You need a whole lot more. You're starting to connect imagination to reality and that's never a good combination if sanity is to be maintained.*

He sucked in hot, desert air that stung his lungs, then wiped sweat from his forehead and paced himself to the Cavalier where he grabbed the remaining Walmart bag and returned to his apartment. He set the bag on the throw rug near the door and returned to the sleeper sofa where he immediately began extricating the desert air from his body.

You are being followed, the hot air seemed to warn.

He took another deep breath. *No. It's a mirage*, the cool apartment air countered.

He exhaled. *Panic is your survival mechanism*, the fleeting hot oxygen maintained.

One more deep breath. *But calm is the only way you'll make sense of it all.*

He exhaled.

And then his heart skipped when the beating of knuckles assaulted the front door. When he opened it, Marcy was standing there, smiling, her painted red lips forced into a lie that her eyes betrayed. She glanced over her shoulder toward the road before she spoke.

"I have great news," she said and stepped into the apartment. Billy closed the door and, with an open palm, offered her a place on the sofa. Her short, white skirt hiked up above her knees when she sat, revealing tanned portions of thigh. "Cooper wants to meet with us."

It took a moment for Billy to comprehend. He was staring at Marcy's legs but he wasn't thinking about them. He was thinking about breathing. He was thinking about exhaling. Marcy crossed her legs and turned slightly sideways on the sofa, patting the vacant cushion to her right as she did so. Billy sat. "Cooper," he said. "You mean the local guide you found on the side of the road?"

"Not found…rescued." Marcy's smile was now much more genuine.

"Ah, yes. Rescued with your broken car and Les the mechanic. I remember now."

Marcy pushed him, her palm against his shoulder, as one child might do to another who was fooling them. "She wants us to come over to her house for dinner tonight. She might have some information that could be valuable."

"Professor Cower?"

"Yes. And probably much more."

"What does she want in return?"

Marcy leaned over and placed both hands, palms down, on Billy's shoulder then rested her chin on top of her knuckles. Her lips were inches from his ear. She lowered her voice. "Same as us…information."

Billy looked straight ahead. Nervous desire warped through him. Cautious tension kept his body rigid. "Who was in the Cadillac?"

Marcy drew back. Her smile faded but did not totally disappear. "I'm not sure what you mean."

"You didn't see the Cadillac parked in your driveway?"

"I heard a car but when I looked out, it drove away. I saw you out there. Is there something wrong?"

Billy forced a faltering smile. "No. I guess not. I just thought…" Marcy didn't say anything; she just kept staring at him, as if she were daring him to start up with his nonsensical talk again. "Oh…nothing."

"You didn't sleep well. Are you sure you're up for a meeting with her? I could go alone and bring back—"

Billy shook his head. "I'm up for it. I just don't know what I'd say to her."

"Tell her what you know of Cower. Tell her what you know of the Cubit. Tell her what you know of the Book of the Djed."

"No!"

Marcy blinked. "No what?"

"As I've said before, no one needs to know about it. I'm paranoid enough just having it here."

"You have it here, still? In the apartment? I thought you said you were going to move it to a safer place, like a bank."

"Changed my mind. I remembered how banks and I don't get along very well."

Marcy gently grabbed his forearm and Billy knew what she was going to ask before she said it. Marcy had been fascinated with the Book of the Djed since she'd seen it slide from under the Cavalier driver's seat back in Las Cruces. Just about once a month since they'd arrived in Sedona, she'd asked to see it. She was fascinated with its power to self-write and she was almost deranged in her desire to know what new etchings had been made to its center spread. He'd given in to her requests only twice, not really wanting to bring the Book out of its hiding place at all, but she'd not asked to see it since Billy had told her he was moving it, which he never did. Frankly, he was curious himself if the center spread had added anything new. Little of it had changed since they'd left Port Aransas; just a few more tail feathers had grown onto the bird at the top of the page.

"Yes," he said. "You can take a look. Actually, I wouldn't mind taking a peek myself."

Marcy nodded, grinned, giggled then pulled the hem of her white skirt forward toward her knees with polished red fingernails. Billy stood and closed the front window blind then entered the bathroom and closed the door. He opened the linen cupboard where he'd hidden the Book and the page torn from it that Alixel had called *the key*.

"Why do you do that?" Marcy said. "So you keep it in the bathroom. You don't have to close the door. We're friends, remember? On a journey together, remember?"

Billy emerged from the bathroom with the Book in hand. "And I'm a paranoid hypocrite, remember? It's just habit. Here." He handed the Book to her. "See, I trust you."

Marcy took it gently into both hands and set it on her lap. "I wish we could read the whole thing."

"Even if we could open it, I doubt we would understand. As far as I know, only one person can open and read all of the pages and she's…" Billy cleared his throat. "Go ahead."

Marcy pinched the leathery cloth cover between two fingers as if trying to open it to the first page. The attempt, again, failed. Instead the Book opened to the center spread, all of the pages in front of it locked together as one big leaf. She shifted it so its spine rested between her thighs. Billy immediately craned his head forward. Something substantial *had* changed.

The glyph of the bird at the top of the right-hand page seemed to have become darker, the black lines of fire streaming from its tail now thicker, denser, almost embossed. It even appeared that the first hint of another color had made its mark within the drawing—a few very thin lines of red traced one of the bird's fiery tails.

The three sixes under the bird had also changed. They were now larger, taking up twice the space they once had. They occupied the left half of the page about a third of the way down from the top and Billy was sure that they had moved from where they'd once been centered under the bird. But they had to have moved to make room for the new drawing that had been added to the right of the last six: three additional numerals, all smaller than the sixes…

999

"What does it mean?" Marcy asked. She turned the Book upside down. "Sixes and nines."

"Maybe Revelation had it all wrong. Maybe John the Apostle envisioned the numerals the wrong way. Maybe it means nothing that pertains to the Bible."

"The mark of the beast?" Marcy traced one of the upside down nines that now looked like sixes.

"And the mark of the upside down beast? The mark of the Antibeast."

Marcy spun the Book right-side up and almost simultaneously both of them said. "The Savior."

Billy grabbed the Book and closed it. "That would certainly make sense." He stood and walked toward the bathroom.

"How so?" Marcy asked.

"Revelation is not only the story of destruction, it's also the story of hope. That is, if you believe those kinds of things."

"But didn't you tell me that this Book was of Mayan origin? They didn't have access to Revelation or the Bible back then."

Billy stopped inside the bathroom door frame. "Alixel seemed to suggest they did. Or maybe the creators of the Bible had access to the Mayans, their culture, their beliefs, their spirit." He closed the door then appeared a moment later. "Honestly, I don't believe the numerals in that Book have anything to do with Revelation. It's just a coincide…"

Marcy stood with some kind of victorious grin spread across her face. "Coincidence, Mr. Scientist? You are coming over to the dark side. Soon you'll be saying that little green men are living on planet earth."

"Well, not exactly green. Walking dead is a better description."

She turned away from him. "We're to meet Cooper at her place at five. She lives about a mile or so up toward the canyon. We should give ourselves about thirty minutes unless you want to drive." Billy shook his head while Marcy went to the front door and stepped out on the welcome mat. She read from it. "God loves you."

"I'll see you at four-thirty," Billy said and waved good-bye.

Cooper Reyes lived near the trailhead to Boynton Canyon. She'd chosen the location for several reasons. Since the destination of most of her tour groups was the canyon, living where she worked provided quick access to all of the ceremonial grounds and spiritual planes that inundated the area. Additionally, her home's close proximity to the canyon provided shelter on days when unexpected storms caught her and her tour group by surprise. On rare occasions she also offered special, private packages to smaller groups, mostly couples, which included a southwestern meal that she prepared and served at her house. Though she enjoyed cooking and would have loved to have expanded such offerings, she was very choosey about the people she let into her home and, therefore, offered less than a dozen such packages a year. There were simply too many unappreciative head jobs out there who wanted more to fill up digital cameras than to really *experience* what Sedona had to offer: real, genuine, spiritual energy.

And that was the biggest reason why she'd chosen this place to live. Nowhere else in Sedona (or in all of Red Rock Country for that matter) was the spiritual energy as powerful as it was in Boynton Canyon. A vortex, it was called: an electromagnetic divining rod where humans connected with their inner selves and outer turmoil.

A place for cleansing.

A place for experiencing.

Her job (as she understood it) was to introduce "vortex virgins" to the experiences that could only be found in Boynton Canyon. That's what she called them: vortex virgins. These were people who had heard about the Sedona vortices, had read about the Sedona vortices, were skeptical about the Sedona vortices but were ignorant of how powerful such vortex energies really were. And like it was for any virgin, each experience was personal and unexpected. Some visitors left the canyon high on new-found purpose. Some totally freaked out, having felt what they termed an "invasion of their soul." Some left unaffected, unconvinced and closed-minded, their spirit forever locked away from any attempt to cleanse it. The former types of people were those to whom she might offer private packages—those that had taken with them something that needed returning: a gratitude for life and the opportunity to live it. The later types of people, those that could never believe, were those she maintained at a safe distance, often referring them to other tour guides when their return to Sedona was eminent. The third type of visitor, the ones that freaked out, she didn't worry about. They would never return anyway.

Because her van (the one she used to transport her tour groups) was in the shop and would not be ready until at least Monday, she'd had to cancel tours scheduled for the next two days. The popularity of the Thanksgiving weekend had made the availability of rentals scarce to nonexistent. But that was fine with her. Applications for the weekend groups had not looked at all promising. Both groups scheduled were completely comprised of vortex virgins from New York City, and with the memory of last evening's craziness still roiling through her senses, she thought that virgins from the city would increase her stress more than the two strangers who were coming over for dinner.

She started organizing her kitchen an hour before her guests were due to arrive. She usually kept her home quite organized but it had gone into slight disarray because of the distractions over the last couple of days. Though she would never admit it, she really was a clean freak—her psychology professor Dr. Doer would have most certainly diagnosed her as obsessive compulsive—not to the extent of Adrian, her favorite character on her favorite television show *Monk*, but a clean freak nonetheless.

Most of her obsessive cleanliness was centered on her kitchen, by far her favorite room in the house. She'd done all of the remodeling herself, following advice from numerous magazines and an occasional episode on one of the home improvement satellite channels. Southwest motifs were a part of every corner and wall, every wooden cabinet, the pots and pans, the floor and ceiling. Her countertops were her most loved renovations. Thick, white veins curled through granite the color of the red rocks at dusk, the veins like lost rivers feeding a barren land suffocating from heat. The island in the middle of the kitchen was topped by the same granite beauty. Iron skillets and grill pans and long chef's utensils dangled on black metal hooks above the island. They hung low enough that many of her private tour guests (particularly the men) had smacked their heads into them, but their height from the floor was more pragmatic to her short stature than accommodating to visitors. A small ceiling fan spun quietly above a gliding porch window which she had opened a few inches so as to circulate the smell of the desert without sacrificing too much of the air conditioning.

She had planned a similar meal to those she served all of her guests which included a combination of calabaza and poblano stew, chile rellenos, cheese enchiladas and a hearty mixture of marinated strips of chicken and beef and fresh vegetables all seared on the kitchen island's grill and served as restaurants do their fajitas: hot, sizzling and meant to be assembled according to one's own tastes. Her guests always loved her soups and entrées but they would rave over her salsa and tortilla chips, both of which she made herself. She'd cooked up a batch of chips just two days ago and felt no need to replenish the lot since she stored them in the refrigerator in air-tight brown bags to keep them fresh. The salsa, however, she would never store except for her own consumption. The salsa for her guests was always made the day of the meal.

Purple onions and fresh red and yellow tomatoes lay in chopped mounds on a thick, wooden cutting board that sat atop the island. She turned to the window and pulled several sprigs of cilantro from the small herb garden that also held vibrant, foot-high plants of dill, rosemary and thyme. She placed the cilantro on the cutting board, then went to the stainless steel, side-by-side refrigerator to get her secret salsa addition: chipotle peppers—not the store bought variety but those purchased straight from the Hopi reservation to the north of town. She'd befriended some of the Elders' wives back when Chris Cower had done the ole' misdirection two-step.

Once everything was chopped to chip-scooping perfection, she pushed the ingredients from the cutting board into a deep ceramic bowl with the back of the knife, sealed the bowl with plastic wrap, snatched another plastic wrapped bowl filled with marinating meats from the refrigerator and set the salsa in its place.

Across from the island and hanging between two framed prints that pictured Arizona Native Americans preparing meals with mortar and pestle was a flat screen TV. She turned it on with a remote intending to navigate to a soft rock satellite radio station but hesitated when the promo for News 5 at Five caught her attention.

"Sedona police remain baffled by the disappearance of one of its officers," the female news anchor said. "The complete story and all of the weather tonight on the Verde Valley's award-winning news hour."

Cooper's immediate reaction was one of self-concern. Had she been seen? And if she hadn't, would their investigation lead them to Luke at the Café Aus who would name her as someone who'd been curiously waiting, all alone, at a table just a block from the officer's last know location?

She tuned the TV to the soft rock station. Ironically, Lindsey Buckingham was singing *Trouble*. She dropped the wooden cutting board into the island's deep sink and pulled out a plastic cutting board from a cabinet door next to her right leg.

I should ruuuun...un..., Lindsey sang.

She rinsed the chef's knife then plucked a chicken breast from the meat bowl and began cutting thin slices.

On the double...

Red marinade oozed from the chicken and marred the cutting board which, coupled by Buckingham's lyrics, made it hard for her to ignore what she'd seen in the alley.

I think I'm in trouble.

If the police did tag her as a possible suspect (or at least a witness) what would she say? The entire truth was not an option. She ignored Lindsey's lyrics and absently kept slicing and thinking, moving the blade dangerously close to the ends of her fingers.

Tell me Miss Reyes. What were you doing at the Café Aus all by yourself so late at night?

I was waiting for a date that never showed.

A date? You mean a man?

Yes. Yes. A man. He stood me up.

Really? That's not what Luke told us. He said that you told him you weren't waiting for…how did he put it…oh yes, a chap.

I don't go telling everyone my personal business.

I see. And does your personal business include killing police officers?

Are you insane? Of course not.

You were in the alley beside Charleys last night weren't you?

Why do you ask?

We have a witness that saw you go in there.

You mean that drunk who almost ran into me?

So you were in the alley last night.

Yes. But it was only to investigate a scream I heard.

Tell us Miss Reyes. What did you see?

I saw the Sun chop off the head of a Jaguar.

Come with us Miss Reyes. You're under arrest for suspicion of being a crazy fuckin' nut case.

Cooper nicked the side of her forefinger which brought her out of the imaginary conversation. She'd drawn no blood but the red marinade spattered across the cutting board made it suddenly difficult to continue the food preparation.

What would she say? What lie could she create? Would they even suspect her?

She dropped the meat she'd already cut back into the bowl, resealed the plastic wrap, washed her hands, then turned to stare out the kitchen window.

And the doorbell rang.

Billy and Marcy easily found Cooper's house; it was the only one located at the corner of Boynton Pass and Boynton Canyon Road. They had agreed that Billy would do most of the talking: one, because Billy knew more about Cower and Cubits and such and, two, because Billy had "forcefully" suggested he do so. He wanted to control the conversation. He didn't trust Cooper. For all he knew she was a cubit. For all he knew, anybody could be one. He also thought that Marcy might say something that could jeopardize further revelations; she might freely give up something he'd told her without getting useful information in return—something that had to do with the Book of the Djed or Hopi princesses or the walking dead. Really, the only information that Billy was interested in revolved around Chris Cower. If he could understand why Cower had come to Sedona, then perhaps he could understand why he was there as well. To save the world, was not good enough.

It took three rings of the doorbell before Cooper answered. She was shorter than he'd imagined and in many ways resembled the Hopi princess Alixel, except for the strawberry blonde curls that framed her face. Strong arms and legs extended from a T-shirt and shorts that blended southwestern pastel solids with the color of the hardwood floor and wall paint he saw within the doorway behind her.

"Hi Marcy," Cooper said. She shook her hand and looked at Billy. "And Marcy's friend?"

"Billy," he said and shook the tips of her small, unpainted fingernails.

Cooper led them inside. The juicy sweet aroma that had assaulted him outside was overwhelmingly delightful as Cooper closed the door behind him.

"That's fantastic," Marcy exclaimed. "Smells as wonderful as what Pedro used to cook up at the Surf Side. Don't you think so?"

Billy smiled. "As wonderful but without the sea."

Cooper looked curiously at Billy then escorted both of them into the living room where handmade Hopi and Navajo rugs overwhelmed the floor and walls. Thick beams of hardwood supported a high ceiling and lamps on long poles dropped down a foot from the beams but were not illuminated; the living room was lit solely by numerous tall windows and a sliding glass porch door through which Billy saw a skirted, round table covered by an umbrella. On the table were a couple of glasses, a pitcher and a setting of three plates.

Cooper led them to the sliding doors past a huge kitchen in which Billy saw a couple of bowls on the kitchen's center island which Cooper grabbed. Outside, an orange-red sun hovered an hour or so above Boynton Canyon's jagged horizon; the table umbrella had been adjusted to block its direct heat, casting a solid shadow over table and chairs. Cooper set the bowls of chips and salsa within the shadow.

"Go ahead and have a seat while I finish up the preparation," Cooper offered. "Some say my salsa is the best in town."

Billy and Marcy sat with their backs to the house and both immediately sampled Cooper's salsa as she disappeared through the sliding doors behind them. Marcy was right. Not only did the smells from the kitchen remind Billy of Pedro, so did the taste of the salsa. The thought of his chef and the memory of his murder briefly made him sad.

Cooper returned to the porch and switched on a round, plastic portable fan near the far corner where a three-step riser of stairs descended into the red earth landscaping. The stream of air circled the table, billowing Marcy's long hair and cooling sweat beads on Billy's forehead. Cooper sat, poured water from the pitcher into each of their glasses, grabbed a chip, slid it into the salsa and plopped the chip's triangular corner into her mouth.

"So why are we here?" she asked, bluntly. "Information sharing?" She chomped the rest of the chip and licked her thumb. "What could I have that would possible interest two visitors from Texas?"

How Cooper knew that they were from Texas, minutely jogged Billy's curiosity. He ignored it. "How do you know Professor Cower?"

"My. We are the in-your-face-type aren't we?" All three of them snatched chips and dipped together. "Nothing like getting right to the point." Cooper settled back on the chair's tan cushion. "We'll wait until after dinner to discuss that. There's more info than there is time before the food will be ready. Perhaps some small talk before we get into…" A small chunk of tomato fell from her chip and landed on her right forearm, and she kissed the chunk into her mouth. When she lowered her arm, Billy saw the tattoo of a djed stamped near her wrist. Cooper noticed this and ended her statement with, "…before we get into Cower and djeds and such." She drank some water then added, "I could make us some margaritas if anyone is interested."

"Maybe later," Billy said. He couldn't stop staring at Cooper's tattoo. The last time he'd seen something similar, it had been dangling from Alixel's neck.

"A gift from Chris," Cooper said to satisfy his curiosity. "And a bad decision on my part. Would you please excuse me? Dinner will be ready in a few minutes. I hope beef and chicken are a part of your dietary constraints. I forgot to ask if either of you were vegetarian."

"Sounds good to me," Marcy said.

Billy nodded agreement. "Thank you for inviting us. It all looks and smells wonderful."

Once Cooper was gone, Marcy proclaimed, "Cower told her about the Djed."

"I suspect. So she probably knows about the Book."

"Maybe she knows the significance of the numbers."

"Doubtful. They weren't there until just recently." Billy suddenly realized that the kitchen window was open when he heard Fleetwood Mac singing *Tell Me Lies* from inside the house.

"Will you tell her you have it? That info could be the bargaining chip."

"Shhh," Billy whispered and motioned with his head toward the window. He sipped water and watched a large hawk circle near the rocky Kachina Woman spire in the distance; it dipped above and below the circle of the setting sun that had moved fifteen minutes closer to dusk. He raised his voice. "Did you get a chance to talk to the man at Vor-Tech's?"

"I did." Marcy nodded her understanding of his change of subject. "He wanted too much for it, so I gave it back to him."

"Really?" Billy was surprised. He'd been convinced that Vor-Tech's proprietor would have given it up for next to nothing. "How much?"

"Five hundred."

"Crap. That's insane. You try to barter with some of your fortunetelling skills?"

"He said he already knew his fortune, so I told him that he, therefore, must know that I wasn't going to shell out five hundred bucks for a broken piece of glass. It was strange, really. He was nothing like he was last night. His wife was much more bitchy, too."

"Maybe they had a bad sales day. Most of their stuff was probably busted by the quake."

"I didn't get that impression. Perhaps they just liked you better."

Billy played with the point of one triangular chip before grabbing and eating it. "Too bad. It looked great right next to your buffalo testicles."

Marcy laughed, hard. "Those aren't testicles. They're scaled down replicas of the ceremonial balls used in the ballcourt games. But I like your idea better."

Cooper poked her head out of the sliding door. "It's ready. Grab the bowls and glasses if you don't mind."

Cooper's rectangular dining table was big enough for six people. Only three places were set up, all toward the side of the table closest to the kitchen. Cooper sat at the head with Marcy to her left and Billy to the right from where he could look out through the sliding glass doors onto the porch. A half a dozen bowls and plates of southwestern cuisine sat in front of them. Smaller cups of salsa, guacamole, sour cream and chopped green onions dotted the festive food landscape. A woven wooden bowl held a warm towel where flour tortillas comfortably waited within. The next fifteen minutes was full of hearty consumption and small talk.

"What's the Surf Side?" Cooper asked Billy.

"It's a restaurant I own in Port Aransas. Seafood mostly."

"And quite a delicious place to visit," Marcy added. "Don't let Billy's modesty fool you."

Cooper tried a smile but it seemed a bit contrived. "Really? So how does my cooking measure up?"

"I was just telling Marcy outside how really great everything smelled and the salsa, as you said, is top-notch. You've grilled the meats to perfection. The chile rellenos…well, this is only the second time I've ever had any but, up until now, I've never thought a chile could taste so good." Marcy nodded as she stuffed her mouth with a rolled piece of tortilla that overflowed with a mixture of just about everything on the table. "I am curious though. Where's the beans and rice? I thought those were staples in the southwest."

"Fillers," Cooper said. "Without them, you get to eat more of the real entrées. Restaurants serve too much of the frijoles y arroz to fill you up and save on the expensive ingredients."

"Makes sense." Billy ate the rest of his chile relleno. "So tell me… where did you learn to cook like this?"

"In college. I lived a short stint with a sorority house where I was designated the house cook. You get really good, really fast with twenty stuck up bitches always hammering you with complaints." Cooper ate strips of chicken without a tortilla, moving the meat trough red marinade before forking it into her mouth. "So what's your story?" She pointed the empty fork at Marcy.

"I also have a business in Port A." The statement was muffled by the huge wad of food in her mouth. She swallowed. "A fortuneteller."

"Marcy Ruminski sees all," Billy said. "And she's quite good at it." Billy thought that he had sounded too callous. Even though he was beginning to believe in mystical influences, his baser instincts still protected him from total immersion. Last night's argument with Marcy hadn't helped. Perhaps, he thought, he should just keep quiet when the topic arose in the future.

"You can see our future?" Cooper asked.

"Perhaps." Marcy quickly replied. "Perhaps you should come over to my place some time and we'll test the waters."

"Not into tarot cards and such," Cooper said. "Never was much of an astrologer either. Fate is what you make of it, and if you're wrong, fate will steer you back on the right path."

"We have a lot in common," Marcy said, wiping her hands on a cloth napkin. "We just call them different things."

Marcy asked for some milk to cool the heat of the meal's chile undertones. When Cooper returned with the glass she said to Billy, "What do you know of the Djed?"

Billy wiped his hands and mouth. "So—who's cutting to the chase now?"

Cooper smiled, genuinely this time. "I thought that's how you wanted to play." She sat. "But we can wait until…"

"No. That's fine. Because, quite frankly, I don't know a whole lot about it. All I know is what anyone with a computer could look up on the Internet. I know that it is a reverent Egyptian symbol. It is connected with interpretations such as 'stable,' 'enduring,' and 'resurrection.' It represents the death and renewal of the yearly cycle. It is mostly known for its connection to the legend of Osiris—the murder of Osiris. Osiris is tricked into climbing into a wooden chest by the evil one, Typhon, so the story goes, and the chest is dumped into the Nile where it wanders into the sea and finds land near a huge tree. The tree grows around the chest until one day, the trunk of this tree, containing the body of Osiris, is cut down and turned into a pillar for the house of the king. I also remember reading that Osiris was born on the three hundredth and sixty-first day of the year, one of five unlucky days. As it was in Egypt. As it was for the Mayans."

"As it is for many cultures," Cooper concluded. "There seems to be a common connection to peoples who lived across impassible oceans in times when water navigation was in its infancy. Makes you wonder if all cultures are all a part of some greater…" She hesitated for the right word. "…some greater existence."

Cooper folded her hands and placed both elbows on the table, straddling her empty plate. Her statement reminded Billy of the images of the Bible's creation story as it was depicted in the Book of the Djed, as

Alixel had explained to him on the night of the hurricane. He remembered not believing her. He remembered thinking that such cross-cultural connections were impossible.

A few uncomfortable minutes passed in silence as the diners finished their meals, then Cooper stared directly into Billy's eyes, never blinking, never flinching and with a threatening undertone said, "Since we are being so blunt this evening, I'll offer this: you want to know about Chris Cower; I want to know if you have the Book of the Djed."

Billy snatched a quick glance from Marcy whose eyes looked apologetically disdain. He thought Cooper must have overheard their conversation through the kitchen window.

"Wait," Cooper said, abruptly. "Before you tell me you *do* have it let us retire onto the porch for a bit of green tea and sunset." She scooted the chair from under the table and stood before either Billy or Marcy could answer. "I'll be out in a moment. Please." She offered her hand in the direction they were supposed to walk.

Outside, the fan still spun a cool breeze across the table but the umbrella was of no use any more; the sun had fallen below Boynton Canyon and twilight had taken its place. Billy collapsed the umbrella, looked over at the kitchen window which appeared to be closed, then sat beside Marcy.

"I don't trust her," Marcy said.

"What makes you say that? Because she doesn't like fortunetellers? Seems lots of people don't like fortunetellers around here."

Marcy slapped Billy's arm. "Enough with the fortunetelling thing." She rubbed the spot she'd just slapped. "I don't trust her because I think she's playing us. I don't trust her because, somehow, I think she's in on this with someone else. She might not be the bad guy but she's working for him. I think you've known me long enough to trust my intuition."

"Yes. Of course I do. But we've gotta give to get. You said as much yourself."

Marcy moved her hand from Billy's arm to brush red-painted fingernails though her black hair. She leaned back in the chair, prompting her chest to rise upward toward the waning light. "You're right. Just be careful. I wouldn't want to lose my favorite man."

Cooper appeared with a tray that held a ceramic pot decorated in bands of red, orange and brown, and three similarly decorated cups. Steam trickled from the pot's closed top. She sat with her back to the darkening horizon and poured each of them some green tea. "I hope you don't mind drinking it straight," she said. "It is the best way to drink green tea…you know without all of the artificial additions."

Billy didn't answer the question but instead said, "I do have it. And to tell you the truth, I really don't know why I have it. I guess it was sort of passed down to me."

"From Chris?" Cooper asked, sipping tea.

"From Janine Bender."

"I don't know any Janine Bender."

"No. You wouldn't. I only knew her for a few short hours before she was killed."

Marcy watched her tea steam but didn't drink it. "She was a wonderful person," she said. "Kicked around and beaten down. She just wasn't at the right place at the right time."

Cooper raised her hands, palms high, in an I-don't-know-what-the-hell-you're-talking-about pose. One red-haired eyebrow lifted up under a curl of hair equal in color.

So, Billy told Cooper the story of Janine Bender, at least as much of her story as she had told him. He recounted details about the destruction of her farm, about Janine's flight to Port Aransas to escape her husband, Albert, who had then followed her to the island. He told Cooper that Janine had saved Cower's life and that she had acquired the Book from him though he didn't tell her how since he didn't know himself. He left out parts concerning the walking dead and all of his friends that had been cubited, and when he had finished, Cooper looked directly at Marcy and said, "So what about the Cubit? You asked about that yesterday."

Marcy directed the answer toward Billy. "He knows more about that stuff than I do. I'm just along for the ride."

Cooper turned a stern look on Billy. "We are going to get nowhere unless we can all be totally honest with each other. You have to understand that the Book and the Cubit are interconnected. How well, I'm not quite sure, but I do know one thing. That Book you have possesses great knowledge and great power. With it, you can become invincible."

Marcy responded before Billy had the chance. "So that's why you want the Book? You're hungry for the elusive and quite fantastic delusion of immortality?"

Billy could not have said it any better. He nodded at Marcy then gazed expectantly at Cooper for an answer.

"It's not delusional. At least that's what Chris said."

"Chris," Billy replied. "Chris Cower, the good professor? He seems to be at the heart of all of this. Why don't you tell us about *him*?"

The final sliver of twilight drifted away from the horizon and Boynton Canyon's skyline became nearly invisible. Perhaps it was the sudden coolness that swarmed through the night air that made shivers crawl up Billy's spine. Perhaps it was the shot of adrenaline that pumped through him as his expectant ears waited for what would hopefully further define his own fate. Whatever it was, it froze his mind into a singular concentration. This is why he'd come here tonight.

Cooper began…

The Rise & Fall
of
Christopher Cower

Professor Christopher Cower had visited Sedona on more than one occasion. The first time was in the fall of 2003. His purpose then was the same as it would be four years later: to provide argument against land developers who were driven to influence reservation and national park leaders that their real estate was useless without their investment. But in 2003, Cower's desire to help had been heartfelt, an altruistic effort, unlike the distractive lies contrived in 2007.

He'd come from a State University in New York—Cortland, perhaps, but Cooper could not remember exactly which one, though she did remember that the school had excelled in anthropology studies of which Cower was a professor. A Hopi Elder named Alixel had asked for his help.

And Cower had run off the developers, using archeological reasoning to reinforce what the Indians and naturalists already knew— that, basically, nature was not short on cash. But something else had happened while he'd been in Sedona in 2003, something that would forever change him and, apparently the fates of many, something that would eventually drive him back to Red Rock Country in 2007. Apparently, he'd found some etchings on walls within a burial site that no one had known existed. He'd stumbled on the site purely by accident, and to hear him tell the story, the accident had been predestined and had almost killed him; he'd literally fallen into it and had suffered a minor concussion, had passed out, and when he'd awakened, he'd found etchings on tomb walls depicting horrific scenes of mass murder and suicide. But the tomb also held something intangible, a spirit, and it had "infected" him; it had prevented him from mentally putting away the images and they had haunted him, forced him into a solitary pledge never to return to Sedona again.

Then in 2005, while hosting a prominent entrepreneur and former professor at his state college, Cower was, again, engaged with the memory he'd tried to quit. The visitor, whom Cower only referred to as "Dick," had engaged him in a conversation that had revealed many truths about the burial site he'd stumbled upon. Dick had told Cower the story of the great Anasazi tribe and of their sudden, complete disappearance and that what he'd seen on the walls in the burial site was sort of a final epitaph, scratched for infinity by one of the tribe's last survivors. This epitaph documented the true reason for the tribe's disappearance and served as a warning. According to Dick, the Anasazi had not died from plague or famine or tribal warfare and they had not been taken to the stars by extraterrestrials. The Anasazi had killed themselves. They had become possessed by an evil transformation that tempted all men, an evil that cared not for compassion unless compassion was a lie that would culminate in the true goal. Absolute Power. Absolute invincibility. Absolute control of the Earth and the Sun and the universe. This aberrant belief had embattled brother against brother and father against son. They had murdered each other, some taking their own lives in mass suicides so as not to be consumed by the evil that would guarantee them great suffering.

As an archeologist, Cower was staunchly curious as to the reason for such mass insanity that could destroy an entire population and Dick had helped him satisfy this curiosity. Dick had told him that the answers lay at the bottom of a hidden chamber that had yet to be uncovered in the Mayan ruins at Chichen Itza.

With directions from Dick, Cower had found a secret room in the ruins and had uncovered the reason behind the Anasazi's self-genocide. He'd also stolen two artifacts that led him back to Sedona in 2007. One of them was a Creation Dagger. The other was the Book of the Djed.

In the fall of 2007, Sedona had come under the influence of another powerful corporation. The multinational company, Phoenix International, whose industries included oil speculation, pharmaceuticals and gambling, among others, had tried to gain a foothold in Red Rock Country through false promises and lots of money. Phoenix International, locally led by a man named Chancey Lett, had wanted to build a casino on national park land that had been leased to the government in a hundred year deal from the Hopi Nation. Because of his success in 2003, Cower returned to Sedona to fight the impossible battle against corporate greed and corruption. But this, of course, was not the real reason he'd returned. His presence as a hero spokesperson and nature preserver was legitimate in the eyes of the Verde Valley residents but it served only as a distraction for the pursuit of his ultimate goal: to return to the burial site because he now understood that it was the entry into the Great Hall of the Anasazi in which he would find the mechanism that had caused the annihilation of the Anasazi and would eventually destroy the world.

The Cubit.

Cower had hooked up with Cooper because of her knowledge as a guide and because he'd lost the confidence of the Hopi Elder, Alixel, whom he'd joined in common cause four years before. Cooper also had a great relationship with both the Indian tribes and the Parks, having presented herself as an advocate for the preservation of all the beauty the Red Rock Country offered. He'd "hired" her to be his personal guide and companion spokesperson because of the respect she commanded in the community. He'd offered her more than money, though; he'd offered her knowledge. He'd shown her things that most humans would never see. And he had fallen in love with her.

Or so he'd said.

Cooper had never known if Cower had truly loved her. There had certainly been lust, but the lust had been mutual. With Cower in the heyday of his sixtieth birthday and Cooper in the heyday of her thirtieth, both had found solace in the comfort of each other's arms. He'd convinced her to get a tattoo (something she'd sworn she'd never do) because, as he'd said, the Djed was the protector against evil and the resurrection of the good. And she'd been convinced of this because he'd shown her the Book.

On the night before Cower had left, he'd told Cooper the story of the Book of the Djed: how it was an instruction manual to prevent the end of days; how it could be used to raise the Djed; how it could make a person invincible. He'd shown her the center spread and she'd seen an invisible hand sketch into a blank page the image of a fiery bird. She'd seen the flames virtually written onto the bird's wings right before her eyes. And she'd become consumed by it.

The following morning, Cower had gone, leaving no trace of his visit. It was only by pure luck that Cooper would see him one more time and that was the night she'd seen the walking dead for the first time. Cower had found what he'd been looking for all along. Cower had found the Cubit and the Cubit had created his evil twin, just like it had done to the Anasazi, just like it did to anyone who touched it. Cooper had seen him slash his own cubit with the Creation Dagger near Café Aus then had watched him drive off in a station wagon with Cubit, dagger and the Book, never to be seen again.

Or at least that's what she had thought then.

"I think he's returned," Cooper said, concluding her story. "I think he's back in town having fun at my own expense. And I think he might be following me around."

Billy immediately thought of Deere-hat man, but Janine Bender had sworn that Cower was dead, that he'd pushed the plunger that had blown up her farm and himself. "Why do you think that?" Billy asked her.

"Someone sent me an anonymous email yesterday morning that said they knew the location of the Great Hall and that they were willing to share the information with me. I only know of one person who would know the location of the Great Hall of the Anasazi."

"But you never saw him did you?"

Cooper hesitated. "No."

Marcy interjected. "Did you get the information?"

"Kind of…" Cooper looked out toward the canyon. The moon had grown one day closer to new. Only a tiny fingernail of it remained in the sky toward the southwest. Its absence of lunar light made the black night a stargazer's feast. Something streaked across the sky, a pinpoint of light that could have been a satellite or meteor. "I'll show you, but first you have to promise me something."

"I won't tell anyone of our conversation," Billy said.

"Thanks. But that's not what I was going to ask for, though I think our mutual confidence in this is paramount to maintaining our sanity in the eyes of others. I want to see the Book. I want to hold it."

Billy didn't hesitate. He'd known she would ask for it eventually. "We can arrange that," he said. Cooper's smile appeared and faded so quickly that Billy wasn't sure he'd seen it at all.

"Splendid," she said. "Follow me."

Cooper led them into the house, past the dining table still littered with uneaten foods and dirty dishes, and into her bedroom. Billy immediately saw the parchment paper taped to the wall. Below the parchment on the hardwood floor laid a copy of the local newspaper and the plastic delivery bag it had been wrapped within. "It's a map," Cooper said.

Marcy walked closer to the wall. "Doesn't look much like a map. Looks more like it does outside: a bunch of stars clustered together into constellations."

Cooper looked surprised. "You're actually not far off." She walked
to her desk and grabbed the Sedona leylines sketch. "Coincidence?" she
said, showing them the paper. "Cower gave it to me a year ago and now
this parchment shows up."

Billy walked closer and Cooper followed. His finger tested the
texture of the parchment then traced patterns that connected the dots.
"The Great Hall of the Anasazi is buried among the stars?" he asked, not
looking at Cooper.

"Well…not precisely. But these dots do represent heavenly
energies."

"Tell me more."

"I think this is the representation of energy lines across the face of
Sedona and the Verde Valley. At least that's what Chris told me."

"Yes," Billy said. "I see them. Literally, it is a star map. One six-
and one five-pointed star." He saw the puzzled look on Marcy's face and
traced the two patterns for her to interpret. "So where is the Great Hall?"

Cooper shrugged. "At one of the points. At one of the
intersections…"

"Or anywhere in between," Marcy interjected. "Some map."

"Marcy." Billy raised his voice. "Can we focus, please?" Cooper
and Marcy moved away from each other and closer to Billy's opposite
sides. "Is there any reason why one of the points might be a more
reasonable choice than another? Do these two symbols have any meaning
to the riddle?"

"Three symbols," Cooper said. "There are three symbols. Here…
my mistake." Cooper grabbed the curled end of a slice of masking tape
from the lower right corner where she'd repositioned it earlier. When she
peeled it away, the third symbol appeared from underneath. "I know that
this is a glyph that represents the sun or ascension and awareness, and
this is a glyph of the jaguar, the ruler of the underworld, but I am not sure
about this one."

"Wayeb," Billy immediately replied. "Dear God." Both
women turned to him simultaneously. "This really forces back some
uncomfortable memories."

Cooper touched his shoulder; it was the closest she'd been to him
all night. "What does it mean? Does it give you any hint to where the
Great Hall might be?"

"No. Not really. It's a Mayan symbol for the last five days of the year…of their year—bad days…unlucky days…evil days. Perhaps that's why it's drawn so far away from the star points. Evil must be kept separated."

Marcy said, "So maybe this isn't a map. Maybe it's some kind of calendar—some kind of countdown."

Billy's eyebrows rose. "Maybe it's both. Maybe it's neither." Cooper's hand was still on his shoulder when he asked her, "And you think Cower's involved? You really think he's alive?"

Cooper shrugged, retreated from the star map and walked to her bedroom door. "So when can I get a look at the Book?"

"Can I call you?" Billy said, following Cooper's nonverbal push to leave her bedroom. "Monday might be preferable."

The night was at an end. For some reason, Cooper seemed no longer interested in their company. She wasn't getting the answer she wanted, Billy supposed, but, quite frankly, he didn't have many; the search for answers was why he'd come to Arizona. But he did have one other piece of information he'd been holding back—something that could be used as a bargaining chip and could be added to the ante. If he was going to find out anything else from Cooper he'd have to play his one last card.

"There's been more written in the Book since you last saw it," Billy offered.

Cooper stopped and stood halfway between the dining room and the front door. "Chris said that would happen." She looked at her bare feet as they shuffled over the wooden floorboards. "More will continue to appear until 2012." Cooper's face turned to him and Billy was struck for the first time with how pretty she really was—not in a beautiful or gorgeous kind of way, and not in the sultry and seductive confluence that defined Marcy's entire body, but a pinch-your-cheek and glow-like-the-moon kind of cute. Even the stern look she gave Billy at that very moment he considered cute. "What is it? What's written there? And if you say something stupid like, 'You'll see when I show you the book' then we can say to hell with our newfound relationship."

Marcy walked to the front door and opened it, a silent retaliation for Cooper's aggressive ultimatum. She was shaking her head *No* when Billy said, "Sixes. Three sixes written under the bird of fire."

Cooper's expression changed in an instant. Now it was her turn to ask for answers. "What does it mean?"

"I think you already know what it means. A warning, perhaps. A premonition. A fortune." He looked at Marcy who stood in the open doorway.

Cooper's mouth hung open as her head absently shook in disbelief. Her eyes wandered across the floor looking for nothing that wasn't there. She, again, turned to face him. "You'll bring it to me on Monday, then; Monday at noon. You bring it here to my house and we'll go for a walk. In the meantime, give the star map some thought. You seem like an intelligent man. Maybe you can figure out if there's anything else to it." Cooper escorted him to the door. "I'm trusting in you. Please understand, beyond anything else, that all of these puzzle pieces we've been talking about are of no value apart. They must come together at the right time and in the right place—by us if we are to save the world; by them if they are to destroy it. The one with all of the cards in the end will win."

Billy didn't say anything; he only nodded. He was struck by Cooper's sudden attitude shift.

"And Billy," Cooper added as he and Marcy retreated from the doorway. "Be careful out there. The jaguar is alive in Sedona."

Cooper had learned much by eavesdropping through her kitchen window. The stolen knowledge had helped her control the flow of the conversation, had helped her make a deal, had guaranteed that she would actually hold the Book in her hands again. But it was what Billy had said at the end of the night that had really flipped her lid.

Three sixes had been written into the Book by the Hand of God.

Well, he hadn't really said "Hand of God" but Chris had suggested as much. And that's why she'd become so obsessed by it. The Hand of God writing clues in the middle of an ancient book that, if understood, would guarantee immortality in the Great Hall of the Anasazi.

She ignored most of the meal's dirty dishes, rinsing just a few and leaving them in the sink, something that she'd seldom done but her obsessive compulsive tendencies had refocused.

Sixes. She remembered Chris telling her his opinion about the sixes in Revelation. She remembered him telling her that they had nothing to do with the mark of the beast or even the Bible. She remembered him saying that the numbers served as a historical marker, that sixes had more to do with calendars that were unrelated to Western ideals or idols. He'd said that the meaning of the numbers 666 had not originated from the Middle East at all but from Central America.

She walked out onto the porch where the half-empty pitcher of water still sat and poured a small amount into one of the glasses though, in her absentmindedness, she was not sure, nor did she care, which glass she'd selected; Marcy's red lipstick faintly colored the opposite side from which she drank.

Monday was such a long time to wait, she thought. The Book was so close yet still too far away. What if something happened to him between now and then? What if something happened to this man who had, toward the end of the evening, began to feel *comfortable* to her? What if something happened to Billy? She might never see the Book again. And her dreams would forever haunt her. The idea of three sixes would remain an unsolved mystery until the end finally came. And she would die never knowing.

Damn Chris Cower for doing this to her. Damn Him!

She threw the plastic glass as hard as she could into the dark brush and heard it clunk off of some distant rock. Farther out, along Boynton Pass, a pair of headlights grew bright as they neared her house. When the headlights turned right onto Boynton Canyon Road, the single streetlamp at the crossroad flashed a shadowy green color from the passing car's metal surface onto the porch's wooden handrail and Cooper's right leg but she paid it no attention.

Sixes...

Three of them...

Did they have anything to do with the map?

Did the map have anything to do with the calendar?

Why was she driving herself crazy?

Obsessing. About the Book. About the Great Hall.

DAMN CHRIS COWER!

Cooper retired to her bedroom and sat on the edge of her bed, to stare at the parchment of dots and glyphs that made no sense no matter how many times she tried to entice the idea of sixes into it. She would eventually fall asleep in the same spot, collapsed to one side, her butt barely on the bed, her legs bent as if she was still sitting, her dreams an agonizing mixture of what she thought she knew and what really was fiction.

They hadn't walked more than a few hundred yards when the car approached from behind them. Billy was trying to understand how Marcy could have been so rude to Cooper and had just finished asking her if she just might be a little jealous, when the car's horn startled both of them. The car traveled another fifty yards then stopped, its red taillights blazing as the driver held a foot against the brake pedal. Marcy grabbed Billy's arm above the elbow and he stood with her on the side of the road, silent. When the Cadillac's door opened, no interior light offered clues to the driver's identity, though the shadows provided every indication that the driver was wearing a ball cap. When it looked at them, its eyes roiled like silver spheres covered in blood.

"I warned you," the guttural, masculine voice said, sending a hallow echo into the darkness that seemed to swallow Billy's spine. "You know what happens when you don't listen."

The dagger in its sheath under his shirt began to warm. His breast sweated. He looked down to see that his shirt was not glowing—at least not yet.

The shadow continued, its voice rising in anger. "If that bitch screws everything up, I guarantee you they'll all die." And then the shadow pointed at him, its red and silver eyes emulsifying into crimson blood spots. The shadow smashed its fist into the roof of the Cadillac, got back into the car, slammed the door closed, and sped off. A rooster tail of dirt carried into the air and dropped in a thin wave on Billy and Marcy.

"What the hell was that all about?" Marcy asked. "Do you know that man?"

"No. But that car looks like the one that turned around in your driveway. And did you notice the ball cap?"

"That guy from Starbucks. You can't be serious?"

"I'm just saying."

"I think it was some drunk who thought we were someone else."

"Maybe." But Billy really did think so. His dagger's warmth had warned him otherwise. He *knew* that the shadow he'd just witnessed was not only Deere-hat man but was also a cubit—the evil dead—but he wasn't going to tell Marcy this. She wouldn't believe him. He only hoped that the faith which Marcy thought she possessed equaled the courage he thought she might need should the Cadillac's driver decide to visit her. "Do you have anything to protect yourself with in the house?"

"Why do you ask?"

Billy pointed at the retreating taillights which quickly faded to black. "That was Deere-hat man and that was the Caddy that was in your driveway." He said it sternly, as if he wanted absolutely no argument.

"Billy Jo Presser. Why you caring fool. I've got a big walking stick but that's about it. Unless, of course, you are making me an offer."

Her smile eased his nerves for the moment before he understood what she meant. "I didn't mean *that*, but I am concerned for you."

"And what about yourself? Perhaps I should be the one concerned about you. It's you that has the Book of the Djed. Do you have any way to protect *yourself*?"

It might have been his imagination but, suddenly, all of the critters in the desert went silent; it was as if all of the hoots of owls and squawks of nightjars, the cries of prairie dogs and howls of coyotes, even the slithering of rattlers and scuttling of scorpions, had paused their nocturnal searches for food and water to await Billy's answer. It was as if their calm was warning him.

Don't tell her, the silence of the critters demanded. *Don't tell her you have the dagger.*

Billy placed his hand on his chest. "But he doesn't know I have the Book. How could anyone know I have it…well, except you and, now, Cooper."

"My point exactly."

The desert night was again filled with the sounds of wildlife struggling for existence. Billy resumed walking and Marcy followed at his right shoulder. "You really don't trust her, do you?"

"Neither do you. Isn't that what you said? You told me to keep my trap shut tonight because you didn't trust her."

"But she did give us some extremely valuable information."

"Assuming it's true."

"Why would she lie about having an affair with an old professor? It seemed to hurt her pretty bad."

"You haven't known many women in your life have you Billy Jo

Presser? I've known some of the worst drama queens God could ever conjure up. Cooper wants what you have and like all women, she's bound to say or do anything to get it. Hell, she screwed an old man for information."

"Sounded to me like he screwed her."

"Yes. Well…all I know is if what she says *is* true and *if* the Book *is* an instruction manual for ending or saving this planet or for becoming immortal or for whatever, then I suspect you'll have your answer soon. Regardless, until Monday, or until you make up your mind if you'll actually show her the Book, I'd keep it in a safer place than your bathroom—some place like a bank vault."

Billy stopped and stood and glared at Marcy without saying a word.

"Sorry." Marcy corrected herself. "Perhaps a bank vault isn't the safest place either, come to think of it."

The rest of the ten minute walk home was silent except for the critters. Again, Billy thought he was imagining it, but it seemed to him like the animals were following them, as if an outer perimeter had been set up by packs of mammals and birds and reptiles and those packs were walking and hoping and flying and slithering in concert with each step he took. This imagination became even more believable when Billy and Marcy stopped at the crossroad of Gringo and Dry Creek Road and Marcy pointed at her casita and said, "I could hide it for you. There's lots of places to hide a book in there. Some of the floorboards are even loose."

And again, the night fell silent.

"Do you hear that?" Billy asked her.

Marcy paused. "No. I don't hear anything."

Don't give her the Book, the silence warned.

"Don't you think that's strange?"

Don't let her know you have the dagger.

"Yeah. It is strange come to think of it. So, what do you think?"

Don't trust her.

"I think that I'll keep a hold of it for now."

Don't tell her anything else.

"So, I'll see you tomorrow then?"

"Not sure. I've got to get a few things done. I'll stop over."

Marcy turned away and as she headed for her front door the animals began talking again. She looked over her shoulder and raised her arms in the air as if acknowledging nature's voices then entered the casita and closed the door.

Billy walked to his apartment and stood for a moment on the doorstep landing. Looking out in the direction of Cooper's house and Boynton Canyon, he saw what appeared to be a huge animal sitting on a large rock. At its distance from him, it was no bigger than a postage stamp and was illuminated by some unknown light source that provided a faint orange hue behind its black silhouette. He knew that it was a cat because of its tail. He knew it was a cat because of its ears. He knew it was a cat because it suddenly snarled loud enough that the echo reached him in less than a second.

What had Cooper said before he'd left her house?

The jaguar is alive in Sedona.

Invasion of Reality

Cooper was awakened by the pounding at her front door. It was ten o'clock. She would have rather taken a few minutes to work the kinks from her neck (sleeping sideways like she'd done had forced most of her upper body muscles into unknown configurations) but the pounding was relentless. It wasn't until knuckles began beating against her back porch sliding glass door that she rose, stretched one time, brushed both hands through red curls and pulled her T-shirt down over her belly button. She took two steps then stood motionless in the bedroom doorway, her groggy-brained alarm clock bellowing shrill warnings that immediately engaged memories of headless jaguars and sword-wielding suns.

The police officer's silver badge bounced sunshine directly at her and she lifted her forearm, the one with the djed tattoo, to block the white pain from reaching her eyes. A second officer roamed the porch decking, looked at the water pitcher but didn't touch it, scanned the desert landscape as if looking for something in particular.

"Ma'am," the officer at the glass door was saying though his voice was muffled. "Ma'am. Could we speak with you?"

She tried not to look guilty even though she wasn't. Oddly, and only for the brief moment that it took her to walk to the door, she feared being taken in for questioning only because such an unexpected circumstance would mean leaving behind a table and kitchen full of dirty dishes. She slid the door open.

"I'm Detective Beets. This here is Detective Dreagan. Do you mind if we come in?"

Cooper looked over her shoulder at the table. "Can we talk on the porch? My house is a mess." Detective Beets' eyes were covered with stereotypical cop sunglasses (big, round and mirrored) but she knew he was scanning the home's interior.

"It's getting hot out here. Heat wave ain't over yet." He paused to entice a reaction from Cooper. When she said nothing, he added, "Okay then. But a couple of glasses of water would be nice."

Cooper opened the door and pointed. "Could you hand me that pitcher?" she said. Detective Beets did so. "I'll be right out."

As she filled the pitcher, she stared at the flat screen TV on the wall, remembering the news anchor's announcement, remembering that she might become a prime suspect. She'd done nothing but she'd seen everything. When she returned to the porch, the table umbrella was open and both officers sat under its shade. She poured them water and sat between them.

"Do you know why we are here?" Detective Beets said, removing his sunglasses. His face, in many ways, mirrored Tom Selleck's, right down to the bushy mustache.

Cooper didn't bite. "It's awfully early for a Sunday. I usually sleep in. Could we just get to the point?"

Sitting to her right, a younger Detective Dreagan removed his sunglasses (also cop-like). He was not as cheerful as his counterpart and he looked nothing like any cop she'd ever seen on TV. In fact, he looked more like a criminal. "You are Cooper Reyes, aren't you? The Sedona guide? One who wakes at the crack of dawn to lead droves of ignorants into our mountains and valley passes?" There was a silent pause. "And you usually sleep in on Sundays?"

Cooper's grogginess caused anger to form quickly. "I had a late night."

"How about Friday nights?" Dreagan said. "Are you up late on Fridays as well?"

Cooper turned away from Dreagan and looked straight at Beets. "So he's the bad cop, eh?" she said, thumbing with her right hand. "Why don't you tell me why you're here on a Sunday drinking water with me on my porch instead of inside a church where people need saving?"

Beets reached into his tan shirt pocket and opened the folded piece of paper he'd stored there; he flipped it onto the table. "Do you know this person?"

On the paper was an artist's sketch. Cooper thought she knew the face, but wasn't sure. She snatched the paper to study it further. "No," she said.

Dreagan again chimed in. "Luke says you were at his restaurant late Friday night."

Cooper continued staring at the sketch. The face was familiar but not the bald head. Even the neck, which abruptly ended at the paper's bottom edge, seemed a part of some recent memory.

"He says you were waiting for someone," Dreagan continued. "Is this that person?"

Cooper shook her head. "No," she repeated.

Beets said, "I suppose you've heard that one of our officers went missing Friday night?"

Cooper nodded. "It was on the news."

"We have a witness that saw the woman in that sketch leave the alley next to Charleys around the same time we last heard from the officer. Café Aus is just a block away from there and you were sitting outside."

Cooper nodded.

Dreagan snatched the sketch from Cooper's hands. "So did you see this woman or didn't you?"

Beets said, "Please excuse Dreagan. The officer that is missing is his best friend."

"I must have left the restaurant before any of this happened," Cooper said, dreamily, since the identification of the person in the sketch preoccupied her mind.

"That's what Luke told us," Beets said.

"Or we would be here arresting you right now," Dreagan added.

"My friend stood me up," Cooper said. "That's all I know. That's all I saw."

"And who is this friend?" Beets asked. "Perhaps he knows something."

"Who says I was waiting for a man?" Cooper stood. "Doesn't matter anyway. It was just another spiritualist who wanted to arrange a personal tour into the canyon."

Dreagan stood and Beets followed. "His name?" Dreagan demanded.

"Chris Cower." Cooper said. "Now, if you don't mind, I have some cleaning up to do. I'm a very busy woman, preparing to lead droves of ignorants into our mountains and valley passes." She glared at Dreagan who returned his sunglasses to his nose.

"Cower," Dreagan said. "How do you spell that?"

"Just like it sounds." She spelled it for him anyway.

"We'd like to ask you more questions should the need arise," Beets said.

Cooper nodded. "Good day, gentlemen."

Once the police cruiser was out of her driveway and down the road, Cooper collapsed onto her couch. The dishes needed washing, her kitchen needed cleaning, her home needed a good hour or two of her attention. But that was now impossible since her mind was overwhelmed with a singular revelation: the person in the sketch, with a lot of long, dark hair drawn in over the bald head, was the woman to whom she'd served dinner last night. The woman in the sketch was Marcy Ruminski.

Billy had intended to ask Marcy if she wanted to walk with him to the library but she wasn't home. Even though she could be annoyingly callous sometimes, he did enjoy her company. Marcy always put a different spin on his thoughts and though it was hard for him to admit, he liked that part of her—always challenging him, and, always doing what women were good at: changing their minds.

He knocked on her door several times and even went around back to peek into the back porch window just in case she hadn't heard him. It was well after noon so he doubted that she was still asleep. "Marcy," he shouted. "Yoo-hoo."

He stood on the porch another three minutes before giving up. When he turned to exit, his attention was drawn to dozens of dark red circles that stained the wooden porch floorboards. Blood, perhaps. There were six large circles about an inch in diameter and many smaller dribbles. He immediately thought about the cubit in the Cadillac and he hoped that Marcy had been correct: that the man had been drunk and that he and she had been misidentified. The blood could have been left by an animal or…there were many possible explanations including ones that discounted any blood at all. Still—

I warned you. You know what happens when you don't listen, the cubit had said.

Billy started his walk along Dry Creek Road, trying not to think about Marcy and their journey home last night which was, of course, impossible. Every vehicle that approached from behind made his skin crawl just a little and, for each vehicle, he stopped, stepped away from the road and waited as it passed, ensuring himself added safety even though he knew that if anyone would have wanted him dead, he would be dead already.

If that bitch screws everything up, I guarantee you they'll all die.

In the thigh pocket of his cargo shorts, he carried a small spiral notebook and mechanical pencil. Earlier that morning he'd jotted down information according to Cooper and his intention now was to do a bit of research, check out her story, ensure himself that she was not a liar. He'd have a couple of hours before his planned dinner date with Lax and his son.

Sedona's public library was conveniently located at the end of Dry Creek Road, about a block from the intersection with Highway 89. Also convenient for Billy was the fact that the library had decided to open on Sundays for the holiday month, something that it had not done before but was experimenting this year thanks to a grant from some local bibliophiles.

Inside, the library was quite busy. Over in the children's section, a group of youngsters sat in a circle as a woman read to them. To the right of the children were computer kiosks but every one of the ten computers was occupied. To burn time while he waited, Billy sat in the reference section where local newspapers hung from wooden poles that rested inside a square rack. He grabbed the pole that held last Wednesday's edition of the *Sedona Red Rock News* and sat at a square, wooden table to read it. Much of the usual small town community news occupied the first section of the newspaper, including stories in which gossip was given a degree of credibility by having it published and promoted. Some community members complained about street construction and the "crooked" way construction contracts were granted. Some congratulated Christian leaders for merging gaps between the local spiritualists and God. The Village of Oak Creek didn't like the fire station that was going to be built there. Cottonwood was worried about increased traffic without the law enforcement necessary to enforce the increased traffic. A few articles devoted column inches to the Thanksgiving holiday season, to shopping, and to recipes.

But it was the front page of the sports section that changed Billy's quick scan consumption to full immersive reading. The bold headline drew him in:

Llama Lunatic Mountain Bike Race Begins Monday

The City of Sedona and the Village of Oak Creek announce the first annual Llama Lunatic Mountain Bike Race to be held on Monday, Dec. 1.

In cooperation with the National Parks Service and sponsorship by BETH Pharmaceuticals, the race will traverse a loop marked by the Llama Bike Trail. National race professionals will be challenged by sharp natural benches, slickrock, big drops and, perhaps, a cactus or two as they traverse the relatively new trail around Bell Rock and Courthouse Butte and up the challenging rise of Lee Mountain.

"This is an event we've been working on for a couple of years," said Gin Arropo, mayor of Sedona. "The beauty of Sedona's autumn will bring in dozens of prominent athletes from all over the country which will be a holiday boon for local merchants."

BETH Pharmaceuticals, manufacturer of the popular Popstar health pill, has guaranteed a purse of over $50,000 to participants.

"BETH Pharma pledges to bring everyone total health," said the company's president, Richard Manson. "We can't think of a better cooperative effort to bring this mission to these superb athletes and to the people of Arizona."

Stretches of the Llama Trail will be cordoned off for spectators along the entire route. The National Park Service reminds you that if you visit any of Sedona's beautiful natural parks to "Take what you bring and leave what you find." Please visit our local adventure merchants for further information.

BETH Pharmaceuticals. Las Cruces. The Popstar pill. The crazy Hispanic lady he'd almost killed. Deere-hat man. Short chunks of memory collided into a maelstrom of coincidental circumstance. He quickly snatched his notebook and pencil and scribbled the connective keyword sentences, one after the other, on a blank page in the center of the notebook. On the last line, at the bottom of the page he wrote the same name he'd seen on the front page of the *Enquirer* at Walmart—the name of the president of the corporation that owned BETH Pharmaceuticals: Richard Manson.

Two of the computers were now vacant and Billy quickly returned the newspaper to its rack. The monitors were only a couple of feet apart and when he sat at the end of the kiosk, the person to his left, a middle-aged woman who did not wear makeup, looked at him and grinned, then returned to her pursuit of keywords that included cacti, first-aid and poison.

He'd intended to begin his research for anything related to vortices and Sedona but found himself more curious about BETH Pharmaceuticals and the odd connections he was making to that company and recent experience. He opened up Google.

BETH, which was an acronym for Bringing Everyone Total Health, was a relatively new company, having become public just three years ago. It manufactured only one product: the Popstar pill. It was the subsidiary of a much larger corporation: Phoenix International. Its ownership was ninety percent in the hands of one man: Richard Manson.

The Popstar pill was the brand name for what many in the industry were calling "the wonder drug." Clinical trials stated that the pill "reacted with the body's chemistry to negotiate a truce with the urge to eat non-nutritious food." Apparently, the Popstar pill had been shown to reduce obesity by "reprogramming the mind to hate bad foods and initiate satiation of caloric intake." Basically, the pill told the body to choose healthy food over junk and to stop eating once caloric intake reached what the body considered enough, not what the mind thought was enough. This, of course, was a panacea to the health industry and a dogmatic attack on those companies that dished out quick, preservative heavy menus. The fast food industry had unsuccessfully lobbied against the FDA's approval of the drug and the Popstar pill had landed in select communities across the country which, in a year, had shown dramatic decreases in obesity rates. Southwestern cities such as El Paso, Las Cruces and Tucson had quickly risen atop the nation's list of healthiest places to live.

Richard Manson, a former professor of biochemistry at Arizona State University had "discovered" the pill. Manson, the biography read, had made his mantra of bringing everyone total health shortly after recovering from a serious surfing accident when he was a teenager. He'd been a fat kid then and he'd always blamed his obesity on the accident, claiming that a healthier body and mind would have prevented it. To fund research, Manson had become a speculator in oil and other natural resources. His savvy investment decisions had soon made him one of *Forbes* richest men in the world, thus allowing him to pocketbook the Popstar pill's development. Today, Phoenix International and subsidiary BETH Pharmaceuticals were preeminent sponsors for several national health- and athletic-related organizations and activities, including the Olympic Games, the X-Games, a bunch of school systems and dozens of charities.

Billy scribbled the information into his notebook then added a single word at the bottom of the notes: Coincidence? He flipped three pages forward. Before going to bed last night, he'd dumped his memory of the dinner date with Cooper into the notebook. Along with notes about Chris Cower's past five-year history, he'd sketched out a reasonable facsimile of Cooper's map. Ten dots were arranged on the notebook paper but he'd not connected the dots to form the star patterns since doing so, he thought, might lock his mind with an answer to the map that might not be correct. Perhaps the dots weren't meant to form stars; he'd wanted to keep his options open.

He'd also stenciled in the three glyphs in approximately the same location that he remembered them: Jaguar, Sun, and Wayeb. He wasn't a very good artist, at least not with pencil on paper, but his memory provided a satisfactory rendition of the symbols. If he saw them on the computer screen, he'd make the connection.

On the notebook page following the map, were several words on individual lines. He'd kept the list short since one search term often led to tributaries of links.

He opened up a new browser window and typed "Sedona vortex" into the search box. Results included links to web pages representing some of the local businesses, including a reference to Cooper Reyes. He clicked that link. The web page that appeared was a directory listing that included contact information and a brief description:

> Specializing in one of the most profound vortex sites in all of the
> United States, Cooper "Clairvoyant" Reyes is your local guide into
> Boynton Canyon. Hikes into the canyon are arranged by special request
> only.

"Clairvoyant," Billy whispered aloud. The woman beside him who was concerned with cacti hunkered forward as if she thought Billy was watching her search habits. He jotted down the contact information into his notebook and added the keywords "Boynton Canyon."

The next link he selected took him to an online pamphlet that defined the four main Sedona vortices and the energies they resonated.

There was a vortex at Cathedral Rock which resonated with "feminine energies," one at the airport which resonated with "masculine energies," one in Boynton Canyon that provided energetic "balance," and the last was at Bell Rock which offered energies that satisfied all three.

Masculine energies, according to the online pamphlet, resonate with people who are self-confident, who take charge of their own lives, who take appropriate risks. The feminine energies strengthen one's compassion, kindness and consideration of others. Balance weighs the two gender-specific energies equally and resonate in those who do not take action without considering the harm they may cause, while at the same time, deter others from taking advantage of them. Balance, Billy read, was the hardest to achieve and because so few had gained this plateau, its absence in the world was the reason for so much suffering.

Billy wrote in his notebook an additional word, separated by an equals sign, beside the words *Boynton Canyon.*

Boynton Canyon = Balance

The next link Billy chose surprised him almost as much as had Cooper's link, and her clairvoyant nickname: Vor-Tech's Glass Menagerie. The web page was an online store with which one could order many of the pieces sold at the brick and mortar counterpart. Billy typed "dagger" into the store's search box. The glass Creation Dagger immediately appeared. The proprietor had even added an engaging green glow around the picture of the dagger that made Billy think of his walk to Starbucks two nights ago. The dagger in the photo on the web page was not broken. Its price was five hundred dollars which, to Billy, was confusing; Marcy had told him earlier that when she had talked to the store's owner on Saturday, five hundred dollars had been his quote…for a broken dagger. Surely, Marcy had simply made a mistake. Vor-Tech's owner (Calvin Alvery, the web page noted) and his wife had been so insistent that Billy take it, they'd pretty much given it to him.

Within the web page's menu along the left side, Billy chose the link "Our Philosophy." Every paragraph he read matched perfectly with his first impression of the couple he'd met. Calvin and his wife, as the philosophy read, promoted the Chakra as the centerpiece of all human existence. The word "Chakra" was hyperlinked for each instance it appeared and when Billy clicked it, he gasped. The cactus woman beside him stood and walked away.

A thorough explanation of the Chakra's human energy systems

was wrapped around a small thumbnail image of what was labeled "The Sedona Landscape Temple." It contained two stars, one six-pointed and one five-pointed. He expanded the thumbnail with a mouse click and the two stars, superimposed over a terrain mapping of Sedona, filled the screen; except for added information about the Chakra, it was the same as the sketch Cooper had showed him the night before. Quickly, he flipped his notebook to the page where he'd rendered the memory of Cooper's parchment star map. On the computer monitor, a line connected seven points of intersection through the two stars and each was labeled with one of the Chakra energies.

Billy plucked one of the scrap index cards sitting next to the monitor and used it as a straight edge to connect the dots and create the stars in his notebook. He drew a diagonal line through the center of the stars, similar to what was on the monitor, and extended the line to the lower right corner of the notebook page where it intersected the Wayeb symbol he'd drawn there.

Once he'd finished, he set the notebook and mechanical pencil down on the table and stared at the geometric shapes. The points of the stars and the intersecting diagonal line now provided place names for sixteen different geographic locations, but nothing provided clues as to the location of the Great Hall of the Anasazi. What stood out most was the lonely Wayeb glyph which now had the extension of the diagonal line through its center. He ran his index finger along the line he'd drawn, starting from the jaguar, tapping each of the three glyphs, then repeated the action in the opposite direction, running his finger up the page and to the left. He did this finger-tracing three more times before deciding that, perhaps, the line represented a directional marker.

He sent the Chakra map from the computer to the library's printer, closed the web browser window, then opened up Google Earth and directed the program to center over Sedona. Using Google Earth's straight line tool, he drew a diagonal line with the mouse on the computer screen across the face of Sedona in the same direction as he'd drawn it in his notebook. Grabbing the lines lower right endpoint, he extended it, then zoomed out of Google Earth's satellite image to reveal all of Arizona, extended the line, zoomed out, and repeated this process until all of the southwestern United States was visible. He really wasn't surprised to find that the further he lengthened the diagonal line, the closer to the Gulf of Mexico it grew until it intersected with Port Aransas, Texas.

"Shit," he said a bit too loud. One of the librarians at the circulation desk glared at him. In the children's section, several of the kids' mouths opened in astonishment. The woman reading to them placed a finger to her lips. Billy mouthed the word *Sorry* but didn't say it.

Out of curiosity, Billy zoomed out of the satellite image once more, knowing what he'd find. Fully extended, the diagonal line he'd drawn began in Sedona, crossed through Port Aransas and ended at the ruins of Chichen Itza in Mexico where Cooper had said that Chris Cower had found the Book of the Djed.

"My God," Billy whispered but was, again, too loud. The woman reading looked over at the circulation desk. A librarian headed in Billy's direction.

"Sir," the librarian said. "If you can't keep your comments to yourself, you'll have to leave." She looked at his notebook and then the computer monitor as if she expected to see something unsavory.

Billy cancelled Google Earth and the screen was filled with his previous search that concerned BETH Pharmaceuticals. "I am sorry," he said. "I get carried away sometimes."

"Well, just keep it down or you can carry yourself..." The librarian pushed her glasses up the bridge of her nose and squinted at the computer. "You a teacher or something?"

Billy shook his head. "No. Why do you ask?"

The woman reading to the kids glared at both of them. The librarian lowered her voice. "That Popstar pill is pretty popular among the schools around here."

"How so?" Billy said, and when the librarian did not immediately respond he added, "I'm not a teacher but I am a researcher. Can you tell me more about it?"

Their conversation was beginning to annoy not only the circle of children and their reader, but also the five other people who sat in front of the computers around them. The librarian motioned for Billy to follow her. He closed out his web searches, snatched his notebook and pencil, and plucked the printout of the Chakra star map as he passed the printer. Billy stood near a line of two people who were waiting to check out books as the librarian disappeared into a small room then reappeared with a handful of newspapers.

"Here," she said. "These should provide you with information." She handed him back issues of the *Sedona Red Rock News*. "Frankly, I don't think our kids need it, but you can be the judge of that. I've never thought a pill was any substitute for good old-fashioned child rearing. Parents are just lazy."

"Thank you," Billy said. "I'll return them in a few minutes."

"Take your time. We're open 'til five."

Billy returned to the reference section and began reading, his notebook opened to his entries concerning the Popstar pill. The six newspapers dated back to the previous fall, around the same time Cooper had said that Chris Cower had changed her life. He read that BETH Pharmaceuticals had made a proposal to the city in which the school system would receive, free of charge, the Popstar pill as part of Sedona's mandate to reduce its student obesity population, which had dramatically risen since 2001. The schools would also receive grant funding to improve, and in some cases rebuild, athletic facilities and cafeterias. A heavy stipend would be included to better transportation, in-school technology and textbooks. The proposal came at a time when the city was considering a new school levy against businesses that would have raised the tax rates by, at least, six percent, so it was no surprise that many local business owners supported the effort.

There had been heated arguments in city council meetings mostly due to the fact that Phoenix International was asking for something in return: the release of some national park land on which it would build a casino. The property release would garner extra funds for the city's coffers but it would also disrupt a chunk of land near Lee Mountain that had been preserved since the days of the first settlers who had used the mountain pass to move across the Arizona mesas. Some council members had been accused of accepting "pleasantries" if the proposal were to be accepted. The controversy had finally culminated in the proposal being placed on the back burner for further consideration and the school levy did not pass.

When Billy finished, he returned the newspapers to the librarian. It was a little after four o'clock. "Thank you," he said. "You helped a lot. But tell me...did the school levy pass this year?"

"No," the librarian said, removing her glasses to wipe a smudge with the tail of her blouse. "But BETH Pharma is still involved with the city. Even though their proposal hasn't been accepted yet, they still remain true to some of the promises they'd made in connection to its acceptance. The company gave some money toward rebuilding the high

school football stadium and…" The librarian replaced her glasses. "…
and it did give the library a bit of funding. That's why we've been able to
open on Sundays."

Billy was quick to pick up on the librarian's frustration. "But at
what cost?"

"At what cost indeed." She nodded. "It's an uncomfortable catch-
22. I hate the idea of this wonder drug but I also love my library. I figure
it won't be long before the proposal is accepted. BETH will buy its way
into the community."

The librarian's disclosure was familiar. Billy had faced similar
circumstances in Port Aransas. Money was always the great influencer,
whether it was for the purpose of building a casino on environmentally
protected land, or building a front hold into the nutrition decision-making
of a public school system.

His denial of coincidence was pretty much decimated, but what
was more significant was that he was willing to accept it. Science was his
passion and had driven his reason for almost ever. But that was over…
over and done with. His parents, of course, would not approve. They
would question his sanity just as he had always questioned those who'd
been dead set on mythological and spiritual mumbo jumbo. He just
couldn't lie to himself anymore. He had to apply the unexplainable more
to destiny than to theory. He had to rely on instinct regardless of what
facts suggested. He had to believe that he was now living the planned life,
one according to the unknown, unseen and unproven greater being.

He realized all of this on the Sedona Roadrunner shuttle as he
traveled Highway 89 from the library toward his meeting with Lax. He'd
connected the dots, literally and figuratively. He'd been "given" the
Book and the dagger for a reason. He'd been led to Sedona for a reason.
He'd met Lax, and Cooper and, even, Deere-hat man for a reason. He
hadn't just stumbled upon information; he'd been led to it. He'd been
manipulated by the hands of either Heaven or Hell to have come this far,
to be sitting on this shuttle, on this day, four years before the Mayans
predicted that the world would end, realizing that, really, there wasn't
a damn thing he could do about it. He absolutely knew that Lax would

further his path toward destiny, that Cooper would, that Marcy would, that, perhaps, even the Roadrunner shuttle driver would.

He could almost feel the puppet strings attached to his hands and feet. He hated the idea but it was comforting as well. Did he have free will? He wondered. Did anyone really have it? He could jump off the shuttle and bust his brains all over Highway 89 at any time he chose. Wasn't that free will? He could screw destiny at any moment. Wasn't that free will? The puppet strings were invisible and they had no power to hold him back, and if that's the way he was meant to go, then so be it.

He caressed his chest and the sheathed dagger. He rubbed the star that had been burnt into his hand. He stared at the notebook page which he'd opened to the star map. A line connected three towns. He'd now been in two of them. He'd collected artifacts in Port Aransas and was sure that he'd find more in Sedona. And he was now certain that destiny would take him to Mexico. Like a character in a fantasy video game, he was stuffing his gunnysack with items that would be necessary to win a final battle. He even knew that fated date: December 21, 2012. If only he knew whose hand was on the joystick. If only he knew which button, the red or the blue, the joystick operator would press next.

The shuttle stopped at the light at Airport Road. It seemed to Billy that this corner had been rather "fated" for him in the past few days. Vor-Tech's was on the far corner to his left. Starbucks was on the near corner to his right. Near the top of Airport Road was the Health Heaven Haven where he'd met Lax and where, according to his recent research, there was one of Sedona's renowned vortices. He thought for only a moment about exiting the shuttle and visiting Calvin at Vor-Tech's; he thought that he should verify Marcy's story. But he didn't. Vor-Tech's was not open and Marcy wasn't a liar. She'd just made a mistake, that's all. But Billy was beginning to wonder; his effort to even consider it was proof. Still, it made no sense why she would lie about such a simple thing. Marcy was an oddity, but she was the only person he could trust. Characters in fantasy games had to collect characters they trusted as much as they had to collect artifacts for salvation.

The shuttle reached The Y a little before five o'clock and when Billy stepped from the shuttle doors and onto the sidewalk, he immediately heard the quick tapping of a car horn to his left. Traffic filled the intersection that connected Highways 89 and 179 and, through the moving melee, he saw a white Ford Ranger on the far side of the road. The small truck was parked along L'Auberge Lane just yards from where he and Marcy had been sitting when the earthquake had shaken his destiny forward. Again, Billy was not surprised. The quaint connections with present and past and coincidental markers with physical constructs were all a part of spiritual momentum. He even giggled. Where else would Lax have been parked?

Once he'd crossed the intersection, Lax's son opened the passenger's door. It creaked a cry of rust infestation and stuck momentarily before Aaron pushed it to its full extension.

"Hello, my friend," Aaron said, his smile comforting and encouraging. "Jump in."

"We are glad you accepted our invitation," Lax added as Billy yanked the door closed.

The front seat was a tight fit but Aaron's thin body made it possible to manage. His poncho tried to tangle the stick shift, adding a degree of difficulty to the truck's navigation.

They headed south along Highway 179 for just a few minutes before Billy said, "Why did you invite me to dinner…I mean really?" He couldn't stop thinking about his sudden revelation with destiny and this made him impatient.

"Are you hungry?" Lax offered, instead.

Billy thought about it. His stomach had not mentioned it to him since his mind had been too preoccupied for it to listen to anything else except the tidbits of research with which he'd been overwhelmed. "Yes," he said. "Yes I am."

"Then that's why we invited you to dinner. Hungry people need to eat."

Billy let it go. Instead, he followed along. "So, what's for dinner?"

Aaron rubbed his stomach. "Maize. Frijoles. Arroz. Pan de horno de pozo. And vanilla flan for desert."

Billy smiled because of Aaron's play between Spanish and English. "Pan de horno de pozo?"

"Pit oven bread," Aaron translated.

"Really? I had some great fajitas last night," Billy offered. "The meat was grilled to perfection but not in a pit oven."

"We don't eat meat," Lax said. "Our ancestors did—they had to. But we are given better choices today."

"Vegetarians," Billy said.

"No," Lax responded without malice and with total contentment. "Respect."

"Well, that certainly puts a new spin on things."

"Indians that don't eat meat." Lax laughed. "Yes. The world is changing—ever changing."

"And I suspect that is why I was invited tonight." Billy's stiffness within the confines of the truck's cab eased and his shoulder and arm relaxed against Aaron.

Lax lifted a heavy eyebrow, his dark-skinned cheek still bunched from his laugh. "You know more than you think you know." He down-shifted as he slowed the truck for a right turn. Aaron's knees accommodated. "Corn and beans and rice and pit oven bread…a magic elixir. Makes a man think about where he's going. Makes a man think about what he's done. Cleans a man out." He laughed again.

They drove along a curiously titled road called Back O' Beyond. To his left rose the grandiose spires of earth known as Cathedral Rock. To his right, and moving closer to them the farther forward the truck traveled, was Oak Creek. Lax passed what seemed to be the last house on the road, drove at least another mile, then parked in front of a single-level, Spanish-style home, reminiscent of just about every other home in Sedona. Billy was surprised only because he'd had the image of the old western in his mind, one in which John Wayne or Clint Eastwood rode into Indian country only to find teepees and smoking fires and food cooking in the sunshine.

"We don't eat meat and we don't live in teepees," Lax said, his smile still strong and vibrant. "But we still love our bows and arrows." He patted Aaron's head twice. "We'll show you."

Lax's home might have looked like something right out of the new millennium from the outside but inside, tradition reigned. There was no clutter. There were no pictures, no paintings, no floor coverings, and it appeared that the room Billy entered (which he assumed was the living room) housed just two electrical components: an air conditioner and a ceiling fan that spawned four light fixtures.

The room was not empty, however. Billy guessed that Lax was a craftsman, schooled in the fine art of woodworking. The couch and easy chair and two small end tables had either been purchased on a reservation or Lax had built them himself. The arms and legs were whittled into compelling logs of intricate patience and had been stained so that the chunks that had been sliced away appeared darker and deeper. The walls, too, were not completely bare. The bow and arrows that Lax had mentioned in the truck hung above the couch. A quill held six arrows. Eight more arrows were attached to the wall in an intersecting pattern that resembled an asterisk. The bow was decorated with six feathers. Again, all of them looked as if they'd been carved by hand.

"Welcome to our teepee," Lax said. "Aaron. Would you please check the fire?"

Aaron disappeared around a corner of the room to the left. When Billy followed Lax to the couch, he saw that the corner around which Aaron had gone beheld an anteroom that was too dark to see through. He guessed that more of the house existed beyond the chamber but its darkness masked any possible confirmation.

"Please, have a seat." Lax offered the easy chair with an open hand. "Tell me what you think. It's Aaron's first piece."

The chair had hand-stitched, brown upholstery that wrapped around the seat and backrest. Its arms of wood twisted into a knob at the end of the arms' length, as if the craftsman had taken individual branches and had turned them clockwise upon one another, similar to a strand of braided hair. The legs of the chair were formed in the same knurled pattern. When Billy sat in it, the comfort consumed him, seemingly wrapping itself around the perimeter of his backside.

"You are one with the chair, yes?" Lax asked.

"Amazing." Billy patted the twisted arms. "I've not seen or felt anything like it."

"He learns very fast. Aaron will be a master craftsman one day." Lax sat on the couch which was made in much the same way as the chair. "It is of learning that I asked you to come here today. It's the reason why you came to Sedona. You are here but you don't know why you are here."

"Yes," Billy said. In front of him was the dark anteroom. His attention was drawn to it as Lax continued.

"What do you see?"

"I don't know what you mean."

"In the darkness. What do you see?"

The more he stared at the dark chamber, the further his consciousness seemed to be consumed by it. He began to feel lightheaded, as if his brain's neurons had suddenly sprang from the top of his head and now floated an inch or two above him.

"I see…"

The darkness twisted, forming lighter shades of shadow across the blackness. And then a face, hazy at first, took shape.

"I think I see a woman," he said.

"Who is she?" Lax interjected.

The face drifted within the anteroom's darkness and formed into…

"It's Alixel," Billy sighed. "But how can that be?" He turned away from the image just for a second and when he looked back, the face was gone.

"She still lives here," Lax said. "Her spirit has never left."

"You know Alixel?" Billy continued staring into the darkness but the face did not return.

"She is my sister. She said you would be coming."

Whatever part of him that seemed to have separated from his body now dropped back into place. He could actually feel its invisible weight. "Then you know all about…If you and she are siblings then…She told me that I was supposed to save the world…And that means…"

"It means that I am also here to help you fulfill that destiny." Lax scooted across the couch to within arm's length of Billy. "Your hand…let me see it."

Billy turned in the chair to offer Lax his right hand and presented it palm up.

"I knew it was you when I saw this yesterday," Lax said. "A sign of divine protection. And there is only one way that you could have received this mark. You have it, don't you?"

Billy said nothing as Lax traced his palm with one fat finger.

"You have the Creation of the End dagger." Lax lifted the finger and pointed at Billy's chest. "I can feel its energy. It has been lost for so long and now it may be the only thing left to prevent an age of chaos."

The last person to see the dagger, besides his best friend whom he'd killed with it, was Alixel. It seemed almost prophetic that her brother would be the next. Billy slowly unbuttoned his shirt to reveal the dagger's white haft and the star etched in it that duplicated the pattern burned into his palm. He reached for it but Lax grabbed his wrist.

"No," Lax demanded. "Keep it there. The next time it is unsheathed will be the moment it saves your life."

Billy's hand hovered over the dagger. "When?" Billy whispered. "Do you know?"

Lax settled back into the couch. He shook his head. "Only the Great Spirit knows that answer. But I can tell you this…" Aaron walked through the dark anteroom at that moment. Billy buttoned his shirt. "The jaguar will try to get it from you and you cannot let that happen." He turned to Aaron. "How is the fire, son?"

"Smokin'," the youngster said and grinned. He watched Billy reattach the last button of his shirt. "It's ready for him."

"Let's cook, then," Lax said then looked at Billy. "Follow us."

Aaron returned to the anteroom abyss and Lax urged Billy to follow. As he entered the dark chamber, Billy was overwhelmed by a feeling of supreme serenity, as if the small, dark space was filled with all of the world's answers, as if he were walking through dark heaven. On the far side of the room, Aaron lifted what appeared to be a tarp that hung from the top of a doorway. A flash of light appeared then was gone as the tarp fell back in place. Billy's hand wandered forward, connected with the makeshift door, swung the heavy obstruction to one side and entered what was certainly a kitchen. Lax followed.

Again, Billy was greeted with the accoutrements of modern day home living. The kitchen was not much different than Cooper's in that it contained many high-end appliances. What the "front" room lacked for efficiency, the land behind the tarp excelled. The most fascinating thing about the space, however, was its glass walls. From the floor to the ten-foot ceiling, sunshine gathered in abundance. Only the corners of the kitchen were not transparent. It was, in all ways, a solarium. Greenery sat and hung in pots and packages everywhere. The smell was pure nature.

Lax pointed as he described some of them. "Basil. Oregano. Parsley. And these over here…almost impossible to find in America." The plants he now tickled with all of his fingers ranged in size and raggedness. Some had flowers. Some looked almost ill. Some looked too deadly to even touch. None of them was familiar to Billy. "This one gives the body defense against water-borne viruses. This one soothes rashes caused by allergies. This one just makes everything come out according to plan. Kind of like the frijoles but much prettier." He chuckled. "And that one over there provides the mind with the ability to awaken to possibilities outside of experience."

Billy walked over to a small tree that stood about five feet high. Small pods that looked like twisted pasta shells hung from several limbs. He lightly touched one of them. "Sounds like a narcotic," he said.

Lax huffed. "A word used by law enforcement to control a person's attempt to break the bonds of the natural world."

"You grew up in the 60s, I'll bet."

Lax just smiled.

Beyond the glass, the home's backyard patio had been laid with bricks that looked as if they'd been formed and fired by hand. Brown and beige and tan and sand colored the earth's floor in artistic patterns that made sense only to those who gave them concentrated effort. Beyond the perimeter of the brick paving and straight ahead from where Billy stood behind the solarium glass wall was a circular indentation in the ground that spewed smoke.

"You are a cook," Aaron said, tugging at Billy's short sleeve. "Come on. I'm hungry."

Aaron led Billy through an opening in one glass wall and out onto the pavers and Billy immediately gasped. The glory of the solarium and the fine craftsmanship of pavers and furniture were miniscule compared to Cathedral Rock which towered before him, its twin spires of sedimentary history nestled between mounds of abutments that were many yards higher. Billy's head craned at an angle greater than forty-five degrees so as to encapsulate the magnitude of such beauty. "My God," he said.

"Our God," Lax added. "But I think that deserves a little latitude."

"There's not much difference as far as I've been able to tell."

Lax shuffled sideways to where Billy stood in amazement. "We are learning, aren't we? Alixel would be proud."

Billy thought of responding but he knew that it was unnecessary. Their silent bond had been secured. And he knew that he'd finally arrived in Sedona.

The food cooked in a clay pot that was buried in the ground. Aaron taught Billy how to cook bread in it by sticking discs of dough against the sides of the pot with a heavy glove. It took only minutes to bake and when the dough was cooked, it fell to the bottom of the pot where it was plucked free with a long, metal fork. Beans and rice and a heaping helping of grilled fresh vegetables and herbs from the solarium sat on a hand-crafted wooden table. There were no plates and only a single wooden spoon occupied each of the food bowls. The procedure for eating in the Lax household entailed the immediate use of the fresh pit oven bread stuffed with whatever assortment of fillings a person wanted. There was no waiting. Since the idea was to eat the bread while still hot, Billy could be eating while Aaron waited for another disc of dough to cook. They took turns, basically.

"It seems that every time I have dinner with someone, the food just keeps getting better," Billy said, catching a strip of green pepper that fell from bread as he nibbled it. He plopped it into his mouth. "Cooper's peppers were good but not this good."

Lax backed away from the clay pot with a disc of baked dough clasped in the claws of the long fork. "Cooper?" he said, his big eyebrows furled with concern. "Cooper Reyes?"

Billy nodded and took another bite.

"She's bad news," Lax continued. "She tried to steal the Cubit."

Billy had just stuck the last chunk of bread into his mouth and now he choked. Aaron came around behind him and slapped his back.

"Of course we know about the Cubit," Lax said. "We are its protectors."

When Billy could breathe again, he drank some water. "She said it was Cower who tried to steal it. Chris Cower."

"He didn't try. He did. But she helped him. Do you know where it is?"

"I used to but the hurricane swiped it away last June."

Lax shook his head. "No. It didn't. It returned to Mexico. It returned to the land of our forefathers. As did the daggers. Our great mother of nature has a way of correcting earlier mistakes." Lax ate his piece of bread without stuffing it. "But we made a big mistake trusting that man, and we'll likely pay for it in the end."

"If you know where it is, why don't you just go and get it?"

"That's your mission Billy Jo Presser."

Billy thought about the notebook he carried in his cargo shorts front pocket, about the map he'd drawn in it, about the line connecting three cities, about his own premonition that he would eventually end up in Mexico. "Chichen Itza," he whispered to himself.

Lax stopped chewing and took a moment to stare at Billy. "You should understand what you will be getting into."

"I already do. That thing killed all of the people I cared about."

"The Cubit doesn't kill anyone. It makes people kill."

"Either way…" Billy sat down in one of the wooden chairs. The sun painted the horizon with the same desert colors as it had the night before. Cathedral Rock glowed within its iridescence. "Alixel told me that there is only one way to kill a cubit." He patted his chest and the dagger. "I saw her use two of these. She sure could take out those damn things."

"One of the daggers was mine," Lax said and sat beside Billy. "We thought that she might need them both." When he broke off another chunk of bread, steam escaped from a hidden pocket and the sudden heat made him drop the bread onto his poncho. When he plucked the bread from his lap, his finger caught the tail of the poncho, and he accidentally lifted it as he brought the bread to his mouth. For an instant, Billy saw an inch-wide scab just below Lax's dark-skinned rib cage, as if he'd been recently stabbed there. He pulled the poncho down, ignoring Billy's stare. "Now they've all returned home as well, except yours, of course."

"That leaves you defenseless," Billy said.

Lax huffed and smiled. "Aaron. Could you go and bring us some dessert, son?" Once Aaron had finished his last bite of stuffed bread and had disappeared into the solarium kitchen, Lax added, "How old do you think I am?"

Billy shook his head and lifted both shoulders. "If you lived in the sixties…fifty-five, maybe."

"I'm more than five times that age, as is my sister. We come from a long line of the ageless. We are never defenseless. Some would even call us invincible, at least up until the time that we accomplish what the Great Spirit has placed us here to do."

Billy really wasn't surprised. He'd given up questioning the fantastic. The energy drain wasn't worth the effort anymore. He accepted what was said as fact and considered Alixel's fate. "So your sister's purpose was to kill Albert Stine?"

Lax shook his head. "If you remember, it was Janine Bender who killed that beast."

It took him mere seconds to realize the correct answer. "Me," he said. "She was there to save me."

"We all have a greater purpose in this world than we can possibly know. She gave you a *chance* to further your own understanding and you took it."

Billy watched Aaron shuffle through the kitchen behind the tall, glass wall. "And your son? How old is he?"

"He's not my son. We can't have children. I adopted Aaron from the Hopi Nation when he was just a baby. He's grown up thinking that I am his father, though."

"I understand," Billy said as Aaron returned with their desserts. "Vanilla flan. That really looks good, Aaron." Billy sliced a chunk of the molded sweetness. A creamy, white filling oozed out. "So if I'm supposed to be going after the Cubit, it sure would be nice to know more about it." He looked at Aaron, suddenly concerned that perhaps that information was not meant for him, at least not yet.

Lax forked a bite of dessert into his mouth and pushed a stray dribble of vanilla filling into the corner of his lip. "That's okay. He already knows. The oral tradition is still quite strong in the Nations."

Once everyone finished dessert and Aaron had retrieved a fresh pot of white tea, Lax sat back in his chair, gazed out over the Sedona sunset, and began…

The Story of
the Cubit

(as told by a Daykeeper)

The Cubit, simply put, is the manifestation of Evil in the Age of Jaguar. It is the physical construct of Evil. It occupies space only so man can understand it, since it is man that it desires. It symbolizes that which drives men mad, that makes the innocent arrogant, that attaches value to materialism. It makes man use the club not for survival, but for power and lust and greed. Man's faulty genetic code harbors that which the Cubit empowers. Fortunately, the absolute influence of the Cubit to control all of life has been kept, for the most part, in check. Good has prevailed. It is the only reason why we are sitting here today, discussing such things, instead of ramming steel blades into each others' chests, instead of dropping warheads on our neighbors' houses.

Still, the Cubit has infiltrated this world in great degrees. The history of man is replete with names associated with the very essence of it. These hopeless humans were those that the Cubit had complete control over. A bully is evil, his genetic code tripping into a need for suffering in concentrated ways, but pure Evil desires the destruction of everything. The real Cubit, the one that represents itself as an innocent wooden crate, desires a human that can change more than schoolyards at recess. The real Cubit desires men with power, men with aptitude, men willing to give their very soul in pursuit of every deadly sin. You've heard of these men. Christians call them Antichrists. Islam calls them Al Mahdi. And, of course, there are dozens if not hundreds of pseudonyms. They are the supreme beings of everything awful, memorialized in mythology, dreamed about in nightmares, realized in places all across the world and throughout recorded time.

And this is Evil's greatest accomplishment, not so much that men exist of such malignity but that men should think that Evil exists at all. It is with the Age of Jaguar that Good and Evil was created, thus giving moral superiority to those who think their Good justifies those atrocities they bestow upon those they categorize as Evil. Just think of all the death and suffering we can attribute to this Age's third creation: Religion. I can justify my God as being more righteous than your God and if you don't believe me, I'll kill you, or have my followers kill you, or have my country kill you. A man who holds the power of the Cubit in his hands can change thousands. A man who holds the power of the Cubit in his hands can control an army. A man who holds the power of the Cubit in his hands can end the world as we know it, thus ushering in the next Age as one of pure chaos, when there will be no hope, no mercy, no love—when murder will be an acceptable means to an end and only the worst of humanity will survive. The Jaguar will be dead, its position as guardian of the underworld gone with it, and the retched population of the underworld will eat upon this earth.

Much of the Cubit's history has been lost in time. The destruction of great cultures almost always included the destruction of their knowledge so as to 'prevent such Evil' from spreading into those who have conquered them. That is why the oral tradition is so important. One can destroy what I write but cannot take away what I remember, and I as long as I tell stories before I die, knowledge is saved. The knowledge of the Cubit in my time, I now pass onto you, so that you, too, will not let the world forget.

The Cubit is uniquely adept at masking its influences, usually destroying everything human so as to silence any transfer of its existence. You, Billy, have seen this as the consumption of human flesh. Those that have been 'cubited' devour their primaries just as Evil consumes Good so as to hide itself, so that no warning can be made, so that Evil is accepted as normal. If this process of transformation is allowed to continue unabated, you can imagine how quickly an entire culture could be consumed. And so was the case with the ancient Maya.

My story begins with the name, Samaal, which in Yucatec Mayan means 'tomorrow.' It should be comforting to know that in the presence of Evil, no matter how consuming that Evil may seem, there will always be at least one who will survive to record the history; there will always be at least one whose charge it is to destroy those men who have come under the Cubit's greatest influences and help prevent Evil from consuming the next population by hiding the Cubit from temptation. Samaal was this man in the ninth century. Samaal was in Chichen Itza when that city fell to the influences of the Cubit.

For many years, the Maya of the Lower Peninsula and present-day Guatemala migrated north. The city of Chichen Itza not only became one of the first great immigrant cities in this hemisphere, it also became the center for trade from cultures outside of the Mayan civilization. Thus, Chichen Itza became what might be analogous to an early Rome or New York City, governed and socialized by an extremely diverse population of customs and histories, which, unfortunately, is the perfect breeding ground for Evil's influence. The more diversity a population has, the easier it is to create dissension, to blame another culture as being the 'bad' culture and to morally lift one's own culture up as being supreme.

But great diversity is also essential to the exploration of human consciousness and the shattering of barriers that tend to prevent the progression of the mind. Though Chichen Itza eventually destroyed itself, it became the center of knowledge for the growth of agriculture, architecture and astronomy…particularly astronomy. The Mayan calendar and the end date that you know so well were edified in the years of the Great City and Samaal had a lot of influence in these developments. That's because, like myself and my sister, Samaal was a Daykeeper, an ancient warrior of the mind if you will, tasked to keep record of all time for all time to come—tasked to guard the Cubit.

Chichen Itza remained prosperous until the Cubit was discovered during the construction of the city's observatory, Caracol. A renowned architect of the time, Ka'at, stole the Cubit from a hidden chamber in which Samaal had placed it. It was not long until Ka'at became very powerful in a city that had no single leadership. Ka'at ruled with might and fury, introducing human sacrifice as a means for control. The Cubit offered Ka'at the power of the universe but ended up destroying him and all of his people. The Maya of that time disappeared from the face of the earth. Scientists, today, can only speculate as to what happened to them. There are also some pretty wacky claims by others concerning creatures from outer space. But we know what happened to them. Samaal passed the knowledge forward, preserving it in writing within the observatory vault from where the Cubit had escaped his protection, and preserving it in the oral tradition as he passed this knowledge onto another Daykeeper.

The Mayans killed themselves as the Cubit's influence spread among them quickly and with intentional malice. Very few escaped this total, self-cultural, massacre. Samaal was one of them and he fled with the Cubit.

The Cubit disappears in history for several hundred years, during the time of the Dark Ages. It reappears right here in Sedona around the thirteenth century. It is guarded by Eka, an Anasazi Daykeeper, and is kept in the Great Hall, a place of worship but forbidden to those uninvited for fear of certain death.

Now, if this story is starting to sound familiar, it is. Daykeepers can only maintain the historical record and can *attempt* to prevent the Cubit from influencing man, but we cannot undo the aberrant genetic code that makes man repeat his own mistakes. The Cubit again finds solace in the possession of the son of the Anasazi ruler and, again, an entire population slaughters itself. The atrocities were cited on the walls of the Great Hall before Eka fled with the Cubit when, again, the Evil is lost in time.

My sister and I became involved in the eighteenth century. Our charge was not only to hasten the capture and protection of the Cubit but also to destroy those who had gained maniacal power over even larger populations of people. The world had expanded tremendously since the days of the Anasazi, and now the Cubit, through one man, could endanger millions.

Alixel was responsible for Napoleon Bonaparte. She 'dispatched' the dictator on the island of Elba in the year of 1821 then took the Cubit across the Atlantic with the intention of returning it to its safe-haven under the ruins of the Caracol observatory at Chichen Itza, but her ship was intercepted by a gang of pirates in the Gulf of Mexico led by captain Jean Lafitte. He commandeered the ship and enslaved Alixel but did not find the Cubit stashed in a hidden cargo hold. When he returned with his new prizes to his home fort in Galveston, Texas, one of his shipmates stumbled upon the Cubit; it was not long before the shipmate's cubit shared this secret with the island of pirates.

Lafitte, who took a shine to my sister, believed her to be a princess of the ancient Maya and gave her that Mayan name, Alixel. He was very protective of Alixel; his men were not even allowed to touch her. But this, of course changed as the men changed. Not touching Lafitte's female treasure only instigated the deed from a growing cadre of cubits.

Late one night while Lafitte and Alixel were sleeping, a band of cubits placed the Cubit in bed with Lafitte and it changed him, his cubit crawling forth to take immediate charge of the dead around him. As you know, my sister is quite talented with her Creation Dagger and she quickly dispatched dozens of them. Lafitte, however, took the Cubit and fled the island on the stolen French ship which he had renamed *The Pride*.

The story from here gets somewhat sketchy since my sister was no longer around to record the Cubit's successive history with Lafitte, but we do know this: the next time the Cubit appears, it is in the possession of Adolph Hitler and I am sent to retrieve it and kill the fuehrer. The Cubit is transported back to the Great Hall where it is kept protected from temptation until the arrival of Chris Cower. From that point on, you probably know more than I do.

"Lax is my real name but you can call me Alaxel or Alax or Lax. My sister preferred Alaxel. She gave me that name. She felt that if she was going to be known as a Mayan princess, then I should be known as a Mayan prince. Honestly, I prefer Lax. It's easier to say and has a kind of ring to it, don't you think?"

"Amazing," Billy said. "Truly amazing."

"And every bit the truth."

"No one's going to believe me, you know."

"The story's telling is not meant to make believers out of mortals. It is told so that it is not lost."

Up on the smaller of the two Cathedral Rock spires that now radiated sunset red, perched a bird that was unrecognizable at its distance. Billy knew that it was a bird only because he had seen it land there just moments before Lax had finished his story. It flapped its wings, just tiny flips of feathery arms against the waning sunlight, then leapt from the spire and plummeted toward the ground, disappearing into the shadows created by the majestic rock. Moments later, Billy watched it reappear, flying low to the ground but now half the distance from where it had fallen and heading straight at him. It bellowed a sharp squawk and this caused both Lax and Aaron to turn toward the noise.

"Osi," Lax said to Billy. "Short for Osiris, the Egyptian caretaker of the underworld. He's been hanging around ever since the earthquake."

"He likes our pan de horno de pozo," Aaron said and stood to add a piece of dough to the earthen oven that still steamed with warmth.

The bird, which Billy knew was a hawk when it flew two feet over his head, landed at the apex of the house's roof where its talons slipped momentarily on clay tiles before it righted itself and screeched once again.

"Una momento, por favor," Aaron said to the bird as he slapped a disc of dough into the oven. A couple of minutes later, he produced a round of fresh bread clasped in the claws of the long metal fork and waved it at Osi. "Come and get it," he yelled. The bird dropped from the roof and dove at Aaron who flipped the bread into the air for Osi to snatch with huge talons. The bird flew off into the growing darkness and landed close enough for Billy to hear its squawks of delight as it feasted.

"Why didn't you call the bird Jag?" Billy asked. "You know…short for Jaguar."

Lax leaned forward, the hint of a grin tickling the left side of his face. "I don't understand. Osi is a good name, don't you think?"

"I mean…You said that the Jaguar was the guardian of the underworld. Why use an Egyptian namesake? The word 'Cubit,' too, is also connected with Egyptian history. For that matter, so is the djed. I'm confused why these Mayan artifacts reference Egyptian ideas. It is historical fact that the two civilizations could have never intertwined. Each was dominant during a different epoch of evolution. Not only that, but they had this gigantic body of water separating them called the Atlantic Ocean."

Lax's grin widened. Aaron remained near the pit oven where he continued to cook more bread for the bird. "Perplexing isn't it? Man is too attached to time and space to really understand that all things are connected by everything that came before, everything that currently is, and everything that will ever be. Jaguar and Osiris and the Chinese Yama are only words. It's the concept and the construct and the comprehension that is universal, not the words. I think that, one day, you will understand. It is a transcendence that few ever attain."

Aaron tossed a fresh disc of bread like a Frisbee into the darkness. Osi squawked its gratitude.

"Until then," Lax continued, sitting straight up in his chair with a new, concerned look on his face, "beware of everything that wants to prevent that knowledge from finding you. Remember I told you that the Cubit has lived in Sedona for many years. In that time, more men than Chris Cower have chanced upon it—more men than Chris Cower have touched it. Fortunately, none of them have been the messiah of death but all who are not the messiah are his servants. And they roam everywhere, in all parts of the world, occupying positions of control and influence and change. Some of these cubits lust for power that is only a delusion; it will always be the case that they exist only because the messiah of death, the Antichrist, allows them to do so. They exist to serve His ultimate fate: the end of the Age of Jaguar and the beginning of an Age of Chaos."

"Who is it?" Billy asked. "Who is the Antichrist?"

"Evil clouds that knowledge from even the Daykeepers. But he lives…now…today. And he awaits the omega point: December 21, 2012."

"Is it true that this…" Billy hesitated, thinking that the word *man* was now incorrect. "Is it true that this *thing* needs the Cubit and the daggers and the Book of the Djed to complete the transference?"

"Alixel told you this." Lax didn't wait for an answer. "Yes. And the necessary ceremony must be done in the right place and at the right time. That's why, other than for protection, you must never give up your Creation Dagger, particularly since it is the Creation Dagger of the End that will either save the world or end it."

"Where?" Billy said. "When?"

"Only the Book of the Djed and Great Hall of the Anasazi can tell us that."

"And where is that?"

"I can't tell you…at least not yet. But when the time is right, we'll go together. And it won't be long. Chances are, I suspect, you'll figure it out for yourself before that time. If so, I warn you that there are many out there who desire its location. The Evil from the Cubit remains in the Great Hall and still produces a mighty influence over mere mortals and the cubits that roam Sedona. The energy of false promises can seem overpowering."

Aaron threw the last piece of cooked bread into the consuming darkness that was now lit only by the house's solarium and the dying embers in the ground under the pit oven. Osi squawked with delight one final time before its wings could be heard pushing the air as it took off to search for meatier snacks.

Cubits, Billy thought but didn't say it.

"Yes," Lax said. "I guarantee you that at least one has been keeping its eyes on you. It wants what you have and will wait until the right time to get it. It will use those around you to get it. And it cannot be killed without that which you carry close to your heart."

An unrelenting silence fell over the triumvirate as Billy sat and stared at Cathedral Rock, its spires somehow darker than the pure moonless night behind it. Again, he was amazed by the absence of any nocturnal rumblings, just as it had been the night before—just as it had been when the Cadillac had stopped in front of them and the shadow with the ball cap had emerged.

He was now convinced that he'd been followed ever since leaving Port Aransas. Deere-hat man was a cubit and it was waiting for the perfect moment to make its move.

"Could I get a ride home," Billy finally said.

Lax stood. "I thought you'd never ask."

He descended a steep staircase that spiraled. The steps were made of red rock sandstone, the edges of which were so sharp that to fall would mean certain death, not only from the multitude of serrations the human flesh would endure but also from the distance the body would bounce toward the staircase base. He had to take each step at an angle and had to use his trailing hand on the steps behind him to maintain balance. Dust and tiny pebbles that had not been disturbed in quite a while skittered under his feet, making the descent even more problematic.

Light was provided from two directions. Up above, the disc of the sun shone dead center through the hole he must have climbed down though Billy did not remember doing so. Below, a much redder light glowed from some hidden source, making the bottom of the stair pitch questionable at best.

His heart pounded so vibrantly that he thought he heard drums beating somewhere beyond the below. The intense hammering in his chest pressed the sheathed dagger against a torn, white button-up shirt and it flexed the fabric in rhythm with his body's pulsing blood.

A voice infiltrated this noisy solitude.

You must save the world.

He stopped on a step and looked around at the dark round walls that were only a few feet from his face.

Now!

The staircase chamber trembled. Dust and pebbles rained down on top of him. His hand lost its grip on the steps behind him and his foot slipped. Down he went, his back scraping the sharp edges of steps that were few compared to the distance above the floor that he thought he'd been standing. He fell only a couple of feet, which didn't make sense, but he was happy to be alive.

He stood and waited as the dust settled around him. Red clouds swirled and twisted in a mixture of blue sunshine from above and the hidden red glow which now appeared to be emanating from a squat opening directly in front of him. He walked the five steps to the opening, his head at the same height as its archway, but stopped before stooping and passing through it. On the walls on both sides of the opening and across the arch was scrawled the glyphs of a history long dead. The story of their own self-extinction pictured men decapitating men and women torturing babies. Animal glyphs of all breeds scattered away from the doorway, away from the human massacre.

Cower, Billy whispered to himself. *This is what Chris Cower found. The Great Hall of the Anasazi.*

But Billy was too scared to pass through the opening. He didn't like the crimson red aura that pulsed beyond it. It reminded him of temptation. It reminded him of the Cubit.

And then his hand started to itch—the one with the star burned into it. He absently scratched it as he tried to find courage but the palm's irritation was relentless, becoming uncomfortably hot. When he opened his hand, he found that one of the star's scar points glowed—the one in the lower right quadrant—the point that referenced the Creation of the End: the fifth point. He lifted his hand in front of him, palm pointed toward the opening, and the red heat from the scared star became a beacon of white light that ripped through the archway, dousing the crimson aura that undulated within.

Then he stepped through, his hand blazing courage, and he screamed. Staring him in the face was…

Himself. And he grabbed him.

Billy's eyes flickered open, or at least that's what it felt like. For all he knew, his eyelids might never have even closed. The room was so dark.

"Billy."

It was Lax and he was standing right next to him in the anteroom just beyond the kitchen solarium. Billy shook his head, the twisted image of himself burned into consciousness.

"I…saw…me," Billy mumbled. He turned to face Lax's dark outline. "I was there," he continued. "A staircase. An opening. Drawings on the walls of horrible death."

"Sit down for a moment," Lax led Billy out of the anteroom and to the couch.

"No. I'm all right." Billy looked back into the darkness. "But why?"

"That room is our place of worship. Spirits come alive in there. All homes of the true Hopi have them. It is a place we go for answers."

"I didn't ask any questions."

"And those are the answers that are most beneficial."

"I don't understand."

"You will."

Aaron came through the front door then. "Truck's ready for departure," he said.

Lax took Billy's right hand, which was still warm from his experience, and led him out of the house. "It's been a long night, now it's time for rest."

Though he was only ten, Aaron drove. Lax sat beside him, his eyes wary with anticipation as his adopted son successfully operated the stick shift between his bulky legs.

Billy was squashed up against the Ford Ranger's passenger side door so much so that he had to hang one arm out the open window. His body sat at a slight angle. He closed his eyes for a moment but quickly opened them since the memory of his garish face remained planted just behind his eyeballs. Cool Sedona breeze helped alleviate the psychological pain delivered by Lax's spiritual anteroom, but it was not enough to sooth the fear that his evil twin would forever haunt him. Every time he closed his eyes, Bad Billy would be there. Waiting.

Other than a few instructional directions from Lax to his son concerning the rules of the road, they drove in silence the entire way to the corner of Dry Creek and Gringo. Aaron parked beside Stephanie's Cavalier.

"Yours?" Lax asked, pointing at the car as Billy opened the door and almost fell out.

"It belonged to a good friend of mine. I don't drive it much."

Lax shuffled from his place in the middle of the cab and closed the passenger's side door. His thick elbow rested within the window opening. "Don't let your memories haunt you," he said. "Life is too short."

Billy was unsure if Lax was talking about Stephanie Drake whom he'd never met, or the vision of Bad Billy whom he'd never seen. Perhaps Lax was simply offering a final piece of humanistic wisdom. Regardless of the intent, Billy thanked him for all of the knowledge that he'd learned and all of the wonderful food that he'd eaten. When he asked if they'd be getting together again anytime soon, Lax did not provide a straight answer. Instead, he ended their evening with humor.

"Watchum' for bad men, Kemo Sabe," he said, playing the role of Tonto. "May the five elements keep you safe."

Billy watched the truck pull out of the lot and head back toward town. Across the street, Marcy's casita rental appeared unoccupied. No lights were on inside. Again, he wondered why she would have lied to him about the cost of the broken glass replica of a Creation Dagger. Again, he thought of the Cadillac and the shadow wearing the ball cap that had groaned obscure warnings. Again, he wondered if the red drops on Marcy's back porch were blood, and if so, from what animal. Again, he wondered if Marcy was safe.

But he wasn't going to let his thoughts haunt him…which was better said than done.

The Vortex

Cooper thought that the last time she had wasted so much of one day was back when Chris was here. They'd spent an entire Sunday doing absolutely nothing except talking and cooking and eating and exploring each other's bodies. She'd taken no phone calls, had not been concerned about giving tours into the canyon, had done absolutely no work of any kind: no house cleaning, no landscaping, no home maintenance—she'd not even left the house, and that was odd, considering how much staying indoors for long periods of time drove her crazy. But it had been a Sunday when she'd thought she was falling in love. At the time, it had been worth it but in retrospect—knowing now what she didn't then—the day had been a total waste. It had been Chris Cower's greatest deception.

Yesterday had been kind of like that—without the sex, of course. After the good and bad cops had left, she'd sat down on her couch, staring at the walls, thinking about nothing and everything all at once. She'd been excited and doubtful and afraid. She'd spent hours reliving the Cower experience, believing that, if she put enough thought into it, she might remember one small piece of the complex Cower puzzle…just one, that would help her understand why she was sitting like a vegetable contemplating it at all. She'd thought about Billy, wondering if he, too, had some hidden agenda—wondering if he, too, would figuratively screw her. And she'd given Marcy a considerable amount of contemplation. From the moment she'd met the red-fingernailed fortuneteller, she'd thought that something was fishy. Woman's instinct had waved the warning flags, and that instinct had been justified when good cop Beets and bad cop Dreagan had shown her the artist's sketch. Had Marcy Ruminski been dressed up in the ceremonial Jaguar costume? Had Marcy Ruminski driven a dagger into the chest of a ceremonially masked Sun? To think of such things was insane. To have seen such things meant insanity. Besides, Marcy Ruminski could not have been the Jaguar…the Jaguar had been decapitated.

Crazy, incomprehensible thoughts like these were what had sterilized her body for all of Sunday after the cops had left. Finally, as late evening had approached, she had picked her lazy ass off the couch and had cleaned up the remains of a dinner that had been stewing behind the porch window glass sunshine for nearly an entire day. Her sleep had been restless and filled with all of the confusion her wasted-day mind-fuck had bestowed upon her subconscious. But it had all been worth it.

When she woke Monday morning, she felt cleansed…her mind

somehow fresh and ready to tackle anything. If the cops showed up again…no worries. If Marcy came hunting for her with a dagger…no problemo. The only thing that could really screw up the day would be if Billy did not bring the Book of the Djed. Her newfound outlook on life really centered on this singular anticipation. It wasn't every day someone would come bearing the gift of eternal life.

She removed the star map parchment from her bedroom wall and rolled it up inside the newspaper just as it had been delivered to her. She then grabbed her Swiss Knife from a dresser drawer; she never went into the canyon without it. She took the newspaper and knife and set them on the dining table as she went to the kitchen to grab a couple of water bladders and some energy bars. From the utility room, she plucked two small backpacks from the nail on which they were hanging. Just before she closed the utility room door, she snatched a pair of men's hiking boots from the floor. She'd stored six pairs in various sizes just in case one of her private tour participants forgot that climbing rocks and walking among desert wildlife was not something for which sneakers—or heaven forbid, flip-flops—were created.

All of the items needed for the hike into the canyon she massed onto the dining table before dressing in cargo shorts and a light cotton shirt that buttoned at the chest. Then she sat and waited. Her intent was to take Billy into the canyon so that if there were any aggressors that wished to follow them with the intent of stealing the Book, they would be on her turf, in a place she knew like the back of her hand, where nooks and crannies and caves and corners made for easy hiding places from those who didn't know they existed.

She drummed fingers across one dark-skinned knee that was crossed over her other leg. It was five minutes before noon and her tension continued to build. She stared at the door.

Was that a knock?

No, just some rattling car as it passed in front of the house.

Okay, what about that? That was definitely a knock.

No. That was a car door slamming.

Why did he drive? He said he would be walking.

Maybe it isn't him. Why don't you get off of your ass and see?

She nodded at the notion and went to the front window. Outside, just beyond the driveway, was an unmarked police car. Cooper immediately recognized the two cops that emerged and now confronted Billy.

Up until the point that the two cops stepped out of their car and asked him his name, Bill Jo Presser was having one heck of a good Monday morning. He'd slept rather well, considering his mind's status before going to bed. Serene, was the word that kept coming to him throughout breakfast. He'd had a serene sleep, the mind at ease as if a mighty weight had been lifted from it. His apartment had a serene comfort level to it: homey, bright and inviting. Even the air outside smelled of total serenity. The heat wave that had taken hold of Sedona since Thanksgiving had cooled down to a more seasonable seventy degrees. Clouds had even returned to the Verde Valley. If the animals could sing, he thought, today would be the day they'd reveal such ability unto the world.

The last thing Billy did before leaving the apartment was grab the Book of the Djed from its hiding place in the bathroom. Shortly after renting the place, he'd found that one of the shelves in the bathroom's linen cupboard had been loose. He'd lifted the shelf from the recessed cupboard to find that the paneled wall inside was also loose. Behind the paneling was the cupboard's two-by-four framing and a horizontal board provided a perfect roost for the Book. He'd kept it and the Book's key hidden there ever since.

His walk to Cooper's house included a skip or two. He was afraid of nothing, was concerned about nothing, and looked forward to a day full of discovery. Such connectedness that he felt all the way up to the point where he turned the corner from Boynton Canyon Road to Boynton Pass, he likened to surfing…not the water and the wave, but the absolute serenity one feels while mastering Mother Nature for a fraction of a moment. He was king of his domain and nothing was going to drag him down.

Except Detective Dreagan.

Apparently, the two cops had been sitting and waiting and watching just a block from Cooper's front door. Billy had absolutely no idea why they were there and his serene attitude, at the moment, really didn't care.

But Detective Dreagan had a way of getting under a person's skin and it took three sentences for Dreagan to prove it.

After confirming his name, Dreagan said, "Hello. I'm Detective Dreagan and this here is Detective Beets. Did you and your girl kill my friend?"

Beets grabbed his partner's arm and attempted a serene smile. "Hold on, Dreagan." He acknowledged Billy with a quick glance then turned to glare sternly at Dreagan. "Forgive him," he said to both Billy and Dreagan. "My partner here has had a difficult day and is sorry for what he said…right?"

Dreagan backed down from his aggressive stance. His eyes fluttered. "I apologize," he offered, but Billy wasn't buying it. It was the cop's smug delivery and his youth that belied his sincerity.

Beets handed Billy a piece of paper. "Do you know this person?" he asked.

Billy unfolded the artist's sketch of someone who looked a lot like Marcy without hair. "Why do you ask?"

"Calvin Alvery says that you and this woman were at his shop last Friday night."

The name sounded familiar. *Alvery*…

"He said that he gave you and this woman a weapon."

"Weapon?" Billy said, still trying to remember the name.

"A glass dagger. One with a broken point."

"Yes. Oh, yes. The owner of Vor-Tech's. He gave us the dagger because of the earthquake."

Beets pulled a second piece of paper from the same shirt pocket as he'd stored the first and handed it to Billy. Dreagan stared indignantly, a smirk pulling the left side of his face into the shape of doubt. Billy shuffled the paper over the face of the Marcy-looking sketch. It was a photograph of a broken-tipped Creation Dagger that looked in every way like the one Calvin Alvery had given him—except for the red stain covering the dagger's broken tip. "Is this the dagger he gave you?"

Billy suddenly felt extremely uneasy. He thought about the real dagger he kept near his heart. He thought about the Book of the Djed which he'd stashed in his short's waistband behind his back. He thought that if they frisked him, he'd be thinking much more about lawyers and courtrooms and jails. He thought that, perhaps, he shouldn't say anything else. Thankfully, at that very moment, the conversation was interrupted when Cooper yelled to him from her front door. "Billy!?"

Dreagan immediately turned to her and yelled, "This doesn't concern you. Get back into your house." Cooper remained at the doorway.

Beets continued. "Is this the dagger he gave you?" he repeated more forcefully.

"How would I know that?" Billy offered. "He gave us a piece of glass that looks like what you have there in the photo, but I can't tell you if that is it."

"Where is the piece he gave you?" Beets asked.

"Marcy has it…had it. She returned it to Vor-Tech's, Saturday."

"Marcy. You mean the woman in the sketch?"

Billy nodded.

Dreagan walked quickly toward him. "Can you tell us where she is, and mind you, your answer will determine if we put you in handcuffs today or tomorrow."

Billy ignored Dreagan. "What is this all about?" he asked Beets. Neither of the detectives noticed Cooper as she walked up behind them.

"Yes," Cooper added. "I'd like to know as well."

"Ma'am!" Dreagan almost yelled. "I told you to get back in your house!"

Beets waved his hands in the air, in a let's-all-calm-down motion. "One of Sedona's police officers went missing Friday night," Beets said to Billy. "A witness saw the woman in the sketch at the scene. Your friend, Cooper here, was near the scene when it happened. That weapon was found near a puddle of blood and was catalogued as evidence, but disappeared from the police cruiser's trunk that same night."

Cooper walked over and stood beside Billy. "Sounds to me like someone wasn't doing their job very well," she said and glared at Dreagan.

Beets' nice-guy approach changed at that moment as he snatched away the papers in Billy's hands. "When we find this woman Marcy," he grumbled, "we'll return for both of you. A missing police officer is not to be taken lightly and we will go to the ends of the earth to find out just what happened. We suspect that both of you are involved and when we find the proof, you'll be spending a lot of time in the Arizona pen."

Billy was about to tell them that the dagger from the crime scene could not be the dagger he'd been given by Calvin Alvery because *that* dagger had been sitting on Marcy's fireplace mantle when he'd awakened on her couch Saturday morning. But before he could say another word, Cooper interjected.

"Good luck with that," she said. "Come back when you have evidence. And don't try to pull anymore of that psychological crap on us because you both stink at it."

"Don't leave town," Beets said.

"Your asses are ours," Dreagan added.

Then both turned away, got back into their car, and spun a rooster tail of dirt that would have covered them both had Billy and Cooper been standing behind it.

"I don't know," Cooper said as if anticipating what Billy was about to say. "I don't know what the hell is going on but your friend is hip deep in it."

She walked back toward her house and Billy followed. "Why would they think that you have anything to do with it?" he said. "You only met Marcy a couple of days ago, right?"

"Right."

"So?"

"So nothing." She stopped at the front door which she had left wide open. "Remember the star map? I got it near where the policeman disappeared. Coincidence, that's all." She walked into the house then pointed at Billy's feet. "Nice hiking boots. They'll do. Come on."

Just who in the hell was Marcy, anyway? Billy had known her in only bits and spurts in the two years that he'd lived in Port Aransas. They'd gotten to know each other because of Joel Canton. Marcy had befriended the poor fisherman and had introduced him to Billy after one of the city council meetings. But other than an occasional run-in with her in the town, a few dinners served to her at his restaurant, and the connection to Joel, he really didn't know Marcy at all. She was separated from her husband or divorced—one or the other. She had two kids, she'd said, and they were staying with their father while she was here in Sedona. She never talked much about her kids and, quite frankly, Billy suddenly wondered why. All mothers talked about their kids…they talked about them all the time. But Billy couldn't, in the past five months, remember her talking about them at all.

And her hair. In Port Aransas it had been long and luxurious, Cher-like, but now she didn't have any at all, at least that's what the cop's sketch had shown. Maybe she'd never had any hair. Maybe she'd worn wigs. Her hair was false—just like her kids were false; just like her reason for being in Sedona was false. At least that's what he was beginning to believe.

Billy's head hit the roll bar of Cooper's jeep as she turned onto an access road that would take them to one of the trailheads into Boynton Canyon. He bounced in the seat, its springs squeaking under him. While in the bathroom before they'd left, he'd placed the Book of the Djed in the small backpack that Cooper had given him. He now held the backpack with one hand between his legs as he grasped the roll bar with the other.

"Marcy killed a cop?" he said to himself, intentionally out loud.

Cooper, who had said little until now, glanced at him, her sunglasses hiding her expression. "It would seem so. She had the dagger, according to you. A witness saw her at the crime scene. Pretty cut and dry if you ask me."

"I thought I knew her better than that."

Cooper bounced up and down. "How much does anyone really know someone else? We're all liars to some extent."

"What makes you say that?"

"Years of reading textbooks. It's a psychological necessity—a part of the classic fight or flight mechanism. We lie to survive." They reached their destination and Cooper stopped the Jeep in a small cul-de-sac that was occupied by two other vehicles. She turned to Billy while dusting off her brown shirt and dropped her glasses on the dashboard. Her red, curly hair mixed conspicuously well with the fire that burned in her green eyes. "So tell me, Billy. Did you lie to me? Do you have the Book and is it in that backpack between your legs?"

Her face was inches from his nose as he nodded. "I have it," he said, remaining close to her face, her small nose, her pert lips. "Now tell me. Are you going to steal it? Is that why you wanted me in Boynton Canyon so that you could bury my body in some dark rattler's nest?"

A curt smile grasped her lower lip. "Why, Billy. Haven't you figured it out by now? The Book means nothing without you. Besides, I think you have way too much untold information for me to be burying you anywhere."

Her head moved slightly closer and for a split second, Billy thought that she was going to kiss him, but she backed away while opening her door and jumped out with backpack in hand. She walked to the beginning of a line of trampled earth that snaked its way around a tall, thin, rock formation that, with enough imagination, looked like what the sign at the trailhead professed it to be: Kachina Woman. "Are you coming?" she said.

He joined her and, together, they started up the trail. "Why did you want to bring me out here? You could have looked the Book over back at your place."

"You don't like my company?" She kept walking without looking at him. Kachina Woman towered above them as they traversed the path around it. "I don't like the idea of not controlling my space. You saw those idiot cops, snooping around, looking for a reason to arrest anyone they find the least bit suspicious. The Book surely would ignite a curiosity I don't want them to have. The last place the Book needs to be is locked up in an evidence room somewhere, just waiting to tempt a lowly clerk into stealing it. Then what would we have: no way to save the world."

"And no way to live to an eternity," Billy added.

Cooper stopped then. "Okay. Yes. That's right. We use it to raise the Djed and we live for an eternity. But that's what's necessary for the world's salvation."

"Is that really what you want? To save the world? Or to save Cooper Reyes?"

"We have a long way to go don't we? I don't trust you and you don't trust me, simply because we are innately both liars. I suppose we'll both have to live with that. Perhaps, the time will come when all that changes. Until then, let's just pretend."

"Pretend?"

"Yeah. Pretend we like each other. That'll make our journey into the canyon much more pleasant. Besides, the energies here don't like negativity. I've had a few tourists succumb to some pretty nasty visions just because their minds were pretty nasty thinkers."

"Okay." Billy gazed up at the head of the Kachina Woman rock formation. Sunshine broke through chunky white clouds directly above it and cast a rainbow aura around the bulbous rock. "We can be friends but I'm not gonna hold your hand."

Cooper laughed. It was the first time he'd heard her do so. It wasn't as alluring as Marcy's laugh was; in fact, it sounded a bit too brash, hoarse, and annoying. She even snorted. "Deal," she said and walked away from him.

It was at the first crest of rock when Billy heard the drumbeats for the first time. Cooper had been leading them forward and Kachina Woman was no more than three hundred yards behind them when Billy stopped and listened. The path snaked its way between rock formations in front of him. The drumbeats seemed to be coming from within the canyon. They weren't very loud at all; in fact, Billy, at first, thought that it was his heart beating.

"What is it?" Cooper asked.

"Drums…I think."

"I suspect you'll hear, and see, a lot more than that before the day is over."

"Vortex energies?"

"Yeah. They are gonna stick to you like glue." Cooper waited until Billy stood beside her. "There's something about you that I haven't felt from anyone else, especially now that we are near the canyon. You exude energies, almost as if you are a vortex in and of yourself."

"Flattering."

"No…Serious. If I was going to come on to you, I would have kissed you back in the Jeep. I'm simply stating a spiritual fact."

"Isn't that what you'd call an oxymoron: a spiritual fact?"

"Smart guy, huh? That will certainly be useful later on."

She turned away and continued her lead, her steps bouncing, her short frame agile, her strawberry blonde hair now denser and darker since the sun was mostly hidden behind clouds and shadow had taken control.

Cooper had not been pulling his leg nor was she hitting on him. She was quite serious. Billy almost undulated with it. She could even see the aura of energy that doctored his body with electrical sparkles. It was alluring and fanciful and, to be truthful, arousing. But, it wasn't the physical nature of the energy that was getting to her—it hadn't been for Chris and, for the most part, it wasn't for Billy, though she had to admit that he was quite attractive. It was something else entirely, something that the two of them had in common. Something like…

And then all of a sudden it hit her. The Book of the Djed. That one wasted Sunday that she'd spent with Chris a year ago had been filled with the same feeling she was now getting from Billy. An intoxication, really, as if someone had put a roofie in her water. That was the day that she'd seen the hand of the Great Spirit write man's destiny into the center spread of the Book: a bird of fire, one of death and of life. The Hopi called it Mochni but it was better known as the phoenix.

Cooper was becoming so excited, she trembled. She even stuttered when Billy asked her about the Yavapai Indians he saw within a narrow ravine as they'd pushed farther into the canyon.

"What are they doing?" he said.

"M-m-medicine wheels," she mumbled. "B-b-building medicine wheels for worship."

"You're shaking," he said, touching her shoulder.

"T-t-took a chill."

And when he touched her, the trembling stopped. She actually saw the red sparkles of the aura around his right hand suck a wisp of something out her body. When he removed his hand she saw the star burned into his palm. One of its points glowed, undulated, but for only a second. As her trembling faded, so did the red point of the star. She'd seen the star before. It looked just like the one that was etched in the haft of Chris Cower's Creation Dagger.

"You've touched one," she said, pointing. "You've held it in that hand."

Billy looked in the distance as the Indians knelt in front of the markers they had assembled out of rocks and twigs and dirt.

"Do you have it?" Cooper added. "You have it don't you. The Book *and* Chris' dagger; you have them both. That's why I feel…that's why you have such energy."

"No," he said. "Only the Book—as I promised."

"A lie?" she questioned.

He stepped in the direction of the worshipping Indians. "I don't have Chris' dagger," he said, absently.

"No," she said and tried to grab his elbow but missed. "They don't take kindly to interruptions."

But as he continued in their direction, the three Yavapai that had been kneeling, stood up. One even waved him forward. And drumbeats…

Cooper now heard them. She'd experienced drums beating in the canyon before, but this was somehow different, louder, rhythmic, meaningful. She followed a dozen feet behind him but stopped short of the ceremonial ground as Billy reached it. The three Yavapai gave Cooper a kindly but stern gaze, then turned their backs to her and stood in a short line, blocking her sight of Billy. Billy remained hidden behind the Indians for ten minutes while the aura of sparkling energy that had encapsulated his body filled the space beyond the Yavapai; their bodies were temporarily engulfed by it just before the energy blaze weakened and died. Billy emerged between them, walking slowly as if dazed, but surefooted. When he finally stood beside her, the Yavapai returned to their own ceremonial labors.

"Chris Cower is not the stalker," he said, dreamily. "Cower is dead and gone."

"Stalker?" She shook his arm. "Billy?"

And then he came out of the trance. "It's Deere-hat man."

"Deere-hat man? Who's that? How do you know? What did you see?"

"Come on," Billy said, taking her arm. "Let's not disturb them further. Lead the way and I'll try to explain."

He'd not been in control of his thoughts or his actions; that's how he explained it to Cooper. But before he could tell her what he saw within the medicine wheel, he had to explain the rear view mirror, the one in his VW Bus, back in Port Aransas. He'd had visions within it, of someone screaming at him, of being chased, of being shot at, of puking. And now he understood what it all meant. Now he understood that what he had envisioned in Port A, and now in much greater detail because of the medicine wheel, was the end of Lenny Bender's life. Creepier still, was that he had envisioned it *through* Lenny Bender, as if he was Lenny Bender. He could feel the bullet nick his ear before webbing the station wagon's windshield. He could smell the acidic stench of a hamburger and fries as it coated Chris Cower's arm. He could hear the sirens of the police cars as they rammed them, metal-to-metal, from the left. And he could see...

He could see inside the state trooper's car. He could see the officer in the front seat, the one on the passenger's side, the one with the radio microphone in front of his lips, the one screaming through the P.A.: *Pull the fuck over, Professor Cower! You ain't got no escape this time! We'll make sure of that!*

It was their stalker! It was Deere-hat man, except, in his medicine wheel vision, he was wearing a state trooper's hat—at least he was wearing it until the wind blew it off. And that's when Billy had been sure. That's when, through Lenny's eyes, Billy had seen the thin flip of blonde-white hair as it slapped against a mostly bald head. And its red eyes with swirling silver sparkles…raging red eyes…crazed red eyes…dead red eyes…eyes and hair and body that had been dead for a long time.

Billy (as Lenny) relived the confrontation with the burnt creature that had been one of Deere-hat man's accomplices as it stood over him, as its charred flesh crumbled into his gaping mouth.

Billy (as Lenny) relived Janine's use of the dagger to magically pull the bullet from Chris Cower's chest.

Billy (as Lenny) relived touching the Cubit, feeling its energy, watching the blue spark of temptation snatch away any chance for future survival.

Billy (as Lenny) relived dying. He relived seeing himself as a cubit. He relived the pain of being eaten alive.

But the worst thing Billy relived was being Lenny's cubit, of eating flesh that was not dead, of feeling no remorse, no guilt, no life. He relived the experience of being stabbed with the dagger by his own mother, of molting into ash and bone. And he experienced…

Floating.

As Lenny Bender's cubit, Billy had become all of the nastiness cubits' encumbered. But after Lenny's cubit finally settled into a heap of bones, Billy had relived a spiritual release, as if Lenny's soul had been imprisoned within the cubit and then rose from the ashes to witness the Bender farm's destruction, to witness Chris Cower as he fell onto the dynamite plunger that incinerated all.

"If you believe that Cower has anything to do with anything going on in Sedona today, you can forget it," Billy said in closure. "I guarantee you that nothing could put all of his pieces back together again."

"Then who in the hell gave me the star map?" Cooper said more to herself than to Billy.

"That crazy bastard that has been following all of us, I suspect—the one that has been manipulating everything. The one who chased Lenny and Cower into the cornfield. The one who followed Marcy and me from Port Aransas. The one who punched a poor Hispanic woman in Las Cruces. The one who is in Sedona, who wears a green ball cap with the words John Deere sewn into it and drives a Cadillac."

"The one who probably has something to do with the missing police officer," Cooper added.

They had been walking for an hour without rest, but now both of them stopped and stared at each other. The canyon, in that time, had closed in around them, the red walls becoming taller and redder on either side. They were now engulfed in complete shadow. Blue skies had become gray clouds. A chill of wind skirted past, whipped up the ground, and dashed its dirt against the canyon walls.

"What do you mean?" Billy asked.

"I saw it all. I wouldn't dare tell the cops that, though. They'd think I killed him. At first I thought that I was imagining things. But listening to you now—well, I guess anything is possible. Still, it's not every day you see two life-sized kachinas going at each other, and one of them loses their head, and can still walk, and can still plunge a dagger into the heart of the one that just cut off its head."

"You're not making much sense."

"There was a man and a woman, dressed up like a jaguar and the sun, in the alley on the night that the star map was delivered to me, on the night that the police officer disappeared. One had a broadsword and the other had what looked like a Creation Dagger, but it sparkled too much. Anyway, the woman dressed up like the jaguar had her head chopped off by the man in the sun costume. I don't think I'll ever forget that damned jaguar head as it rolled toward me and I know I'll never forget watching that headless woman stab the guy in the chest with the dagger."

"Then what happened?"

"I don't know. I ran just when the cop showed up. I heard him scream as I got the hell out of there."

"Did you see Marcy anywhere around there?"

"I think she was the jaguar and she had the dagger that dickhead Beets showed us in the picture."

"How can that be? You said the jaguar's head was chopped off."

"How can it be that you saw all the shit you just told me?"

And then an absolutely horrifying notion came to him, one that knocked his knees right out from under him and caused him to fall to the red dirt canyon floor. Cooper sat with him, suddenly understanding as well. He opened his mouth but she said it first.

"Marcy's a cubit!"

Billy shook his head in denial but thought that there could be no other answer. It made all the sense in the world, except that, Marcy didn't act like one—at least, she didn't act like what Billy thought a cubit would act like. "Shit," he moaned. "If she can pull it off then we are totally screwed. Who knows what person out there is one of them." He glared curiously at Cooper.

"No way, José," she said, bringing both hands out in front of her. "I'm all pure woman. I'll prove it to you if you don't believe me."

The temptation was almost too good to turn down but Billy thought that now was not the time. He had to agree, though, that screwing someone would be a damn good way of finding out who was a cubit and who was not, but the idea of choosing poorly made his skin crawl.

"As far as Marcy's concerned," Cooper said, "there's one good way to find out if she was at The Y, Friday night."

"And that is?"

"Pull her hair."

Cooper, at that moment, reminded him of Stephanie Drake and how she'd seen logic so simply. Billy smiled, that inkling of sound reasoning tickling his fancy. "First chance I get, I will. You better believe it." He looked around and up and down. "Is this a good place?"

"Good place for what?"

"You know what I mean."

"Good place to prove I'm a woman?"

Billy reached out and gently pulled a lock of her curly red hair. "All woman…like you said." This made her laugh and, again, snort. "I'm talking about the Book."

"Excellent place," Cooper quickly replied while grabbing the hair that Billy had just released. "Give it to me."

Her breaths came fast and furious. She felt totally and completely turned on. Billy's energy and his honesty overwhelmed her. Every word he spoke was nuanced in her mind with sexual connotation. That's how Chris had done it to her. That's how Billy was going to do it to her. She wanted to prove that she was all woman. She wanted to rip her clothes off right then and there. And when he touched her hair she thought that she would bust. A snort of laughter escaped because there was absolutely no way she could hold back the air that was building in her lungs, air filled with words that she knew should not be spoken but she said them anyway.

"Give it to me."

And when Billy did, her desire magnified beyond what she was mortally capable of maintaining. When Billy handed her the Book, the energy that pulsed through Boynton Canyon centered on her, raged within her blood, fused with her brain. All of the power of all of the ages consumed her. Her life flashed before her, every piece of it, every person in it, every place she'd been to, every touch her fingers had ever stroked—all in the span of an instant. She saw the Book's center spread... the phoenix bird undulating under her fingers, the sixes and nines twisting and turning and becoming nines and sixes and sixes and nines. She even felt the grooves that the Great Spirit had carved into the very fibers of the Book's papery texture, grooves that now beheld clues that would save or end everything.

Her heart beat faster. The clouds bunched down around her. The canyon walls fell on top of her. But Billy was there, his body thrown over her like an invincible cloak, protecting her from the deluge of her growing insanity. Billy was there on top of her and he held a weapon. He held a Creation Dagger. And he plunged it downward.

When Billy dropped the backpack from his shoulders and unzipped its main pocket, he heard something but ignored it. When he grabbed the Book and pulled it free, he heard it again and looked around. Part of his outer body experience in the inner body of Lenny Bender had included the young man's obsession with Clint Eastwood. This synthesis into his own consciousness had Billy looking to the cliffs on both sides, looking for those outlaws who would have been tailing Eastwood in every spaghetti western he'd ever starred in. He looked for glints of reflected metal. He looked for, and listened for, falling rocks. A hiccup or a cough or a tactical word of some kind would have determined the source of the sound, but there was none of that. The noise he now heard for the third time didn't even come from the towering rocks encircling him. The sound, actually, came from his feet.

He handed the Book to Cooper and she opened it at the exact moment that the rattler struck. Because she'd been sitting with her right hand on the ground for support, that arm was easy pickings for the diamondback. It struck her twice before quickly slithering away. When Billy looked at her arm, the djed tattoo was now punctured four times, one snake fang incision occupying each of the tattoo's four crosses. There was very little blood but an immense amount of swelling. The snake had struck her brachial artery and the poison was working very quickly. She swooned and fell and the Book toppled and closed beside her body.

Billy quickly yanked the backpack from Cooper and furiously searched its contents. A newspaper was in there as was her water bladder. He turned the backpack upside down and a Swiss Army knife dropped at his knees. It was good to have such a valuable tool but Billy had no idea how he could use it against four venom holes. He knew that to cross cut the skin and suck the venom from the body was one survival method that he'd been taught as a Cub Scout too many years ago, but the way that Cooper's arm was swelling made him believe that he could cut and suck all day and she would still die.

So there was only one option.

He didn't know if he should stab the snake bites with the point of the Creation Dagger or simply set the long blade across the wounds as Alixel had done to the cut across Joel Canton's throat back in Port A. He opted for the later and immediately understood that it was the correct decision as crimson light spewed from the dagger and from his hand. He placed the seven-inch blade on top of Cooper's mounding, puss-filled skin and the magic did its thing. It was amazing to watch. Lenny Bender's view of his mother pulling the bullet out of Cower's body was of no comparison. The dagger's blade actually sucked Cooper's arm. It sucked the infiltration of poison from the wounds. It sucked the mounded skin

full of infection and venom and spit long rivulets of moisture from the
very tip of the blade and onto the red dirt ground below. In a moment that
was quicker than a moan, the dagger had completed its task.

Billy studied the dagger still resting in his palm. The last and only
time he had unsheathed it was to kill his best friend and that had been five
months ago. Now, at this moment, sitting between majestic canyon walls
with a women he'd met only days ago, squirming at his knees, venom
and blood splattered around her in broken Rorschach patterns, and a bird
squawking an echo of resolution from some hidden recess, he considered
how valuable it must be—it was the last of its kind. It was the Creation
of the End. It had blazed brilliant red while sucking the life back into
Cooper, but now only twinkled a timid glow from its haft. Curiously, and
this is why Billy kept staring at it, the haft was positioned in his hand in
exactly the same way he'd held it when he'd killed Bottlenose, when the
star in the haft had burned its likeness into his palm. The fifth point, the
one in the lower right quadrant which continued to undulate a faint red
aura, was precisely aligned with that same point in his hand.

In quick succession, his experiences from the Yavapai medicine
wheel and from Lax's ceremonial anteroom flashed before him. He saw
himself as Lenny Bender creeping through barn shadows, looking for
his mother, only to find his cubit and his own death. He saw the low,
arched entry into the Great Hall of the Anasazi decorated with massacre
and fleeing animals, and he remembered the light that had blazed from
his hand, from that single point, the fifth point, the point in the lower
quadrant, the one that symbolized the end. He remembered that light,
penetrating the darkness, revealing his own ghastly face, a warning, a
threat.

Cooper moaned and this brought Billy out of the trance, but
he continued staring at the dagger, which had now stopped glowing
altogether. He continued staring at it because something kept his mind
boiling with calculation. He continued staring at it because the dagger
would not let him go. Cooper's star map did point to the location of the
Great Hall and now Billy knew exactly where it was.

He looked curiously at the canyon walls then quickly returned
the dagger to its sheath and the Book of the Djed to his backpack. The
thought of Eastwood-hungry outlaws became nervously prominent
because, somehow, he knew that they were being watched.

The three Yavapai Indians that had shown Billy the light, disappeared from the cliff's edge shortly after Cooper regained consciousness. They made very little noise as they returned to their medicine wheel and added a new centerpiece to the circular alter. It was not dead but was frozen in coiled infamy. The centerpiece was the rattlesnake that had bitten Cooper Reyes.

"Phoenix," she moaned. "Sixes. Nines. Dagger."

Cooper's eyes flickered and fluttered and Billy wiped sweat from her forehead with the back of his palm. She sat up, her hands propped behind her for support. He fed her water until she coughed. The intense energies that had taken control of her were now gone.

"Damn," she said. "I've seen that happen to those I've brought in here but it's never happened to me—not like that anyway."

"You've never been bitten by a rattler?" Billy said while pointing at her arm.

The lower part of her right arm throbbed as if it had fallen asleep and was just now coming back to life. She lifted it into her lap and studied the tattoo. When she touched it, a blaze of pain shot up her arm. One red circle occupied each of the djed's four crosses. Each puckered a tiny smear of blood. "Rattler?"

"You don't remember."

"I thought it was the vortex. I thought I was having an experience."

"You had an experience all right." Billy offered her more water but she waved it away.

"Two bites in the main artery. I shouldn't be alive."

"But you are." Billy took a deep breath. "You're right about this canyon. Mysterious. It has the power to take life or give it."

"No." Cooper shook her head. "It doesn't work that way. You must have done something." She saw her Swiss Army knife lying on the ground. "My knife…" she began, then reconsidered the snake bite: four holes and nothing else. "But you didn't use my knife did you?" The top button of Billy's shirt was loose and Cooper saw the hint of leather strapped to his chest. She pointed.

Billy grabbed the pointing finger and gently lowered it to her lap. "I know where the Great Hall is," he said.

Cooper answered with an astonished expression.

Billy looked around them. "Being out here in the middle of nowhere is suddenly making me very nervous."

He helped her stand. "You should be," she said. "You know where the Great Hall of the Anasazi is, and you have the Book of the Djed and a Creation Dagger. Who wouldn't be nervous?"

A camaraderie was born between them in the hour that followed. There was no denying that the masculine and feminine energies alive in Boynton Canyon had much to do with this transformation, but it was more so because Billy had saved Cooper's life, and in doing so, threw off all doubt about her true intent. The dagger had not only sucked the venom from her, it had sucked out a bit of her very soul that Billy's energy was able to taste, to sample, to judge. He *knew* that her desire for the Book had been driven by Cower's deceit, his false promises, by the unseen and unknowing, by her true want for human survival. The professor had been the real false prophet, guaranteeing her a life of power and immortality: a false prophet with a false promise set on a slick stick like a carrot before the horse. Cooper's strength and intelligence had been no match for mortal lies combined with whatever ancient influences on mortals that the Book and the dagger, together, possessed. Cower was dead, but his manipulation of her remained cold inside and this was apparent as they talked.

To raise the Djed…that's what all of this was about: raising the Djed and immortality. Cooper didn't know how to perform the ceremony but she knew that the Book and the dagger were necessary. Cower had never surrendered any specifics. The Book would explain, he'd said. And the dagger…well Cower had admitted that he'd never known exactly what to do with it (other than to kill cubits) but he knew that it was important.

Billy told Cooper where the Great Hall was located: in the fifth point, a representation of the fifth element, and the fifth creation. It was located on her star map and she reached into her backpack as he explained. He assumed that whoever had given her the parchment had meant for her—and most likely both of them—to find the Great Hall and this scared the hell out of him. When she unrolled the map from within the newspaper and looked at the ten points that imagination could easily connect into six- and five-pointed stars, she pointed where Billy had intended her to point: Lee Mountain, symbolized on the map as the fifth point.

Of course, Cooper had needed to know how he knew. Magic and logic, he'd told her— the two greatest forces and foes man had ever been challenged to understand.

First, he told her about magic, about Lax, about his own visit to Lax's house, about the anteroom, about his visions within the anteroom and how his palm and the star burned into it had lighted the way. He told her how, after he had saved her life with the dagger, the fifth point in its haft had connected with his skin, as if it were trying to tell him something.

He told her about logic, about Chancey Lett and the acquisition of Port Aransas beach front property under false pretense, about how Phoenix International wanted to acquire land for the same said purposes on Lee Mountain, which, logic would suggest, meant that something there, too, was hidden in the earth and was the real target of interest.

According to Billy, logic and magic were manifest in the Book of the Djed, particularly its center spread. The very existence of the writings was the magic. Trying to understand what they meant was the logic. The phoenix, he reminded her, was the symbol of birth and of death, of giving and of taking and logic would dictate that its place in the Book meant that Phoenix International was part of the big puzzle.

Cooper suggested that the second set of symbols in the Book, the three sixes, must therefore mean that Phoenix International was the Antichrist. Billy admitted that he'd already considered that connection up until Saturday, moments before they'd had dinner together, when he and Marcy had opened the Book to find the added triple nines. If the phoenix represented the antithetical hypocrisy of life and death, Billy said, then what must three sixes turned upside down mean? Antichrist and savior? Perhaps, in that sense, one could read into the symbolism that Phoenix International was the world's savior, but Billy said he was not ready to go that far, particularly because of the corporation's connection to oil, pharmaceuticals and gambling.

Billy then told Cooper more about magic, about Lax's other revelations, about Daykeepers and their responsibilities, about their immortality, about ancient civilizations that were destroyed by the Cubit, about Napoleon and about Hitler. And he furthered his ideas concerning logic by telling her about Jean Lafitte, about finding Lafitte's treasure in Port Aransas where Chancey Lett had wanted to build his casino, about the Creation of the End Dagger that he'd found within Lafitte's treasure and how he had used it to kill a good friend, the same dagger that he'd kept covertly hidden, the one that he'd used to save Cooper's life.

Logic and magic. Good and Evil. Antithetical hypocrisies meant to live together in the Age of Jaguar, in the age of Mankind where absolutes could never exist.

Between them, while sitting in Boynton Canyon under increasingly cloudy skies, Billy and Cooper came to understand beyond a doubt that they were in this thing together, and that, just perhaps, they always were. They came to understand that the only way to survive was not alone and that the cubit that had been following them had been providing tiny clues, had been pushing them on toward the Great Hall, had wanted them together, had wanted Billy and Cooper and the dagger and the Book for the purposes of immortality. And they *knew* that this cubit, be it Deere-hat man or Marcy or both, would eventually create that chance.

It was only at the very end of their conversation that both realized the presence of the Yavapai Indians who now revealed themselves on all sides of the canyon walls. There were at least a dozen of them. As Billy and Cooper continued their journey out of the canyon, the Yavapai followed, taking up positions in front of and behind them but always maintaining their distance among the red rocks. Nothing could harm them with the Yavapai present, they thought. Nothing could harm them until they were out of the canyon.

It would be dark soon and a storm was brewing. It was Cooper's idea to have dinner at Café Aus. She didn't feel like cooking and Billy said that he had nothing substantial in his apartment. Besides, he'd said, his kitchen was much too small for entertaining.

The temperature had dropped to a more seasonable sixty degrees. Many of the people who sat en masse around Billy and Cooper in the restaurant's outside patio wore light jackets.

"You cold?" Cooper asked.

"Not a bit," Billy said, chewing on a tortilla chip he'd just dipped into salsa. "I'm quite comfortable. Really." He studied the chip. "You know. Your salsa is the best I've ever tasted, but I gotta admit, this ain't bad. Kind of fruity and crunchy."

"Luke…he's the owner…added a bit of his own country to it. The sweetness is from the muntries and the crunch is macadamia nuts."

"Muntries?" Billy grabbed another chip and dipped. "That flavor would be excellent on redfish."

A waitress had taken their order but Luke brought their entrees to the table and set them down.

"I see you found your mate," he said to Cooper, smiling. "You know, a couple of the local blue heelers have been snooping. I hope I didn't put you in a wrong way by telling them your name."

"No…no," Cooper returned his smile. "Everything has worked out just fine."

"Wheew! Never thought of you as a killer." Luke chuckled but when neither Billy nor Cooper replied, he said, "Can I refill your dipping bowl?"

Billy handed it to him. "You have a recipe for this that I could steal off of you?"

"How about I give you a sack of some to carry with you after the supper, no charge?"

"Sweet." Billy said, as Luke wandered away from them to acknowledge the finger gesture from a diner two tables away.

Cooper devoured her plate of mango chicken. Billy finished his plate of the same order but it took him twice as long since his attention was drawn to the crowded patio. She sat there drinking water and considering his nervous tension while he slowly forked the last chunks of chicken into his mouth.

"What do we do now?" she asked.

Without looking at her, he said, "We go to Lee Mountain." Then he pointed out toward the street at a line of tables that were loaded with at least a dozen young men who wore the commercialized outfits of professional mountain bikers. "Isn't that Richard Manson?"

Cooper turned in her seat. Among the cyclists, sitting at a table next to the patio's iron fence and all the way over to the left corner, were four people dressed in casual slacks and shirts. She knew all of them. "Yes. And that's Bill Tate, Cheryl Mokier and Pat Roberts, three of our city council members."

"Uh-huh," Billy said. "And you don't think that's kinda strange?"

"In what way?" she said but was quick to answer her own question. "You mean Manson? He's the president of Phoenix International."

"We were just talking about that back in the canyon."

"Okay."

"And now here he is."

"Okay."

"Sitting with city officials."

"I still don't get where you're going."

"He sponsored the bike race that has a course that runs through Lee Mountain. He wants the property to build a casino. He's sitting with council members of the city which can grant those rights. They are violating the open meeting law statutes."

When Billy said that, all four of them turned in unison. Only Manson was smiling. In fact, with the low light conditions in that part of the Café Aus patio, that's all Cooper could see of his face: white teeth curled up into a smile. Of the council members, all she noticed was their eyes. It was hard not to. All three sets glowed crimson red. She shook her head, quickly, as if trying to erase a vision that couldn't be real. She blinked and so did the six red eyes, then Manson and his friends turned back toward their meals.

"Did you see…" Cooper pointed and Billy quickly grabbed her finger.

"Yes. And that means it won't be long before the decision about Lee Mountain is made. A three-to-two vote is guaranteed."

"We'll have to go tomorrow then."

Billy let go of her finger. "No. Tonight. We can't wait any longer. I suspect you have the gear necessary for a night hike?"

Cooper nodded.

"Hopefully we can take them by surprise."

"Who?"

"Whoever it is that has been waiting for us to bring the Book and dagger and ourselves to the Great Hall."

Manson and the three council members rose from their chairs at the very moment a streak of dry lightening lit up the sky. The foursome blinked in and out of sight for a split second, then started walking in Cooper's direction. She sat stiff and turned her face away as they approached. The three council members walked by without a word, but Manson hesitated as he stepped behind Billy. "We know who you are…" he whispered, looking straight ahead at Luke who was standing there with Billy and Cooper's check in one hand. "…and we know where you live." Manson then thanked Luke for a wonderful meal and followed the council members into the restaurant through the patio's double doors.

"Richest man in the world," Luke said. "In my restaurant. What a hum dinger, don't you think?" He handed the check to Cooper.

"Hum dinger," Cooper repeated. "He's a real hum dinger all right."

Lightning flashed again. This time it was accompanied by a spine-jerking clap of thunder that shook the entire restaurant.

Dry lightening creased the night sky in greater magnitude and quantity as Cooper parked in front of Billy's apartment. One streak caused the sky to brighten so intensely that Billy saw SpongeBob, seemingly quivering, sitting beyond the Cavalier's windshield.

"I'll pick you up in about an hour," Cooper said as Billy exited the Jeep. "Dress warm and don't forget the essentials."

"Already packing them." Billy patted the backpack strap on the right side of his chest and the sheath of the dagger on the left then waved as the Jeep exited the parking lot and headed up Dry Creek Road.

Across the street, it seemed that every light was on in Marcy's rental casita. Shadows moved behind drawn blinds. He thought about going over there. He thought he needed to know if Marcy was a cubit. But then he denied the act. He denied the want for knowing. It was better that way. If she *was* a cubit, she would try to kill him. If she wasn't a cubit, she'd soon find that he had left and that it was time for her to return to her children. If neither was true and she was dead, then it really didn't matter and whoever it was casting the shifting shadows inside the casita would certainly be unfriendly—

—Just as unfriendly as his apartment now became as soon as he opened up the front door, switched on the light, and found that someone had absolutely destroyed the place. Food and drink and clothes and the guts and broken bodies of furniture and appliances and cabinetry were combined into such heaps that he could not tell which piece once went where. Plasterboard walls were torn from wood framing and large chunks lay within the massacred contents of the room. His attention was drawn abruptly to the bathroom where he'd stashed the key to the Book of the Djed when something shattered from within its dark recess.

He slipped the backpack onto both shoulders before moving toward the bathroom. His first step landed on a protruding nail that could not penetrate his hiking boot's thick sole. A small chunk of sofa stuck to the boot and Billy had to shake his leg to get it off. He pulled the dagger from its sheath. It did not glow but it was warmer than the sweaty palm of his hand. He stood frozen and waited for a full minute that was filled only with the nocturnal meanderings of the desert beyond the apartment's open front door. He then rushed into the bathroom and slapped a wall switch that illuminated one single bulb in a light fixture filled with two others that had been broken; the sounds that he'd heard were fragments of busted bulbs falling to a floor filled with the rubble of broken sink porcelain, shattered slivers of mirror, a broken toilet seat and tank and a twisted array of towels and other linens. He tried to gain access to the linen cupboard but the mess on the floor prevented him from moving the bathroom door.

"Billy!" Marcy screamed. "Billy. Oh dear God you're alive." He peeked out from the bathroom to see her standing in the front doorway. She saw the dagger in his hand, gasped, and pointed. "You have it! I knew you did. I just knew it. Hurry," she urged. "My house!"

When she turned to run, Billy yelled, "Wait!" Marcy stopped but didn't turn around. "Wait a damn minute! What the hell is going on here?!" He moved quickly through the busted room to where Marcy stood, her back to him. She turned then and Billy expected the worst, had the dagger ready to plunge it into her if necessary. She still looked like Marcy. She still wore red lipstick and black mascara. Her luxuriously long hair was as jet black as it had ever been and he reached forward, grabbed a tangle of it and yanked, hard.

"Ouch!" she screamed. "What the hell?"

"Just wanted to make sure you were you."

"Who else would I be?"

Billy had a thousand questions. Where had she been? What had she been doing? Was she a murderer? But the opportunity was truncated when she turned and ran, yelling out, "Please hurry. Someone is in my house."

Billy stood, indecisive. He had to get the key, if it was still here, but when he watched Marcy cross the road toward the casita, he saw the green Cadillac pull into the driveway. Marcy entered her casita and a fat bolt of lightning blasted the sky, killing all of the lights everywhere: the ones in her house, those in Billy's apartment, and the few that lined Dry Creek Road. The only electricity remaining existed in the jagged bolts of blue that swarmed overhead. There was no thunder and there was no rain—just bursts of blue and white, as if a very old black and white movie was being flash photographed with a twenty-first century digital camera.

Someone was getting into the Cadillac. He took one step and…

Flash!

Another shadow appeared from behind the house. Billy walked more briskly. He stepped out into the road…

Flash!

The Cadillac rolled out of the driveway, its headlights dim. It turned south toward town, carrying occupants that remained hidden in the…

Flash!

The driver wore a ball cap but the passenger—he couldn't see more than its black outline. Someone also sat in the back seat: a third shadow that…

Flash!

He heard a shriek from inside the house and immediately crossed the road. Slowly he moved up the driveway, his senses alerted to every nuance within the black night, every slither, every slough, every…

Flash!

This blue light carried an immense and immediate crack of thunder that dropped on top of him like an anvil, causing him to jump two inches off of the driveway pavement.

Billy circled around back. When he stepped onto the porch and looked through the bay window, the absence of lights inside made it impossible to see anything. Even the double Flash! that now illuminated the landscape did nothing more than…

Wait. There was someone…lying on the floor. The blue light infiltrated the window, outlining a body, and then it was gone.

He went to the sliding glass door and shoved it open on squeaky rails that caused his teeth to grind. When he entered, the body on the floor did not move.

"Billy?"

He looked at the body, confused by the source of the sound of his name.

"Billy? Is that you?"

The voice came from further inside the darkness.

"I think you are too late. They killed them."

It was Marcy's voice, but he couldn't see her. Even when the next blue flash struck and snuck into the house through the sliding glass door and bay window panes, all that was visible was the body on the floor. He knelt toward it then fell back on his ass.

Flash!

It was Detective Beets! His teeth were clenched between lips that were fat and puffy. His eye, the one that looked up at Billy, had been abused to great extent. Blood that looked blue-black in the flash of lightning oozed from the socket and drooled into his creepy grin.

"Billy. Help me."

"Where are you?" he said.

"In the bedroom. Please…"

Billy stood and walked cautiously brisk to where he remembered her bedroom to be located.

Flash!

He saw the doorway but not the second body that lay across its threshold. He tripped and fell on top of it.

Detective Dreagan.

Two more quick lightning strikes revealed that Dreagan's body had been torn into a couple of pieces. The detached leg was the part that he had tripped over. The head seemed to be attached but only by a thread of tissue.

"They were looking for the Book," Marcy said from within the bedroom. "Those cops just got in their way."

Billy, again, rose from the floor. "Who?" he said. "Who was looking for the Book?"

"Deere-hat man," Marcy's voice responded. "You were right. Oh God, you were so right."

More lightning, flashing through a window to his left, revealed

Marcy's bed and Marcy who was sitting on it in a shadowy, cradled position. Billy shuffled toward her while looking around the room. "Are you hurt? Did they hurt you, too?"

"No," she said. "He didn't hurt me but said that he would unless you gave them the Book and the dagger."

Billy sat at the foot of the bed, his backpack to Marcy whose feet stretched out to touch his waist. "Well, they're not going to get 'em. And you aren't going to be harmed, not with me by your side."

Her arms suddenly encapsulated him. He felt her added body weight against the backpack. Her hands roamed down over his shoulders and grasped both of his breasts; one of them stroked the dagger from tip to top. Her breaths, deep and furious, blew into his right ear.

"My hero," she moaned. Her breathing heaved against him. "We can get through this together."

He lowered his head to look for her roaming hand that had found the haft of the dagger under his shirt. Her lips were now on his ear; their moisture leaked across the lobe. She whispered.

"It will soon be over and we will be free." Her hushed and excited breaths increased. Billy raised one hand to her head, caressing the hair that he knew was jet black. She was there for him. She had always been there for him. And then her fingers pulled forcefully on the haft of the dagger.

Flash! BANG!

Billy jerked forward, his hand still twisted within her hair. His arm fell to his lap and in the blue flash, he saw…

Her hair. Her wig. Long and luxurious. Just like Cher's. She clamped onto his back as he rose in sudden shock. He tried to pry her hand from the dagger but its vise-like grip was unrelenting. Together, they fell to the floor and rolled on top of the pieces that once were Detective Dreagan. Billy beat at the appendages around him. He shoved with buckled legs against the shadowy body that covered him. Lightning struck the ground outside the bedroom window, igniting a fire that illuminated the darkness within the bedroom and someone who was not Marcy…but was.

Except for the bald head and the fresh, red scar that encircled her entire neck.

"Give me the fucking dagger!" Marcy's cubit growled. "Give it to me or she dies!"

The combative force of both of their hands against the haft of the dagger sent it reeling out of its sheath and through the bedroom doorway. The Marcy cubit rose up on knees that were straddling Billy, and brought both of it its fists, clasped into one fleshy hammer, down.

Billy rolled. The cubit's fists slammed into the floor before it flipped forward out of the bedroom to search for the dagger. Billy groped the floor. His hands found Dreagan's arm and when he tossed it aside, the entire appendage came loose, flailed across the room and shattered the bedroom window. Heat from the lightening fire wafted into the room.

Billy rose to his knees to find Marcy's cubit towering over him, its black outline framed dead center within the bedroom's doorway. "You putrid excuse for a human," the Marcy cubit exclaimed. In its hand glowed Billy's dagger. Then the cubit leapt at him.

He jumped out of the way as the cubit fell to the floor. Billy blinked. Heat from the fire outside sucked the moisture from his eyeballs. He blinked again. On the floor, two shadows fought for the possession of the dagger: the cubit and …

Cooper!

Her arm wrenched at the dagger that the cubit was not willing to give up. Both shadows stood, wrestled, turned and twisted in all directions, then fell through the shattered window and disappeared from view outside. A screech followed that was louder than the thunder that hammered the darkness. When Billy crawled to the window and stood, he saw Cooper raise the dagger for a second strike to the back of the Marcy cubit's bald head. The cubit convulsed on the ground for an impossibly long second before succumbing. Its head fell off of its re-stitched neck then all of its flesh turned black, molting and melting and disintegrating, the lightning fire behind it providing visual evidence of the cubit's final writhing existence.

Billy jumped through the window and stood beside Cooper in time to see the green Cadillac that sat, idling, at the Boynton Canyon Road intersection. Farther up the road, a pair of headlights from an old Ford Ranger raced toward the Cadillac and within the truck's headlights Billy saw the occupant in the Cadillac's back seat.

It was Marcy Ruminski.

Breathe

They'd left Marcy's casita shortly after Lax had arrived and Billy had returned to his apartment to retrieve the torn page from the Book of the Djed that he'd hidden there. Billy had almost forgotten about it, but Lax had reminded him of its need. The death and destruction they'd left behind for the Sedona authorities to figure out.

Now, the three of them sat at the small, wooden table in Lax's backyard, which provided a spectacular view of Cathedral Rock and the lightning bolts that cracked the black night behind it.

"Where's Aaron?" Billy asked.

Lax's legs were crossed and he leaned back against his wooden chair. "Dropped him off at a friend's house on the way out to see you two. I didn't think that he was mature enough yet to witness exactly what cubits are or what they are capable of."

Billy and Cooper sat next to each other on the opposite side of the table from Lax, watching heaven's light display for several silent minutes when Billy finally said what they both were thinking. "You knew."

Lax sat up, his legs uncrossing. "I knew." he said, his voice deep but calm. "I knew that the woman you call Marcy had been cubited. I didn't know that her primary had been kept alive."

"I thought Daykeepers were all-knowing," Billy said.

"We know what we have experienced and since we live so long, that knowledge encompasses quite a bit." Lax then looked directly at Cooper. "I must apologize to you."

Cooper shrugged. "Why?"

"I saw you Friday night, around the corner, watching. You witnessed me taking off the Marcy cubit's head.

"The sun kachina," Cooper said to herself.

"Yes."

"So why all the ceremonial garb?"

"Because it's tradition for two invincible warriors. And to protect my identity."

"Whatever." She dropped her hand on top of Billy's.

"I thought you were like the professor," Lax continued. "I thought your spirit was not clean."

"None of our spirits seem to be clean." Cooper sat back in her chair as blue lightning played with the strawberry red colors in her hair, her fingers drumming against Billy's knuckles. "We all have a little bit of cubit in us."

Lax scooted closer, his face an expression connoting solemn thought. Both of his elbows slid across the wooden round tabletop and he craned forward. "Young wisdom," he said, studying her. "It never ceases to amaze me. This world truly does have a future." He glanced quickly at Billy whose attention had also been drawn away from the unique display of nature in the night to the center of the table. "I think you two are the perfect choices."

Cooper stared at Lax. It was almost impossible to turn away. His slate gray eyes pooled hundreds of years of experience; the irises were magnetic. "What do you mean by that, old man?"

"I mean that when I tell the story of 2012, it will include wisdom and youth and, I might say, a great sense of humor."

Billy interrupted. "So what's our next step? We were thinking that we have to act quickly, before Phoenix International gets ownership of the land.

"Wisdom requires patience," Lax said. "I don't think Phoenix International is going to be buying anything anytime soon. You saw what happened when they tried to buy beachfront property in Texas."

"Hurricane," Billy quickly responded.

"Makes you feel enlightened knowing nature is on our side, doesn't it?" The dark skies lit up with multiple strokes of dry lightning that illuminated the entire face of Cathedral Rock. "Do you even know why you desire to venture into the Great Hall?"

"It's why I came to Sedona," Billy said.

"And you?" Lax asked Cooper.

She hesitated. "I think…well, I used to think that it was to become immortal."

He grabbed Cooper's free hand and she let him. "Nothing ever dies," he said. "We exist in this flesh to complete cycles that have no beginning and no end. Unfortunately, we are told otherwise. Humans lie because they don't understand. Science lies because it doesn't understand. Faith makes excuses for the lies and packages misunderstanding in convenient collections of knowledge that is distributed as argument. Like you said, every one of we mortal beings have a little cubit in us and that, Cooper, is why death even has a definition. Death has a materialistic understanding, one that can be used against passion and hope and love. It is a bargaining chip."

Billy asked, "So why *are* we going to the Great Hall?"

Lax released Cooper's hand and sat back in his chair. "To make sure that the definition of death does not become the definition of life. And to save your friend."

"Marcy?"

"Yes. There can be only one reason why she has been allowed to… live."

"The Book," Cooper said.

"And the dagger," Billy added.

"And the future," Lax concluded. "What did Professor Cower tell you about immortality?" he asked Cooper.

"He said that to gain immortality, you have to raise the Djed, and the only way to do that is by conducting a ceremony in the Great Hall with the Book and the dagger."

"He was wrong," Lax said.

"About immortality?" Billy asked.

"He was wrong in his understanding of what immortality means. And he was wrong about the location in which immortality is gained."

Cooper stood then and walked to the perimeter of the brick-laden patio. The pit oven that had cooked bread for Billy and Lax and Aaron and the bird called Osi was at her feet. She looked at it, curiously. "So the reason we are going to the Great Hall is to find out the location where the raising of the Djed is supposed to take place?"

"Young wisdom," Lax said. "And now there is an innocent life at stake. The use of death against love. Even if we thought we had a choice, we do not…not if Marcy is to live."

"And the Book will tell us?" Cooper added.

"The Book will tell us where it is that the Djed can be raised," Lax confirmed.

Billy stood then and joined Cooper, placing his arm around her shoulder. Lightning was now only sporadic, providing little illumination.

"You have done this before," Billy said to Lax, his back to him, Cooper's head leaning into his arm. "If you are hundreds of years old then you must be protected by the Djed. Just like your sister was. But I saw her die."

Lax now rose and joined the couple at the patio's perimeter. He stood a couple of feet away as a thrust of desert wind careened into them. "She had completed her purpose, as I will soon complete mine." A second, mightier gust of wind billowed Lax's poncho open; the Djed amulet hanging from a leather necklace, jumped out from under it and bounced against his chest. He turned to them then, the amulet twinkling though there was no light source to provide such reflection.

"Only one more exists," Lax said. "And it is for you Billy Jo Presser. You are to be immortal until *your* journey is complete. The Djed will protect you from all harm as it has all Daykeepers. Daggers and bullets and even the Cubit are of no consequence once you, too, have raised the Djed."

What would it be like to live for a hundred years? Two hundred? Five hundred? The complicated answer to that question kept Billy awake.

His true destiny had now been outlined for him and this "journey," as Lax had put it, would begin shortly. First, though, Lax had demanded that each of them rest. They'd have no chance against Evil without sleep, he'd said. Tomorrow morning, they would go to the Great Hall to save Marcy and to find out where the journey would take them next.

Billy looked up at the dark ceiling. Aaron's bed was comfortable but small. His bare feet dangled out from under the bed sheets and beyond the edge of the mattress by several inches. Lightning still played a minor role in illuminating the small bedroom, and with each faint flicker that entered the space through one single-paned window, Billy looked at his feet, wiggled his toes and thought about growing older.

Fear and fantasy dominated the conversation in his head. One thought centered on Superman, the comic book icon. Would he be able to leap tall buildings in a single bound? Would he be able to stop a speeding locomotive? He wouldn't be able to fly would he? Of course not. That fantasy was pure fiction.

Perhaps he'd be able to fearlessly ride the treacherous waves off of Tahiti. Better still, he fantasized about riding waves in the wake of a monstrous hurricane, one that would lift the surf fifty feet above the ocean's surface. He'd become something like Silver Surfer, and would ease his surfboard into every port of call that necessitated superhero intervention. Bad guys wouldn't have a chance against Captain Daykeeper.

He giggled while staring at the square of window glass glow and then sat straight up in the bed. His toes retreated under the sheets and he massaged his legs.

Immortality. The meaning was beyond comprehension. A fantasy and a fear. Lax had said that bullets and blades would not harm him. But he had also said that immortality had an end. A few hundred years. Or longer. Or sooner. It all depended on when Billy completed his journey, which really meant that he wouldn't be immortal at all. According to Lax, nothing began and nothing ended. In a world like that, immortality had no meaning, and that had been Lax's point all along. So what would the Djed do for him other than bounce against his chest for the rest of his not so immortal life? He'd be able to sling Creation Daggers like a whirring buzz saw and take out droves of cubits, of that he was sure. It would probably make him a lot wiser, more spiritual, and reduce the stress in his life…it would probably eradicate the stress in his life. If a bullet and a blade couldn't kill you, what the hell was there to stress about?

Oh, nothing—except the end of the world.

That thought caused him to get out of bed and walk to the window. His breaths, now deeper and heavier, quickly fogged the glass. He wiped his hand across the moisture then started a simple doodle with one finger: a star, just like the one in his hand…just like the one in the dagger. A star was important for saving the world. He didn't know why or how, but he knew.

Another heavy breath nearly erased his finger art but its smudgy, wet edges remained. A flash of lightning redefined it further. And then it moved. Billy blinked and rubbed his eyes with both fists but that didn't make the star on the window pane stop moving; its top point which Billy had draw straight up, turned a half circle and now pointed straight down. The fifth point, the one that represented the Creation of the End, the one that was burned prominently into his hand, was now resting in the ten o'clock position. Billy continued to stare at it, the fifth point, as it began to glow a dull crimson; then it undulated, the crimson strengthening then weakening, bright to dull, in perfect rhythm with his heart.

Mmm…..mmm….. Mmm…..mmm…..

That sound…he'd heard it before.

Mmm…..mmm….. Mmm…..mmm…..

It had come from within the bank vault at the Port Aransas branch of the Big Texas Bank.

Mmm…..mmm….. Mmm…..mmm…..

It had come from the Cubit!

As impossible as it seemed, the pulsing fifth point drawn into the window glass broke away and fell to the window sill where, as an animated triangle, it continued to glow and hum. Billy picked it up. It was tiny, about half the size of a guitar pick, and its edges were very sharp. They sliced into the thumb and forefinger of his right hand, causing a thin line of blood to emerge.

Mmm……mmm….. Mmm…..mmm…..

Billy's attention centered on the pulsing triangle of red. It was like staring into a looking glass—a crystal ball shaped like a triangle—and in it he could see…

A face. But it was so small he couldn't make it out. He did, however, hear what the face was saying. Mixed in with the numbing humming, were the words:

We are the creation of the end. Follow with me to your destiny.

And then the tiny, unrecognizable face disappeared and was replaced by giant balls of fire pelting a tiny rendition of the earth. Billions of people screamed from within the fiery triangle, and Billy woke up.

Their breakfast was very simple: some berries, bananas, small corn muffins and tea. Billy never said anything about the dream. He never said anything about believing that it was not a dream, that he thought what he'd seen might be prophecy. He did ask to clarify what an upside down star signified. He'd always believed it to be the sign of Satan, though that could easily have been misguided by blockbuster movie theatrics.

Cooper was the first to react. "Just another way man has defaced divine symbols for use in scare-tactic strategies." She ate the last piece of her banana and tossed the peel on the patio's wooden table. The skies were much cloudier today; they drooled in gray at the horizon.

"A pentacle," Lax explained. "turned upside down means nothing. It all depends on which way the top point is pointing.

Cooper nodded. "Top point to the north and you invoke positive energy, protection of the spirit from the underworld and the divine principle. Top point to the south and…"

"Just the opposite," Billy finished.

"Satan is a religious icon for negative energy," Lax added. "It is the ignorance of materialism which clouds a person's natural ability to deny ego and accept the divine that rests hidden, and always ready to be unlocked, within each of us."

"Is that what we'll find today," Billy said. "Our divine selves?"

Lax snatched all three empty wooden bowls from the table, stacking them one inside the other, and stood. "I suspect we'll find both. There's a little bit of cubit in all of us." He grinned at Cooper. "We should probably be on our way."

"I am curious about something before we go," Cooper said. "You've never asked to see the Book. I think that's a bit strange considering how valuable it is."

A half a dozen corn muffins remained in a tray on the table. Lax grabbed the tray with his free hand and jettisoned the muffins out into the desert landscape, then set the empty bowls on the tray. "The Book is of tremendous value, but not for me…at least not anymore." Osi appeared out of nowhere and landed among the tossed corn muffins. The giant hawk ate one of them in a hurry then offered its gratitude with a sharp screech. "You're welcome, my friend," Lax said to the bird.

All of their gear, packed into three backpacks, sat near the solarium kitchen door. Once Lax had finished inside, they prepared for the hike that would take them to Lee Mountain. Though the star map had already served its purpose, Cooper stuffed it, still rolled in the newspaper, into her pack. Billy double-checked that the Book of the Djed and the key were safe and secure in his pack then zipped it up and followed Cooper and Lax around the side of the house.

"Ironically, Phoenix International has provided us a bit of camouflage by sponsoring the bike race today," Lax said as all three climbed into the Ranger. "It'll take us right to the Great Hall under Lee Mountain."

They weren't on the trail more than ten minutes before a light rain started saturating the ground. The organizers of the Llama Lunatic mountain bike race had done a wonderful job of flagging off a pedestrian traffic lane from the main course, but because of the terrain, the two paths were adjacent and in some places, intersected. Pedestrians had to remain attentive to avoid being run over by racers. What some spectators probably had not considered was the rooster tail splashes of red mud that pelted their bodies in turns and in areas where puddles had formed. Some of the spectators (women included) reveled in the mud and rain, having taken off their shirts to write explications across their bare chests. Others, who were certainly tourists, stood rigid, frowning at their red blotchy clothes; one family looked absolutely miserable and Cooper tried to ease their pain as she walked past.

"What's done is done," she told the father of the triumvirate. "You'll need to soak those clothes as soon as you get home or else Sedona will forever remain in the fibers." The man glared at her. The mother asked if they could leave now. Their boy, who was no more than eight years old, smiled, his face dotted with mud. "Who's your favorite rider?" Cooper asked him.

The boy pointed at the bicycle that was heading in their direction. "Cobra Diego," he yelled. "He's in the lead and ain't nobody gonna catch him." Cooper instinctively backed a few steps as Cobra skidded across the bike path, sending a fresh tail of red mud over the head of the boy and into the faces of his mother and father. The mother wiped the mess from her mouth and exclaimed, "That's it! I'm outta here." She shoved past Cooper who was amazed to see that the woman was wearing flip-flops; she slipped on a rock and almost fell.

"Come on," the father said to his son. "We better help her or she's gonna bust her butt." The boy looked totally crushed as he watched his favorite racer disappear around the next turn, but he grabbed his mother's hand and all three headed back down the hill toward the trailhead.

Lax and Billy, who had continued on when Cooper had stopped, waved at her from the rocky turn that Cobra Diego had just managed. After three additional racers passed, she stepped out onto the course and headed up the gentle slope to meet them.

They stood a few yards away from the course as rain continued to mist the area. Clouds broke at one point and, for a few minutes, a rainbow appeared in the direction that Lax said they should go, which was straight ahead, across a wide, flat plain filled with multicolored autumn brush and cacti, toward the base of Lee Mountain about a mile and a half away. To their right, the bike race continued along the west rim of Lee Mountain, snaking its way up treacherous slopes, across flat and rugged ground, around corners where the racers disappeared momentarily before reappearing to continue their slippery journey toward its apex. To their left was a set of smaller hills that had not yet gained prominence in the presence of the more sensational red rock monoliths promoted in the area.

As they descended a short slope to flatter land, Lax explained that it was in this plain where trailblazing pioneers had moved between Arizona and Utah in the late 1800s. The mountain was actually named after one of these men who settled nearby.

"I'm sure it came with great cost," Cooper said as she scraped mud from the bottom of her hiking boot with a broken juniper tree branch. She handed the stick to Billy who followed the same procedure.

"All men have a right to the land," Lax said. "But not when that right is defined by self-serving policy." Lax took the stick and cleaned his boots, using Billy's shoulder for support. "You are right, though. White men pioneered on the backs of dead natives. The policy was called Manifest Destiny—to settle in the name of American progress. But we all know who the real Americans were then and still are today. Progress for America by killing Americans. That tune sounds familiar, doesn't it?"

"One that doesn't make much sense," Billy offered.

"And never will," Cooper concluded.

Once their boots were a pound of mud lighter, they started across the plain, following Lax's lead. Rain continued but it was light, and unlike on the hillside, the ground beneath them now was stitched with enough autumn tobosa grass that their boots did not collect much of the earth. Considering that the terrain was densely populated with desert flora, the trek was not encumbered: they walked a trail, it seemed, though no footprints or other signs of passage was present.

Throughout the hike, Cooper kept thinking about their conversation the night before, about the idea of immortality and the implications for those promoted to its promised hierarchy. She wondered if Lax was telling them the truth. It certainly wasn't inconceivable that it had been Lax all along who had wanted them and the Mayan artifacts together in the Great Hall. That thing around his neck could be any one a thousand lookalikes sold at any one of a hundred shops in the Verde Valley. This could all be one big ruse to find out for himself exactly where the real Djed could be found, she thought. He'd then kill them both with the help of his accomplice, Deere-hat man. He'd kill them, then kill Marcy and flee to Mexico…to Chichen Itza where Cooper suspected the Djed lay in wait. Lax had told Billy that he would become immortal only to gain his confidence. Just as Cower had used her own ego against her, Lax was using Billy's against him. The promise to live forever could not be ignored by mere mortals.

They stopped once for rest and water and this is when Cooper had to ask. "Why should we trust you?" Billy looked shocked, as if he'd never even considered such blasphemy.

"I've given you no reason," Lax said, simply.

"Then this is as far as we go." Cooper looked to Billy for support. "Right?"

Billy suddenly seemed defeated and helpless. "But we do trust him…don't we? We've come so far."

"I'm not Marcy," Cooper grumbled. "*We* haven't come far at all. I was taken on a carpet ride to the Land of Liars before. It's not happening again."

"Please," Lax pleaded. "This is unnecessary. I can prove that I am who I say I am."

"A Daykeeper?" Billy asked.

"Yes. I can tell you what is contained on just about every page of the Book except the center page, the one that is being written by the Great Spirit, and the pages that will be revealed by the key."

"What do you mean?" Billy asked, taking one step away from Cooper and one step closer to Lax.

"The center page reveals clues that guide the end of the Age of Jaguar. The key reveals where to find the Djeds and how to seal the Cubit forever."

"The Djeds…plural?" Cooper said, suddenly feeling a bit ostracized.

Lax wiped accumulated mist from his forehead. "Right now, the key reveals three locations. The first is of the Great Hall itself where the revelations are made. The second is Chichen Itza where my sister raised her Djed."

Cooper looked confused and Billy clarified. "Alixel."

"The third location revealed by the key is where *my* Djed was raised." Lax tapped his chest where the bulge of the amulet pressed up against his wet poncho. "Puerto Morelos."

"Where's that?" Billy asked.

"In Quintana Roo…on the Riviera side of the peninsula. It's a small fishing village very much like your Port Aransas."

Billy pulled his backpack from his shoulders and started to unzip it.

"Stop!" Cooper demanded. "What are you doing?"

"I'm going to see if he's lying."

Cooper stepped to him and gently but firmly grabbed his hand. "He could have opened it last night while we were sleeping."

Lax's face spread into that cavernous grin of his. "Wise but paranoid," he said to Cooper. "I guess there's only one way to find out then. Billy, you know what to do."

Cooper released Billy's hand and he gave the pack to her. "What's he talking about?" she asked him. "Wait…you don't mean…"

But before she could finish her sentence, Billy had already unleashed the Creation Dagger and plunged it into Lax's ribs, then quickly withdrew it. The seven-inch blade was coated in Lax's blood; the dripping point hovered over the crimson hole in Lax's poncho. Cooper looked across the landscape, wondering if she should cry for help. Up on the rim of Lee Mountain, the ant-sized shadows of bike racers continued up the slope in earnest. Then, appearing out of nowhere, flew the hawk Lax had called Osi. She ducked, slipped forward, and fell to her knees. She'd never seen a raptor that big. It continued to hover overhead while Lax's body proved its immortality.

While the dagger remained an inch from the wound that it had just inflicted, the blood on its blade jumped from the metal surface and onto the hole in Lax's poncho. It was as if the blood had suddenly been frightened by the reality of being pulled out of its home and was now desperate to return. Every ounce of it drained in a thin rivulet from blade to body. The blood soaking the fabric followed in retreat. The magical procedure lasted only a minute and when it was over, Lax lifted up his poncho. Cooper then realized that Billy had struck Lax in the exact same location that she'd seen the Jaguar stab the Sun last Friday night. The wound had already started stitching itself, sucking any remaining blood around the vertical opening until nothing but a thin scar remained.

Billy returned the dagger to its sheath and said, "Believe?"

Osi screeched above them, circled once more, then flew off in the direction they were headed.

At the far end of the plain, Billy was surprised to find a cemetery. It would have been hard to detect from just about any vantage point, even one that looked out over the plain from high up on Lee Mountain. The headstones, about a dozen of them, were located behind an outcropping of rocks from which short but bushy broad juniper trees had grown. From the ground, the rocks hid the headstones. From above, the juniper trees provided camouflage.

In addition to the flora that seemingly guarded the cemetery, an obviously angry mass of fauna encircled it as well. Billy counted ten rattlers before he'd even crossed the rocky barrier into the cemetery. Skittering across the rocks themselves were more scorpions than he'd seen since coming to Arizona. There was even a coyote sitting and watching them on a short rocky shelf a hundred yards above them. But none of that mattered since, as Lax led them forward, all of the desert creatures parted as if they were either scared or respectful of his presence. The only threat to their passage into the cemetery came from one stray rattlesnake that slithered up behind them and tried to snag Cooper's foot. Osi again appeared as if out of thin air, swooped down, and snatched the reptile within its giant talons. It took to the sky and disappeared beyond the mask of the juniper trees, the snake writhing into a question mark.

The headstones were chipped and eroded; some had fallen over; some were broken in several pieces. Billy read from the five that still offered legible epitaphs.

Ole Man Jacobs d. under his tractor Oct. 1886

Robert Kenny d. Apr. 1900 Typhoid Fever

Mamie Baker d/o Ben and Ella d. shortly after birth

Wife of G.W. Johnson d. on Lee Mt during the Civil War

Unknown Child d. 1865 Starved to Death

Lax continued through the cemetery then stood by a mass of one- to two-foot sandstones that lay in scattered, half-circle disarray.

"Over here," Lax said. "The earthquake opened up the door to the well."

Billy stepped onto the scattered stones and Cooper followed. They helped each other across the stones' wet surfaces until they stood beside Lax. The rain began to fall more aggressively as Lax pointed at the shadowy hole in the ground.

"The well," Billy said. "I saw this well in the vision."

Lax nodded. "Remember—both of you." He waved a finger. "Remember the purpose of the Great Hall. It served to imprison that which was the mechanism for the creation of Evil. And it is protected by the Jaguar—the undertaker of the underworld."

Billy took the lead. Gray sunlight was the only source of illumination and this provided a glimpse at only the next five steps below his descent. Just like in his vision, the stairwell spiraled downward and each step was as narrow as the width of one foot. As fascinating as it was to be actually living a dream, he felt his concentration could not chance a state of wonderment since, with each step, his footing was challenged not only by the tapered steps and their sharp edges, but also by the running water that cascaded from the opening above and washed a slick residue under his boots.

This staircase seemed to be much deeper than it was in his dream-vision. The farther down he went, the darker the well became until, at one point, only the next step could be seen. He stood there for a moment and Cooper's hand fell on his shoulder.

"What is it?" she asked, her voice hollow as if she were speaking from inside a tin can.

"I can't see the steps."

From above, Lax urged him onward. "You know where they are. You've walked these steps before."

"Yeah. But I fell that time," he said, referring to the dream-vision.

Water rolled down the steps at an ever-increasing rate, flooding the sole of his boot as he stepped downward once more. The light from above disappeared altogether but the well did not become completely dark; below, a dim red glow lit the bottom. The red hue provided a view of the rest of the staircase but grew only faintly brighter by the time he finished the descent. He helped Cooper and Lax down the remaining steps and the three of them looked up at the twisting staircase, at the rain water which was now tumbling down and splashing profusely. Red froth collected at their feet and within minutes, the water had risen above their ankles. To their right was the source of the red illumination. It peeked through a stone obstacle that blocked the arched doorway. The obstacle's seal, however, was too tight to allow the deluge of water an escape. It now rose to their knees.

"This wasn't here before," Lax said and quickly sloshed over to the doorway. "Give Cooper your pack and help me push this out of the way or we're all going to drown. And Cooper…keep the pack out of the water. I don't know if the Book has ever survived submersion but I don't want to find out now."

She took Billy's backpack and held it with both hands over her head as the water rose to her waist. Billy and Lax wrestled with the stone obstruction, wrapped their fingers into a narrow crevice, pulled with combined force to the left.

The water rose to their chests.

They tried rolling the stone to the right.

The water rose to their shoulders.

The weight of the water was now draining their strength. Together, they pushed as hard as they could.

The water covered their mouths.

Briefly, Billy looked back at Cooper. All that remained of her was two arms sticking straight up with his backpack clamped between her fingers; short curls of hair swirled within the rising water. He turned then, and with every ounce of strength he could manage, pushed through the water and into the obstruction. The stone toppled backward and the immediate rush of escaping water sucked them through the arched doorway. Billy fell on top of Lax and Cooper fell on top of Billy. Cooper gasped for air, her face inches from his.

"The pack ain't wet," she said and coughed, then crawled off of the body heap with Billy's backpack in her hands. She offered her hand to Billy, then Billy helped Lax to his feet. Water continued rolling through the doorway, hitting the round stone obstacle and cascading off of it to each side. The streams rushed into small slits that had apparently been carved into the rock walls of a long corridor in which they now stood.

"The underworld," Lax said. "She is quite thirsty today."

"And very pretty," Cooper added.

Billy turned around to see Cooper standing in the middle of the Great Hall; it was a two-hundred-foot-long, twenty-foot-wide, twenty-foot-high corridor that dead-ended into a stone wall. Her entire body reflected shades of red that fell from the high ceiling. Her silhouette mixed dark shadow within the red hues and she looked kind of demonic.

"It's a chemical brought up from the Yucatán," Lax said and pointed toward the very top of the walls where a rounded shelf of rock housed the chemical source of the red light; the shelf was continuous, as was the light, and ran the length of the corridor along both walls. "It was produced from a combination of plants that are now extinct. The chemical reaction is self-replicating; it never goes out and never needs to be reenergized. It would have been invaluable in today's resource-hungry world."

Billy thought of some of the chemists back at MIT that would have sold their mothers for a chance to be standing where he was now. Ancient Mayan plants now extinct, providing perpetual light for an underground corridor built by the Anasazi.

And, suddenly, that didn't make sense to him. "Wait a minute," he said. "Are you implying that the Anasazi visited the Mayans? That can't be. There's a three- to four-hundred-year difference, not to mention a couple of thousand miles that separates the two cultures."

"I am not implying that at all." Lax sucked in a deep breath in a way that made the air seem precious.

"Unbelievable." Cooper gasped. "Look at these walls. I'm no archeologist but this looks like a convergence of ancient Mayan and old Native American writing."

"No." Billy shook his head. "Really? The Mayans were the Anasazi?"

"Not precisely," Lax corrected. "But the surviving Mayans had to migrate somewhere. Remember what I told you about Samaal and Eka?"

"The Mayan and Anasazi Daykeepers?" Billy answered. "The influence of two cultures colliding. The transference of knowledge."

Cooper stroked the walls, fingered the striations. "You are supposed to be the next one aren't you?" she said to Billy. "Don't you see? You are supposed to be the next Daykeeper. Lax is passing the knowledge on to you right now." She looked at Lax. "You are a clever one aren't you, my Hopi friend—if you really are Hopi. My guess is that you and your sister are descendant of the last surviving Anasazi."

In the red luminescence, Lax's big, fat grin made his teeth look bloody. "She's sharp, Billy. I'd hang on to her if I was you."

"But you're extinct," Billy said.

"Nothing ever dies," Lax reminded him.

Billy turned his attention to the wall's deep etchings of pictographs and glyphs that told stories with lost meanings. Hunters stalked bison. Lizards swirled around twisted trees. There were many four-legged creatures and orbs that Billy guessed represented celestial objects. As he walked along the corridor, the simple pictographs began to transform into the kinds of glyphs one could find in the ruins of the Maya. Deep chiseled etchings of frogs and serpents and men with fantastic headdresses merged with the more simplistic pictograph scratches. The farther he walked, the more transformative the drawings became until there remained only Mayan glyphs.

He stood near the end of the corridor and looked back toward the well opening. The wall drawings presented a chronological move forward in history, but at the same time told of a recession in intellect. The Mayan glyphs closest to him were meticulously crafted, some chiseled into three-dimensions all stacked in rows one on top of the other. But as the corridor continued toward the well, the drawings lost their third dimension and became scattered, simple depictions that reminded Billy of something he might find in a kindergarten class.

When he turned back around, Lax and Cooper were waiting for him in front of a narrow vertical opening of about five feet wide that split the dead end wall from floor to ceiling. Billy stood there for a moment longer because of the sound he heard behind the wall.

A humming noise.

"Hey. Do you guys hear that?" he asked as Lax and Cooper disappeared into the vertical slit. Billy followed.

When he emerged on the other side he gasped, the one breath seemingly stuck in his open mouth. The temple face in front of him really didn't look like anything the Anasazi might have constructed. It looked Mayan. A rectangular door carved an entrance through the middle of the temple face and it glowed a dim white. To each side of the door stood a statue of a jaguar-headed human; their noses pointed down toward the doorway which was a couple of feet shorter than the statues were tall. Ceremonial accessories of feathers, small animals, carnivorously sharp teeth and a slithering snake were chiseled across their bodies. The walls to the left and right of both jaguars were filled with glyphs set in horizontal rows. Some of the glyphs were stained in red, some in blue, some not at all.

"What does it say?" Cooper asked Lax, pointing at the glyphs beside the statue on the left.

"In a roundabout way, it says we better not enter unless we want our souls ripped from our bodies and sacrificed to the underworld."

"Wonderful," Cooper moaned.

"And on this side?" Billy asked.

"It names the Daykeepers from history. We are the only ones whose entry is guaranteed safe."

"Then I'm good," Billy said, studying the glyphs, their arrangement, their representative iconography. "Where am I?"

"You aren't a Daykeeper yet. You still have quite a demanding journey ahead of you."

Billy wondered what it would take to get his representation chiseled into the temple wall. What labors would he have to accomplish to be awarded with such reverent gratitude? The thought scared him. He should have known that the ascension toward immortality just might kill him in the process.

Cooper walked over to that side of the temple. "So, you are inscribed into the last row?" she asked Lax.

"It's not written in such linear terms nor is it written to be translated as English," Lax explained.

Billy interjected. "That would go against everything the Mayan culture believed in: no beginning and no end, just one long, unending cycle. Kind of like all of the 'begots' in the Bible: a lineage of ancestry without chronology dating back to the beginning of human history. The importance is that one came before and one came after and not when those links were created."

Above and in front of the temple face and attached to the ceiling, was a row of what Billy thought were stalactites. Inverse conical sandstones, their sharp points hovering directly over his head, seemed almost like teeth and when Billy realized that an equal set of conical shapes stood upright across the entire base of the temple, he was sure that is what they represented. Lax verified his assumption.

A single sandstone step sat in front of the doorway like a welcome mat and Lax now stepped onto it. "Let us enter the mouth of the underworld," he said. "The Wayeb Chamber awaits." And then he stepped through the doorway.

Ya'axche'

As it always has been and as it always will be, spiritual ceremonies and mystical ruminations remain central to all human cultures throughout time. For the Maya, the sacred ceremony Ya'axche' represents the center of life on earth and is the connection between Heaven and the Underworld. Only the wisest of men are allowed to perform the ceremony which has, as its central symbol, the Tree of Life: the ceiba tree. Found in all parts of the Yucatán, Central America and the Caribbean, la ceiba is fundamental to survival. Its wood is used to build shelters and canoes and containers, and provides a base from which are constructed handicrafts and wondrous artwork. Within the tree's numerous seed pods grows a cotton-like fiber with which clothes are made and the seeds, themselves, provide fertilizer for crops. As one of the largest trees in the tropics, its gray-white trunk, which is inundated with protective thorns, rises several feet before branching into a canopy of leaves and seed pods high above the ground. The most striking part of the tree, and that which is considered connected to the underworld, is its roots. Standing tall and thick above the ground, the tree buttress roots are often taller than the height of a human. It is at these roots where X'Tabay waits for unsuspecting men.

Legend has it that X'Tabay is a deadly spirit of the night; she is the goddess of suicide. During a full moon, she awaits unsuspecting male souls as she sits atop the ceiba tree roots, stroking her long black and beautiful hair, her body and eyes so seductive that men are helpless to deny her advances. This deceitful, dark spirit sings tones of increasing sensuality, luring her victims into her embrace. Men cannot escape as her arms turn into thorny branches, her face into razor-sharp spines, and her mouth into a cavernous pit that devours them alive.

For Cooper, it was the ceiba tree, standing in the center of the temple's ceremonial chamber that first caused her to gasp. Its twenty-foot tall, four-foot thick, white trunk rose into the ceiling where it spanned out into a canopy of many leafy, pod-bearing branches. The tree seemed to continue straight up through the sandstone where, from above, very dim rays of daylight found spaces within the dense canopy and provided dull illumination throughout the vast chamber. Cooper knew the ceiba tree very well. She'd grown up understanding its tremendous material and spiritual value in Puerto Rico. At an early age, its use was required learning, particularly since her hometown was named after the tree.

For Billy, it was the woman tied to the ceiba tree roots about thirty feet away, that first caused him to gasp. In almost every way, she resembled what legend described as X'Tabay. Marcy's long black hair flowed over a thin sheet of cloth that covered most of her body. Her eyes, though open and staring straight at him, did not appear conscious of the reality around her. She sang a soft hum through slightly-parted red lips, a sensual tune that locked Billy's attention. Her body was tied to the tall roots with lashings of vines that prevented all movement except for her head.

"Marcy?" Billy said and took one step forward but was held back by Lax's arm. She continued staring at him, her soft hum never changing its harmonic pitch. Lax glanced around the chamber, at the numerous shadows that hid the depth of the red sandstone walls on all sides.

"Go ahead, Presser," a hidden voice echoed from their left. "X'Tabay wants your young soul. And she wants to know where the final Djed will be found. Show her, or she will die."

A spear flew through the air from the shadows and missed the middle of Marcy's forehead by a couple of inches; it impaled the tree root directly above her head and a feather tied near the spearhead, swooped down over Marcy's glassy eyes. It fluttered each time a humming breath emerged from her lips.

"To the Cubit's throne with the Book," the voice urged. "Hurry!" Another spear flew overhead and struck the tree root to the right of Marcy's head.

Lax and Billy walked cautiously toward Marcy.

"Not you, Daykeeper," the voice demanded. "Just the boy."

"Go on," Lax said. "I'll join you shortly."

Billy looked at Lax curiously, but did as he was told. As he neared the tree, he realized that a square pedestal made of stone sat at Marcy's feet. Billy guessed that it was what the voice had referred to as the "Cubit's throne" since it looked a lot like the Cubit, right down to the red star that was centered and glowed just an inch from the stone's top edge. A green John Deere ball cap sat on top of it. Billy slapped the hat from the pedestal, then pulled the backpack from his shoulders. From inside, he grabbed the Book of the Djed and the single page that had been ripped from it. He had no idea what he should do with them except to set them on the Cubit's throne, which he did.

"Go ahead," Deere-hat man said from the shadows. "Open it. Do your thing. Show us the way."

Billy opened the Book to its center spread. The strokes of heavenly lead depicting three sixes and three nines had become thicker; the tail of phoenix bird of fire had become more colorful with swirls of red and orange and yellow. He picked up the stray page and examined the symbols that were written on one side, trying to understand what he should do next. He dropped the page on top on the center spread but nothing happened. He tried to turn a page in the Book and couldn't.

"Hurry up, boy," Deere-hat man grumbled.

"He can't do it," Lax said. "Only Daykeepers can, or have you forgotten that too, cubit!"

"I'll drill her in the forehead," Deere-hat man said. "I swear it."

"Yes. Of that I am sure."

Lax quickly walked to Billy's side and turned the page. Billy immediately noticed the serrated remainder of the key page sticking a half an inch up from the binding. The page that was visible included sketches in three of its four corners. In the top left corner was the face of the temple that he now stood inside, complete with two Jaguar statues and the glyphs etched into the walls beside them. In the bottom left corner was drawn a structure that looked a lot like an observatory. The sketch in the top right corner looked like a sinkhole and Billy guessed that it was located where Lax had said he'd acquired his Djed in Puerto Morelos, Mexico. The lower right corner was blank.

"This is why the key is so important," Lax whispered to him. "Without it, we would never know the fourth location and you will not know how to seal the Cubit forever."

Lax took the key from Billy and when he placed it into the Book, it automatically re-stitched itself to the serrated edge, becoming whole and firm again.

At that same moment, the chamber shook once, as if the God of the Underworld was either overly pleased or massively pissed off that the Book was again whole. Dust rained down from the dark ceiling. Seed pods from the ceiba tree dropped like tiny grenades. Leaves fluttered to the floor all around them. Much of the falling debris nearly struck Marcy's defenseless body but she did not flinch, the drug within her so strong that it blocked all thought of self-preservation. Billy, wanting to protect her, stepped around the Cubit's throne but, again, Lax's hand came down across his chest.

"No! Not yet," he urged. "You have to be strong, Billy. The

ceremony is incomplete."

Lax's strength knocked Billy backward and he tripped and fell, hitting the back of his head on the hard, sandstone floor. A seed pod struck him in the nose.

"The dagger," Lax demanded. "Give me the dagger!"

Blood ran from Billy's nose and into his mouth. His vision blurred from the force of his head's impact with the floor. Lax wanted his dagger, but Billy couldn't give it up for anything. Even Lax had told him so. It was all that could protect them from the cubits. It was all that could save Marcy. It was all that could bring him…

The chamber's trembling stopped and Deere-hat man showed himself. His three cubited accomplices who had been hiding in silence, also appeared: the three city council members that Billy had seen seated with Richard Manson at the Café Aus. Councilwoman Cheryl Mokier grabbed Cooper and Councilmen Bill Tate and Pat Roberts rushed to either side of Lax, grabbed the big Indian, and wrestled him to the ground. Billy didn't have to see the flip of blonde-white hair to know that the man now standing over Lax, wearing a feathered serpent headdress, was the cubit that had been stalking him every since he'd left Port Aransas.

"Ain't living forever a total thrill?" the Serpent said to Lax as he stood over him.

Lax no longer wrestled against the strength of the two councilmen cubits. "Evil never wins," he said to the Serpent. "And your pretension as Lord of Reincarnation is blasphemous."

"Is that so?" The Serpent grabbed a large chunk of sandstone that had fallen during the tremor and dropped it on Lax's chest. The crunch of ribs reverberated throughout the chamber but Lax refused to cry out. "Immortals can feel pain, can they not? At least your kind of immortals can." He picked up the stone and dropped it on Lax again. "Can they not!" he yelled. Then he turned to Billy. "Come on, boy. Show us what you got. Complete your destiny or the next throw crushes his face."

Billy wiped the blood from his nose and sat up, still woozy from his fall. He didn't know what to do. Cooper screamed, "Kill him!" and was immediately slapped to the floor by the cubited councilwoman.

And then something peculiar happened. It felt as if he were suddenly back in the dark abyss of Lax's spiritual anteroom. A memory surfaced that was not his. A voice emerged in his head that had been a part of another time. Thoughts of a boy now one-year dead, became Billy's thoughts. When Lenny Bender had been faced with a moment of truth in a Kansas cornfield he had thought about Clint Eastwood. And now, so did Billy.

You gotta start living or you gotta start dying, the voice suggested.

The dagger's warmth quickly grew against his chest. His hand itched. The star in the top edge of the stone throne pedestal began to brighten. Billy looked at his palm. The fifth point blazed with crimson light. The dagger against his chest became so hot that he had to free it. And then…he understood!

With the Creation of the End Dagger in his right hand, the star in its haft perfectly aligned with the scar it had burned into his palm, he approached the Cubit's throne and thrust the dagger's point into the glowing red star in its top edge. From above, the light infiltrating through the tree's canopy that had been merely miniscule suddenly blazed bright white, sending a beam down onto the Book. The key page acted as a filter, using the light from the tree to stamp an image into the page that followed it. The fourth location. Billy blinked once, a snapshot planted in memory, just before Deere-hat man, feathered serpent headdress and all, snatched the Book from the pedestal and raved, "That's it! That's it! After all of these long, long years." The cubit grabbed Billy's hand and tried to wrench the dagger from his grasp.

That was when the light above the tree died and the earthquake started.

Deere-hat man screamed when a boulder crushed his foot, having not fallen from above but thrown by Lax who had freed himself from the retreating councilmen cubits. The Serpent released Billy's hand and Billy immediately withdrew the dagger, slashing out at the back of the Serpent's head but missed it by inches.

Out of the chamber, the Serpent ran with the Book of the Djed in hand as rocks fell all around him. The cubits that had pinned Lax quickly followed. The cubit that had held Cooper was now under Cooper's foot. She waved at Billy who threw her the dagger and Cooper quickly planted it in the back of the cubit's skull.

Another large rock hit Lax and he groaned loudly as he fell onto his back. He tried to protect his face, but it was futile.

Up against the ceiba tree, Marcy remained unharmed. The broad canopy above her deflected much of the debris that pelted Billy and Cooper and Lax.

"Over here!" Billy yelled to Cooper. "We have to get him under the tree!"

With dust and sandstones falling at her feet, Cooper ran to Lax's side and, with Billy, wrestled the big man up across the stone pedestal and rolled him against Marcy's feet. The four of them remained under the protection of the Tree of Life until the earthquake subsided.

"Did you see it?" Lax moaned. "Do you know where the Djed is to be raised?"

Billy knelt at his side and wiped red, sweaty mud from his brow. "I saw it but I am not sure what it is. You have to help me. You have to stay awake."

Lax grabbed his hand. "You will," he said, his voice hushed. He smiled then, that big grin parting his face from cheek to cheek. Then he closed his eyes. "Find the Gormen," he whispered. "The Gormen will be waiting for you."

"Who?" Billy squeezed his hand. "What do you…"

"Billy. Remember what I told you about immortality? You too will serve like us, to protect from man what he should not know. But first you must fulfill your own fate."

"What do you mean?"

Lax coughed up blood. "Find the Gormen. Find the Djed. Assume your destiny." Then he blinked once and exhaled with words that faded as did his body. "Tell Aaron I do love him so."

And Lax lay still.

From above them came a screech that tore through the chamber's acoustics. Billy and Cooper looked up to see a giant bird roosting in the canopy of branches that were now bare except for a few leaves and seed pods. The Djed remained hidden underneath Lax's poncho but it now became so green-white bright that the edges of the four crosses were easily discernible through the fabric. The green-white aura quickly encapsulated Lax's entire body and Billy felt its energy pulse beneath him. The aura rose, sparkles of green diamonds swirling within it, until it connected and was absorbed by Osi. The bird, now wrapped inside green-white light, flapped its wings twice, sending a wave of energy downward that Billy would forever remember as being pure spirit. It then hopped the branches up the tree canopy and disappeared from sight.

"Billy?"

It was Marcy's voice.

"Billy? Where am I? I feel so…"

"Stay here with her," Billy said to Cooper. "I'll be right back."

Billy exited the Wayeb Chamber to find that the stalactite teeth had fallen from the ceiling and were now in broken ruins as was much of the corridor in front of him. At the far end, the opening to the water well had collapsed and was sealed shut. The remaining plant chemicals that provided eternal light from above cast the crumbled path into broken red shadows that only served to enhance the sight of its destruction.

Billy turned back toward the temple and noticed that both of the jaguar statues had suffered little, if any, damage. The glyphs noting the dire warning on the left wall had been chipped by falling debris. The glyphs on the right, those that enshrined the names of Daykeepers, had been saved except for…

Billy walked to the wall and just stood there, trying to remember…

The last row of glyphs had changed; he was sure of it. He knelt and leaned closer. One new glyph had been added—one that looked just like a bird. Its sharp beak and piercing eyes seemed to be looking at something and Billy followed its gaze. Poking out of a short pile of sandstone rubble was the corner of the key page from the Book of the Djed.

"It must have torn free," Billy said to the bird glyph. "Thank you." He snatched it, returned to the chamber, and told Cooper that the well had collapsed and that they were sealed inside.

"No." Cooper shook her head, then led him to the back side of the broad tree trunk where long spikes rose to the ceiling like rungs in a ladder. "We'll follow his spirit. We'll follow the Great White Hawk."

Though Cooper knew that she would be a suspect in the deaths of Detectives Beets and Dreagan, it was not the primary reason she wanted to go with Billy to Mexico. She hated the idea of just picking up and leaving her life behind. She had a good job, a great reputation (at least up until recently), and she really loved her house. But everything had changed. All that she'd experienced in the last four days had taken her life on a different path. To be with Billy was something she was meant to do. Cooper was unequivocally convinced of this. Besides, there was absolutely no way in hell she was going to miss watching Billy "raise the

Djed."

After they had escaped the Wayeb Chamber by climbing up the ceiba tree, they had returned to Lax's home with the hope of finding Aaron. They needed to tell him what had happened to his father, but Aaron was not there and none of them had any idea where he might be. So Billy left him a note:

Aaron:
Your father has joined the Daykeepers in Heaven. I believe you knew that this day would come. Please do as your father has asked of you. Your home is now among the tribe of men. Take care.
-Billy

All three of them now sat in Cooper's home at her dining table. Marcy had just finished telling them her story: about how it had all started in Port Aransas. As he'd done with many other business owners on the island, Mitchell Bone had lured her into the vault at the Big Texas Bank where she had come in contact with the Cubit. That same night, while she'd been asleep in her home, her cubit had paid her a visit. It had been a nasty looking thing, she recalled, having been out of the box for only a few hours. It had snarled at her and had cursed and had threatened to tear her apart. The only reason it had not, was because it had been on a steel chain leash; its handler had been the one whom Billy had named Deere-hat man, the one with the flip of blonde-white hair—the Serpent who had drugged her and had tied her to the ceiba tree.

We have your daughters, Deere-hat man had threatened. *If you ever want to see them alive again, you'll do as I say. Your cubit, here, is quite thirsty for your flesh but it can be appeased by snacking on your offspring. You wouldn't want that to happen, now would you? I can assure you that it would be a most horrific and painful death for both of them.*

So, Marcy had been told to: *Keep an eye on Billy. Make sure he gets to Sedona. Find out if he has the Book. Find out if he has the dagger. And never forget that we will be watching. Never forget the innocence of your daughters that will be brutally ravaged if you even hint any of this to that young prick.*

"I'm sorry, Billy," Marcy said. "But that thing Cooper killed at the casita would have eaten my daughters."

Billy, who sat to her left, massaged her shoulder. "What else could you have done? Your daughters are safe now."

Cooper smiled at the shared compassion but knew that it was time to move on. "We have to figure out what to do next." Billy and Marcy nodded. "I think we already know where we are headed."

"Chichen Itza," Billy confirmed.

"And we have to lay low. It won't be long before they find Beets and his buddy in pieces at Marcy's. I figure we'll all be suspects."

"I'm not going to Mexico," Marcy said. "I have to see my daughters. I have to go back to Port Aransas. I have an entire life that I was forced to leave behind."

"Can you prove that?" Billy asked, his hand still on her shoulder. "I mean, can you prove that you were being blackmailed with the lives of your daughters?"

Marcy had apparently already considered the possibility. She turned her head to Billy, her eyes still swimming with the remnants of the drug she'd been given, her lips still full and beautiful even though they were scratched in places. She leaned forward and kissed Billy on the forehead. "The authorities are looking for a woman with a bald head." She draped fingers through her long, black hair. "They really don't have any other proof than an artist's sketch made by a drunken pedestrian. Besides, I think they will be quite interested in the goings-on of a couple of their city councilmen. I suspect they were the ones that destroyed your apartment and they certainly helped my cubit in the slaughter of the two detectives."

"So what are you saying?" Billy said.

"There really is no other choice. You both need to continue with your own destinies. I have mine to contend with. I'll stay here as a diversion while you and Cooper get a big head start. Your names will be suspect, for awhile, but I figure their investigation will soon stray away."

Cooper asked, "Where will you say we've gone?"

"To Port Aransas, of course. That would be the most logical place… at least it would be for Billy. It also has the added benefit of getting local authorities involved with the threats made to my daughters."

All three of them stood simultaneously. "We'll need to get going immediately," Cooper said. "Before our names get placed on a computer. Getting into Mexico will be impossible then."

"We can't fly and we can't take your Jeep," Billy offered. "The Cavalier. We can make it to the border by nightfall."

Cooper packed as much as two suitcases could hold then locked up her house, hoping that she would soon return. The three of them walked the wet road to the intersection of Dry Creek and Gringo.

Billy went to his apartment to get as many of his personal effects as he felt was needed, then placed them in the trunk. Cooper was already in the passenger's side front seat and was playing with SpongeBob, grabbing his rubbery hand and shaking it. He then hugged Marcy long and strong, and whatever desire he'd had for her in the past completely vanished as their embrace sealed a friendship of love that would last forever.

"Be careful," Marcy whispered in his ear. "You come back to Port A once this is all said and done, okay? You promise?"

Billy nodded. "Marcy," he said, releasing her. "We couldn't have done it without you."

"Nor could I have without you." Marcy turned away and did not look back, even as Billy pulled out of the parking lot and beeped the horn.

The last thing he would remember of Marcy Ruminski would be her long black hair as if shifted and shuffled behind her through the casita's front door.

Part

Three

Welcome to the Jungle

(Friday, ten days later)

At sunrise, Evan jumped from the Cessna two thousand feet higher than usual. His boss had demanded it. The added altitude would give them ten more seconds of freefall.

His new helmet-mounted camera wiggled a bit as air rushed past at a hundred and ten miles an hour, but that was of less concern to him than the accuracy and comfort of the earplugs which he'd added to the helmet's interior within the last week. They were experimental, of course, as was so much of what he did for his boss. Richard Manson demanded perfection from untested inspirations, a bear of an attitude to have, especially if one served as his right-hand man.

Today, Manson had decided to take his sky surfing prowess to the Gulf of Mexico. Below them, there was nothing but water, dark blue and hard, a sheet of bone-crushing liquid that looked intimidating even from this height. Manson's intent was to have fun, defy death, and in the process, get some knarly footage that could be used to pump up the next X-Games for which his company was a major sponsor. As his cameraflyer, Evan knew exactly which angles would not only portray sky surfing as the ultimate in extreme sports, but would place Manson dead-nuts center as the single most important influence in getting the sport accepted, once again, into the competition. If this old man could do it, anyone could. Age-defying beauty, Manson had called sky surfing, and in the process had called out all of the young bucks who still thought the sport was too dangerous.

Today's experiment included synchronization to music. Manson thought that the old-school method of adding music to action only after the action had ended was boring and bogus. Anyone with a few dollars worth of computing muscle could simulate the sky dance with flash cutting and mashup mixes. What Manson was interested in was the real thing, a sky dance on a sky board set to real-time music. The grabs and side slides and barrel rolls and inverted flips would all be orchestrated in flight to the fast-paced, in your face, feels like flying into space lyrics of R.E.M.'s *It's the End of the World As We Know It*. The only way this could be accomplished was if the cameraflyer (Evan) and the sky surfer (Manson) were both listening to the same tune at the same time. Manson would perform as the cameraman repositioned himself for the sweetest angle, one that rocked to the beat and rolled to the rhythm.

To accomplish the synchronization, Manson had "borrowed" one of Steve Jobs newest gadgets: a wireless, waterproof iPod. The two CEOs had always acted as if they were best buddies but few-to-none had ever believed it. The rich did what they needed to do to remain rich and if acting all chummy was a part of that ritual then that's what the public got. What Jobs got was a heavy investment from Phoenix International and media blitzes every time Manson showcased one of Apple's products. Manson got brand association and influence with the young pop group. It was hip to be on the Apple bandwagon and Manson was about the hippest old dude on the planet.

Almost fifty seconds had elapsed since they'd jumped and Evan stepped off of the bottom of Manson's board, the camera pointed at his boss who soared upside-down, just as R.E.M repeated the chorus which magnified what he believed would be some of the best sky surfing footage ever. The actor and the cameraman had been in perfect sync, married to the performance, a director's dream. With the red-orange sun ball rising atop the horizon and the indigo marble of water twinkling underneath, no studio in the world could have provided a more perfect setting.

Evan pulled his chute as Michael Stipe rolled on with the words *Slash and burn, return, listen to yourself churn.* Immediately, his body jerked hard as his relative speed went from a hundred and twenty to ten miles an hour in a second. Evan looked around for Manson, expecting to see his infamous phoenix-painted canopy nearby; Evan always added this extra footage for outtakes that included some pretty hilarious gestures from his boss.

But the parachute was nowhere on the horizon.

Evan looked up, then down. Manson was below him and his chute was not open. In another six seconds, the man would hit the surface of the Gulf traveling at over a hundred miles an hour. Evan angled his head down at the receding dot that was Manson and adjusted the zoom ring in his helmet camera. From fifteen hundred feet up, he knew that he'd only capture Manson's small, white dot of a splash as his body hit the water but, considering that he'd never been told of his boss's intent, he'd not rigged anything more powerful.

Suddenly, Stipe's voice stopped on the words...*a tournament of lies.* Below him, a ripple no larger than that made by a pebble in a pool, encircled the white, frothy center where Manson had landed. Two hundred yards away and speeding atop the water was their chase boat.

Evan angled his parachute toward the pickup zone and when he was a hundred feet from splashdown, the music returned...*of the world as we know it, and I feel fine.* To his left floated the shattered remains of Manson's skyboard and a few feet farther out, Manson, whose arm was in the air and waving.

Evan missed his own landing on the chase boat's deck because he was too busy filming Manson's rescue; instead, he landed softly in the water just a dozen feet from the deckhand's struggles to pull Manson's body up and onto the boat's rear platform. His camera was still zoomed way in and it captured the essence of Manson's screams.

"God-damn, that was great!" Manson bellowed. "Wasn't that great, fellas?" All three deckhands nodded in unison while one of them fished the chute pack off of Manson's back and another helped him stand on legs that were twisted in physically impossible directions. Evan swam to the boat's rear platform and pulled himself aboard. "You get that, Van? Christ that's gonna make some good Youtube." Manson removed the iPod earplugs.

"Totally banananonkers," Evan replied. His language was often this kind of twisted amalgamation: combining two words into one; in this case, bananas and bonkers, which really meant crazy and irrational. He removed his pack and pulled in the canopy and stringers from the water's surface, then took off his helmet cam and stood beside Manson.

Manson pushed on the joints in his legs until they were, again, straight. "That was like hitting concrete," he said to all of them, combing back short, silver hair with his fingers. "Just think what a mile-wide asteroid would have done sixty-five million years ago. Those dinos didn't have a chance."

The sky surf was only ancillary to the real reason why Richard Manson had come to this location, twenty-five miles offshore from Mérida, Mexico, where the alleged dinosaur-killer asteroid had struck. His vast oil exploration resources had recently found that such a speculation was, perhaps, fact. Perimeter demarcations and unusual sea bed densities had been detected three thousand feet under the very spot where the chase boat now floated. Geologically-speaking, such an impact and the associated heat should have compressed the earth with such ferocity that oil pockets could have formed underneath ground zero. Richard Manson was convinced that it had.

"Dinos didn't have a chance," the youngest of the deckhands replied to Manson. He was a wiry man of about twenty years; Evan really didn't know his age. Manson never asked about ages when Evan brought in new hires, though his boss did tend toward the younger crowd. The deckhand's name was Jessup or Jester or—it might have even been Jesus—all that Evan could remember was the *Jes*. The young Hispanic had been a part of Manson's "executive team" for only a month and he had yet to earn any brownie points, mostly because Manson had not yet trusted him enough to assign him duties other than piloting the chase boat and ordering take-out. For the time being, Jes was a Yes Man, something Manson loathed.

"What did you say?" Manson asked Jes, his silver eyebrows uncurling into sharp edges.

"The dinosaurs didn't have a chance. The asteroid wiped them out just like you said."

Manson ignored the response. "And what about your hair? Didn't I tell you never, NEVER! allow it to grow below the neck."

"Yes, sir."

"So why are you still standing in my face. Cut it!"

Jes looked around at the other deckhands, then at Evan. Manuel, who had been a part of the executive team for more than a year stepped forward, taking Evan's non-verbal signal to do so. "Cut him," Evan told Manuel. Manuel was twice as wide and twice as heavy as Jes and he easily escorted the youngster to the front of the boat.

The thrill of the jump had seemingly dissolved from Manson's immediate memory. Evan could tell by the way Jes had so easily pissed him off. "What's next on the agenda, Van?" Manson asked.

Evan quickly walked to the boat's cabin to retrieve his iPhone. Beyond the cabin, through the front windshield, he saw Manuel, with scissors in hand. He turned away and returned to Manson, opening up the cell phone and scrolling through the day's appointments as he managed the boat's rocking motion. "The sheik will be in Mérida at…" A scream and then a splash from the front of the boat interrupted him for a moment. "He'll be at the Tower for breakfast at nine," Evan continued, watching in his periphery to the right as Jes's body floated face down, a trail of new blood streaming across the shallow, choppy waves, the blade of the scissors still stuck in his neck. "At noon you have lunch with the team from Explorer One. They will update you on their recent core drill results. The mayor of Mérida also asked for the pleasure of your company today though I don't have him scheduled yet. And…excuse me for a moment. There's a message here from Bartholomew." Evan listened to the message. "Bartholomew says that our guests have arrived."

This brought a huge smile to Manson's face. His attention transformed again from all business to all fun. "Excellent," he beamed. "Isn't that excellent?"

Evan did not say *yes*; he only nodded and watched Jes's head bounce against the chase boat's rear platform.

"I want to see the footage you grabbed today. We'll put together a Youtube clip tonight then get it out as soon as possible. Make sure Jobs knows. Call him personally. Maybe the son-of-bitch will finally make some time to talk face-to-face. It's been too long. We gotta get sky surfing back on the X-Games map."

Again, Evan avoided the word yes. "Done," he told his boss. "And Jes?"

Manson squinted, the sun now blazing across the early morning Gulf. He thought about it for only a moment, looked down at the deckhand's floating body, then said, "Too bad. I almost liked him." He walked away toward the boat's cabin, his legs still wobbling at the joints, the boat's rocking motion making it even harder for him to maintain balance. "Sharks gotta eat, too," he added, then started the boat's engine.

Entering Mérida was no different than entering the other, few, major metropolitan cities that had intervened in their drive from Arizona to the Yucatán. Mexico had seemed inundated with these kinds of topographical short stories that emulsified globs of poor around centers of wealth. Cardboard boxed walls provided shelter for most citizens that couldn't afford, by wallet or by wiles, the scrap plywood squares of existence that dotted the brown perimeters leading into the cities of gold. Mexicans ran naked, peed naked, lived naked, outside the invisibility of progress. If, by airplane, one flew into the progress, you, as an average tourist, would ignorantly dodge this true flavor of Mexican reality, an experience that now had Cooper wishing for Nexpa.

Not all of Mexico was as depraved as it was on the outskirts of the big cities. In smaller towns, the lack of greed and fruit of labor combined to form a self-sufficient unit of people, animals, plants and possessions that were wondrously symbiotic. Taking too much advantage of any one of these meant that the whole community suffered equally and, in this regard, was self-regulated. Nexpa, a surfing spot on the Pacific Ocean, was one such town.

Billy had suggested that they stop for a day or two to "chill out." He'd said that they should take Lax's advice about preparing the spirit for battle, and Billy had taken the advice one step further. He'd explained how rest and relaxation was the elixir of life. You either lived it or you searched it out and stuck it into your 365-day calendar at some point to prevent insanity. And, according to Billy, there was no better way to rest and relax than to jump on a seven-foot long board of fiberglass and attempt to ride it atop ten-foot swells of salty extreme, as were the waves that pounded the Nexpa shores five peaks at a time.

Yes, Billy had become quite a philosopher in their ride south of the border. During the long, dry stretches of roads leading to Nexpa, the spirit and the soul and the self had been popular topics. He'd talked about good versus bad, right versus wrong, and love versus hate. These were men's words, Billy had suggested. They were created for social control. Their abstractness was intentional, to be easily manipulated by those who demand that life be led not for the purpose of spiritual oneness but for the purpose of conformity. Those who held such reins of power wished only to make us slaves to our own emotions by using these brilliantly orchestrated words. Billy had even brought up the conclusions of Dr. Carl Jung, at least those that he wanted to remember from his Intro to Psychology class back at MIT. Cooper had been impressed with the accuracy of his memory and though he'd not quoted verbatim, he'd presented the essence of Jung's thoughts as they pertained to one's psychological turmoil.

When an inner situation is not made conscious, it happens outside as fate. The individual remains divided, unconscious of his inner opposite, and the world acts out the conflict, tearing the individual into opposing halves.

Opposing halves. Of all that he'd said, those two words had stuck in Cooper's mind, reverberating, reiterating and reinforcing her recent experience. She'd seen the physical manifestations of such psychological premises. After all, that's exactly what the Cubit was all about: it ripped the opposing half right out of you and then presented that pure Evil to you at your bedside, during black nights full of nightmares that detailed the agony of being eaten alive, of being literally consumed by your darkest half.

Mérida was like that, too: opposing halves—the haves and the have-nots; a juxtaposition so evident it was blinding. Of particular magnitude was the monstrous Phoenix Tower that beamed its materialistic might of steel and glass reflections onto the timid block and stucco facades of the centuries-old buildings around it. Simple shops and single-story homes stuffed with families cowered under its forty floors of new world order.

Cooper leaned forward as far as her seat belt allowed, her forehead not quite touching the windshield or SpongeBob's incessant happy open arms and happy open grin. She'd asked to remove the toy from the dashboard only once in their ten-day adventure, but Billy had adamantly denied the request; he had apparently anointed the character to the iconic position of guardian angel and had demanded that its removal would "alter their good luck." She'd moved it from directly in front of her face to the middle of the dashboard so that she could see the road ahead without staring between the toy's spindly yellow legs but she had not removed it—not once.

SpongeBob's hand caught in a strawberry red curl as Cooper gazed up the side of the Phoenix Tower, watching as the morning sunshine was snatched away by the building's girth. On the shadowy west side of the tower, the word BETH was anchored in bold blue letters above the fortieth floor windows. "Where do you suppose he is?" she asked while settling back into her seat.

"Maybe we're not looking for a man." Billy straightened the toy arm that had tangled in Cooper's hair. "Maybe we're not even looking for a person." He maneuvered the car very slowly through the deluge of pedestrians that apparently found jaywalking through moving traffic to be a perfectly viable option for getting around town, and did not divert his attention from them until he stopped at the next intersection. Just ahead, sunshine awaited just beyond the tower's sharp shadow. He looked at SpongeBob and then at Cooper. "Maybe we're looking for a group of people. The Gormen kinda sounds like a tribe or some other collective." The traffic, again, began its slow creep through the pedestrians and Billy returned his attention to the front of the car. In Cooper's opinion, he was being way too cautious. If he'd just pick up the pace the pedestrians would get out of the way—at least that's what the cars in the left lane were doing—and they could get the hell out of this city and on toward their destination. "So I've been trying to think of all of the words that begin with 'gor' and perhaps uncover some kind of clue as to the origin of Gormen. For example gorilla men, but that doesn't make sense to me. I don't think they have gorillas in the Yucatán do they?"

"No. I don't think so."

"How about gore men, like in a violent group of men who shed blood?"

"Why would Lax want us to hang out with a group like that?"

"I don't know. There's just not many words that begin with gor."

Cooper thought that Billy was putting way too much effort into this line of thinking, but she didn't tell him that. She honestly believed that the Gormen was a single individual. "How about gorgeous?" she offered with a smile.

"Gorgeous men…" Billy chuckled. "I think we came to the wrong city for that."

The sunshine returned in full force, blazing heat against the side of Cooper's face. Unsure of what the pedestrians might do, they had rolled up their windows before entering the city. Cooper now rolled hers halfway down. "Why are we even concerned about this guy…or this group of guys? We already know that Chichen Itza is our current destination, don't we? The star map and the Book and even Lax said so."

Billy turned to her then, uncaring of the woman and her two children that quickly ran away from the front of the car. "Because Lax said that we should. What do we do when we get to Chichen Itza? We know that there's a secret chamber but where? I gotta believe that whoever or whatever the Gormen is knows the answer. I gotta believe that Gormen knows a lot more than we do."

"Okay. So, I ask again: Where do you suppose he or they are?"

"Gorilla men!"

"What?"

Billy pointed toward Cooper's side of the street. They were now a block passed the Phoenix Tower plaza. The buildings on this end of town looked as if they'd been recently restored. Historical in stature, they included the only multi-storey structures Cooper had seen so far. She guessed correctly that these were public buildings, housing government entities, religious sanctuaries, and a rather profound number of museums. The building that Billy pointed at was the History Museum of Mérida. A banner above its entrance read in both Spanish and English:

December is the Month of the Gorilla Men

"Coincidence?" Billy asked, a curt grin capturing the left edge of his mouth.

"What in the world does that mean? There are no gorillas in Mexico, at least none that haven't been brought in for zoos."

"You hungry?" Billy didn't wait for an answer. "Yeah. Me too. They gotta have some fresh tortillas around here somewhere."

Cooper really didn't want food but she knew they weren't going to eat anyway. "You mean like inside the History Museum of Mérida?"

Billy nodded and immediately began looking for a place to park.

The concept of coincidence really didn't compute for Billy anymore. He now saw the world as a never-ending collection of checkpoints where markers to future "coincidences" awaited his eventual arrival. Things that people said and how they acted, objects and places that intervened in daily routine, even his dreams, were all there to move him forward, to help him step into and through the next arm of the maze toward the end, whatever that was.

Such was his new attitude that was quite comforting and frightening at the same time. All he had to do was keep on moving forward, accept intuition, and keep his eyes and ears open for the signs, regardless if they were filled with good intent or malice.

Like *Gorilla Men.*

It was ridiculous to even consider that one of the final pieces of advice passed on to him from a Daykeeper would have anything to do with gorillas. *Gormen* was an amalgamate of gorilla men? He just didn't see it. Neither did Cooper. Maybe the Gormen was a single individual. Maybe it was a group of savage tribesmen. But gorillas? Intuition couldn't even remotely confirm such an idea. Intuition did, however, roar an *it-just-can't-be-coincidence* alert when he passed the history museum and saw the banner, not because it had anything to do with the origin of the word Gormen but, more so, because he and Cooper had been talking about it at the exact moment they had driven passed the Phoenix Tower, owned by Phoenix International, the corporation that seemed to have been following him ever since Port Aransas. They had been discussing the Gormen in the shadow of the tower and then, as soon as they'd emerged into the sunlight, there it had been: the red banner with the black words *Gorilla Men.*

How could he not stop?

Billy was surprised to find an underground parking garage within a block of the museum. When he got out of the car, he grabbed his backpack from the back seat and slung it over his shoulders. The backpack had now become as much a part of his daily routine as had the dagger which he still kept sheathed against his heart. Inside the pack was the page from the Book of the Djed that had fallen free during the Serpent's retreat from the Great Hall. He'd thought of simply folding it for easier transport in his pocket but something—that intuition thing—had told him not to, that he should keep it free of creases and protected from nature and man.

Together, they emerged from the parking garage into a mass of pedestrians that was only slightly less crowded than those roaming around the Phoenix Tower plaza a block away. The sun quickly drew sweat onto his forehead. Cooper's curling bangs moistened and stuck to one eyebrow. He'd not walked more than ten steps when the incessant collisions with others' shoulders prompted enough caution that he removed the backpack and cradled it in both arms in front of him. Few of the Mérida Mexicans looked directly at him but those that did forced an extreme discomfort—a feeling as if he was intruding, as if he, alone, was responsible for all of the repression that imperialism had bestowed upon their land. His white skin and the Phoenix Tower were inseparable according to these pedestrians' expressions. Whatever the tower meant to them, which was most certainly loathing, Billy had caused it. None of them looked at Cooper like this. Her dark, Puerto Rican complexion prompted indifference in most (and hungry grins from a few men), but none looked at her with loathsome contempt.

They were twenty yards from the entrance to the museum when Billy noticed that the long, tall shadow from the Phoenix Tower was slowly creeping toward them. To the left of the tower, the sun's orange ball moved in a slow rising arc that would, very quickly, find a hiding place behind steel and glass. For each step forward and another shoulder bumped into, the shadow gained two steps on them in the opposite direction. Billy looked around as if he might find the source of this manifestation, as if he'd see some guy sitting atop a trash bin with a remote control in his hands, twisting joysticks and thumbing knobs that careened pedestrians into him, slowing him, so that the tall shadow that was also being manipulated could catch him, and Cooper, before they gained the safety of the museum.

Billy freed his left hand from the backpack and grabbed Cooper's forearm, his fingers wrapping around the four rattlesnake fang scars in her djed tattoo, and led her double-time through the crowd. Some Mexicans cursed at him in Spanish; others parted like the red sea for the American who suddenly looked as if he'd run them over if they did not move.

The tower shadow and he and Cooper were now equidistant from the three steps that led up to the museum's front door, over which dangled the *Gorilla Men* banner. The shadow seemed to speed up the closer it approached and appeared darker than shadows had a reason to be; it ate up the cars and bicyclists, the sidewalks and the people, the plaza's squat, imported palm trees and other non-indigenous plants. Billy was now running, Cooper in tow behind him, the pedestrians jumping out of his way. Only a small sliver of orange sun glow remained just to the left of the big BETH sign above the tower's fortieth level. Now in front of the museum, Billy leapt the final three steps, pulling Cooper up and away from the shadow that snatched at her heels, trying to eat her, too. They entered the museum as the eclipsed sun enveloped the rectangular doorway in darkness. Automated lighting flickered on in the museum's small front lobby.

"Help you?" a Hispanic guard said. Billy's breaths rushed conspicuously fast. The guard had, no doubt, seen his share of suspicious characters.

"Gorillas." Billy took two deep breaths in an attempt to calm himself. "There aren't any gorillas in Mexico."

The guard, who wore a standard blue uniform trimmed in red piping, looked at him as if he were insane. "Perdón?"

"The banner. It says you have gorillas."

"Amigo," the guard said but was only being polite. "We no have gorillas. We have statues." He pointed. "This is a museum not a zoo."

"Yes, of course," Billy said. "We came to see the statues." Billy stepped forward, still panting.

"No puedes entrar!" the guard demanded, holding his arm out like a traffic gate.

Billy looked at Cooper. "You can't enter," she said.

"Why?" Billy said to Cooper then looked at the guard. "Why?" he repeated.

"The bag." The guard pointed at his backpack. "What is in it?"

Billy hugged the pack closer causing the guard's eyebrows to rise further. "Research papers," he said. "I…" he looked at Cooper. "…we are from the university."

"Universidad? Que uno?"

"Cancun," Cooper said.

"I have to look in," the guard demanded. "O no puedes entrar."

Billy looked past the lobby and into one of the large display rooms where he could barely make out the large statue of what could have been an ape. Closer to him and just beyond the counter that the guard stood beside were two stanchions, standing hip high and separated by about five feet: metal detectors. The Book's key inside the backpack was suddenly secondary to his concern for the dagger which would certainly set off an alarm.

"Fine," Billy said. "Then I will wait here. My research is much too important for just anyone's eyes."

The guard obviously did not understand everything Billy had just said except the part about waiting. "Wait outside," he said, pointing to the dark, shadowy entrance.

Billy opened the backpack and pulled out his small notebook, the one in which he'd scribbled information from the Sedona Public Library, and handed it and a pencil to Cooper. "You remember what we are looking for?" he said to her. "Gor…Men."

Cooper nodded though Billy could tell she was confused; still, she played along. "Of course," she said and handed the notebook to the guard who flipped nonchalantly through pages that were certainly gibberish to him. He actually didn't even look at the pages; his attention squared on Billy and the backpack.

Cooper walked through the metal detector as Billy turned toward the door. He took several cautious steps, looking over his shoulder only once to see Cooper enter the room with the apes, and the guard whose expression was of anger, before walking into the rectangle of Phoenix Tower shadow.

Cooper had rarely been separated from Billy since they'd left Arizona. Even during their three-day layover in Nexpa, she'd not been out of ear shot for more than ten minutes at a time. Until this very moment, when she saw Billy disappear through the museum's entrance and into darkness, she'd not realized how important his company had been, how comfortable she felt around him, how much protective energy he provided. She'd gotten quite close to him in Nexpa. He'd taught her how to surf and she'd taught him a thing or two about making really great Mexican salsa. They'd snorkeled together, had ridden horseback together, had swum in the lagoon together, and had eaten every meal together. And when the days were done, they'd watched three beautiful sunsets together while nestled under a lean-to made from the branches and leaves of nearby plants. It had been during moments like these, with the waves crashing in soothing loud bunches and the colors of the Pacific dusk illuminating wide, white beaches and the salty, gritty wind tickling every hair on their bodies, that Billy had talked about life. His thoughts had been so deep at times that Cooper didn't understand what he was talking about. But the words, though sometimes unintelligible to her, were full of wisdom—the wisdom from a mortal who'd recently discovered that immortality was within his grasp.

Cooper had indeed fallen for Billy, but it was an emotion unlike any she'd ever had before. It felt a little bit like a girlish crush, a little bit like sibling friendship, a whole lot like life-saving gratitude, and, with a pinch of lust thrown in, it was all very surreal. She cared about him…a lot. And when he disappeared from view, emotional alarms went off that made her think she might never see him again.

She stood there, in the anthropology room filled with artifacts but no people, her eyes fixed on two statues behind velvet ropes that did, indeed, look like gorillas, wondering that if she screamed right now, would Billy even hear her.

The guard was watching. She didn't turn in that direction but she felt his gaze at her back. She opened Billy's notebook more for show than for purpose, and flipped through the pages, wondering why he had left her. Several pages were filled with lists of words: BETH Pharmaceuticals. Las Cruces. Popstar. Crazy lady. Deere-hat man. Richard Manson. On another page was written her phone number and the words Cooper Clairvoyant Reyes. A smiley face was sketched next to her name.

She wasn't very clairvoyant now, she thought. *She didn't even know why he had left her, unprotected.*

On another page, he'd sketched a reasonable facsimile of the star map, had connected the dots to form two stars, had drawn a diagonal line through their centers, connecting the line to three tiny glyph scribbles of the jaguar, sun and Wayeb; beside the Wayeb glyph he'd written: Port Aransas. He'd told her that the Wayeb meant five evil days.

She knew some martial arts but she didn't have the dagger. And anyone could be a cubit. Especially here, in Mexico.

She flipped through a couple of empty pages, thinking about the dagger and then she turned toward the lobby, toward the guard who quickly looked away. The metal detector…Billy couldn't enter because of the metal detector.

You remember what we are looking for, he'd said. *Gormen.*

She walked to the side of the two statues; one stood slightly taller than the other, about five feet in height, and both presented bloated chests and thick arms that hung almost down to their feet which disappeared into square blocks of stone.

She was looking for the Gormen…or perhaps she was waiting for the Gormen to find her! Yes. That's it, Clairvoyant Cooper. Billy left you here not to find someone but for someone to find you!

Again, she looked behind her then around the room which displayed important artifacts against bland white walls. Acting like a researcher from Cancun University, she flipped through several more pages, looked at the gorilla statues, flipped through pages, looked at the statues. The notebook had lots of sketches in it; they weren't particularly artistic but she knew what they were: memories from the Great Hall of the Anasazi, including some of the cross-cultural glyphs from the corridor, the Mayan glyphs from the outside temple walls, the pedestal on which the Cubit once rested, and a drawing of the *fourth destination*, the one that the Book had produced behind the key page that Billy now carried in his backpack.

She looked at the statue then back at the notebook.

She could tell that Billy had given the fourth destination more artistic effort. The sketch in the notebook had been meticulously rendered, right down to the mortar joint lines between the limestone blocks of the structures presented.

She looked at the notebook then back at the statue and paused for a moment. What was that? At the foot of the taller gorilla? Something was written there. A Mayan glyph? She leaned forward, her body arching over the velvety rope that warned her not to do so. She blinked and the glyph seemed to move. She leaned farther forward, grabbing the stone at the foot of the statue for support. What was that? And then it occurred to her. She'd just seen that glyph while flipping through Billy's notebook. Still leaning forward, she brought the notebook to the foot of the gorilla and thumbed a few pages backward to the sketch of the Wayeb. It filled the entire page and was as intricately drawn as was the fourth destination. She moved the notebook next to the glyph on the foot of the statue to find that they matched.

Billy had been standing on the top step in front of the entrance to the museum for ten minutes, watching the melee of activity that partially rushed and partially meandered around the intersection where the modern façade of the Phoenix Tower plaza met the colonial Spanish restorations of all the city blocks around it. He hoped that, at any moment, Cooper would come strolling out with the answer to the Gormen question. Who was it or who were they? And why the hell had they stopped in the first place? It had to be more than stupid coincidence. They'd been talking about it and then he'd seen the banner—he'd seen the sign!

It was past noon and the plaza's numerous stone benches and plush, rolling landscape of green grass and cobblestone paths was littered with people eating, talking, and relaxing. It was too industrialized, too first-world, too American, Billy thought. No one seemed to care that the Phoenix Tower had gobbled up all of the precious sun. No one seemed to care about anything.

The sun's ascent finally found the top of the tower and the right half of shadow, that which was farthest from the museum, disappeared. The people that had been enjoying that side of the plaza suddenly stopped what they were doing and stood, almost in unison, as if they had been programmed to do so. Now immersed in sunlight, most of them walked off toward whatever chores or jobs or sightseeing they had scheduled for the rest of the day. Those that remained walked over to the dark half of the plaza and sat among those who, with few exceptions, had not moved. To Billy, it was an unnerving sight: the left half of the plaza was crowded, the right half contained only sunshine. It seemed that no one wanted to enter the plaza square that was sunlit, opting instead for every inch of real estate that marked its north perimeter. This made passage by foot or vehicle around the square almost impossible.

And that's when Billy saw him. He absolutely, and without hesitation, knew that it was the Gormen. The man stood in the center of the sunlit side of the plaza all by himself and, even at this distance, Billy knew that he was staring straight at him. He was huge and black, the dark skin protruding from khaki shorts and white shirt a stark contrast to the sun's glare. He didn't move. He waited.

Billy left the museum's front steps almost in a trance, not looking at anyone around him, holding tight to his backpack. Spanish exclamations came fast and furious; he was almost hit by more than one car as he crossed the intersection and stepped onto the cobblestone path that led from the street, through the plaza and directly toward the black figure. Billy was not afraid but he was cautious. The sun continued to rise and escape the south side of the Phoenix Tower and in his periphery, Billy saw that people evacuated in time with the movement of the sun-to-shade terminator.

As he approached the stranger, he began to realize just how damn big this man really was. Billy's first thought questioned how he'd ever gotten his massive arms and legs into his clothes. The second thought came almost as quick: John Coffey; the man that stood in front of him was almost as big as the character from the movie *The Green Mile*. He had been reincarnated right here in the middle of Mexico, his body a near splitting image (bald head and deep voice included) of the black savior falsely accused of murdering two little girls.

"Weird, ain't it?" he said to Billy. He waved one massive arm out in front of him, as if offering the plaza to Billy. "Just about every day—except Sundays when no one around here works—it's the same thing. When the sun gets over the tower and none of the shadow remains, everything returns to normal. Watch." The man folded his meaty forearms and looked to where the last remnants of shadow contained a sliver of pedestrian life. Once the sun was full overhead and for an additional five seconds, no one except Billy and the black man stood anywhere within the city block that contained the Phoenix Tower plaza. The black man counted: "One…two…three…" When he got to five he snapped his fingers, obviously already knowing what was about to happen. That's when the crowds stuffed at the plaza's perimeters began filing, again, onto the sunlit cobblestone paths and grassy knolls; the plaza returned to its average, everyday, out-of-place, industrialized, America business park. "Like a force field or something, ain't it?" the black man said, his slight southern drawl becoming more apparent. "I been around these parts for years and still I can't figger it out."

"Ritual?" Billy offered. "Respect for the sun god?"

The black man laughed one, big fat Hah! "I like the way you think. My name is…"

"Let me guess," Billy interrupted.

"If you say John Coffey, you gonna make me awful upset. I get tired of vacationers from the states calling me that."

"Well," Billy said. "I don't know what the hell they are thinking. You look nothing like him. John Coffey wasn't so handsome."

"Hah!" The black man's teeth blazed sunlit reflections. He reached out his hand and Billy released his stranglehold on the backpack, then slipped his right hand into the black man's palm where it was consumed by mighty fingers.

"I am Billy Jo Presser and you are…" Billy hesitated. The black man was staring at his hand, at the star that was burned into it. His expression turned from one of commandeering jocularity to one of reverence. "You are the Gormen?"

The black man's big lips were parted but no words came out. A few Hispanics passed on either side, giving wide berth to the two men still clasped hand-in-hand. "Who are you?"

"Billy Jo…"

"No. I mean, how do you know that name?"

"Lax sent me looking for you."

The black man released Billy's hand but did not stop staring at his palm as Billy's arm fell to his side. "Alax," he whispered to himself. "My dear friend Alax. He's dead isn't he?"

Billy replaced his right arm against the backpack. "He would not call it that but, yes, he is no longer a part of this world. How do you know that?"

The black man didn't answer the question but instead said, "Alax always messed up my name. It's not Gormen, it's Gordon. John Brown

Gordon."

"The abolitionist?"

"Maybe in a past life. Today I'm a guide. And as good timing would have it, I'm your guide. It's what Alax wanted." And then both of them turned simultaneously toward the museum. "You hear that?" John said.

"Cooper!" Billy yelled and then ran.

Cooper lost her balance, the rubber sole of her right sneaker slipping on the vinyl tile flooring. Her right hand slid to the left across the foot of the statue and intersected the Wayeb glyph she'd been studying. The glyph jumped from the stone to her hand and for a moment, Cooper thought that she was hallucinating. She blinked, but the glyph did not go away. It sat amongst the knuckles and veins on the back of her hand.

"Very nice," a hallow, deep Mexican accent said from behind her. Something rubbed her butt which was prominently displayed in her bent-forward position. "It's against the law to touch such things."

Cooper quickly pushed off of the gorilla statue, nearly toppling it over, and turned around. The man was quite close to her and his breath smelled of beans gone bad. She immediately realized that the glyph drawn at the foot of the statue had not been drawn there at all. It had been a shadowy reflection of the man's earring: a Wayeb glyph dangled from his left earlobe.

"I'm a researcher…" Cooper started to say.

"Yes. From the Universidad. So I've been told."

The man was big but not tall, thick but not fat and he *was* much too close to her. She felt cornered. Beyond the man's shoulder, she saw no guard, no people, only the rectangular entry doorway that was still filled with Phoenix Tower shadow.

"You know what they do with lawbreakers in Mexico, don't you, researcher?"

"I haven't done anything wrong," Cooper demanded, standing her ground even though her fear was skyrocketing. "I'll scream."

Her threat did nothing more than bring a grin to the Mexican's mouth. "Why would you do that? I am a guide, sent to help you find what you and your boyfriend came looking for."

Cooper stepped sideways then backward to open up space between her and the man with the Wayeb earring. "Gormen?" she asked.

The man continued to grin but his eyes had that moment of confusion that one could see only if one was staring intently into them, as Cooper was doing right now. The eyes' split-second consternation was accompanied by cloudy swirls of silver and red flecks that were nearly hypnotic. "Gormen," he said. "I will help you find Gormen."

Cooper knew she was in trouble and she knew screaming would not help her but she screamed anyway. Not only was she certain that this man was not the Gormen, she now understood that the guard was in on it too when he closed and locked the museum's front door. The big man in front of her grabbed her, covered her mouth with one bean-smelly hand and pushed her up against the gorilla statues.

Why had Billy left her there? Why had he left her unprotected?

On the fortieth floor of the Phoenix Tower, high above the plaza, Richard Manson opened his eyes and looked out at his building's long shadow while thumbing through his iPhone. He pressed a couple of screen images and turned to Evan, who stood near the pile of lobsters that had been picked clean by the sheik and his entourage a half hour ago. Evan thought Manson was going to ask him about the sheik's bad manners, about how the man's pompous attitude was probably not the best business sense one could bring into a meeting with Mr. Manson, but that's not what he asked.

"You think we could build a tower tall enough to see the Gulf from here?" he said.

Evan opened the office door and several bus persons took the tray of red carcasses and empty wine glasses. "Allamah has one in Abu Dhabi that is said to look out across the Persian Gulf all the way to Iran."

"Fucking ass," Manson said. "He's a fucking ass. I'm not sure I should be doing business with such an ass tool like that."

"That's not why you want his alliance."

Manson gritted his teeth so hard, the screech was almost deafening. As much as he wanted to, Evan didn't cover his ears. His frankness often pissed of his boss but it was the reason why Evan was his right hand man…his Watcher. It was his responsibility to watch out for Manson particularly where stupid humans were concerned. Manson slammed the iPhone onto the oak desk but didn't break it this time.

"Van!" he raged. "Shit!" He turned back toward the window and looked down at the plaza. "He's made contact," he said in a more evened tone.

"Yes," Evan said.

"And Manuel?"

"Removing one of the trouble spots as you asked."

"Don't kill her," Manson warned. "If he kills her there will be hell to pay."

Evan took this literally. He'd seen way too many people who'd met the hellfire that Richard Manson could put on flesh and bone. "Manuel can be trusted."

"You can't trust things like that," Manson turned from the window. "They live for the sheer delight of causing as much misery as possible. I should know."

"Of course."

Manson picked up the iPhone and started pressing the screen with one finger. "Any luck with Jobs?"

"He won't return my calls."

"Why do I put up with these goddamned assholes?"

"Because you need them."

Manson looked up and smiled, but it was not the kind of smile that made one feel all good and happy; it was a smile that only added to the uncertainty that Manson innately created. "When are we going to look at the footage from this morning?"

"Anytime you want. I quickly zipped through some of it. I think you'll be very pleased."

"This outta get Jobs attention. We need him for the X-Games. We need the influence."

Evan nodded.

"When Manuel returns, call me and we'll set something up."

Evan nodded again and left the office.

As soon as the door closed, Manson returned to the tall glass window, gazed down toward the History Museum of Mérida, then closed his eyes. He tasted refried beans though he hated them and stunk like the ocean though he'd showered since returning from the Gulf earlier in the day. But these were palatable inconveniences that came with his projected experiences, especially when those experiences included the rape of puppets.

She'd killed two of them. She'd taken Billy's dagger and had thrust it into the back of the cubited head of Marcy Ruminski and the councilwoman named Cheryl Mokier. That act had made her feel strong and fearless. The dagger had filled her with a sense of overwhelming comfort, an assuredness that nothing could harm her as long as she wielded the magical weapon. Invincibility was the furthest thing from her mind now.

Mr. Bean Breath's eyes boiled red; thin swirls of silver occupied the pupils. His hands covered her mouth while the other wrenched at her thigh, trying to pry her legs apart. The guard came around to her right and pulled her right knee in that direction. Her struggles caused her back to scrape against the rough edges of the gorilla statues. When she looked up, the worn simian faces ignored her, looking directly over the top of her curly hair to the locked entry door.

"Tengo ganas poonta," Bean Breath cackled. "Tienes ganas?"

The guard pulled and fully flexed her leg but fell backward when his hands grabbed her shoe and it came off. "Chinga usted chorra poonta," he yelled from the floor.

They were cursing at her, she knew that much, and she was sure that she was going to be raped. If only she had the dagger. If only Billy had not left her. She kicked with the leg that the guard had released but it was useless. The big Mexican's hand grabbed the button of her blue jeans and yanked, hard.

"Leave some for me, Manuel," the guard pleaded.

Suddenly, the museum's front entry door broke wide open. Sunshine infiltrated the space and Manuel turned, loosening his grip enough that Cooper kicked off of his chest, dropped to the floor and rolled away. Her head smacked against the plaster wall and dazed her long enough that she doubted the vision she saw standing in the doorway. It was big and it was black, its head barely clearing the doorway's top frame. Manuel was big, but this thing was twice his size. The guard scrambled to his feet and ran in the opposite direction of the advancing black behemoth. Manuel was not such a coward; cubits never were.

The black man said nothing as he entered the anthropology room. Manuel, on the other hand, would not shut up. He spewed so much Spanish so quickly that Cooper could not understand a word of it except, *Geechee*, which she knew was a derogatory term associated with skin color. He screamed it over and over again, particularly as he was lifted off the floor and thrown against the wall opposite from where Cooper laid. Manuel's neck and right arm broke on impact but he stood anyway, his head lolling to one side, his arm dangling because the humerus was sticking an inch out of his skin just above the elbow. He ran like that at the black man, his head bouncing up and down against the shoulder which supported an arm that flapped uncontrollably. When he was a foot away, the black man stepped aside and, behind him, stood Billy with the dagger out and ready to strike. When Manuel saw him—saw the dagger—he immediately flipped and flopped away from Billy who slashed at the back of Manuel's head, missing the kill spot and slicing off a quarter-sized chunk of the cubit's cheek and the earlobe from which the Wayeb earring dangled. Manuel left his pieces on the floor and ran out the front door where he quickly disappeared into the crowd. Billy spun the dagger two full circles across the palm of his hand then sheathed it in one smooth motion.

"Dammit!" Cooper yelled. "Don't ever leave me like that again." Her adrenaline had soaked into every bodily function and now, as the intensity of the moment faded, all of that energetic rush caused her body to tremble. She stared at the earlobe chunk on the floor—the Wayeb earring—thinking how close she'd just come to being…

And then she cried.

Billy came to her, knelt beside her, pulled her shoulders up against his chest, allowed the tears to soak his breast while John searched the rest of the museum for the guard without success.

"Time to leave," John said, the depth of his voice echoing through the room.

Cooper gawked at him as if she'd never seen a black man before.

"John's the name, ma'am," he said to her, offering his hand. "You know me as the Gormen."

They'd left Mérida and were now heading east toward Chichen Itza along the *autopista*, a four lane government highway that was inundated with toll stops where Mexican soldiers with carbines stood at attention, waiting for anything suspicious to pass their lines of sight, waiting for anything that would mercifully cause them to move from their stoic, sentinel stances. One toll stop featured a soldier still in adolescence who stared at the car as Billy handed the attendant fifty pesos. Billy averted the boy soldier's threatening stare, realizing that the soldier probably wasn't even looking at him with John stuffed into the Cavalier's back seat. The soldier pointed at them, said something to another soldier ten feet away, and both soldiers smirked. Billy wondered what would happen if they suddenly ran to the car, guns pointed forward, yelling commands in Spanish. What if they searched the car? What if they searched him? How would he explain the dagger? A simple stare or a big black man might be all the instigation they needed. He left the toll stop, his attention on the side view mirror, but nothing military followed.

John fit in the back seat of the Cavalier like a size twelve foot in a size ten shoe. He looked uncomfortable, but John had made do, his big body slung out across the entire width of the seat, his head in one hand that was supported by an arm that rested within the open window. Wind beat at his eyebrows; his checks flapped a bit when he turned his head in just the right direction. He rubbed his bald head with his free hand then let it fall forward onto the headrest behind Billy. Billy jumped.

"Sorry," he said. "Not many places to put the meat hook back here." Billy saw John looking at him in the side view mirror. "They act as if they never seen a blacky before, don't they?"

"They probably haven't," Billy said. "Particularly one as big as you."

"I suppose you're right. Seems like every time I come through here, they get younger."

Cooper turned to him. "You visit Chichen Itza often?"

"Used to. I serve as a private guide mostly in Mérida where I run a scuba dive shop. The really special people, though, I used to take on tours through several of the ruins around here, from Uxmal to Chich to Ek Balam."

"Special people?" Cooper asked.

"Yeah. Those that really wanted to learn. Them that wasn't scared to experience new things. The kind that didn't take advantage of God's graces. They were rare but they were the best kind of turistas."

"Hablas Español?"

"Si. Y Tú?"

"Solo Un Poquito." Cooper turned back around and absently reached out to tweak SpongeBob's arm which sat directly under the rear view mirror. "I know what you mean by special people. I ran tours through the red rocks of Sedona and met some people you wish you could just through back. No respect at all."

Billy asked John, "What made you stop?"

"Takin' people to the ruins?"

Billy nodded.

"Too much danger in it anymore." John pushed himself up in the seat as much as headroom would allow. "This whole place has changed. Foreigners have infiltrated and bunkered themselves in. They take and take and don't leave nothin' but bad spirit and bad people. They've turned the locals into bad people. It's a you're-either-with-me-or-against-me mentality and it's led to a lot of mistrust. It's becoming just like the Middle East where you don't know if your neighbor is the one's gonna blow your head off from one day to the next. All depends on if you follow this new religion of greed the resort and oil industry thugs have created."

"Looks pretty subdued from what I can see," Cooper said, watching endless swaths of flat Yucatán jungle bush pass along both sides of the car.

John looked out the window. "Naw. It's out there. You just can't see it. It doesn't look like what you imagine. It's not about big buildings and lots of roads. It's in the small villages, those that have homes built of rocks and food supplied by the jungle. It's something inside." He pounded his chest and it made a solid thud. "Promises and lies. It's one of the reasons I took up the dive shop business. Only place to get away from these crazy vibes is to drown'em…with some good scuba gear on, of course."

"Is that how you met Lax?" Billy said.

"Lax?" John was still looking at him through the side view mirror reflection. "You mean Alax…yes. And his sister. They came down a couple of years ago wanting me to guide them into Chich though I wasn't sure at the time why they needed me. They seemed to know the layout of the joint quite well. Of course, I know better now. I was their camouflage, their diversion, their legitimacy for being there and for doing what they did. And to set up a future that would lead you to me."

Billy didn't have to ask. John saw the question in his eyeball reflections.

"Yes. I know why you are here. You came to get one of them amulets that hung around Alax's and Alixel's necks. You came to tell stories. You came to remember."

"And why are you here?" Cooper said, again turning to him.

"What…you don't know? I'm a black man in a brown man's country. I'm here to stir the shit up. I'm here to pick fights and throw them damned dead things against walls. I'm here because of a promise, one without lies, one that will hopefully end all this bad vibe shit forever."

"You're here to protect us." Cooper said. "Like you did for me in the museum."

John looked into Cooper's eyes but didn't say anything. Then he looked at the back of Billy's head and brought his big hand up to his mouth, patted the fat lower lip, and looked out the window.

"No," Cooper said. "That's not it at all, is it John?" John wouldn't look at her. "You promised to protect *him*. How could you have known he was going to bring extra baggage?" She turned back around. "I'm not supposed to be here, am I? I mean, according to the way this whole story is written, I don't get more than a movie extra's role."

Billy was watching John's expressions in the mirror as Cooper revealed what was obviously true. He remembered how close Cooper had been to death, how he'd just left her in the museum because of his own selfish desire to find the Gormen. "She's the reason I'm here," Billy told John. "Without her, your promise would not be worth squat."

"I know that," John said. "But there'll come a time when a decision has to be made. Just like it was in Gulf One and Two. In the pit of battle, some live, some die."

"I tell you what," Billy said. "You watch my back and I'll watch hers. I'm not asking for any favors but I'm not gonna lie to you either. Having a bodyguard such as you, one who has apparently spent some time fighting wars, definitely makes a stranger in a strange land feel at bit more at ease. But if it comes down to it, I'll not leave Cooper and we'll, *together*, have to deal with it—that is, if you are to uphold your promise."

Cooper looked hard into Billy's face but Billy kept his eyes on the road ahead.

"Alax said you would be strong," John said. "My promise is to protect you, Billy, to make sure you get to where gettin' needs be. And that's what I'm gonna do, at least until you don't need me no more."

Another toll stop loomed ahead. A military Jeep with a soldier stationed behind a machine gun sat parked on the right side of the road. Directly above the soldier's head and attached to a thick, overhanging pole was a green highway sign noting that the road to Chichen Itza veered right immediately after the toll stop. As the Cavalier passed the Jeep and the soldier turned to look at them, Billy knew that if the soldier suddenly decided to spray the car with machine gun bullets, John would leap between the seats, between him and Cooper, and take round after blazing round while Billy watched Cooper shred into pieces beside him.

Cooper was thinking about Manuel, his cold hands, his bean-smelly breath, his Spanish gibberish, his piece of earlobe and the attached Wayeb glyph which she had snatched from the museum floor and now carried in the pocket of her khaki shorts, when John said, "I hate them gawd-awful things. Harder to kill than a dug-in Taliban on the cliffs of Khyber."

"You served in Afghanistan?" Billy asked.

"And Kuwait and Iraq and, if truth be told, Iran and Pakistan, too."

"We're not at war there."

"You sure? Lies of the heart. Lies of the media. Lies of presidents and pastors. We believe what we hear."

"Army man," Billy interjected.

"Marine," John quickly corrected. "Semper Fi—Hoorah!" He lifted his arm quickly and accidentally punched the car's roof, creating a dent. "Sorry. Got carried away." He fiddled with the roof's new irregularity.

"They got cubits in Iran?" Billy asked.

"That what you call them things? Cubits? We call 'em Mu'bä 'round here: poor souls that have just been buried and are unable to move peacefully to the afterlife because they are called forth by someone on earth to obey whatever commands the master makes; they're flesh eaters…zombies basically."

"And you believe there are actually dead people walking around and eating people?"

"Yes, and so do you—so do these Mexican Mayans who live their lives drowning in such mystic BS. That's why they're so easily manipulated by the greedy ones. Every tree and flower and bug and rock has some meaning and some purpose and something to do with life and death. Drink too much alcohol and the Mu'bä will become part of your nightmares. Sleep with your neighbor's wife and the Mu'bä will come take you away. Fight the industrialists and the Mu'bä will kill you and your entire family."

Both Billy and Cooper said in unison, "Sounds familiar."

The rural road to Chichen Itza was much narrower than the more modern four-lane highway they'd traveled on from Mérida. Every time a truck or bus or any vehicle that was larger than the Cavalier passed in the opposite direction, Cooper cringed, her legs stiffening, her thumb pressing harder against the piece of Manuel that she'd stashed in her pocket. Scattered intermittently along the right side of the road were old women riding on the back of three-wheeled bicycles that their old men pedaled, their short, stocky legs easily maintaining momentum regardless of the size of their women. A large vehicle approached head-on at the same time they were trying to pass one of these bicycles and Cooper closed her eyes. The Cavalier shook when the truck passed and when she opened her eyes to look in the side view mirror she saw that the old man and his passenger had not even flinched even though she swore she'd heard the bicycle's rusty handlebar scratch her door.

No one said a word for a good fifteen minutes. Cooper used the time to consider her own safety as their journey moved them closer toward what she was beginning to regret, particularly since John had basically told her, had told both of them, that Billy's life was more important than her own, and that if it came down to it, John would let her die. Why he had saved her from Manuel she could only guess, but she figured it must have had something to do with Billy's survival as well. Perhaps keeping her alive was for no greater purpose than to keep Billy happy. John couldn't sacrifice her if Billy's emotions would also be sacrificed. How could a brokenhearted Daykeeper save the world? It was a flimsy basis for denying insecurity but it was all she had. Her big gamble, though, was the feeling that Billy really *did* care for her in the same way she cared for him which promoted a dilemma. If he cared so strongly for her, he just might sacrifice himself to save her and then where would they be? All of their lives wouldn't be worth shit and John's promise would be null and void.

She looked over at him and became absorbed by his tanned, strong chin that had not been shaved since Nexpa, his dirty dishwater blonde hair that was wavy and waving through the wind that wiped within the car. He looked at her and smiled and she averted his gaze for a moment to hide a blush. His hand crossed the invisible divide between the bucket seats and dropped atop hers which still played with the earlobe that Billy had sliced off.

"He approves," Billy said, his voice hushed. She thought, at first, that Billy was referring to John, but when he nodded toward the dashboard, she realized that he was talking about SpongeBob's happy grin. Of course, its frozen expression of toy joy approved of everything but its happiness did have a contagious way of making things seem okay in the midst of imminent gloom. Perhaps, this was a secondary reason why Billy clung to it so much. The primary reason was certainly Stephanie Drake.

He'd told Cooper about Stephanie during their layover in Nexpa. Her memory had been deeply rooted and was particularly attached to surfing. She'd known this because on at least three different occasions while he was teaching her to surf, he'd called her "Steph." Finally, she'd asked him why he kept calling her that and, after admitting he hadn't even realized he'd said Steph's name, he'd told her about the bank, the beach, her horrible death. He'd told her all about Steph on their last night in Nexpa while they'd been huddled under the hand-woven lean-to, watching the surf rise and fall like clockwork in front of a sunset that was more purple than red. Cooper had known then that Stephanie Drake would forever be a part of his soul and that the chance of losing another person he cared about would, for a long time, make him cautious in a way that would prevent him from telling her how he really felt.

The car slowed as they entered, Ikil, a small scrub of a town turned tourist hotbed with one of the Seven New Wonders of the World just up the road. A huge concrete speed bump made Billy almost stop the car completely. The wheels crawled over the yellow-painted obstruction, giving a few of the locals a chance to market their wares while following the car's slow advance. In their pleading hands were maps and trinkets and facsimiles of artifacts that were sworn to have healing powers and protective powers and reproductive powers.

Ikil was not very big but it was very crowded and in most ways resembled nothing of the bush jungle they'd traveled through so far. Apparently, the Mexican population had somehow gotten it into their heads that foreigners loved bright pastel colors and they loved them plastered onto everything, but Ikil had gone a little overboard. The town's main thoroughfare made Cooper think of a highway stop along Interstate 95 at the border of North and South Carolina. *South of the Border* it was called, the tourist trap of all tourist traps. That place proved that even Americans believed that Americans loved bright pastels. And like that American version of a Mexican town, Ikil had its share of small shops, pressed side-by-side, on both sides of the road. Above and surrounding them were many bold neon signs that promised luxury, entertainment, and spirituality all at "rock-bottom" (Ikil businesses apparently also knew that Americans loved the word "rock bottom") prices. Though the signs were dormant in the afternoon sunshine, Cooper imagined what the pastel-ridden, mile-long stretch of shops would look like under them at night: unnatural, industrial, over-bearing and materialistic. What had John called it? Lies of the mind?

Billy, like Cooper who was also too engaged by the touristy feel of the town, did not see the second speed bump. It was not painted like the first one and when he hit it, even at the slow pace they traveled, all three of them jumped off their seats, the Cavalier's springs wining with the sudden impact. SpongeBob fell to the floor and Cooper quickly replaced it on the dashboard. John fell forward, his torso wedging itself into the floorboard space behind Billy's seat. He pushed himself up, but when the car's rear wheels contacted the speed bump, he fell back in.

"Sorry," Billy said. "Those things come out of nowhere."

"Topes for dopes," John murmured as he rolled back up and into his stuffy position across the rear seat. He rubbed his bald head. "That's what they call 'em around here. And damn, that one was really topey. I don't remember them puttin' one in the middle of freakin' Main Street." Another young merchant ran up to the window where John's head glistened in the sun. He tried to hand John a flyer and John bellowed, "Get outta my face! Váyase!" The flyer fluttered from the boy's hand, flapped through John's open window, and fell to the floorboard where his head had just been. He reached down and picked it up. Then he laughed. "That boy's got some business savvy. Maybe it was him or his old man that put that damn tope there in the first place. This flyer, here, promotes something about undercarriage car repair. And this flyer…" John shuffled the two pieces of paper he'd plucked from the floor. "Why, this ain't a flyer at all. It's a computer printout. Why would a kid in the middle of Mexico have a computer printout? Why would a kid in the middle of Mexico have a computer?"

Billy stopped the car for a plentitude of pedestrian traffic. "Can I see that?" When John gave him the paper, it took Billy only a second to realize that the paper must have been under the driver's seat all of this time; it was a computer printout from the Big Bank of Texas, Port A branch, and the names listed were people he knew, people that had owned businesses on the island, people that had been cubited.

Car horns urged him forward. Billy had not realized that he'd been idling there, right in the middle of downtown Ikil, thinking about the list of names for a full minute after the pedestrian flow had passed. More local youngsters approached the car as Billy lowered Steph's computer printout onto his lap and eased off the brake. The boys shouted Spanish at him but he didn't understand a word of it.

Canton Andrews, Madeline Black, Charlotte Broughton…

Slowly, the traffic crawled forward until it crossed the town's third speed bump, painted yellow, then gained momentum as the view became less American modernized and more Mexican rural. Most of the traffic turned left at a beautifully sculptured wooden sign that read "Sacred Cenote." An arrow painted in pastel red, orange and yellow pointed the way. An "Enjoy Coca-Cola" sign dangled underneath it.

Lewis Kennedy, Noel Kilpatrick, Jeffrey Lemmon…

Another hundred yards up the road, a half a dozen not-so-modern motels, in various phases of reconditioning, sat only partially occupied. They looked much older than the buildings within Ikil, having somehow been left out of the loop when Ikil went the way of the Western world. None of them had paved parking lots and only one of them had seen a fresh paint job in at least a decade.

Professor Theodore Nelson, Dr. Shasta Preston, Manny Rodriguez…

As Billy passed the last of the buildings, the memory of faces attached themselves to the names. So many people had died. So many people had been cubited.

John broke his concentration. "Turn left up there."

A dirt road led into dense bush and thick trees and Billy turned onto it. The road was in desperate need of repair and Billy had to use its entire width to slowly navigate the craters, some so huge that he could have parked the car in them.

"Where are we going?" Cooper asked.

"A friend," John said. "We can't go into Chich in the middle of the day. We'll have to wait for nightfall."

"But isn't that dangerous?"

"Yes. That's why it's good to have friends, especially those that have worked at the site for as many years as he has." John, for the first time since they'd left Mérida, rose to a sitting position. His back hunkered forward and, with his head lowered against the dent in the car's roof that he had punched earlier, he shuffled against the bucket seats, his chest filling the space between them. "So you gonna tell us about the printout? When I handed it to you, you looked like you seen a ghost."

"Mu'bä," Billy said. "A couple a hundred of them…from Texas."

"You got a list of the walking dead? How'dya manage that?"

"I didn't. Steph did."

John looked perplexed.

"We killed most of them before we left the island. The hurricane got the rest."

"We? You mean you and this Steph?"

Billy swerved to miss a crater that wasn't very wide but was deep enough to disable the car. "Long story. If I have time, maybe we'll get into it."

"You're the Daykeeper," John said. "That's what you do."

"I'm not one yet."

John's hand came around Billy's left shoulder and dropped, his fingers delicately but firmly massaging the meat. "I'll get you there. I'll get you both there." He purposely grinned at Cooper but did not hug her. "Here it is." He pointed with a finger that still rested on Billy's shoulder.

There were actually three buildings spread out in a wide one-acre plot that had been cleared of plants and rocks. All three of the buildings looked similar in size and construction, with walls made of irregularly shaped limestone boulders and simple gable roofs made from the trunks of the trees that suffocated the perimeter of the clearing. The density of the jungle around the plot helped shade the open area. Billy parked beside a rusted, old Chevy Impala that was propped up under the front axle by two large rocks; its wheels were missing.

A window made of Plexiglas was centered in the front door of the building nearest them and within it, a head quickly appeared then disappeared. John pulled himself out of the back seat of the Cavalier as a man with intense gray hair, a worn, scraggly cowboy hat, and more wrinkles than Billy had ever seen on one face, emerged from the building with a shotgun in both hands but not pointed at anything in particular.

"A hundred pesos says ya can't hit the side of a taco stand with that thing," John teased.

"You know I hate fucking taco-th," the man said, his accent a mixture of Mexico and Texas that lisped behind the two front teeth that were missing. "You bring me a new toy to play with?" He pushed his gun in the direction of the Cavalier but did not point it at the car. Billy and Cooper exited and Billy walked around to stand beside Cooper.

"Chill," John told Billy. "He's not referring to Coop. He likes the car."

"Another trip into the ruin-th, Johnboy? It-th the only time you come thee me. Been a coupl'a year-th now."

"Chich ain't the same as it used to be, my friend."

"Got that right. Who-th the gringo-th?"

"Tourists," Billy quickly answered.

"Really," the man said. With the barrel of the shotgun, he tipped a crumpled bend in his cowboy hat, uncovering an abundance of wrinkles in his forehead. "Where from?"

"Texas," Billy said and looked at Cooper. "And Arizona."

"Thun-of-a-bitch!" the man said. "Thun-of-a-fucking-bitch! Did you tell 'em to thay that, Johnboy?"

John waved Billy and Cooper closer. "This here is my friend," he said to them. "He's really quite gentle unless you do him wrong." The man nodded and then smiled, revealing the dark hole where his two incisors once existed. "Honestly, I can't tell you his first name since I don't know it myself, but I've come to know him as Strykor. At least that's what we called him in the Gulf."

"You guys served together?" Billy asked.

"We didn't therve any whore," Strykor said. "We killed a bunch of mother-fucker-th though."

"Strykor's from Texas, too. Galveston, isn't it?"

"Damn thtraight. Was an oil drillin' man before them peckerhead-th in Iraq thtarted thcrewing everything. You drill oil, thun?"

Billy shook his head. "No. I used to own a restaurant."

"Yeah?" Strykor said. "Plannin' on thtarting one in Ikil?"

John interrupted. "He came to see the well."

Strykor's eyes popped a bit more open. "Really? And what-th your thtory muchacha?"

"They both came to see the well," John said. "I thought you were going to get some new teeth? You sound like a damned snake."

"Thhhh…" Strykor hissed, his tongue firmly pressed against the open space. "And ready to thtrike. Like old time-th, eh buddy?"

"This guy just couldn't be killed," John said to Billy and Cooper, thumbing in Strykor's direction. "That's why the captain always sent him in to do the dirty stuff."

"Don't give me all the glory," Strykor said. "You got yourn." Strykor walked casually to them, an odor following him like Pigpen dirt that wafted over Billy the closer he came. Strykor smelled acidic and unwashed and a bit like tree bark that's been freshly ripped from the trunk. "What do ya want for it?" he asked Billy.

"Want? For what?" Strykor tapped the hood of the Cavalier with the barrel of the shotgun. "You want to buy my car?"

"Naw. Ain't got no money." Strykor squinted and his face wrinkles rolled into new positions. He studied Billy, his head lolled backward, the missing incisor hole a black rectangle until his tongue moved behind it. "We trade in theeth part-th."

A little spittle launched from the tongue-in-tooth hole and landed on Billy's cheek which Billy, on instinct, refused to wipe away. Disgust for this man's spit could upset him to a point that he might suddenly relive one of his glorious, covert missions in the Middle East. Instinct also told him not to ignore Strykor's request. Billy had had no intention of selling Steph's Cavalier, at least not up until this point in time; John had said nothing about it, had in no way prepared him for such a quandary. He'd not even known they were going to meet such a man as Strykor, let alone be subjected to a decision that would leave them all without a means to transport them farther, toward the fourth destination, wherever

the hell that was. Even though reason told him that John would interfere
with any attempt by Strykor to harm him, instinct told him that such an
intervention would not be necessary. If only he had the right answer. What
was Strykor really saying? This was a test—it had to be. *We trade in
theeth part-th.* Trade? Cooper grabbed his elbow.

"Can you get us safely to and from the well?" Billy asked Strykor.

"Doe-th a dog thit in the jungle?" Strykor said, studying Billy's
face.

"What's in the well?"

"We'll find out together, I th-pothe."

"And I suppose nothing is free around here."

"You got that one right, gringo."

"The car for your guidance, then."

Strykor didn't smile but Billy could tell he'd said the right thing
since, after he'd said it, Strykor pointed at John with the shotgun and
said, "Th-arp gringo. You brought me a th-arp Gringo, Johnboy. Now
let-th eat!" He slapped Billy on the back then slung the shotgun over one
shoulder. "What would you make on a hot mother-fucker day like thi-th,
rethrant man?" he said to Billy as he walked away.

Instinct told Billy the answer. "Snake, I suppose."

Strykor laughed, his boisterous bellow echoing within the acre of
jungle he called home.

Billy had eaten snake on two occasions, both while back in
college, which, ironically, was before he'd moved to a state known for
its slithering inhabitants. In Cambridge, it had been "a thing to do,"
something different, something daring, something not affordable to
the "average" person. A good section of rattler could cost upwards of
fifty dollars a plate and, prepared well, was worth the money, more for
bragging rights than for the purpose of nutrition.

Billy hadn't paid for it. His parents had been visiting on both
occasions and had insisted. They liked doing what others did not have
the opportunity to do—at least his father always did. Billy suspected his
mother just went along for the egotistical ride, not really enjoying such
"upper class" snobbery but supportive of her husband regardless of how

she really felt. Billy remembered how wonderful the snake had tasted. When prepared correctly, it tasted just like chicken, just like Strykor's snake did on the eve of their journey to Chichen Itza.

They sat on four shaded tree stumps around a fire pit that had been carved into the limestone ground between two of Strykor's buildings. "What's that sweet taste?" Billy asked the cook. Strykor stirred the fire then grabbed Billy's stick and stabbed another portion of meat he pulled from a wooden bowl. He gave the reloaded meat stick to Billy and Billy immediately stuck it in the fire. John asked for a refill and soon both sticks of rattler were hissing in the open flames.

"A theecret," Strykor said. "Caribbean thnake. What about you, honey?" he said to Cooper. "You like my thnake?"

"It's good," she said, chewing slowly, a half piece of blackened snake still clinging to her stick. "It would go really good with my salsa."

Even Billy could tell she was lying. She ate the snake but was in no way enjoying it. She drank way too much water even though it looked muddy.

"You don't have to like it," Strykor said. "Unfortunately, I haven't made it to the thtore recently. When we get back from the well tomorrow, we'll get thum thtuff for your thal-th…your thal-th—" He spit all over his chin. "Your thal-tha."

"Teeth," John said. "Get some goddamn teeth and you can yell out salsa from the top of your lungs."

Strykor suddenly stood and quickly walked into the cottage he called home. Billy thought that John had just pissed him off and that Strykor had gone to get his gun, but when he returned all Strykor had in his hands was another wooden bowl of marinating snake. He sat on his stump and said nothing for the longest minute.

"More," John said. "And this time don't be so stingy." Strykor reloaded John's stick but still did not say anything. "What the hell's wrong with you? I've never known you to be this quiet."

"Thalsa," Strykor said under his breath as if he was really trying to work on that one word. "Thalsa," he repeated a bit louder. "Salsa."

"Whoa," John said. "How'd ya do that?"

Strykor grinned then and all three of them looked at his mouth, squinting simultaneously. The black rectangle of missing incisors was now filled with two oversized blocks of white that hung over his bottom lip. Carved 'em myself. What'da ya think?"

John's lips puckered because he was struggling so hard to keep his laughter inside. His eyes, which were quickly moistening, rolled in Billy's direction and Billy was certain he would bust at any moment. His expression tickled Billy so much that when John finally did release it, Billy started laughing, too. "You sound much better," John finally managed, wiping his eyes, "but you look like…you look like…"

"I know," Strykor said. "Bugs Bunny." And then he started laughing. "Carved 'em out of a coyote's ass."

Cooper, who didn't seem to know how to react, added her own small bit of shy laughter but, again, it was a false response meant to please the status quo.

"Come on, Coop," John said. "Liven up."

But Cooper stopped laughing and just stared at her meat stick.

John snickered through the last bites of his second helping and pointed at what was left of Cooper's meal. "Ain't ya gonna eat that?" he said, and before she could respond, he plucked the last bite from the charred stick and plopped it is mouth.

What in the hell were they going to do without a car? Cooper was not about to be stranded in the middle of the Yucatán jungle. She had survival skills, but come on!

Throughout their entire meal, that's all she could think about (along with an overwhelming feeling of dehydration and a careless attitude about the color of water she drank). Billy was going to give up their ride for a guided tour into Chichen Itza? And what about John who seemed to go along with all of it? Billy had a destination and it wasn't "Chich." Chich was a place for raising a Djed of the past, not of the future. And another thing: why didn't the big son-of-a-bitch give a shit about her? She was beginning to second guess her belief that he would keep her alive if for no other reason than to keep Billy happy. To hell with cultural excuses; women in Mexico remained among the low rungs of the social ladder—but not women named Cooper. She wasn't cooking anything and she wasn't cleaning anything and she wasn't bearing his children but she still demanded respect, dammit! She still deserved some fucking protection!

His buddy Strykor was no different. She didn't like his crappy snake meal…so fucking what! Why didn't he offer something different? Some goddamned tortillas would have been just fine. Why didn't he have any goddamned tortillas? All Mexicans had tortillas! And those teeth. Stupid. What was so goddamned funny about teeth that looked like Bugs Bunny? And if he said the word salsa or thaltha (or whatever and however he called it) one more time, she'd scream…she'd absolutely lose her fucking mind!

But it was when John took the food from her stick without asking, whether she liked what was wrapped around it or not, that had been the final straw. Her mind did flip. Her anger exploded. Fucking sexists! Goddamned them all!

The last thing Cooper remembered before she passed out was John telling her to liven up.

At about the same time that Cooper fell into Billy's lap, Sedona councilmen Tate and Roberts met with Evan at an outside taco stand a couple of miles away in Piste. Tate was round and fat. Being cubited only intensified his voracious hunger. He ordered five more fish tacos.

"Manson is pissed as hell you fuckers let Cooper get away," Evan said. "Now we've got to do this the hard way."

"Blow me," Tate growled. "It was your piss ant Mexican dumb shit that got his head all broke."

Evan punched him square in the face. Tate's fat, squishy forehead easily absorbed the blow. No one at the taco stand, not even the American tourists, paid any attention. Tate rubbed his face then dug into his refried beans with his fingers.

Unlike Tate, Roberts' cubit had maintained some of its primary's self respect. It even wore a coat and tie and polished shoes. "They hooked up with another missionary Marine," Roberts said.

Evan slammed a fist on the makeshift wooden table, causing Roberts' glass of cheap wine to topple on the table. "Strykor!"

For a cubit that was only a couple of month's fresh, Roberts had transitioned particularly fast. Its expression mimicked a real person's surprise. "We knew that was going to happen, didn't we?" he said. The waitress brought Tate's five tacos and he immediately dug into them, smearing their contents all over his face and table. "Disgusting," Roberts added and sipped the rest of what had not spilled from his wine glass.

"Yes," Evan said, ignoring the pig sounds that emerged from Tate's feeding. "But only after the transformation." He reached over and slapped the half eaten taco from Tate's hands. "Listen, you pathitiful fool! Remember why you are here."

"The Serpent screwed up," Tate said through a mouth full of slop. "Not me."

"You all screwed up. That book ain't worth jack shit without the key." The cubits stared at him expressionless and frozen, as if some internal springs had died and needed rewinding. "You work for me not that Serpent idiot. You remember that or hell will feel like heaven once Manson gets through with both of you."

Tate picked up another taco and began chewing. "We gob it cobbered."

Evan, again, slapped that taco from his hands. "You have nothing covered. Manson has it covered and you fucked it up."

Roberts said, "I thought we were going to take them in the well."

"*We* are not going to take them anywhere. The Serpent will do our bidding for us. Has Manuel made contact with him yet?"

"The camp is all set," Roberts said. "We'll roast all four of 'em."

"Stupid! Both of you are the dumbest…" Evan looked around the outdoor restaurant and lowered his voice since everyone was now looking at him. "You will not hurt Presser. Even the Serpent knows that if Presser dies there will be no *raising* of anything except your heads from your shoulders."

"No cares," Tate said, grabbing for another taco. "The Cubit will make more of me."

"I wouldn't be so confident if I were you. Even the Cubit has a master."

"Like I am the master of this taco," Tate said and took a bite.

Evan knew it was useless to talk any further. Roberts, perhaps, would still be of some use but Tate was a lost cause; he'd make arrangements for his disposal later. Right now, Evan had to do what the two cubits had not been able to do: recover the key to the Book of the Djed. The Book and the key and Presser had to be together on December 21 or else Manson was going to destroy all of them. Evan took a deep breath, snatched Tate's taco from his hand and dropped it on the table.

"Leave," he said to both of them. "You have work to do, don't you? The camp? Remember? You fuckin' idiots."

The two cubits left Evan to stare at the remnants of Tate's slop. A waitress came to the table and apologized to Evan for no reason as she cleaned up the mess. "Agua, por favor," he said to her and a moment later she returned with a plastic bottle of water.

To rule in the New World. That had been the deal. Manson had promised that when all of this was over, Evan would have everything he could ever want. He'd have his choice of cities, of the people in them, a chance to be somebody. He'd be able to make all of the decisions and not just wander in the shadows as he'd done his entire life. He'd finally have respect and admiration and if anyone disagreed with him then, well, he'd make sure they never disagreed again...in a similar way that he was going to make sure Tate would never disagree again. Unfortunately, you couldn't really threaten a cubit, but the people that remained after 2012... they would be flesh and blood and controllable. If the world as it existed today was any indication, he'd be able to control masses with just words, his words, the things he believed in, the things he desired—the way Manson controlled the cubits: with promises. The Serpent, like all cubits, was simply a pawn in Manson's great scheme. All cubits thought, in their cubited little brains, that they were in total control.

Promises...

Promises for errand boys.

Kind of like how Evan was an errand boy but dramatically different. The latitude that Manson gave him with disagreement showed how much Manson needed him. All cubits needed human counterparts, at least all cubits that expected to remain hidden from human discovery.

"La cuenta, por favor," Evan said to the waitress with a wad of pesos in hand. Without the diversion of Tate's gluttony, he now found the young woman to be extremely pleasant but he was too damn shy to ask for her. He certainly had the money and she certainly would give herself to him. That's just the way it worked around here. Still...

The time would come when money would no longer be necessary. Demanding was so much easier.

The last of the sunlight had disappeared an hour ago and all Billy was left with was an oil lantern, a hard cot, a sparse room, Cooper who rested on a second cot beside him, and his thoughts.

Strykor could not have apologized enough. He'd taken his hand-carved, coyote-ass teeth out and had kept repeating, over and over, "Tho thorry. I'm tho thorry." Apparently, Strykor had thought he'd brought all of them water that he'd distilled for drinking. Accidentally, Strykor had grabbed one of the tumblers in which he kept well water, stuff that he had not boiled, stuff that he used for washing his hands and wiping his face.

Cooper had drunk all of it and there was no telling how many parasites had entered her body, Strykor had said. He'd thought that the snake marinade had masked the odd taste of the well water and so, Cooper had not known any better. He'd also said that the parasites could easily turn a person insane, could knock them out cold, or both. Fortunately, Strykor had been prepared. He'd said that he'd made the same mistake himself only once and the madness that had ensued had been so bad that he'd never wanted to take such chances again. Since then, he'd kept plenty of what he'd called "antidote," which was a prescription from the pharmacist in town. It would work quickly, he'd promised. She'd feel some nausea when she awakened, but the parasites would be gone and so would the madness. She'd be ready to travel by midnight, the time Strykor had set for their excursion to Chichen Itza.

Except for one young man who had maintained a revolving occupancy in the last cottage in the row, Strykor's "motel" had been vacant for quite some time. This was the same cottage that Billy and Cooper now lay in. Strykor had said that the young man rarely came around on the weekends and never before midnight since he worked long hours at the ruins. The cottage had only a single room. There was no bathroom; the shithouse was out beyond the cottage at the end of a path that had been chopped through the jungle. Strykor had dissuaded Billy from going out there after dark without him, and had urged Billy to "take care of business" before the sun went down.

The stone walls of the cottage had two openings: one for a door made out of tree limbs that were tied with strips of bark, and one for a window that had no glass—just a screen to keep insects out. Beyond the screen, a full moon broke through shuffling clouds and its white luminance fell angelically on Cooper's sleeping face.

When she'd passed out and had fallen off her tree stump into his lap, Billy had been quite concerned. He'd thought he'd seen blood smears at the corners of her lips but John had assured him that it was nothing more than Caribbean snake marinade. Still, the memory of concern remained strong and he hated it. It made life much more complicated when you cared for someone else, especially when recent experience reminded him how Steph had been so heinously taken from him, how her cubited naked body had been one of the scariest things he'd ever seen, how she'd mewled for him to come closer. How she'd demanded a kiss.

The soft pitter-patter of rain rustled the roof's natural construction and jostled some of the jungle bush outside the cottage. The moonlight still roamed intermittently through the window and Billy stood, momentarily glanced down at Cooper when she softly moaned, then walked to the window. More clouds than clear filled the moon-glow horizon and Billy figured they'd have a wet hike ahead of them. To the left were the other two cottages; John was in the center cottage and Strykor was at the end. Between them, glowing embers from the fire pit sizzled whenever a raindrop found them. To his right was jungle. Even with the moonlight, it was hard to see very far into it. A path had been cut into the jungle but it curled away to the right so that the shithouse could not be seen from the window. There was, however, something else sitting along the path. It wasn't predatory. In fact, it wasn't even animal. He opened the cottage door for a better look, blinked, looked right then left, blinked again. It was still there. The VW Bus was still there.

He walked to the head of the path with only enough caution to prevent him from tripping over the tree roots underfoot, his gaze centered on the VW's round, broken headlight. The vehicle sat in a small clearing to the right of the path and as he neared it, he kept telling himself that it couldn't be his VW, the one from Port Aransas, not all the way out here. Besides, the hurricane had taken it, hadn't it?

His heart hammered harder. The VW's driver's side window was missing and when he looked through the opening and into the vehicle's interior, he saw cabinets, just like the ones he'd built into his own VW, the cabinets where he'd stored his computer equipment, the computer equipment that controlled his robot, the robot that had infiltrated the bank, the bank that had housed the Cubit, the Cubit which was the reason why he was standing here in the first place.

He walked around to the back of the vehicle to find more evidence. The rear bumper was missing and when he bent down to look under the VW, moon glow revealed that the brackets that had held the bumper were twisted wrecks of metal, as if something had literally ripped the bumper right off of it.

Albert Stine's twisted image flashed through memory, how he had held the VW by its bumper, how he and Steph had escaped only because the bumper had torn free.

Billy slowly opened the rear door panel and crawled inside. The cabinet doors were open and empty. Still, Billy was convinced that this was his 1963 VW Bus. For final confirmation he tapped the floorboards with his knuckles and a small door popped open on spring hinges. He flipped up the door and found what he expected to find: electronic parts. The compartment contained a couple of solar batteries, some replacement solar cells, a small remote control, a tiny robotic insect that he'd given up on repairing and a Ziploc containing various circuit board components. Billy pulled up the tail of his shirt and piled into it the compartment's contents. When he pulled out the Ziploc, a can of Budweiser rolled into view. He looked at it curiously, not remembering when he'd put it in there, then shrugged and plucked it out, sticking the can into a pocket in his shorts before closing the floorboard door.

He shuffled backward through the VW's rear panel and stepped out into the light rain while juggling the contents in his shirt tail. Quickly, he returned to the cottage where he squatted and spread everything out onto the limestone floor. He removed the beer can last and set it among the pile of components. Rain drops rolled down the Budweiser label. He snatched up the can, flipped open the tab, and took a long swallow.

How in the hell did his VW Bus get here, he wondered, licking foam from his lips. Coincidence, for him, just didn't exist anymore. But thinking about it right now made his head hurt, so he turned to the electronics and the solace they represented, turning each piece in the palm of his hand, examining it, remembering what purpose it served. He'd not gotten to play with his robots in so long. The excitement made him giddy and, coupled with the beer which he now finished in one gulp, Billy felt right at home in the middle of the Yucatán jungle.

Both John and Strykor had machetes though Cooper wondered why. The purpose was not for trailblazing; the path they walked seemed as if it had been traveled frequently. She assumed that the machetes were meant for something in the jungle that she could not see, which was very unsettling.

She'd awakened about an hour before they'd departed. Her stomach had ached something horrible but the crazy thoughts had gone. She'd become so angry, so quickly and if she'd had a gun, she probably would have shot them all. A shiver of that thought had accompanied her awakening and when her eyelids had finally unglued themselves, she'd found Billy toying with scattered pieces of electronic components on an earthen floor within a circle of broken moonlight. He had been giggling, and his head had bounced back and forth as he'd assembled some of the pieces into objects that were, apparently, making him very happy. His giggles combined with her lingering thoughts of murder had only made her nausea worse.

Billy had told her what had happened and how apologetic Strykor had been, and as they'd prepared to leave the makeshift motel courtyard en route to Chichen Itza, Strykor had treated her like a queen, asking her time and again if there was anything she needed, anything at all, to just "thay it and it-th your-th." All she could think of at the time was to request that he reinsert his makeshift incisors so that she could understand him.

But Strykor said very little during their journey to the ruins. His only commentary was in response to Billy's question concerning the resident of the cottage in which she'd slept off the poison's influence. "Yes," he said to Billy. "Pedro is his name. He traded a box of artifacts he said he'd recovered in Texas for a job at the ruins. I helped him return them to the well and gave him a place to stay."

John, too, said very little. He warned them about some of the surrounding plants, particularly the skinny tree that leaked poison which he called the chechen negro. Getting some of its sap on the skin would guarantee misery, he said. Oddly, a tree that always grew right next to chechen negro was the chacah, a tree that provided nectar which neutralized the chechen's poison. John stopped them for a momentary

explanation he felt was necessary to ensure that Billy and Cooper knew
what to look for in the future.

The canopy of the jungle wasn't very high but it was very moist.
Light rain earlier in the evening had now turned to pure mist and, in the
full moon shine, it cast an eerie blue hue against everything, dripping
that blue sheen downward, a surreal curtain filled with dire consequence.
Visibility increasingly diminished the farther they walked; at one point,
Cooper lost sight of Billy's backpack when she stopped for only second
to assure herself that the tree closest to her right arm was, indeed, the
chechen. If it had not been for one swooping sound of a machete against
bush, she might have lost her way.

An hour into the journey, they emerged from the jungle into a
clearing that revealed a white road of inlaid limestone (which looked blue
under the current conditions); John called it a *sacbe*. About a hundred
yards ahead, at the other end of the sacbe, loomed the misty outline of a
squat pyramid centered among two other shorter, rectangular structures.
Strykor put his hand out to stop their forward progress.

"The Nunnery," he whispered. "There will be a guard stationed just
around the corner and a second one should be walking the perimeter."

As if on cue, a guard appeared in front of the pyramid, walking
right to left, the misty haze wafting behind him as he moved. Strykor
sidestepped to the cover of wet bushes and trees and the rest of them
followed. He dropped his backpack from his shoulders then removed his
boots, his shirt and pants. Underneath, he wore what Cooper assumed was
the dark blue uniform of the Chichen Itza guards. He shoved his outer
clothing into the backpack, slipped back into his boots and inspected
the blade of a commando knife that he then stashed in a strap around his
calf. "They know me," he said to Cooper. "But just in case." He took out
his fake teeth, handed them to her along with his backpack and machete,
then ran off along the edge of the jungle bush. He continued, stealthily, to
where the jungle's camouflage ended halfway to the ruins, then he stood
straight up and walked casually, as if he had every right to be there.

When Strykor waved an arm, John stood from cover. John
whispered, "Coast is clear." John told them to leave the machetes and
they moved quickly to where Strykor stood.

And then, all four of them jumped when a small dog appeared,
seemingly out of nowhere. It started barking incessantly at the intruders.
When Strykor flicked a small rock that hit its hindquarters, the dog only

momentarily quieted, ran into the shadows, then returned, barking even more aggressively. Strykor snatched a much larger rock and Cooper grabbed his hand.

"Not that way," she insisted. Strykor hesitated, the endless folds of wrinkled face flesh scrunched prune-like into disbelief. "You said you'd do anything for me. Don't hit the dog."

Strykor dropped the rock just as someone shouted, "Parada! Quién es eso?" John yanked both Billy and Cooper backward and into the space between two of the stone buildings. A flashlight beam missed revealing them by half a step.

Cooper peered from her hiding place and out beyond the centuries-old buildings. Strykor was out of sight and just beyond the moonlight blue misty corner of the ancient building and to the right. Billy stood behind her and John was next to him, his dark skin a perfect complement to the shadow in which he stood. A little déjà vu attacked Cooper's senses. It had been exactly two weeks ago that she'd stood in another alley, hidden beyond another corner, listening to the conversation of two other people she did not know.

Most of the Spanish she understood though Strykor's lisp made the conversation harder for Cooper to decipher. Strykor apparently didn't know the guard but the guard accepted him as a co-worker. Strykor's additional lies included statements pertaining to him arriving late for work, a request of the guard to not tell the boss, an offer of two hundred pesos to forget they'd even seen each other, and a question concerning who was watching a *caracol*, though she had no idea what *caracol* meant.

"Julio y Pedro," the guard said. The dog started barking again. "Perro! Tranquilo!" the guard yelled and did something that made the dog yelp. The dog ran past the space where Cooper hid. It looked at her and for a moment, she thought the dog was going to give them away, but it kept running, tail between its skinny legs.

"Grathia-th," Strykor said. "Buena-th noche-th."

Billy kept shaking his head. Pedro *was* here and, according to Strykor, had brought with him the Cubit.

"What is it?" John said, his deep baritone whispering like a bass drum in his ear. "You act like you just saw a ghost."

"Yeah," Billy said. "More like, heard a ghost."

"Don't deny intuition. It's about all we have left."

Strykor popped his head around the corner and Cooper yelped. "Come on," he said. "The Caracol i-th juth around the corner."

Cooper handed Strykor his fake teeth. "Please," she said. "What you have to say right now might be too important to be misunderstood."

Strykor grabbed the teeth and his backpack and reset both, then stepped cautiously along the perimeter of the Nunnery's colonnade of structures, leading the group between a square building on the right and the short pyramid on the left. The moon and the mist really screwed with Billy's pre-conceived notions of the great city of Chichen Itza. It certainly looked nothing like the pictures on the internet or in any brochure, pamphlet or flyer he'd ever perused. Not only was everything blue, it was shadowy blue, eerie moon-white blue, misty wet-to-the-bones blue. His right hand ran across the mortared limestone blocks of one of the oldest buildings in the city, the twenty-foot tall Iglesia, and the faces carved into them stared back with what Billy thought were shocked expressions of open-mouthed men who were gasping because of the superstitions they attached to blue nights. Even with the protection of two Marines, he could not help the chills that raced through every nerve in his body. He'd read (in some of those pamphlets and on some of those web sites) that to visit Mayan ruins in the middle of the night invited malevolent ferries into the human spirit, ferries that could easily drive a person to madness, ferries that would never leave until the body they infested was dead. Perhaps that was the chill he felt: ferries scratching their way into his soul, clawing at his very essence, anchoring themselves there forever. Perhaps the ferries were the only thing that could kill an invincible Daykeeper apprentice, and a whole legion of Marines couldn't do a damn thing about it.

When they rounded the far corner of the Iglesia, they came upon a large, vacant plot of land that had once served as a great Mayan center for trade. On the far side of the open area, stood a building that looked nothing like the ones he'd seen so far.

"Caracol," Strykor said, pointing at it. "The well is in the Caracol."

To Billy it looked almost like a modern day astronomical observatory. The dome had partially crumbled, leaving only four window openings in the front half and a big hole in the back; in the blue haze, the entire structure, the dome and the three platforms it sat atop, seemed to glow with invisible energy. Strykor and John both looked in directions that Billy did not: to the far left where jungle infiltrated the marketplace square, to the near right where rows of stone columns that no longer supported roofs stood next to the Caracol's second-level platform like frozen soldiers awaiting long forgotten commands, and behind them where the scrawny dog sat silent in the shadows, sniffing the air and watching.

Strykor adjusted his teeth before he spoke. "When I say go, we all run to the platform with the standing columns. Stay low, silent and quick." Strykor looked around and made some hand gestures that probably meant something to John then returned his gaze to Billy and Cooper. "Ready...Go!"

Strykor left the cover of the Iglesia first. Cooper and Billy followed in quick pursuit. John took up the rear and the scrawny dog followed him. As if it had understood everything Strykor had said, the dog stayed low, was quicker than all of them, and didn't make a sound. By the time the foursome had dashed across the fifty yards of open space, the dog was already sitting between two of the limestone columns, waiting and wagging its tail. All four of them took a different column, positioning their bodies so that if someone was perched above them, they could not be seen.

"Pedro will help us," Strykor said. "Not sure who Julio is but I'm sure Pedro can create a distraction. He's done it before."

"The Pedro from your motel?" Billy asked just to reassure himself that he already knew the answer.

"Yeah. The one who owns the VW you broke into." Someone appeared in one of the dome's windows. "Never mind that now. Pedro can settle with you later." Strykor squatted and pressed up against his column, and the rest of them followed his lead. He placed a finger to his lips.

It was, indeed, Billy's chef that now stood in the domed observatory window. The last he'd seen of Pedro was on the beach in Port Aransas. He'd heard Pedro scream. He'd thought Pedro was dead. But there he was, standing within a rectangle of darkness, his incessant grin still beaming incessantly white teeth that sparkled even at this distance.

And if Pedro's presence wasn't shocking enough, below him, laid into the dome's stone structure, was a pattern of blocks that looked exactly like the Wayeb.

Life was without coincidence. Life was without control. The Wayeb had been a part of his very soul, following him, marking his progression, verifying his journey. The face represented Evil's infiltration into the world; it occupied the top of the key to the Book of the Djed that was now stored in the pack on Billy's back; it had been inscribed on the fin of a mystery surfboard Billy had found on the Port A beach; it had been imprinted on the coins found in Lafitte's treasure on the night of the hurricane; it had been the title of the chamber that had housed the Cubit in the Great Hall of the Anasazi; it had dangled as an earring from the rapist that had tried to hurt Cooper in the History Museum of Mérida. And now, here it was, like a stamp marking the proverbial X.

Under the inlaid Wayeb face was a doorway into the dome. Pedro disappeared from the window above as people emerged from it.

People…In the middle of the night…Appearing from within a building more than twelve hundred years old.

And not just one or two people, but dozens. They labored when they walked; at least one of them dragged its left leg like a dead stick. A couple of them tripped and fell from the top platform, down a dozen stone steps, to the intermediate platform just above Billy's head. One of those that had fallen, a woman, slowly rose and staggered in his direction, her flip-flopped feet skittering recklessly across the limestone mortar joints. She stopped and stood just above him. Apparently, she didn't see him or didn't care that he was there, even when the scrawny dog took off back in the direction of the Iglesia. More people filled the Caracol's platforms. More fell down the hard steps. More filed onto the open marketplace grounds. And none of them made any sound whatsoever.

"Mu'bä," John moaned.

The woman standing above him suddenly took one errant step forward and fell straight down onto the top of one of the columns, her head cracking against its surface, her body twisting in the air and toppling to the floor at Billy's feet. Her face turned up to him; it was slathered with blood that appeared gray in the light blue misty hue. Billy knew the woman. Her name was Madeline Black. In fact, when Billy started concentrating on the faces of all the twenty-five or thirty people that had emerged from the observatory dome, he realized he knew most of them.

They had at one time been residents of Texas but had made the mistake of applying for a security box just to enter a contest at the Big Texas Bank. And every one of them was listed on Stephanie Drake's computer printout that John had found under the Cavalier's front seat.

Across the open marketplace square, the cubits wandered aimlessly in multiple directions, seemingly lost, walking as if drunk, as if they'd just been reborn as something beyond dead—not really zombies, not really Mu'bä. Still, the blue mist that wafted around them made Billy think of the classic George Romero living dead movies. Even Michael Jackson drifted into thought, and how, even at two years old, the *Thriller* video had made such a psychological impact on him.

Broken Madeline Black, owner of Black's Café in Port Aransas, Texas, rolled onto her side and grabbed Billy's foot. Billy couldn't help yelping which caused all of the wandering cubits to turn around.

John grabbed his arm. "Gotta get," he said.

Strykor and Cooper had already taken off, hunkering low against the first stone platform of the Caracol; Strykor's commando knife was out and ready. Billy unsheathed the dagger and held it in front him in similar fashion.

"Ain't gonna need that just yet," John said.

Billy stared at him long enough to replenish his trust then replaced the dagger, even though the cubits were moving in on them, and followed John up the first set of steps. Ahead, two cubits (Lewis Kennedy who had owned the Mustang Ranch and Charlotte Broughton who had been a Port Aransas real estate agent) writhed on the steps. When Cooper stepped over them, Charlotte grabbed her ankle. Strykor quickly separated the arm with his knife and Cooper swatted the severed appendage from her leg which then tumbled down the steps a few feet from Billy, the fingers still grasping for a leg that was no longer there. The foursome ascended the remaining steps two-at-a-time and stopped in front of the doorway that led into the dome. Pedro appeared within the internal darkness.

"Hola," Strykor said to him. Pedro only nodded then disappeared.

Billy stood there, dazed and wondering. Had Pedro really survived? Certainly, a man like Strykor would have known better. If a cubited Pedro had shown up looking for residence at his makeshift motel, the Marine, with all of his training in covert operations, dealing with the worst kinds of people this world had to offer, would have detected something fishy. A cubited Pedro would have slipped up at some time during the past five months and Strykor would have put it down. But the two seemed too conspiratorial for that. They actually seemed chummy. Strykor and Pedro in collusion. Strykor and Pedro.

And then a thought sunk Billy's heart right down into his stomach. What if both Pedro and Strykor were not "alive?" What if both of them were actually…

"Watch out!" John yelled and pulled Billy to one side. Out from the dome's doorway stepped a man dressed as a guard. It wasn't Pedro and it didn't struggle with its body's functions as did the mass of cubits that now were fumbling up the first set of steps behind them.

"Parar!" demanded the guard whose name was Julio. He had a pistol and he waved it at the heads of all four trespassers. "Manos arriba!"

Cooper immediately raised her hands. Strykor, who had stashed the commando knife behind his back, raised only one. John lifted both of his arms and urged Billy to do the same. Half of the cubits behind them had completed their awkward ascent of the first platform and were now attempting the second flight of steps. One of them raised its arms.

Poor Julio never saw it coming. As Strykor slowly brought his knife out from behind him, gunfire rang out from within the dome's shadowy doorway. The bullet exited Julio's head just above the nose and he fell forward, tumbled down the steps and took out five cubits like a bowling ball crashing through pins. Smoke curled from the barrel of the pistol that Pedro had fired.

"Hurry!" Pedro said. "Before they catch us."

Billy walked straight into an interior wall of a secondary dome that was built inside the Caracol's outer dome. The parallel domes created a five-foot wide passageway that wrapped in a circle within the entire structure. Billy rubbed limestone dust from his nose and turned left, following John whose enormous body in the narrow passage prevented him from seeing that Pedro led Strykor and Cooper ahead of them. A quarter of the way around the passage, the shadows began to glow in the same blue hue that had been cast by the full moon across the entire city of Chichen Itza. Halfway around the inner dome, he stopped and stood and looked up just as John and Cooper were doing. The full moon, hidden behind sparse clouds, was centered within the dome's broken opening.

Pedro and Strykor had entered the core of the Caracol through an opening in the interior wall to his right. Except for the viewing platform from which ancient astronomers had peered into the skies through the windows at the top of the dome, the entire core was filled with a single spiraling, stone staircase. It curled down from the viewing platform forty feet above him, which, along with the dome, had been sheared away over time. Four of the dome's stargazing window openings still remained, one of which Pedro had been standing behind a few minutes ago. The winding staircase, during "regular" visiting hours, would have ended at the floor but tonight, a large hole had been opened and the stone steps disappeared into it.

The well, Billy thought. Lax had told him that this was where Alixel had raised her Djed, that this was where the Cubit had been kept by Samaal back when the Mayan civilization eradicated itself, that this was the secret well that housed the secret room in which Professor Cower had stolen the Book of the Djed.

It was like walking down the center of a giant snail. The experience was eerily similar to his descent into the well at Lee Mountain in Sedona, except that these steps and this stairwell were much wider and much older and seemed to have been constructed with much greater effort.

He was at least as far down the stairs as the Caracol's dome was high before he saw the red light; it dimly illuminated the end of the spiral steps. Pedro stood at the base of the stairwell and when Strykor joined him they walked together out of sight, as if right through some wall that Billy, from this distance, could not see. John was a few steps below and in front of him and his bald head shined with a mixture of the red glow emanating from the bottom of the staircase and the blue hue from the opening above. Billy looked up. The faces were small but recognizable: Port Aransas cubits. Six of them hovered over the opening and, to Billy, it looked as if they were considering the ramifications of an attempted descent. They were learning quickly, Billy thought. Stumbling down the Caracol's platform steps outside had served as lesson number one. Still, one dumb cubit stepped into the opening and toppled forward, bouncing ten feet down before coming to rest in a twisted heap. It twitched, its back arching upward, and tried to stand on limbs that were no longer useful but, instead, rolled down another six steps.

When Billy got to the bottom, the first thing he saw was the jaguar. Cooper yelped a hallow echo that seemed to spiral upward toward the cubit faces which were now very small. This statue was different from the two that had stood majestically outside of the Wayeb Chamber in the Great Hall. This jaguar stood menacingly on all four legs just inside a wide cut that had been made into the side of the well wall, its sneering face and saber-like teeth a purposeful greeting of dread and discontent for any and all trespassers. Red light blazed from two red jade eyes that had, at their centers, swirling twists of silver that reminded Billy of cubits' eyes, of the insanity that twisted inside their twisted minds, of the insanity that would surely snatch his own soul and store it here, in the underworld, if he continued staring into them. But Billy couldn't will himself to look away and it took John's tug on both shoulders to finally free him from the trance. As he and John joined Cooper in the sacred room Billy wondered if the statue had anything to do with all of the people he now saw carved into the limestone walls.

Circular in shape, the room had no corners, its forty-foot ceiling a dome of carved rock. Much of the room that was closest to him was illuminated in that same red jade glow provided by the jaguar's eyes, but farther back, the room was hidden in shadow. All around him and chiseled into the wall were dozens of Mayans, some in complete ceremonial outfits, some bare-naked. There were men and women and children and they rose from the flat floor all the way to the apex of the dome, a Michelangelo-like rendering of the people who existed a thousand years before the Italian Renaissance artist was born. The people in the wall were not happy. In fact, they looked absolutely miserable, scared and suffering. Billy looked over his shoulder at the jaguar statue and thought, again, about his own soul.

Billy, Cooper and John stood shoulder-to-shoulder. Strykor and Pedro stood together twenty feet in front of them in the center of the room, their faces turned away. When Billy stepped forward, John's meaty hand grabbed his shoulder.

"What are you doing here?" Billy asked Pedro.

"Doing what you and your fellow Daykeepers failed to do," Pedro said not turning around, his Spanish accent completely gone, his voice sounding nothing like the Pedro, Billy once knew. "We're keeping Evil in its place…for now."

"We?" Billy asked.

Strykor's head shifted from what he was looking at directly in front of him to the shadows in the back of the room to his left.

"Strykor and me and a whole lot of others," Pedro said, again talking as if someone else controlled his mouth.

"You son-of-a-bitch," John said to Strykor. "After all we've been through."

Strykor still said nothing and continued staring at the shadows.

"Don't blame him," Pedro said. "Actually, all of you should praise him. He helped me return the Cubit to its proper place."

At that moment, Pedro stepped to the right and turned. His eyes were red and swirled with silver just like those in the jaguar statue. Strykor, however, did not move, his attention seemingly frozen. Billy leaned forward.

Behind Strykor and beside Pedro was a stone pedestal that was nearly identical to the one in the Wayeb Chamber of the Great Hall of the Anasazi. It differed only by the Cubit that sat on top and the three glyphs on its front face. Engravings of two Creation Daggers were chiseled in opposing directions, their seven-inch blades dipping down at forty-five degree angles, the tips coming together in the center of the pedestal. Below the V-shape created by the daggers was a Djed—or at least it appeared that a Djed used to be there. Unlike the daggers which were carved in the same three-dimensional style as the Mayan occupants within the domed wall, the Djed seemed to be missing. The shape of the Djed remained, its center column and four crosses recessed into the stone, but it was empty, as if something had pried the Djed from it.

Pedro stroked the top of the Cubit's wooden surface. "It's the end of the world as we know it," he chimed. "And I feel fine." He laughed loudly, once, then added, "To bad Strykor doesn't feel the same. When I saw my cubit for the first time, I was also absolutely terrified."

From the direction that Strykor was staring stepped…Strykor. The folds in the face of the cubited Strykor were much more pronounced than were those of its primary. The cubit, apparently, hadn't had the time, or know-how, to carve its own artificial incisors and when it spoke, it lisped so badly it was almost impossible to decipher.

"Thha-pri-thh, Thh-trik-thor. Drop-th ta yor-th knee-th an' make-th thi-th eathy on aw uff uthh." The cubited Strykor stepped fully from the shadows carrying a broadsword with a blade that was as long as his leg.

The fight that ensued ended so fast that none of them could have reacted even if they had wanted to. The real Strykor stabbed hesitantly at the cubit with his commando knife. This provided his cubit an opportunity to chop off the thrusting arm, impale the attacker in the chest, and decapitate the Marine, all in swift, succinct motions. The body fell in three pieces to the limestone floor next to the Cubit's pedestal. The Strykor cubit then backed John off with the sword and wrenched Cooper from her grasp of his arm. She screamed as the cubit pulled her in tight and, using her as a shield, shuffled backward to the jaguar statue. Billy stood by himself a few feet in front of the Cubit; John was between him and Cooper.

"Billy...poor Billy," Pedro said. "You came all of this way based on the lies of an Indian and a nigger. What did you actually think you'd find here other than death?"

"I didn't think I'd find you." Billy's hand moved to his chin to scratch nothing that itched; he just wanted to get his hand closer to the dagger under his shirt.

"Life is a fuck in that way. You never know what you're going to get." Pedro grabbed the lid on the Cubit. "You know what's in here?"

"Evil, of course," Billy said, still nonplused by the way Pedro talked as if someone else controlled his mouth and vocal cords.

"Evil? How simplistic. Evil isn't in here. Evil is in you. Evil is in all of us. You think Alax was almighty pure and honest and good? You think Johnboy here is some kind of fucking angel? He's murdered more innocent lives than there are sinners forever frozen on these walls." He raised his arms and looked around the domed room. He picked up on Billy's confusion. "Ah. I see. They didn't tell you, did they? They didn't tell you the real reason they brought you here."

Billy ignored the deception. "How do you know Lax? Even in life, you'd never been to Sedona."

"What do you mean 'in life?' This is life. I can dance." He shuffled his feet and shook his scrawny butt. "I can laugh." He whaled one short guffaw that rebounded throughout the room. "I can even cook one hell of a Caribbean shrimp platter just like I did back at the Surf Side. Life is what you make it. Mine holds a more realistic future than the one you follow so blindly, one cooked up by the goody two-shoers of the world. What you fail to understand is that everything exists to feed on something else. Politicians feed on your fear of taxes. Pastors feed on your false sense of morality. Cancer feeds on the body. Maggots feed on death. Right down to the microscopic and macroscopic levels, this consumption is eternal. You're a scientist Billy Willy. Certainly you understand that something always has to be feeding on something else, or else how could life exist at all?"

"Who are you?" Billy said. "You might look like Pedro but you talk like…"

"I talk like one intelligent son-of-a-bitch that would never deceive you as your so-called friends have." Pedro stepped away from the Cubit and halved the distance between himself and Billy. "Go ahead. Ask him. Ask the abolitionist what his promise to Alax really was."

Billy turned toward John as Cooper grunted, "Don't listen to him," before her mouth was sealed by the Strykor cubit's hand.

"I brought you here so that you know where the Cubit must stay for an eternity," John said.

"And…" Pedro urged.

"And nothin'."

Pedro continued. "And that, as a Daykeeper, he'll have to remain a prisoner in here for the rest of his immortal life. Go on…tell him."

John looked at the red-glow-gray limestone floor. "Alax said that to keep the Cubit out of the likes of people such as this asshole, you'd have to remain close to the ruins."

"Not close. In the ruins."

John shook his head and looked up. "No. That's not right. Alax never stayed in the Great Hall. He was never a prisoner there."

"And neither did his sister. And see what happened. Those two shirked their responsibilities and let the Cubit get out. It's because of them all of this shit is even happening. So you see Billy: raising the Djed is nothing more than a prison sentence, one that continues for an eternity. Now who wants to live life like that, hmm? No loves, no adventures, no children. If you want to know where Evil comes from, I gotta believe you've found it." Pedro pointed at John. "He wants to take everything human away from you."

"No," Billy demanded. He stuck his hand under his shirt. "I don't believe you."

"I don't give a shit what you think you believe, but the truth remains. Johnboy brought you here so that the process of immortality could begin. You raise the Djed and come back here for an eternity." He pointed at the domed wall. "At least you'll have company. I think there might even be a couple of Daykeepers in here that pretty much lost their minds and the jaguar added them to his collection. So, shall we get started?"

"Started?"

"Processing you for immortality." Pedro looked at John who again looked down at his feet. "Hah!" Pedro laughed. "Son-of-a-mother-fucker. You really do suck, Johnnie. You know that, don't you? Why, you didn't even tell him that… You were too much of a coward to let him know about…"

Suddenly, the top edge of the Cubit began to glow red. The box looked as if it were trembling atop its pedestal. The lid, which had no hinges and no hasp, very slowly started to rise, the crimson from within growing brighter the farther it opened.

"Well I guess we'll have to put the induction of Billy into the land of immortality on hold for a bit," Pedro said. "Looks like another of our island friends is coming out for a visit." He offered an open hand toward the Cubit as if he were some kind of model on a TV game show. "Isn't it beautiful? Isn't it just like every movie and every novel and every fantasy adventure you ever saw or read? The Cubit, returned to its proper place, returned to where it will usher in the End of Days…the alpha and the omega. An oracle satisfied, one that has nothing to do with the Bible, or the Torah or the Qu'ran or any of the fucked up religions this world has suffered under. This oracle was set many ages before such foolish notions such as Man was ever conceived. It is the oracle of the beginning and the end, of a complete cycle in which hope and love have screwed up everything. The universe feeds upon itself—there is no hope in that. Everything that lives, also dies and is reborn again and again and again."

The lid on the Cubit stood straight up and crimson light streaked from inside, creating deeper shadows toward the back of the circular room, further detailing the stone-frozen Maya that were forever entrenched into the wall. The intensity of the Cubit's red light magnified the three-dimensional depth of the suffering faces that seemed to cry out for salvation.

Billy's attention was drawn to the figure etched into stone at the domed apex of the room. He wondered if that man had been a Daykeeper and had lost his mind while guarding the Cubit as Pedro had suggested. He wondered if he, too, would become part of the suffering mosaic. He wondered if Pedro and whoever it was manipulating him was telling the truth. Immortality meant living no life whatsoever.

It was Cooper's muffled scream that returned his attention to the Cubit and the two hands which flopped up from the inside, the fingers curling over the edge. Its shoulders, which inhumanly appeared before the head, were too wide for a comfortable emergence but that didn't matter. Its bones were like jelly and squished through the top of the Cubit with ease. When its head sprung from the shoulders, the cubit stood from the box, a bright red aura encircling its entire body, and crawled carefully down to the floor. It turned around and Billy gasped, his dagger becoming so hot that he had to pull it from the sheath.

"Your buddy, Crabman, used to be a great surfer," Pedro said to Billy. "But those days are over. He makes a much better Mu'bä don't you think? Hell, this is your fourth rebirth isn't it, Crabby? And the more we return the faster we learn."

"Da more we weturn da faster we wearn," repeated the Crabman cubit.

Billy waved the dagger underhanded, the curved blade pointed forward.

"The only thing you are going to do with that is give it to Crabman," Pedro said.

"I'll give it to him all right," Billy warned.

"We can make this easy or we can make it hard. Give him the dagger and then, won't you be so kind as to give him the key as well. It's in your backpack, right?"

"I don't know what you are talking about." Billy waved the dagger at him.

"Sure you do." He lifted a finger toward Strykor. "Hand them over or your girlfriend's head comes off."

"She's not my girlfriend. She's just a hitchhiker we picked up on our way over."

"Now who's a liar?" Pedro lifted his arm over his head. "One last chance."

That's when John reacted. He spun around with the dexterity of a man a hundred pounds lighter, crouched, slung one leg out, and smashed the back of the Strykor cubit's knee with the heel of his boot. The cubit only flinched but loosened its grip on Cooper enough for her to drop to the floor. John took off from a three-point stance like a massive lineman after the quarterback, snatched the dagger from Billy's hand, and pounced on Pedro. Billy ran to Cooper as John missed Pedro's kill spot in the back of the head, brought the dagger up and thrust downward for a second attempt. The Strykor cubit swatted Billy aside and grabbed Cooper by her curly hair, pulling her up and into his grasp once again. When Billy rolled to his knees, he saw John plant the dagger in Pedro as Crabman lifted the Cubit from its pedestal. Pedro screamed one last time, "Take her fucking head off," before succumbing to the blade.

Billy looked at Cooper whose head was between Strykor's hands. Her eyes told him what they both knew was about to happen. He yelled, "No!!!" then took one step in her direction and saw in his periphery the flying box of wood just before the Cubit knocked him cold.

He didn't know how long he'd been out but he suspected that the sun had risen somewhere above him; it was the pinpoint of light at the apex of the dome that made him think so. The one inch twinkle of white was the only source of illumination other than the shadowy fraction of light peeking in from the stairwell beyond the jaguar statue; the twinkle peered down at him from the eye of what Billy had believed was the stony, etched reverence to some past Daykeeper. The beam fell directly on the center of the Cubit's empty throne like a spotlight. John sat, leaning against the pedestal's two daggers and empty socket where a Djed had once been carved, his knees drawn up to his chin, his big forearms clasped together around his shins. His head rocked ever-so-slightly back and forth, lightly tapping the stone with his bald skull. He hummed a melody that was distantly familiar but was too low and broken in volume for Billy to identify. Halfway between his feet and John's distant stare was the Cubit. It sat upside down on the limestone floor. Next to it was Billy's backpack; it had been unzipped and the contents dumped. Lots of individual electronic parts and his notebook lay scattered in front of him. The Book of the Djed's key page, he assumed, was gone.

When Billy cleared his throat, John looked up. "I'm so sorry," John said. "I couldn't save you both. I had to choose. I had to choose you. It was a promise and I couldn't break my promise again."

"Where's Cooper?" Billy stood.

"They took her."

"They have the key, too."

"I'm sorry, Billy. It's just that…"

The bone-ash remnants of Pedro lay just beyond the dimmest part of the overhead spot of light. "Here," John said, uncurling from his fetal position to reveal the dagger clasped in his left hand. "You're going to need this."

The Cubit was at Billy's feet and when he leaned forward to grab the dagger, he understood what John meant. The Cubit had knocked him out; it had touched him. John looked from the box to Billy and then to the dagger. He nodded. "When?" Billy asked.

"I don't know. No one ever knows. That's what's so damned scary."

Hearing such a mountain of a man even say the word "scary" was scary. Billy returned the dagger to its sheath. He'd always known that its blade would one day become paramount to his salvation but he'd never really thought about coming face-to-face with his own cubit. Living vicariously through Lenny Bender's grotesque murder had been horrific enough. His imagination immediately began searching the dark recesses within the room.

"Not yet," John said. "Been sittin' here watchin' it."

"Can it open turned upside down?"

"I figure the Cubit can do any damn thing the Cubit wants."

"So we just sit around and wait?"

"Course not." John stood, pressing the dust from his shirt. "They took Cooper and we are going to get her back."

"How do you know she's still alive?"

John stepped around the Cubit and patted Billy's shoulder. "Because…you are."

"I don't understand."

"Get your stuff and let's get out of here. If we seal it in then maybe it'll be trapped here as well."

Billy looked at the Cubit and thought about what his Evil half might look like, imagined it poking its head out of the toppled box, wondered what manifestation of malfeasance an anti-Billy would master. He swept all of the electronics and his notebook back into his pack, slung it over his shoulders, and followed John past the jaguar statue; it's eyes were dead, the snarling face no longer as menacing as it had been a few hours ago.

The stairwell was drearily lit by the shadowed opening fifty feet above them. John led the way, never talking his eyes off the steps above and in front of him. Billy, on the other hand, kept staring back down, watching for red glowing clues that would signal the emergence of the dead from the Cubit.

"Be careful," John said. "Watch where you're going, not where you been. Falling from here might take your life and I really wouldn't want that." He stopped about thirty steps from the top and urged Billy to take the lead. "If something comes, I'll be ready."

When they exited the well, Billy couldn't help looking down once more. A red hue glowed at the bottom but he wasn't sure if its source was from the reignited eyes of the jaguar, the reincarnation of life from the Cubit, or just pure imagination.

John grunted beside him. "A little help."

John grasped a thick pole of wood and was using it to slide a slab of limestone that was a bit larger than a standard-sized door across the floor and over the stairwell opening. Billy grabbed a second pole and pried it under the slab. Together, they muscled the stone forward, covering only half of the entry into the Cubit's chamber. John led him to a second, equally-sized piece of limestone and they pushed it to where it interlocked with the first stone, completing the camouflage that had, with few exceptions, kept the Cubit secret for hundreds of years. Both dropped the poles when they heard Spanish chatter from beyond the dome. Apparently, a couple of guards had found last night's casualties.

John led Billy into the inner hallway created by the overlapping domes and moved clockwise, away from the footsteps that shuffled toward them in the same direction. They walked when the guards walked and stopped when the guards stopped and entered the center of the dome. Billy pressed his face up against the wall to hear them questioning each other just beyond its nine-inch thickness, then reenter the inner hallway to move, again, in their direction. John yanked his arm and shook his head at the rectangular doorway that opened onto the platform outside. Together, they ran.

Guards roamed near Mayan structures that were distant enough for Billy and John to go unnoticed. They quickly scuttled down the Caracol's three sets of steps and Billy saw what looked like blood but no body parts. Within another minute they were crouched under cover in the jungle bush just beyond a large pile of stones that Billy guessed had once been a part of the observatory. When he looked up, the face of the Wayeb that had been inlaid just below one dome window stared down at him, and Billy wondered how much the Wayeb truly knew about the future.

They retrieved the machetes they'd left in the jungle and razed a trail back to Strykor's motel in a different direction than they'd come. The bush was still wet and this made chopping messy. About thirty minutes into the trek, Billy finally asked. A lot of the things the Pedro cubit had said hadn't made much sense and his preoccupation with the information had nearly caused him to severe a chechen negro twice.

"That didn't sound like the Pedro I knew," Billy said, slashing at a knee-high plant that had triangular leaves with prickly edges."

"Most likely, it wasn't." John dodged a crop of bushes and urged Billy to do the same.

"How's that?"

"It's like glossolalia. You ever heard of that? Back in Georgia, it happened a lot, particularly in those backwoods churches. Most people called it 'speaking in tongues.' Words come out of the mouth that aren't their words but are thought of to be channeled through the greater God." John stopped and turned around. "In this sense, we are all just vessels that think we are in control of our own condition when actually we are just tools…a means to an end. What you heard from that guard in the well were words spoken by his real master."

"The Devil?" Billy's mouth worked faster than his mind had to reason.

"I wouldn't call it that. Devil's too simplistic. Devil's too Catholic. Whatever is out there that's caused the world to know Evil…that's really what we're talkin' about. And with cubits, you can always tell when it's happening."

"How?"

John turned back toward the jungle and resumed slashing at plants that were taller than his waist. Up ahead, a small building sat in a ten-foot wide clearing. "Their eyes," he said. "They turn all red and swirly-looking. That's when their master is in control."

"How do you know this?"

"Alax…and experience."

"He never told me such things."

"I suspect Alax never told you lots of things. How long did he know you?"

"A day or two."

"A lifetime of knowledge in a day or two…unlikely, particularly since we both know how old he was."

"So my destiny is to become immortal and sit in that god-awful secret chamber with all of those god-awful people chiseled into the walls just so the Cubit doesn't get out and screw up the world more than it already has?"

They'd made it to the clearing and the smell from Strykor's shithouse blew into their faces as a gentle breeze changed direction. The path to the motel cottages wound through the jungle ahead of them. John stopped once again.

"I'd say that your destiny, right now, is to save your girlfriend. What you really gotta learn, Billy, is to focus on things you can control. Concentrate too much on the end and you'll lose the now, and then your destiny will certainly take a turn for the worst."

"How do I save her when I don't even know where she is?"

"I think I know. It's just a hunch but a good one. The sacred cenote near Ikil is infamous for Saturday night partying. It's a closed invitation kind of thing…a rave kind of deal. They got lots of drugs—some really bad ones. Los Zetas—a paramilitary group that are enforcers for the Gulf Cartel—hang out there to deal heroin. Some say they even make sacrifices to the cenote but that may be more scare tactic than reality."

"Sounds like the perfect place for cubits to hang out."

"Yes. And a perfect place to recruit them."

Billy looked at his machete's fat blade. "Not much use against a force like that," he said. "Got any machine guns or tanks or missiles?"

"Faith," John said. "You gotta have faith." Then he stepped into the shithouse and closed the door.

In her mouth was a foul-smelling rag that, for all she knew, could have been an ass wipe for any one of the several dozen men and women that she heard talking and screaming and laughing around her. She kept her eyes closed and tried to refrain from gagging.

"When do we get to do her?" The voice was Mr. Bean Breath from the museum and he was much too close to her.

"Keep it in your pants," another voice said that she also recognized.

"Anything happens to her before I say, and I'll cut it and your floppy head right off."

Rocks skittered close by. Deep breaths that were distant moved closer to her face. A hand swept through the curls on her forehead and wiped away the cool moisture. "Cooper. Wake up, Cooper."

She sat against what her spine thought was a tree. Her arms were bound behind her. It wasn't raining but she could smell mist. She continued her act though the stinky cloth in her mouth was nearly unbearable. *The voice...who was that?*

"They're coming for you, Cooper. Fret not."

Who in the hell was that?

"Not as luxuriously sexy as Marcy, but you make a fine X'Tabay nonetheless."

The Serpent! That's exactly who knelt in front of her. She heard his voice fade and more rocks skitter so she opened one eye just a fraction of a slit. Her head leaned too far forward for her to see anything more than two legs below the knees walk away from her. A second set of legs moved closer and she immediately smelled the beans. "Sexy," the rapist said then licked her forehead sweat. "And tasty."

For another hour, she continued acting as if she was unconscious when, suddenly, music started playing. Its volume went from low to loud as the beat turned furious. The music was American heavy metal that sounded as if it was being covered by Mexican artists. It was an odd mixture, listening to *Sweet Child O' Mine* being sung by a pseudo Axl Rose Mexican imitator. The guitar licks were spot on but the voice...it just didn't quite work.

When someone screamed right in front of her, she finally opened her eyes and lulled her head back against the moist, round root of a ceiba tree. She guessed that it was around noon but dense clouds masked the sun's true direction. Under the gray light she watched what she thought was some kind of party rave. She sat bound in a jungle clearing thirty feet from a small fire around which four men gyrated to the Mexican Rose. All four of them wore green uniforms that looked like those she'd seen the guards wearing at the autopista toll stops. Pistols were strapped to their waists on gun belts and all of them waved long sticks of charred meat above their heads. One of the men fired his automatic rifle into the air every time Mexico Rose screamed "Sweet Child O' Mine."

To the left and farther away from the fire were dozens of people, stamping the dirt and twisting their bodies to the hidden source of music. Few of them had any rhythm; in fact, it looked almost as if none of them had any control of their muscles whatsoever. Some fell to the hard dirt and others fell over those that had just fallen. They laughed and screamed and cried and yelled. Two men were kissing at one point during the song, then suddenly they were beating the shit out of each other as *Sweet Child* ended and a non-AC/DC version of *Dirty Deeds Done Dirt Cheap* began.

To her right and much farther away, she saw several people gathered around what looked like a sinkhole, or *cenote* as they called it in Mexico. From where she sat, she could barely see the cenote's far side limestone wall as it curved raggedly inward, about fifty feet in diameter, toward the numerous onlookers who gathered around a platform that had been built at the forward perimeter. In front of and over the heads of the onlookers, an axe appeared that quickly swooped down and out of sight. The group chanted as a headless body was thrown into the cenote. The head was then lifted up by the hair, the chant became louder, and the head was thrown into the cenote as well.

Cooper looked down when one of the chanters saw her looking at him. She closed her eyes but it was too late. A minute later, he was beside her.

"You like what you see?" Cooper remained motionless. "Come on, love. I know you saw it." A hand grabbed her chin and gently lifted her head. "Don't worry, Cooper. We're not going to throw you in…at least, I'm not going to throw you in." She opened her eyes. The man was rather skinny but athletic at the same time, Cooper thought—something like an endurance athlete—a distance runner, perhaps. His black hair was about as straight as any she'd ever seen; it was trimmed around his forehead in a half-moon from temple to temple; its length stopped at the earlobes. His eyes were pure gray. Not one speck of any other color occupied any part of the irises which only made the pupils look much, much darker.

"Allow me to introduce myself. I'm Evan Santinal and I'm here to protect you." He reached forward and loosened the knot on the smelly twist of cloth in her mouth. Immediately, she spit it out. "Here." Against her lips, he tilted a plastic bottle filled with purple liquid; the word *Gatorade* occupied the center of a label that, besides that one word, was inundated with Spanish. "If the taste is anything like the smell, this will seem like god-juice." Cooper drank half of the contents in one gulp; the man named Evan had to pull it away from her. She coughed. "Manuel wants to do some very unheard-of things. I think he's a bit cookoo—well, I know he was a bit cookoo in real life. The shit he used to do to women…Sad." Evan took the smelly rag from her face and threw it away as if it were a disease. "What do you think of him? Do you want me to kill him?"

Cooper's tongue still played with threads from the shit smelling mouth rag. She spit but the thread only launched as far as her cheek. Evan wiped it away. "He's already dead," she said.

Evan smiled. "Aren't we all?" He turned his attention to the gathering by the cenote. Manuel emerged with an axe from the center of inhumanity. His head still flopped to one side, bobbing up and down on his right shoulder as he strutted toward them. "You're a psychologist. What's your diagnosis of such a bumbling fool?"

Cooper gasped and as soon as she did, she regretted it. It seemed that this reaction was exactly what Evan wanted.

"Yeah. We know," Evan said. "We know everything." He smiled.

"Fuck you," Cooper squawked, her throat unable to enforce the vocal strength that her mind demanded.

"Fuck seems to be the pivotal word here, doesn't it?" Manuel walked up to her, holding the bloody axe like a trophy. "What do you think Manuel?" Evan said to the grungy Mexican who smelled less like beans and a lot more like the rag that had been in her mouth.

"Fuck is good," he moaned, apparently excited by the mere mention of the word.

"Billy's gonna make you wish you never existed," Cooper grumbled.

Evan turned toward Manuel and yanked the axe from the cubit's grasp. He held it awkwardly, as if he'd never held an axe before. "Bring it on," he said, his skinny face puckering into an expression of fortitude that was so much a lie Cooper almost laughed. He planted the blade into the tree root well above Cooper's head. "In fact, if he doesn't show his coward ass and 'make me wish I never existed,' Manuel will make a permanent part of you between his legs."

She looked at Manuel who grinned with a sour looking set of teeth that were set at an angle in his lolling face. Her memory of his aggression made the skin crawl up the back of her neck. "And if I tell you to kill that ugly bastard, then what?"

Evan knelt in front of her and gently grabbed one of her strawberry curls. "You really have no idea what's happening here do you? I can only hold these monsters off for so long. I take one out and it just comes back to life. What I really need is the dagger. With it, I can put all of these creatures in hell for good and you'll never have to worry about any of them fucking you or your boyfriend. I really mean that…from the bottom of my heart."

"You're not one of them," Cooper said, jerking her head away from his touch.

"Correct. Like I said, I'm here to protect you." Manuel suddenly reached forward and touched the top of her head. Evan punched away the forearm. "Not now, you stupid ignoramus." He returned his attention to Cooper and smiled. "But I'm not gonna be able to for much longer. They are more like zombies than they are given credit. Living flesh absolutely drives their desires banananonkers. I hope your boyfriend shows himself pretty soon."

"And if he does show?"

Evan bent closer for a whisper. "Then I'll take the dagger and get rid of Manuel for you. You'll never have to worry about him again… except, maybe, inside your nightmares, but I can't do a damn thing about that."

She nodded in the direction of the man with the flip of blonde-white hair who was dancing with a couple of degenerate cubited women. "And what about the Serpent? I'll bet he's the one that tied me up like this. He's got some kind of fetish for women and ceiba trees. Will you take care of him as well?"

"No can do." Evan looked over his shoulder. "He's the boss man. He's the one that set you up. He's the one that's been setting all of this up. If it wasn't for him, none of you would even be here and I wouldn't have a job. He wants Billy…and not just his dagger."

"Why would he want Billy?"

"You're a smart girl. You can figure it out, can't you?"

Cooper remembered their encounter in the Great Hall. "He took the Book."

Evan nodded.

"He already knows the fourth location."

Evan nodded.

"So why doesn't he just show up and raise the Djed himself?"

Evan shrugged.

"And why does he need the key? I saw that Crabman thing take it from Billy's backpack. The key has already revealed all he needs to know." She watched the Serpent walk toward her."

"Perplexing isn't it. I wish I could tell you. I wish I knew. Maybe you should ask him." Evan stood.

"I see she's awake," the Serpent said. "Hello delicious."

Cooper scowled.

"I mean you really do look delicious sitting there all tied up to the ceiba tree. Tantalizing, don't you think?" Manuel hungrily agreed. Evan simply nodded and smiled. "Marcy was tastier, but you'll do."

"Shove it up your ass," Cooper growled.

"Temper…temper. Anger makes the meat sour."

"Who the hell are you anyway?"

"The boss man. Like Evan said."

"You've got everything you need. Why don't you just leave us alone?"

"But I don't have everything. If I had everything, you would be dead."

"So my death is important for raising the Djed?"

"You give yourself too much credit. You're nothing but a pawn—a goddamned, no good poonta. You were used by Cower. You were used by Billy. Now I'm using you. That's really the only purpose you serve. It's your only value in life. Evan may say he's going to protect you, but we both know that's a lie. He's a really good liar." Evan, again, nodded.

"If he's a liar then you aren't the boss man," Cooper said. "You must be a pawn, too. We have a lot in common."

The Serpent slapped her. "You tie your tongue or Manuel will be the very least of your worries." He turned away from her and called over one of the men dressed like a soldier. "Give her a taste," he said. "The experience will set her straight."

The soldier, whose forearm had the injection point tracks of a junkie, presented a hypodermic needle and knelt beside her.

"Feed her Djed," the Serpent ordered.

The soldier reached around the root of the tree, plunged the needle into one of Cooper's rattlesnake scars and emptied the amber fluid into the djed tattoo. The effect was almost immediate.

"How do you like the taste of heroin?" The Serpent asked. "It is the elixir of life."

John's faith would have to be strong enough for both of them. The man was big. The man was strong. The man was a Marine, schooled in tactics that Billy had only seen portrayed in the movies where actors playing Rangers and Seals and Green Berets almost always reminded their fellow soldiers—and the theatre's audience—that the trained mind was more powerful than any arsenal of weapons. Still, it was hard to see how two men with no firepower could rescue a woman held hostage by dozens of trained killers. Billy's faith eroded even further when he stepped from the shithouse path to the cottage clearing to find that the Cavalier was gone.

"It's close enough to walk," John said when he saw Billy's concern. "It'll take a couple of hours but I wasn't going to suggest the car anyway."

"It's not that," Billy said. "It's just that…"

"Sentimental value." John walked over and stood in the spot where the car had been parked. "A concept that's of absolutely no use to us right now."

Billy shrugged. He couldn't help his emotions. The car had been such a part of his life for over five months, even if it had just sat in the parking lot outside his Sedona apartment. Of course, it wasn't the physical construct of the car that had mattered most; it was the value association to lost friends and a lost life. Port Aransas had been the last place he'd ever expected to live. He'd built a business from scratch and had connected with nature in ways that most people would consider fairytale. But more than that, the car represented freedom: freedom to have chosen Port Aransas in the first place; freedom to have had the courage to drop out of college and decimate his parents' hopes for him; freedom to start a new life, to accept the desire for another person into his soul, to ride the waves of Mother Nature. The car represented the freedom to flee when these freedoms were taken from him. The car represented freedom from *this* God-forsaken place.

"Wait," John said. "What's this?"

Billy walked over to where John was pointing. A little yellow hand stuck up from the ground. Billy knelt and scooped away the dirt around SpongeBob's smiling face. He plucked the toy from its burial prison and blew dust from its yellow, sponge body. He wanted to hug the toy right then and there but thought the timing was a bit inappropriate. John smiled, perhaps even expecting a joyous embrace, then waved for Billy to follow him into Strykor's cottage.

The interior of the cottage was a complete mess. It wasn't destroyed like his apartment had been; it was simply a pigsty and it smelled like one, too.

John walked to a waist high refrigerator that was brown dirty and littered with magnets promoting all things military, from the USMC logo and several bulldogs, to antique pinup girl magnets—the kind that might have been distributed during the World Wars though Billy didn't think refrigerators were very popular back then. "We'll need to eat and reenergize before we tackle the impossible."

"You kind of sound like Lax…eh, Alax."

"Naw. I think he got that idea from me." He opened the refrigerator and pulled out a couple of Mason jars filled with liquid slurry surrounding what were likely indigenous meat chunks. "Not sure what it is but if he can eat it, so can we." To his armload he added a milk jug that was hand-labeled *CLEEN* and a block of yellow cheese that thankfully looked as if it had been purchased rather than handmade. "Grab the tortillas and let's go start us a fire." He pointed to the round metal table that was cluttered with tools and towels and bowls and cups and a bag of ten-inch tortillas.

"You seem to know Alax quite well," Billy said. Next to the tortillas was a soldering iron and a circuit board that was about the size of a pack of cigarettes. He looked at the board curiously before taking it and the tortillas, then followed John outside. "Did you guys serve in a war together or something?"

"We both served, but not together." John placed the food and jug on one empty tree stump then walked to the back of the cottage and brought out an armful of wood which he dropped onto the black ashes inside the fire pit.

Billy set the tortillas on the same stump, removed the backpack from his shoulders, dropped the circuit board and SpongeBob inside, and went to grab a second armful of wood. "You handle a Creation Dagger pretty well," he said from the back of the cottage.

"Is that what you call them things?"

Billy added his wood to the pit. "John. I'm not that stupid. You saw me use it on that thing from the museum and you never said a word. You asked for it in the Chichen well as if it was yours. You knew exactly how to use it."

"Yeah…well. I used to have one of 'em." He sat on one of the stumps then reached down to where a notch had been carved into the wood. From it, he plucked a small tin with the rusty words *Altoids* printed on it. He opened it and grabbed one of the matchsticks inside, then struck it against one of the limestone rocks surrounding the pit and threw it onto the wood pile.

"What happened to it?"

"Cower."

Billy sat, hard, onto a tree stump.

"I see you know the name. Son-of-a-bitch tricked me and I had always thought that was impossible. Sucker like that humbles a person."

"He took it from you? How could anyone take anything from you?"

"Don't remind me." The fire grew to a gentle blaze. "Throw me that cheese and a tortilla will ya?" Billy flipped him the cheese but took out two tortillas from the bag before passing them. "Cubits ain't the only twisted shits in the world—don't you ever forget it." He broke off a chunk of cheese, waved it at Billy's face and slapped it into Billy's open hand. He saw the burnt star scar in the palm but didn't say anything about it. "The really bad thing was that the ass was so damned nice and honest-like. I mean, he really could have sold ice to Lucifer. Where I come from, you don't come off trustworthy then betray it. With people like that, even *you* can't save this world from itself."

The fire grew hot enough to cook in; Billy handed John the jars of mystery meat and two of the charred sticks they'd used to eat snake the night before. John wrapped a big chunk of cheese with one tortilla and shoved the whole thing into his mouth. He peered at Billy from the corner of one eye as if he knew what was about to asked. While turning the cap on the Mason jar he said, "Alax told me. In fact, the promise I made to him did include protecting you, but that wasn't the big promise." He sniffed the contents of the jar and shrugged, then fished out a couple of meat cubes and stuck them on his stick. He did the same thing with Billy's stick and set the jar on the ground. "Whoever was behind Pedro's eyes was correct in one way. 'Processing you for immortality,' as he so gracefully put it, took one giant step this morning."

Juice ran down Billy's stick as he stared at John who would not look at him. "I'm to raise the Djed." Billy said.

"Mmm hmmm. Won't do you no good unless…" He lowered his stick into the fire. "You gotta meet and beat that which no man ever wants to confront." As he grabbed Billy's hand and urged it and the stick toward the fire, he stared hard into Billy's eyes. "My promise was for you to touch the Cubit. You have to confront your worst fears, those which make up the darkest part of your very soul. You have to face your own cubit and *You* have to kill it."

The memory of Billy's vision from Alax's anteroom came thundering back into his head. *Bad Billy* had been waiting for him, beyond the doorway, in the darkness. He shivered at the thought of being eaten alive like Lenny Bender had been, like Pedro had been—and Steph…the flesh had been hanging from her lips…she'd wanted a kiss… and that had taken him over the edge. "I don't think…" he mumbled. "How can I possibly…"

"You have no choice any longer."

Billy dropped his skewer, his fear quickly transforming into anger as he gazed into the fire. "You! You took me there. It's all your fault. You motherfucker!" Billy's fist flew and connected with John's jaw with such force that the Marine fell off his stump; his stick of meat skittered across the ground. Billy looked at his hand as if it didn't belong at the end of his arm.

John pushed himself to a sitting position. "I guess I deserved that. But you gotta remember. At least we sealed it in there and it doesn't have any place to hide. You'll have the upper hand."

"I don't want the upper hand. I don't want any of this."

"Christ, Billy!" John stood and for a moment Billy thought he was going to return the punch. "Grow up and accept it. You think your own cubit is bad…wait 'til we get to the party tonight. At least cubits aren't among the living. What you should really be afraid of is real humans, especially these."

Billy's stick had caught fire. The meat cubes on it had burned so badly that the black chunks fell into the flames. He tossed the stick aside. John walked around the fire, picked up the stick he'd thrown when Billy punched him and snatched the jug of water. He washed the dirt from his meat cubes, sat back down, and resumed cooking them. "I get the feeling that Alax never had the chance to tell you how important it is that you don't give up."

Billy stared into the fire, unresponsive and pouty.

"Answer me one question. Why aren't you dead?"

Billy was tempted to look at him, but his concentration on the flames had promoted a vision of Cooper Reyes with flesh hanging from her lips.

"He could have killed you in Texas."

Cooper's mouth sucked up the hanging flesh and Billy could almost hear the slurping-sucking noise it made.

"He could have killed you in Arizona."

Cooper's mouth was smeared with the blood from her own sinew.

"All the way through Mexico, he could have sent any dozen men who would have killed you for a couple a hundred pesos."

Cooper puckered her gruesome lips.

"In Mérida. In the museum. In Chich. In the well."

Cooper wanted a kiss.

"BILLY!"

Billy shook away the fiery trance.

"Why aren't you dead?"

Billy turned to him then. John peered sternly, like a professor waiting for an answer before resuming his lecture.

"I had the Book."

"Gone."

"I had the key."

"Gone."

"I still have the dagger."

"You didn't in the well, remember? You gave it to me, which means you were defenseless, without the key and without the Book. Strykor's cubit could have easily taken Cooper out then you."

"But he didn't kill either one of us."

John pulled the stick from the fire and gave it to Billy, who wrapped a tortilla around one hot chunk and pulled it from the stick. He didn't eat it; he just held it for a moment as he tried to understand. "They need the Book and the key and the dagger to raise the Djed," Billy said, thinking out loud, again turning toward the dancing orange flames. "The Djed provides immortality. But a cubit is already immortal in the sense that it cannot die. Unless you stab it with the dagger. So if a cubit gets a hold of the Djed…" He looked at John, astonished that he knew the answer. "The dagger cannot kill it."

John nodded.

"They didn't kill Cooper because they wanted the dagger. They want me to bring them the dagger."

"They want *you* to bring *you*."

"A trap?"

John ate his meat chunk and chased it with a piece of cheese.

"You're getting warmer."

"Dammit! Just tell me. Okay? I have a destiny…fine. I'm supposed to be some kind of Daykeeper…fine. I live for an eternity, telling stories or I live in a dark-domed well with a bunch of creepy stone carvings and a pet rock jaguar…whatever. How I'm supposed to save the world is irrelevant since you aren't going to or can't tell me anyway. But all of this is mute if they…if he…" Billy's eyebrows lifted. "Deer-hat man? The Serpent?"

"Of course. But that doesn't answer the question."

"Was it the Serpent who was staring at me through Pedro's eyes?"

"No. Someone much more powerful. The cubit you call the Serpent is only a self-serving pawn, just like the rest of the cubits."

"Who?"

"Not totally sure but he wants you alive…for now."

And then the answer to the riddle came to him; it simply popped into his head as if it had been trapped in a bubble that had just burst. "I'm the only one that can become a Daykeeper. I'm the only one that can raise the Djed. The recipe includes the Book, the key, the dagger and me!"

"Hallelujah!" John bellowed at the clouds above him. "Now you've got the *who* and the *with what* now all you need is the *when, where,* and *how.*"

"Jesus…we're not going to spend the whole afternoon playing twenty more thousand questions are we?"

"We could and I probably would if I knew *all* the answers. I like playing these intellectual games with you. Stimulating."

Billy huffed. "I think I know the *when* and I have a clue as to the *where* since the Great Hall showed it to me."

"When?"

"December twenty-one."

"And what grand piece of reasoning tells you that?"

"The end of the Mayan cycle. The winter solstice. The turn back toward the living. And, it begins the five-day cycle of the Wayeb when the underworld is given a chance to enter into our own."

"Impressive! You know a lot more than I gave you credit for."

Billy jammed his entire wad of tortilla-wrapped food into his mouth and immediately grimaced. "What the hell is that?"

"Iguana, I suspect. Not Strykor's best effort."

And that's when Billy, for the first time, saw real sorrow attack the big man's expressive face. No doubt he was thinking about his friend. Billy actually thought he saw a tear on the far side of John's face but he scratched that cheek so fast, Billy wasn't sure. He slapped John on the back as he chewed then stooped to his right to grab his backpack. "It's not very good but I'm starving," Billy said. "The cheese helps considerably. I wouldn't mind another piece."

While John assembled more food for the fire, Billy reached into his pack and pulled out his notebook. "The *where*," he said while flipping through the pages. He folded the notebook back along its metal spiral spine and presented the page where he'd sketched the image he'd seen in the Book, noting the fourth location. John wiped iguana juice from his hands and traded the notebook for the cooking stick that now held two more pieces of meat and what looked like small onions. Billy stuck it in the fire. "Recognize it?"

"You weren't an art student, I take it."

"Funny man." Billy smirked. "Robotics, actually. I can do some pretty fine mechanical drafts but that necessitates a table, square and a few other drawing utensils. As for freehand. Well, there you go."

John studied the sketch until the food was cooked. He turned the notebook upside down and sideways several times, said, "Hmm" at least twice, then swapped the notebook for the fresh tortilla wrap Billy had made for him.

"Anything?"

"Yeah," John said, studying his tortilla. "That looks like El Castillo in Tulum…at least part of it does. Don't know what that chicken scratch to the right of it is supposed to be." He took a bite. "Hey. The onion sure changes the flavor."

"You sure?"

"About the onion?"

Billy scowled.

"Yeah, yeah…I know." He chuckled. "Not a hundred percent. If that is El Castillo, it is pictured from an angle that looks in from the ocean."

"The Serpent saw it. He must also know."

"Most likely." John finished his food and swilled from the water jug as Billy took his first bite. "You keep calling him the Serpent. Why is that?"

"It seemed more fitting than Deere-hat man."

John's eyes rolled. "I don't think I want to know. But I think you should know."

"What? More revelations you've been holding back from me?"

"Daykeepers are supposed to figure these things out for themselves."

"I will as soon as you tell me."

"Why Billy. The answer, like every other answer so far, has been staring you right in the face ever since you started to believe. You need to open up your mind much more in the future." He handed Billy the water jug. "Here. You better clear your throat so you don't choke."

Billy drank water even though he hadn't eaten anything in several minutes.

"He set up that entire ordeal in Texas. He used Albert Stine who used Chancey Lett who used Mitchell Bone. The excavation of the beach was solely for the purpose of recovering the dagger which you now possess. And all of the other pieces just fell into place for him after almost two hundred years."

"Who?"

"Someone who knew Alax's sister quite well."

"Who, dammit!"

"Captain Jean Lafitte, of course."

Evan didn't think Mr. Manson gave him as much credit as he deserved. Dealing with all of these ignorant peons, whether dead or alive, took all of the willpower one man could muster. He would have much rather been skydiving or scuba diving or splicing and dicing extreme footage on his gigantic Mac system back in Mérida—secluded, by himself, the only challenges being those that his own mind and imagination placed in front of him. He so hated people: all of them. He was introverted to the max and this made dealing with morons so much less pleasant. He had zilch people skills and zilch patience. Even the avatars in World of Warcraft had more spine than these simple-minded freaks.

But he had to maintain the illusion. The pirate had to continue to believe that he was in control of the entire situation. The pirate was the boss and what he said was the word. Unfortunately for Evan, following the commands of a two-hundred-year-old pirate was one of the most unpleasant chores he'd ever been given. Every time the inverted ponytail bastard returned to the peninsula, Evan's imagined future utopia seemed to slip farther away.

The pirate's reasoning was all screwed up. Evan didn't like the way that he'd used Billy's friend, Marcy. He should have simply sent his minions in to take what he wanted. These stupid mind games drove Evan crazy but the pirate seemed to get off on them. He'd done the same with Chancey Lett and Albert Stine and who knows how many other people in the past two centuries. Now he was working on Cooper. Was it really necessary to pump her with heroin? Was it really necessary to put her through the hell of watching all of these addicts rave and rant and revel in their perceived almighty drug lord power trips? There had to be an easier way. But then, again, Evan wasn't one of them. He was much smarter. He would bide his time and get his just reward. Soon, he would be the boss and if the pirate was lucky enough to live that long, Evan would introduce him to Davey Jones' Locker, whether Mr. Manson agreed to the deed or not.

"Evan. I said get your ass over here!" Lafitte stood near an unmarked box truck which had pulled in off the dirt road a few minutes ago. He'd just opened the rear doors. "Rapido!"

Evan took one more look at Cooper. The effects of the heroin were evident. Her open eyes were glassy, she smiled a goofy grin, and her head lolled to one side, kind of like the way Manuel's head was now permanently attached. Evan giggled short and sweet, not because of Cooper's situation but because of Manuel's. He absolutely hated that smelly-assed cubit and couldn't wait to execute Manson's orders to erase the problem; its failure at the museum was, after all, the entire reason why he was standing here in the middle of the jungle taking orders from a power-tripping dead pirate. He casually walked to where Lafitte stood. Without warning, Lafitte hauled off and slapped him.

"Thirty cases of beer! Thirty!" he wailed. "Not twenty-nine. Not thirty-one. The Zetas are precise in what they desire." Lafitte looked behind the stacked boxes that were labeled *Coors Light*. "How many kegs?" he asked the truck driver. The short, chubby Latino looked at his manifest.

"Ocho," he said and flinched as if Lafitte was going to slap him next.

Lafitte glared at Evan who was rubbing the hand print on the side of his face. "At least you got that right. You really make me wish I'd a saved Pedro. He was much more efficient and unquestionably loyal."

"But he's dead now isn't he?" Evan couldn't help it. Perhaps he was a glutton for punishment. Lafitte swung at him again but Evan dodged the blow.

"Get this shit off the truck and into place," Lafitte ordered. "And would somebody please turn that fucking music off? They'll be here shortly and they like their own tunes."

Tonight's rave at the sacred cenote was a cover for the drug deal that was about to go down. Everyone knew it, the local policia, the Mexican gobierno, the citizens of Ikil. But it really didn't matter. These were Los Zetas and they'd be well packed. They'd bring enough firepower to knock out a platoon if need be. Besides, many of the recipients of tonight's exchange would be local, state and government officials, all non-cubited non-law abiding citizens of the country's corrupted underbelly. Money was to be made and power was to be dealt during a moiré of fanatic partying by both the living and the dead. And that's exactly how Lafitte liked to play it. The goal to raise the Djed was important to him since it would ensure his ever-lasting menace to the world, but it was not a priority. He had until December twenty-one and he'd use every last day, leaving absolutely no room for error. Above all else, Evan hated Lafitte's patience the most. It unnerved him. Evan wanted to get shit done and move on. If Lafitte would only play it like World of Warcraft. You have a goal which garners you power and you go about collecting all the pieces necessary to attain that goal. If it had been Evan, the game would have been solidly in his hands a year ago. Cower had possessed most of what they'd needed—But no! Lafitte had to play his stupid fucking mind games and the key had gotten separated, and the Kansas woman had disappeared with the Book, and Albert had disappeared with the dagger and...

"Shit!" Evan yelled. Lafitte stood behind him.

"If you can't do such simple tasks, I'll find someone who can.

Strykor looks like a willing and able subject."

"He's an idiot," Evan said. "He just came out of the box this morning. He can't even tie his own shoelaces."

"Then perhaps Billy, when he shows up."

"He's not gonna help you do anything except stick a dagger into the back of your head."

"Not that Billy, dumb ass…the one in the well." Lafitte laughed then, mostly because of the expression on Evan's face. "He'll make a wonderful concierge, don't you think? Even as a cubit he'll be much smarter than you. You should know by now that I've only kept you alive because of your knowledge concerning 2012. I suspect Billy knows as much if not more. And, given time, so will his cubit. Then I'll have the pleasure of watching you replaced. Until then, please try not to screw anything else up?" Lafitte whistled and two of the men dressed in military uniforms came over to the truck to help unload it.

It was so hard for Evan: taking this kind of abuse and receiving no credit. Manson would surely see his sacrifices. Manson would surely reward him. But he'd have to wait and patience was not his greatest virtue.

It really was impossible to get his head wrapped around it all. Ice in the spine…that's what it felt like: a creepy, freezing, alien tiptoe up his vertebrae. His brain looped through theatrical tones that had tied current circumstance to his meager mortal memories.

You are the one, Neo.

Mos Eisley Spaceport. You'll never find a more wretched hive of scum and villainy.

You gonna draw them pistols or whistle Dixie?

I'm sorry, Dave. I'm afraid I can't do that.

How could he be the one if he was dead?

He had one dagger, one machete and one Marine. How in God's name was he going to save Cooper and save his ass and save the world?

He sat on the floor of the cottage formerly rented by Pedro's cubit, his backpack at his feet, the notebook flipped open to the sketch he'd made of the fourth location…of what John had identified as El Castillo.

John said that they would be leaving in a couple of hours which would allow them enough time to walk to the sacred cenote and arrive after nightfall. In the meantime, rest was priority one.

Better said than done.

SpongeBob's yellow hand poked out from between the pack's zippered pocket. He lifted the pack's flap and SpongeBob's big smile and blue eyes caused him to grin and grimace in rapid succession. He dropped the flap. Lifted the flap. Saw the happy face. Dropped the flap. It was a goofy attempt to try and humor himself but it was working. Billy finally smiled and pulled the toy out.

"What would SpongeBob do?" he asked it. "Something totally off the wall, no doubt. Something that made no sense whatsoever. Something that would have nothing to do with responsibility." He moved SpongeBob's hand as if in salute against its sponge head.

"Aye, captain," he mimicked the toy's voice. "You think any Mexicans have ever seen a walking sponge before?"

He moved the toy back and forth across the floor, imitating a walk. "How could they Spongy?" he said in his own voice. "They're too busy getting stoned and killing innocent Daykeepers."

He set the toy down and pulled the circuit board from his backpack. He'd been curious as to why a recluse in the middle of the jungle would have such a thing but, until now, hadn't had the chance to give it much thought. He set the circuit board on the floor beside SpongeBob and said, "Hey Sponge. Meet your new partner in crime." He tried to think of a superhero kind of name for the circuit board and drew it closer to read the manufacturer's stamp on the top edge. *Zogg's Boards*, it read. Billy blinked then turned the board over in his hand, examining the soldered components. He'd always purchased his electronic components via mail order from a place called *Zogg's*. It was a small Mom and Pop shop outside of Cambridge with which he'd stayed in contact once he'd moved to the island. The irony of the name and its association to the infamous surfboard wax, plus the always reliable and inexpensive components had made him a permanent customer.

And then he remembered that the computers had been removed from his VW. Apparently, they were somewhere in Strykor's cottage. He picked up SpongeBob, searching its big blue eyes for inspiration. He examined the circuit board, dumped out the rest of the electronic parts from the backpack, thought about his computer surveillance equipment, wondered if it had been salvaged. His mind whirled, the icy infiltration that had grabbed his spine now melting. An idea was emerging. It might not be much but…

"Nautical nonsense, my ass," he said to the toy. "You're a genius!"

She was no longer bound but that really didn't matter. Heroin controlled her. She tried standing only once but the euphoric buzz was too much. She fell back against the ceiba root and slid to the ground. The tree was her only salvation, now. Its thick trunk and broad leafy canopy above provided a false sense of security from the melee that danced without music in psychedelic terror all around her.

What was real and only imagination coalesced into one big fat mind fuck. It seemed that night had fallen but she really wasn't sure. It seemed that the fire had grown from infant to inferno, but again, her sweaty eyeballs could not gauge any truth. Instead of considering the reality of the brutal sacrifices that raged around the fire and on the platform of the cenote farther away, she stared at her forearm, at the djed tattoo, at the pinpoint incision that the hypodermic needle had added to her flesh's landscape. Men screamed for salvation but she ignored them. Women pleaded for second chances and she clasped her ears with both hands, drawing the djed tattoo closer to her face.

In the flickering firelight, the djed tattoo did things no tattoo should do. It became animated, dancing with the heavy metal schizophrenic pace of *Chop Suey*. The four snake fang scars turned into snake fang imaginations, launching themselves at her face, stretching the forearm's epidermis beyond anatomical reason. She tried to grab the elastic illusions with her left hand but the skin fangs sank quickly back into veins.

"That-th creepy. Th-kin fang-th."

The Strykor cubit's folded, wrinkly face hovered over her. Toothpicks were placed between its cheeks and forehead like lean-to poles to keep the skin from folding over its eyes—but, of course, this too could have only been her imagination. Strykor walked away and Manuel took his place. "You're sexy," he mewled. Manuel's face had molted since the last time she remembered seeing it; white splotches pockmarked its entire surface as if a thousand rattlesnakes had planted two thousand fangs into it. "I just hope they leave enough for me." His panting increased as his shoulders turned his broken neck toward a caravan of military vehicles that rolled into the clearing and parked a good distance from her. Blurry men dressed in blurry uniforms carrying blurry guns jumped from the vehicles. "Manuel!" someone screamed, and the smelly cubit left her there to struggle with the heroin's effects.

Music, which had been silent for quite some time, resumed with a Mexican covered version of the Backstreet Boys' *Larger Than Life*. The heavy metal versions of pop were bad enough, but even in her drug induced fantasia, she thought that the vocals that now infiltrated her brain could have easily driven a straight person insane.

Night took control of the party thirty minutes later. At least a hundred people danced around a huge fire to her left and the boy band cover songs kept coming. The effects of the heroin had diminished quite a bit in the short time span and Cooper attributed it to the small quantity she'd been given. Regardless of her recovery, she continued acting stoned. On several occasions, soldiers stood in front of her, yelling Spanish expletives while gyrating too many body parts too close to her face.

To her right, around the sacrificial platform of the cenote, drug deals were in the process of completion. At this distance, she couldn't actually see the money trade hands but the exchange was evident. Large plastic wrapped cubes that twinkled in the firelight went one way and cloth satchels bulging at the seams went the other. Vehicles entered and vehicles left; all tolled, Cooper witnessed the transfer of too many pounds of heroin for too many paramilitary-supporting pesos.

Once most of the deals had been made, she overheard a conversation between a bearded militia man and the Serpent; most of it was in Spanish but she understood the gist of it though the connotation was disturbing. Apparently, the Zetas were ready to start their target practice and the militia man was asking the Serpent how the game was going to be played tonight. *Duck shoot*, is what Cooper had translated and that was the confusing part. Moments later it became evident.

All of the Zetas took up positions near their vehicles. All of them had cash that they tossed in small wads onto the hood of one Jeep; a bet of some kind. To the right, the sacrificial platform remained faintly illuminated by the firelight and was unoccupied. When the Mexican covered version of 'N Sync's *Bye Bye Bye* began, one of the Zetas took a kneeling position and brought his pistol up, clasped in both hands. From the dancing pack around the fire, one man suddenly ran to the right toward the cenote. When he was a few feet from the sacrificial platform, the Zeta soldier fired. The man flinched and fell on top of the platform. The other Zetas howled and took chunks of cash from the hood of the Jeep. Apparently, the kneeling soldier had lost the bet. A second Zeta remained standing and set his scoped rifle against one shoulder. Money flooded the Jeep's hood as another cubit (a woman that Cooper recognized as one that had stumbled down the steps at the Caracol) ran toward the cenote. The moment the cubit stepped on the platform, the Zeta fired his rifle. It lifted the woman off her feet and she disappeared over the far edge. A split second later, a splash resounded and the rifleman turned and snatched the cash from the Jeep's hood.

The game continued but Cooper could no longer watch. She lowered her head but flinched every time a shot was fired. She counted two more splashes before the bearded leader of the Zetas grabbed her chin. He was kneeling in front of her and smiling. Cooper tried to continue her act but the man was wiser.

"Not interested in our game play, chica?" he said. Cooper thought that the man was strangely attractive for a murderer. His hair and beard were well-groomed and his teeth were straight and white. "You don't need to fear me or any of this. I will be taking you with me at the end of the night. You'll be quite comfortable in my mansion on the hill." He gently twisted one of his fingers through one of her red-haired curls. "Fresas. Beautiful." When he released her hair, he waved the hand and another soldier appeared with a syringe. "This will help you enjoy the rest of the night. We'll see you in a couple of hours."

The soldier dumped another hit of heroin into the vein in her arm and her eyes returned to glass just as another shot-splash crashed into her ears.

When they were available, Billy and John followed trails that had been cut through the jungle by some of the local tribes. For the most part, though, they had to chop their way toward the sacred cenote. Billy was getting good at trailblazing and he was obtaining a great education from John about the indigenous plants of the Yucatán. At one point, Billy amazed even John by pointing to a small tree that stood chest high. Small pods that looked like twisted pasta shells hung from several limbs. "This one here provides the mind with the ability to awaken to possibilities outside of experience," he said.

John grinned. "Maybe you should give some to your sponge toy. I'd say the little fella will soon be experiencing some major outside possibilities." Another trail appeared just ahead and John cut a path to it. Together they stood on the trail which was one of the widest so far—about six feet. The faint sound of music trickled through the bush. "You really think it'll work?"

"I may not be a military man but I've watched my share of westerns." Billy patted his chest. "Alixel was able to take out a couple dozen cubits but she had two of these and there were no real live Mexican mobsters to deal with. Even Clint Eastwood knew when to say when."

John's eyebrows perked up. "This ain't no movie western."

"Maybe not. But they got something in common with Marines and survival. You know what it is?"

"SpongeBob." John smirked.

"Come on, John. You need to open up your mind. The answer is staring you right in the face."

"Okay. All right. I get it." John scratched his chin and acted as if he really was giving it some thought. "I give up."

"A distraction. You get the enemy going one way while you plant the bomb, or rob the bank, or break your buddy out of jail."

"Or save the girl."

Billy nodded. "Or save the girl."

"But a toy? How in the hell is a sponge toy going to create a distraction?"

"Well while you were resting back at the motel, I was busy with…"

At that moment, Rally Panini, alias Crabman, emerged from the jungle. "Goddammit you're hard to track down," he grumbled. Even as a cubit, he was still unnaturally red and impossibly skinny. John could have screamed loud enough to knock him over. "How's the bump on the head treating you? Ya'know what happens when you touch the Cubit." He snickered.

"Why don't you stay dead?" Billy said, waving his machete.

Crabman pointed at the back of his scrawny skull. "Kill point.

Remember? You gotta get to the kill point." He took a step toward them. "And you gotta have a dagger to do it."

Billy waved his hand in a come-and-get-it motion. "You want the dagger? I'll give you the dagger."

Crabman took another step. He was less than ten feet away. "I overheard you talking about distractions and I gotta tell ya: I agree."

Just then, Bill Tate fell from the tree in which he'd been hiding. His weight had snapped the branch where he'd roosted and he tumbled onto the path, crushing bushes and flattening small plants as his fat body rolled onto the trail. He stood, stumbled once, then said, "Tada! Now hand over the blade." He pulled a small pistol from his pocket and pointed at Billy.

"You won't hurt me," Billy said. "You need me."

"You know. You're right." And Tate turned the gun on John and fired. The caliber of the weapon was small and when it only grazed John's left bicep, he ran remarkably fast to Tate and took his head off with one swipe of the machete. A second gunshot rang out from behind and John spun around while grabbing at his back as if trying to scratch a relentless itch. A blood spot grew from a bullet hole that had entered his shoulder blade just to the left of his spine. Pat Roberts stepped from the bush on the opposite side of the trail as John fell. Smoked trickled from the barrel of his much larger caliber rifle.

"What'cha gonna do, Billy?" Crabman said. "What'cha gonna do when they come for you?"

The cubit's eyes started to glow—crimson red irises with swirling silver pupils—and Billy wondered who was behind them. The master of all Evil was now staring straight at him and Billy took the opportunity to tell him exactly what he thought.

"I know who you are," Billy said. "You're a bumbling fool who likes to play with pirates and little boys. And you're a coward. Why don't you come out of your hidey hole and face me like the Antichrist you are. Do I frighten you that bad?"

"Suffering," Crabman said, his voice now very similar to the Pedro cubit from the Caracol's well. "It's all about suffering. Janine suffered. Joel suffered. Stephanie suffered. Marcy suffered. Cooper and John are suffering. All of your friends, everyone you know has, are, or will suffer. My 'hidey hole' is in your mind and I think I'm playing with it quite fantastically. Look at him. He's dying. Doesn't that frighten you? I'd hope it does considering that, without him, you have absolutely no hope left."

Roberts came up from behind and stuck the barrel of the rifle into Billy's backpack. He shoved hard, forcing Billy to drop his machete and stumble toward Crabman.

Who lives in a Pineapple under the sea?

The sound came from within the backpack. Roberts looked at it, curiously.

SpongeBob SquarePants!

The force applied by the rifle's barrel wavered.

Absorbent and yellow and porous is he.

When he longer felt the barrel pressed against him, Billy spun around, blocked the barrel with his left hand, and punched Roberts in the jaw. The rifle fired and Crabman jerked backward, grabbed his face, and fell onto the trail. Billy never realized how hot the dagger had become as he unsheathed it, flipped it in the air to readjust his grip on its haft, and kicked Roberts who fell to the ground face-first. Billy jammed the seven-inch blade into the back of Roberts head then turned toward Crabman.

"You won't be coming back again," Billy growled as he stood over the writhing cubit, one of its eyes now missing. "Your suffering ends here." One, quick, downward thrust and Rally Panini morphed into bone and ash.

"Gunshots," John moaned. He kicked dirt while his hand wandered across the hard ground. "They'll be coming." He tried to crawl but his strength was fading as fast as the blood that flowed from the bullet wound. "T-t-t—take cover."

Billy replaced the dagger and ran to John's side. He tried dragging the big man by the arms but lacked the strength.

"Your-s-self," John pleaded. "Not m-me."

"Shhh," Billy said. "You have to protect me, remember? You have to keep your promise." He scooted John's body so that it was parallel with the trail then rolled him into the bush. A sharp embankment helped John's forward rolling momentum as Billy pushed from the side until his body came to rest beside a ceiba tree about twenty feet from the trail. The tree's buttress roots were tall enough to hide them, but moving John's body to the backside of the trunk seemed impossible.

"I need you to help me," Billy urged. "Come on. Push!"

And John did. With what little strength remained, John crawled as Billy pushed and yanked and pulled until they were nestled in between two tall roots.

John's breathing came in rapid pulses. His eyes were closed and Billy wondered if he was even conscious. "We're going to get through this John Brown Gordon. You hang in there with me, you hear?" The front of his shirt was soaked in blood and Billy pressed the palm of his hand against the wound just as three men came walking down the trail toward them. He hunkered over John, hoping that his body would hush John's breaths.

The men spoke Spanish and their vocal inflections told Billy that they were confused about what they'd found on the trail. All three of them chambered their guns. Feet shuffled into the bush on Billy's side of the trail. The rustle of plants stopped no less than five feet from him. "X'Tabay," the man said. "Donde está usted, X'Tabay? Tengo algo para usted."

Where are you X'Tabay? Billy understood that much. And then the man fired his gun into the tree, sending chips of wood down on Billy's hunkered head. Another voice yelled at the gunman and he responded, again to the tree, by yelling "Vete al infierno!" then he fired two more times and shuffled away.

It took a full ten minutes before Billy felt it was safe enough to curl up from John's body. John's rapid breaths had transformed into wisps of inhalation so shallow and weak, Billy feared he was too late.

"John," he whispered. "John." He lightly slapped both of his cheeks and lifted one eyelid though he did so more because he'd seen doctors do it and less because he really knew what a rolled eye in the socket really meant. After checking his pulse at the throat, Billy knew he had to act immediately.

He stretched John out at the base of the tree and flipped him over. The entry wound had produced much more blood than the exit wound. He drew the dagger out and, for no reason whatsoever, kissed the star in its haft, gazed up at the ceiba tree's canopy, and looked for hope, looked for a giant hawk. He stuck the dagger's blade gently into the hole and the single fifth red point in the star immediately grew bright. John jerked and Billy almost thrust the point too quickly at an angle which could have severed the heart. Not wanting to take the same chance again, he inhaled deeply then buried the dagger in one swift motion, all seven inches of it. The dagger grew so bright and so hot so quickly that it literally blew Billy off of John's body, knocking him back into the ceiba tree roots where he fell onto his butt. Billy looked back toward the trail and throughout the jungle. He thought that the gray clouds overhead coupled with the waning sunlight would have made the blazing spectacle that encircled John's body easily visible for at least a mile. But no one came and Billy just sat there, watching, as the blade did its thing, reworking and restructuring and re-stitching human flesh while slowly rising, inch by inch, out of John's back. The point tottered on his shoulder blade for an impossible second, the entire dagger erect and defying all physical laws, before its light blinked out and it tottered off of John's body to the ground.

"Am I in heaven?" John said while slowly rolling onto his side and blinking. "Ah shit…Ain't no way in hell."

It was very garbled with intermittent static but Cooper swore she heard SpongeBob. The soldier had filled her with twice the heroin she'd experienced the first time around so the voice, she believed, had to be imaginary. But voices and visions were two different things altogether. Not only was she hearing the damn thing, she was seeing it, too. SpongeBob stood just inches from her left leg and looked at her. She tried to swat it away with her knee but it backed up on its eight metal legs, which really freaked her out.

"If nautical nonsense be something ye wish," the eight-legged SpongeBob said.

She blinked and tapped her ear against one shoulder. It didn't even sound like the SpongeBob captain…it sounded like Billy.

"SpongeBob SquarePants!"

"What the fuck is that?" It was Lafitte and he was standing halfway between the assembled Los Zetas and Cooper. The modified SpongeBob toy scuttled away into the dark bush, repeating its name in Billy's voice as if stuck in a loop.

SpongeBob SquarePants… SpongeBob SquarePants… SpongeBob SquarePants

"Hey! Come back here." Lafitte turned from the toy and yelled at the good-looking murderer with the trimmed beard and white teeth. "Captain Teigas. Surveillance!"

SpongeBob SquarePants… SpongeBob SquarePants… SpongeBob SquarePants

"Atención!" the paramilitary captain yelled. "Federales!" He pointed where Billy's voice reverberated relentlessly.

SpongeBob SquarePants... SpongeBob SquarePants... SpongeBob SquarePants

Lafitte grabbed the captain's arm and the captain looked at the hand as if he'd just desecrated a priceless object, but when he looked up and into Lafitte's glowing eyes his expression immediately changed. "It's not the government," Lafitte said in a voice that was not his own. "It's that fuckin' kid. Remember, don't kill him."

"We won't, mi jefe," the captain said, looking away.

"Your life in the jungle will never be the same if he dies," Lafitte warned.

Captain Teigas ran with his scrambling platoon, yelling orders not to kill the intruder and guaranteeing every one of them what horrible consequences awaited for disobeying.

Several dozen ravers remained around the fire, dancing hypnotically in complete oblivion of what was taking place around them. Gunfire and screams of aggression went unnoticed. Cooper watched Lafitte join the dancers, his ponytail flip of blonde-white hair whipping back and forth as he maintained a pretty good hip-twisting rhythm to the boy band beats.

And then a hand grabbed her from behind which almost caused her to swallow her tongue as she gasped. She turned to see a familiar black face. She really didn't think the face was real so she just smiled and slurred, "Why, he-wo b-yout-ful. Ya come ta join ma rave?" The whites of John's eyes became tracers that twisted and swirled.

"Be still," he said. "We've come to rescue you."

"Why? Am havin' such good times." She giggled. "Did yooo see Spund boob?"

"Hush," John repeated.

"Spider Spund boob," she giggled again.

Gunfire and commands were moving closer. John stepped around the ceiba root and cradled Cooper in his arms. She kissed his cheek and said something that was meant to express her appreciation but it didn't come out that way. She giggled once more and slapped the bicep that Bill Tate had grazed with his .22 caliber pea-shooter. John grimaced and whispered, "Please, Coop. Hush."

"Why you big black chaco-, choca-, shocolate thing you."

John ran with her into the bush unnoticed by everyone except Evan who had been standing and watching the entire rescue from within the cenote's sacrificial platform shadows. He kicked one bullet-riddled cubit into the cenote water and smiled as John disappeared with the bait that Evan had let off the hook.

Billy sat in a thick mangrove tree as the soldiers ran under and away from him. John had painted his face and arms with mud which made his fingers' manipulation of the tiny joystick slippery whenever sweat rolled a dirty wash down his wrist and into his palm. The tree had been chosen for its angle to where Cooper sat, but it was not a good roost for determining his robot's whereabouts once it ran from the clearing. He had mind-mapped a path for the robot he called SpongeMod, and felt comfortable that the range of his wireless joystick would be efficient enough to provide John the time he needed. He had not anticipated the audio recording malfunction and was happy when SpongeMod finally shut up.

Strykor had indeed scavenged his computer equipment, and Billy had been able use the parts to modify Stephanie Drake's SpongeBob toy with an ability to create a diversion. The hardest part had been the legs. Bipedal motion would not have worked. Fortunately, Billy had been working on a new spider-like robot while back in Port Aransas. The parts for that creation, he'd found in the floorboard compartment of the VW Bus. Once the leg mobility problem had been solved, everything else was pretty straightforward. SpongeMod was one creepy looking robot, John had told him. Billy had agreed. It would certainly accomplish its mission as a diversion.

Billy thumbed the controller and looked to where he thought SpongeMod should be. There! At the edge of the clearing. He pressed the red button and the robot started rambling again, repeating its name in Billy's recorded voice.

SpongeBob SquarePants… SpongeBob SquarePants… SpongeBob SquarePants

Billy walked the robot to the center of the clearing near one of the military Jeeps, then snatched his backpack from a tree limb and dropped the controller inside. John appeared under him, Cooper cradled in his arms seemingly unconscious. "Let's get," he whispered.

"Getty yap," Cooper moaned, but not loudly. "Yee-haw."

Billy dropped from the tree and the three escapees ran off into the jungle.

Evan heard the giggles recede into the shadows as Captain Teigas and his men surrounded the annoying toy.

SpongeBob SquarePants… SpongeBob SquarePants… SpongeBob SquarePants

Lafitte entered the small circle and screamed, "GODDAMMIT!" Then his foot came down and crushed SpongeMod. He punched the captain then left the circle to rage internally elsewhere. Captain Teigas drew his .44 Magnum, pointed it at the back of Lafitte's head, then turned it down toward the toy that still would not shut up. He emptied all cylinders into it.

Evan sat and laughed. He was beginning to understand how patience and manipulation were, in fact, quite exhilarating, almost as much as dropping from the sky at a hundred and twenty miles an hour.

He still had a week. While Lafitte continued to try and satisfy his own selfish goals, all Evan had to do was wait.

La Calma Que Precede a la Tormenta

(Saturday morning, one week later)

Billy had been sitting on the vacant Puerto Morelos beach and staring at the ocean for the past two hours, smelling, tasting, listening, thinking. It was like being back in Port Aransas…almost. He'd risen before the sun, he'd walked down to the beach, he'd found himself the perfect seat in the sand, and his mind had been taken away. The wind that blew his hair into comfortable disarray was unlike Port A's in that it had no sea smell to it. He'd run his toes and fingers a dozen times through sand that was white and not Port A brown. He'd sat just beyond the high tide's farthest reach and had relished the cool aqua-white water that looked so much more inviting than the green Gulf. Birds were different, too, as were the creatures that ran through the soupy froth looking for early daybreak snacks.

He wiped sandy fingers on his T-shirt that was silkscreened with the words Pat McGee's across the chest. He'd found it under the driver's seat of his VW Bus a few days ago, and hadn't even questioned why it was there. Really, none of the whys even mattered anymore. It was easier to accept what was offered and appreciate each gift. They had so little time left. Tomorrow was the winter solstice.

Like the calm before the storm, the past six days had been full of wonderful serenity, particularly since none of them had spent the time worrying about a future they couldn't control. Billy had seen it in both of his comrades. Cooper tended to make funny faces in response to lighthearted comments and had, on occasion, spontaneously danced outside local restaurants that broadcast live or recorded Mexican music. She'd stick out her tongue and give just about anyone the raspberry for no other reason than to draw laughter from those on the receiving end, especially children. She'd even done her hair differently, having set it in a more greased-back version of something right off a retro Annie Lennox *Sweet Dreams* album cover.

John, too, had transformed during the days they'd been in Puerto. He smiled a lot more and Billy swore that he'd lost a few pounds, though on a frame like his, it was not evident to those beyond friends. The wound near his heart and the one in his bicep had healed completely and there wasn't a day that went by that he did not thank Billy for saving his life.

John had also treated all of them to the wonders of the sea. Though they had not known it then, he had been preparing them. Over the first three days in Puerto Morelos, he'd taken them offshore to some of the best dive spots he'd visited in the past. They'd marveled at the barrier reef, a sunken ship, and an underwater cave which they had entered only once and for only a short time. They'd not become professional divers in that short time frame but they'd learned enough—at least John had said they'd learned enough to get them to the third location denoted in the Book of the Djed: a cenote they'd finally visited last Wednesday.

A local friend of John's, Sebastian Bondager, had driven them to the cenote which was located just off the coastal highway about halfway between Puerto Morelos and Tulum. As a half Latino and half Scottish retired divemaster, Sebastian knew just about every place there was to take a tank of compressed air throughout the Riviera. If there was a point of interest and it was under water, Sebastian knew how best to get there, what dangers to avoid, and what features were most notable. But as far as the third location was concerned, Sebastian had never heard of it. The cenote they'd visited didn't even have a name, at least none that was publicly popular.

The morning sun was now a good ten degrees above the horizon. Local weather reports had forecast a couple of beautiful days ahead and Billy was going to take advantage of every last ounce on this final Saturday. He looked around for a seashell to toss back into the water but there were none. The barrier reef two hundred yards offshore effectively limited such surfside collectibles. The reef was also the reason why there was no sea smell. According to Sebastian Bondager, the reef blocked the passage of algae and, therefore, few feeding fish could be found between the barrier and the shore. According to Sebastian Bondager, Puerto Morelos was special in many ways and he'd told them as much as he'd driven them to the remote cenote.

Cooper had been sitting in the back seat of the smoky Chrysler Caravan and had been quietly talking with John about the revelation he'd laid on her that morning concerning the man she'd know as the Serpent.

"How can anyone live for two hundred years?" she'd asked him.

"We both know someone who lived much longer," John had reminded her.

"But the Serpent—Lafitte? Surely someone would have busted his cover in that amount of time."

Sebastian, whom they had only met that morning, had become interested. "Jean Lafitte?" he'd questioned in a peculiar accent that merged Scotland with Central America. "Of course he lives. Mu'bä never die. They attach themselves to a place and never seem to leave."

Billy, who had sat in the passenger seat, asked, "So you've seen it… um, him?"

"Many times, but more recently just yesterday. Ain't never seen a Mu'bä drive before but by God that's what he was doin'."

"In Puerto Morelos?"

"No. Over in Playa del Carmen." Sebastian had huffed then, shaking a head of old skin that was sun baked and crackly. "You'd think a ghost would be ridin' a motorcycle or something but not this one. Drivin' a damn Chevy."

"Cavalier?" Billy had asked.

"Yep. How'd ya know?"

"What color was it?"

"Why the hell should that matter?"

"Just curious."

"White, it was. And he had passengers. A Mu'bä driving a damned Chevy with passengers. And I thought I'd seen it all."

It had been confirmation and hadn't surprised any of them. All of the players were where they should be. Billy needed the Book and the key. Lafitte needed Billy and the dagger. Tulum was the setting and Sunday was the date prescribed.

The cenote had been located near a highway rest area. Such rest areas in Mexico were unique (at least along the stretch of road that connected Cancun and Tulum) in that they not only provided a place to use the bathroom, but, at many, you could also take a quick dip in a nearby cenote. Sebastian had parked at one of these rest areas but the cenote they were headed for was not the one populated by weary travelers. They took their scuba gear with them in a different direction, led by John, through pleasant-looking plants that towered and flowered all around them. About a half a mile from the highway they came across a big hole in the ground. It was only ten feet wide and the only reason Billy knew it was there was because of the thick rope that dropped into it.

"There's a limestone shelf below where we can assemble before the dive, but we'll have to gear up here," John told them.

"How do you know about this?" Sebastian asked.

"Don't you really want to know how *you don't know* about it?" John replied, smiling. "It isn't the case that you can't teach old dogs new tricks, eh?"

Once they assembled below ground, Billy was greeted by some of the most beautiful water he'd ever seen. Somehow, it was illuminated from below, casting a sapphire glow against dark cavern walls. When he slid into the water, he felt as if he were standing somewhere man was never supposed to stand—either that or he was in a place granted to only those few humans who had passed the test, who'd gotten it right, who'd deserved such otherworldly payback for well done deeds. It was as if God's hand was wrapped around a blue sapphire and he was about to dive into its depths, to find what lay at the center of life.

John submerged first and Cooper followed him. Billy and Sebastian took up the rear. Parts of the journey through the underground caves necessitated their flashlights. Other areas were faintly lit from above. At one point, Billy swore he could see the tiny feet of several bathers as they waded far above him.

Stalactites and stalagmites were everywhere. Coral stuck to some of them and Billy took extra care not to disturb them. Fish and other aquatic life were sparse but he identified at least one catfish which surprised him. Cooper pointed at it, then chased it like a curious child for a few seconds until it zipped out of range.

They were in the water for almost thirty minutes before John's flippers started to ascend. Billy broke the water's surface moments later and was surprised two find two other people already in the chamber that housed another Cubit throne pedestal. The smell of pot was strong though neither young male diver revealed its source.

"You guys scared the crap out of us," the teen with bald head and flimsy mustache said.

"You're trespassing," John told them. "This cenote is governed by the federals."

"No way," the second teen with a crappy short haircut said.

"Way," John said. "Historically preserved and banned from all that don't have permission."

"Says who?" baldy said.

Billy spoke up then. "The penalty is death."

That, and John's massive size, had been enough to take the young divers' paranoia over the edge. "Sorry man," crappy haircut said. "We won't tell nobody." They were in the water so fast, they forgot to re-seal their bag of dope and it scattered into the ripples as their heads submerged.

The chamber, like that under the Caracol, was domed but the apex was only a few feet higher than John was tall. Unlike the well under the Caracol, there were no etchings on the walls, no jaguar statues, no Cubit. It was a dark and dank place that was filled only with chunks of ceiling that had fallen over time, the Cubit throne and the surrounding water.

"Not so glamorous as the places we've already visited," Cooper said. "If I was going to hide the Cubit, this would be it." Sebastian looked at her curiously, but didn't say anything.

The pedestal was a clone of the one at Chichen Itza. A star was centered at its top edge. Two three-dimensional glyphs of Creation Daggers were etched at an angle below the star, their points touching in the middle of the pedestal's face. Below the points was the hollowed home of a Djed amulet now raised.

"Alixel got hers in the well," John said, pointing at the vacant Djed outline. "Alax got his here, in the cenote."

The journey to the third Wayeb Chamber in the cenote had been quite spectacular. Standing in the blue sapphire under the earth then diving into it had made the trip worthwhile. Even the looks on the faces of the pot-smoking teens would have been worth an admission. But the Cubit throne and the etchings on it and the domed room and the feeling that Evil was all around them really wasn't special anymore. He'd been there and done that two times already. He knew the routine. It had been a different story for Sebastian who thought he'd seen and done everything there was to do along the Mexican Riviera, but for John, Cooper and himself, nothing had been added nor subtracted from the mystery of the Djed, the Cubit and the end of time.

On Thursday, Billy had gone off by himself to do some sketching. He'd chosen three locations in the town to do this. One was where he sat now. Another was at a metal table under a metal umbrella just up the shoreline near a pier where numerous snorkeling and dive boats moored themselves between excursions to the reef and points beyond. The third location was in the town's center square, just a block or so from the pier. This had been his favorite place to sit and think, and to scribble into his notebook everything about the Book of the Djed that he could remember. He'd spent the entire day doing this and most of the second half of his notebook was filled with such memories. Though he wasn't particularly good at it, doodling was a way to get the creative juices flowing. Doodling was an exercise in memory recall. Doodling, he thought, just might reveal someone, some thing, some clue, or some direction in which he should proceed that he had not yet thought of. What the hell was going to happen Sunday? What was it that he was supposed to do? "Why" may have been relegated to uselessness (he knew why he was going to Tulum) but "How" (in this case, raise the Djed) certainly remained an important mystery that could not be ignored.

The hardest parts of the Book to remember where those that Alixel had shown him on the night of Hurricane Antiago; he'd never been able to look back upon these pages since he'd only been able to open the Book to its center spread. While sitting on the beach Thursday, he'd scribbled into his notebook the random images of the Story of the Fifth Age, starting with the Creation of Good and Evil. On one notebook page he'd drawn a miserable replica of the Arc of the Covenant. On the opposite page he'd drawn a much better rendition of the Cubit. Under the metal umbrella by the pier he'd logged what he remembered about the Creation of Man, drawing scattered images of quirky masks and stick figures hanging from stick trees. Sketches of massacred pieces of human body parts inundated an entire page in his notebook and he was uncertain if these memories were from the pages that Alixel had shown him or were more so from his actual accounts of the glyphs he'd seen written on the entrance to and on the walls of the Great Hall of the Anasazi. He'd then relocated to the town's square to finish his doodling exercise that covered the Creation of Religion, the Book's center page spread, the key, and the page noting the four locations. While sitting on an unnaturally green patch of grass, he'd taken greater effort to draw much more stylized renditions of Adam and Eve and snakes and the proverbial tree of knowledge, which, in his notebook, looked a lot like a thick-trunked, buttress-rooted ceiba tree.

Before finishing his doodling exercise, he'd decided to take a brain break and eat a late afternoon lunch at one of the numerous restaurants that surrounded the town square. Le Café D'Amancia was a small, open-air coffee shop that had become his favorite in the short time he'd been in Puerto. The fare was tasty and inexpensive and was served by a friendly family that offered salutations to every customer regardless of creed or color. The family's dog even added to the shop's uplifting atmosphere as it often lay sprawled across the floor in front of the counter, offering a reticent grin as customers happily avoided its tail and legs.

Sitting at one of the shop's small tables with a fresh cup of Oaxaca-grown black coffee in one hand and a mechanical pencil in the other, he'd begun sketching out the remaining pieces of the Book of the Djed.

The bird of fire he meticulously scratched in lead, its streams of flames quite elegant for a hand not given much credit for its knack at artistic improvisation. But it was the sixes and nines that had kept him seated inside the coffee shop for more than an hour. He'd kept tracing them over and over again until he'd finished his fifth cup of coffee, carving such deep impressions into the paper until, at one point, it had finally torn.

The recreation of the key page was the easiest to render. It had contained only two glyphs: a Wayeb mask and a thumbnail version of a Creation Dagger, both set at the top of the paper, and both of which he'd encountered numerous times since Port Aransas.

Jazzed on an extreme influx of caffeine, he'd returned to the town square patch of grass to finish his writing exercise: the recreation of the four locations, each taking the space of one corner of the notebook page that immediately followed the key. These sketches, except for the last, he'd recreated directly from experience. The fourth location, he had recreated from the previous drawing that he'd shown John.

Once he'd finished, he'd sat there, flipping back and forth through his notebook, absorbing the images, adding a flick of the pencil here and erasing any extraneous parts that didn't make sense. But it was the sixes and nines that continued to attract him the most. Perhaps, he'd thought, his incessant attention to the center page was based on the same obsession that had consumed Cooper: the idea that these images had been drawn by the hand of God coupled by the curiosity of what would be entered next. These were clues, signposts, warnings. The bird of fire certainly alluded to the antithetical idea of birth and death. But it also encapsulated an ancillary meaning, one which he and Cooper had believed identified Phoenix International as serving some importance. The sixes and nines, too, were antithetical if for no other reason than one was the mirror image of the other. But what ancillary meaning did they serve? What was it about them that he wasn't getting? Was it as simple as Antichrist versus Savior? Did the Bible have anything to do with it? Did Mayan history have anything to do with it?

And his thoughts had centered on that one idea: Mayan history… Mayan chronology…The Fifth Age. Did sixes and nines have anything at all to do with the Mayan calendar? If so, the ramifications of such coincidental (not an amiable word for him anymore) occurrence both in pre-classic Mayan culture and that of Christianity would be incredible.

The first tourists of the day finally showed up on the beach and yanked Billy from his thoughts. The young couple quickly ran into and out of the surf, screaming because of the water's chill. They walked past him and waved, and Billy returned the greeting. The index finger on his right hand was moist and sandy and, again, he wiped it across his Pat Mcgee's T-shirt. As he watched the couple saunter up the waterline, he noticed that he'd absently written three sixes and three nines into the sand.

Cooper saw Billy on the beach thirty minutes before she decided to go down and sit with him. He acted just about the way she had felt all doped up on heroin back at the sacrificial cenote. He stared at nothing and everything, the morning breeze pushing sand in his face, a stray spoonbill hoping around his legs, plucking the ground with its long beak. He was writing something in the sand but not looking at it, as if in a trance. She knew exactly how he must be feeling: lost, separated, distant, consumed by every feeling associated with every person who'd known the battle was coming but was uncertain of its outcome.

His spell broke when the couple wearing the matching purple swimsuits showed up. He didn't notice that she was standing right behind him and gasped when she spoke. "Billy…sorry. Didn't mean to startle you." She saw the sixes and nines in the sand but didn't say anything. "What'cha thinkin' so hard about?"

He patted the sand to his left and she sat there. "Oh, nothing and everything."

"Anything to do with numbers and a Book?"

He looked hard into her eyes; the intensity of the stare reminded her of Nexpa, of their three days of escape from madness. "Perhaps. What have you been up to?"

"Pretty much the same as you, I suppose. Soaking it all in. Enjoying the beauty of the world. Enjoying this little patch of paradise." She dipped her toes in the sand. "I can see how Tony dumped his entire life for one in Puerto Morelos."

"Tony?" Billy turned his attention back toward the ocean. Cooper thought that she'd seen a tinge of jealousy in his reaction.

"A California businessman I met near the pier yesterday. He and his

wife…" she purposefully added a little bit of emphasis on that word and
Billy smiled without looking at her. "…they left great jobs, a great home,
just about everything they knew, and moved here about a month ago. He's
starting up a small bakery just north of the square."

Billy gently grabbed her wrist, massaged the multiple scars from
snakes bites and needles. "We'll have to visit him once he gets it up
and going." His expression attempted reassurance and she was thankful
for that even though they both knew the truth. "You ready for a walk?
We've got about an hour before John and Sebastian meet us by the old
lighthouse."

She didn't say yes; she simply stood without releasing his hand.
They brushed sand from clothing they'd purchased in town and Billy
kicked sand from his blue Keds which, last Thursday, he'd proclaimed
was the best find any westerner could have made in the Riviera. He led
her to the water's edge and they began walking.

"Could you live here?" Cooper asked. "I mean, there's not much to
do."

"I know where you're coming from but I think a wily person could
find plenty if they wanted to. Our scuba expeditions are proof of that.
Besides, I think what makes this place so alluring to people like Tony and
his wife is the very idea that you don't *have* to do anything. As long as
you can feed yourself, the rest lies in the hands of God's good graces."

"God?"

"Yeah," he smiled. "The Great Spirit. The Holy One. Zeus.
Whatever you want to call it. Whatever it is that ensures that such
complex creatures on a complex planet don't completely destroy each
other."

Cooper stopped and stood and yanked his hand, pulling his attention
to her. Her new hairstyle did not move with the wind nearly as much as
Billy's dirty blonde waves did. "Are we going to die?" she asked.

Again, his intense stare sent Nexpa-like chills into her very soul.
"On the eve of immortality?" he said. "Let's hope the Great Spirit does
not know the term irony." They started walking again. "Truthfully, I don't
think anyone can be sure. We'll try to avoid any obvious mistakes. That's
why we're heading out to sea today. We can't expect the cubits to think of
everything, especially an incursion by sea. It's a good plan. It should give
us the early advantage."

"You know they aren't all cubits. There was one named Evan and he's definitely among the living. I think he let me escape."

This time Billy stopped and stood and squeezed her hand. "Let you? How?"

"He was standing over by the platform among all of those bodies." She coughed. "He was standing there while Lafitte and all of the soldiers went chasing after your robot. And when John freed me, he didn't say a word."

"And you think that's odd?"

"Don't you? I mean, the only reason I was there was to lure you in."

"And you did. Sounds to me like he's got different priorities."

"He told me that Lafitte was his boss."

"But you said he let you go. Maybe his real boss is someone else."

Cooper must have looked as confused as she felt.

"Look," Billy said, his voice even and soothing. "We can't waste energy asking ourselves 'why.' I think it's logical to assume by his action that Evan doesn't work for Lafitte. Why he would pretend to and why he would let you go is irrelevant, in my opinion. I do suspect we'll see more of him, though. I suspect he'll be at the Castillo vying for the Djed and the dagger and not for the purpose of helping Lafitte. He either wants them for himself and his own immortality or he is doing the bidding of his real boss."

"Real boss?"

"Phoenix International." They started walking again and Billy explained his hunch based on the Book's center spread. "The bird of fire is symbolic for the corporation; I think that assumption is correct. But I also think the bird of fire is a warning. I think it is a clue. The mythological bird lives in cycles; it dies and is reborn within a fiery blaze. Life from death. The alpha from the omega."

"And the sixes and nines? Does the phoenix have something to do with that?" More people started to appear on the beach the closer they came to the pier. They stepped over thick ropes that tied small fishing boats to metal anchors in the sand.

Billy continued. "That whole center page, once it is completely written, is going to present us with a story that is reliant on each clue but, at the same time, each clue will be a story unto itself, each also having multiple meanings that warn and reveal and exemplify. Stories within stories. Innuendo on top of innuendo."

The pier was growing quite busy as early morning snorkelers

assembled beside their assigned boats. Billy led her up the beach, past the twenty-five-foot-tall vacant lighthouse that sat at an angle as an icon for the town. He shuffled through confused vacationers, leading Cooper by the hand through the melee until they found a small green patch of grass in the center of the town square.

"Still think you'd want to live here with Tony?" Billy asked while squatting.

Cooper nodded. "Just got to time your daily activities, I guess."

"Yes, well, about the numbers."

Cooper raised her hand. "Wait. Let me take a stab at this. The sixes represent Evil, a.k.a. Phoenix International. The nines represent Good, a.k.a. Billy and Cooper and company."

"Maybe. But the mere fact that they are turned upside down is symbolic imagery denoting extreme ends like the phoenix is symbolic for life and death."

She could see it in his eyes. "But that's not all, is it?"

"No. At least I don't think it is. I keep going back to the reality that so much of all of this revolves around the Mayan end date. Therefore, the symbols must also incorporate Mayan culture or history or something."

"Sixes are from the Bible."

"Well, maybe when John wrote Revelation, he was reading them upside down."

Cooper's eyes popped wide then. "You really are grabbing at straws now, aren't you?"

"Am I? Really?"

"What you're saying is that the Maya and the Christians had something in common before the Christians ever came to the Americas."

"Yes."

"That's cra…"

"Crazy? I used to think so, too. Now I don't ask why and it makes believing so much easier."

"So, how are sixes and nines interrelated?"

"That is the sixty-four million dollar question and one I can't yet answer. But if we survive this thing tomorrow, I'll be bound and determined to figure it out, starting with what is really at the heart of this entire drama: the Mayan's calendar which has given us December 21, 2012, as the end of days."

A voice interrupted from behind. "Anyone mention end of days?"

John stood in the middle of the sunshine, casting a giant shadow over both of them. "Might as well get it on. Sebastian's got the boat hummin' and waitin'. Shall we?"

They weren't going to let rest and relaxation slip away too soon. Sebastian had planned an afternoon filled with fishing and scuba diving before they would head south toward their rendezvous with destiny.

His boat, a restored thirty-five foot Sea Ray, had an upper captain's deck and a lower bedroom cabin that was loaded with everything life at sea could need, including two beds, a toilet, and a small kitchen nook he'd built that contained a gas grill, a small sink and counter, and a short refrigerator. He'd spent quite a penny on the boat ten years ago after selling his "dirt" home for the one at sea and he hadn't regretted it for a second. He'd said that living at sea was like being reborn and he was determined to prove it to Billy and his friends before Sunday morning.

They spent an hour diving about a half a mile out, exhausting one complete set of tanks to explore the waters at a safe depth of about forty feet. Billy was amazed at the sights and sounds of underwater life. He'd spent so much time atop the water, always attempting to stay one step ahead of the surf's need to dunk him under, that he'd never really given the life below his board and feet much thought. The multitude of colors was beyond amazing. And he could hear them. As strange as the experience felt, he really believed that the schools of tropical fish were trying to communicate. Perhaps it was only his imagination; after all, everyone wished they had a little Dr. Doolittle in them.

But that fantasy was enlivened when the bottlenose dolphin showed up. Cooper would later tell him how absolutely awestruck she was with the mammal's antics and incessant devotion toward garnering Billy's attention. It was as if the dolphin had been his long lost friend, only now finding him after so many years apart. It talked to him. It hugged him. It kissed him. If dolphins could love, then this one loved Billy. What really screwed with him, though, were the emotional feelings he shared with the dolphin—human emotions that made him think of Stephanie Drake. And he would forever swear (but keep it to himself) that the dolphin, indeed, *was* Stephanie Drake in every way that Osi, the giant hawk, had become

Alax.

Nothing ever dies, Alax had said. *We exist in this flesh to complete cycles that have no beginning and no end.* Billy had thought at the time that Alax had been referring strictly to human flesh. He now understood better.

The encounter with the dolphin pretty much destroyed Billy's and Cooper's desire to fish for the rest of the day. Sebastian and John understood their sudden intimate relationship with the sea, but they argued that they still had to eat. Certainly, God would never reincarnate man into the body of a yellowfin tuna, Sebastian suggested. To turn man into something man ate? He wasn't buying it. But Billy wondered. The Great Spirit often delivered lessons in forms not easily understood.

John and Sebastian fished while the boat slowly sailed south toward Tulum. When dusk took control of the colored shadows that twinkled off of the water's surface, Sebastian dropped the sails and anchor while John cleaned their catch. Once the tuna steaks were cooked and sizzling on the gas grill, the four of them sat on the long foredeck and ate. Billy and Cooper had opted out on the fish though its spicy aroma was certainly tantalizing. Cheese, bread, a helping of fried potatoes and several pieces of fruit were good enough for them. In fact, Billy wondered if he'd ever eat seafood again and how such a change in attitude would affect his ownership of the Surf Side Restaurant once, and if, he returned to the island.

The shoreline abutting the Tulum ruins remained a good distance from their anchor point; still, El Castillo's unique shape and height was discernible in the waning sunlight, especially since tourism had demanded that spotlights be placed around its base. The half moon sat directly above the pyramid and the Big Dipper was circling around from the north.

"Just like it was when Stephens and Catherwood discovered it in 1843," Sebastian said. "Just like it was when Samaal fled from it." All three of them turned to him in unison. Sebastian grinned, knowing he had their complete attention. "Ah. I see you like stories. Very good."

"Samaal," Billy said. "What do you know of Samaal?"

"Just an old myth, really; one that includes a vicious tyrant."

"Even better," John's deep voice added with an air of menace. "And appropriate." He nodded toward the shore.

Sebastian flung his legs over the deck where they dangled as an invitation for the rest of them to do the same. Billy and Cooper did so but

John remained where he was, leaning on his side with an elbow propping him up.

"Story goes that Samaal was a great leader of the Maya in Chichen Itza. Now, scholars'll tell ya that the kind of culture that ran things in that big city had no single leaders, but they be wrong. Samaal was one of 'em and he ruled with an iron fist. Ballgames were won and lost on his behalf. Hundreds lost their heads."

Billy interrupted. "Are you sure about your story?"

Sebastian looked sternly at him. "You heard different?"

It wasn't the time for argument, Billy thought. Besides, how could you argue against myth? He'd already learned that lesson. "No. Sorry. Go ahead."

"Yeah…well, you see, this Samaal was beginning to piss a lot of people off. Tyrants can't maintain control forever. I think we can all agree with that." Cooper shrugged so that only Billy could see; her eyebrows curled with an expression of what-the-hell-is-he-talking-about. "There was an uprising and they threw Samaal out of the city—sent him packing as it were.

"But Samaal wasn't the type to just accept defeat; he was too power–hungry. Besides, he still had a lot of followers, military types and such. So he did what every good tyrant does: he relocated. He wanted revenge and he was determined to get it. He created this city by the sea, built up the walls to prevent attacks, and trained a new army. But none of that mattered. Sometime in the thirteenth century the neighboring cities came together and forced Samaal and his followers into the sea. In their retreat, they sailed from the Castillo right across this very spot. Unfortunately, Samaal's concentration on land battles had caused him to ignore the rules of the sea. Poorly built boats took on water and sunk right here, right below us. Legend has it, his ghost and that of his crew returns to Tulum every winter solstice, which of course, is tomorrow morning."

"You're so full of shit," John said, sitting up. "Now you know very well that ain't the right story. Why do you go and carry on so?"

"Better story than believing some damn box made Mu'bä out of everyone and Samaal was some hero who built the Tulum walls to ward off zombies."

Billy looked into the dark water knowing but not knowing how he knew. "It was the final battle for the possession of the Cubit," he said. "Samaal was trying to protect it; he was trying to keep it out of human hands. And he must have fled from Tulum using the sea as an escape."

"Cubit?" Sebastian said. "That what you guys were looking for in the underwater cave?" He took their silence as confirmation. "Ain't no such thing."

"So you've heard of it?" Cooper asked.

It was Sebastian's turn to remain silent.

Billy said, "That's okay. You don't have to believe."

"Tell them a different story," John suggested. "One that's true. One that will help them survive. Tell them what you know of Jean Lafitte." John moved over to the edge of the boat next to Sebastian, swung his legs over the water, and gave his friend a big squashing grip on the left shoulder. "Sebastian was just a little kid in these parts when the Nazis came looking for Lafitte and his treasure. You're interested in the oral tradition aren't you Billy?"

"Yes. Very." Billy understood what John inferred. As a future Daykeeper, Billy would be spending a lot of time listening to first-hand accounts of historical experiences. "Go ahead."

He was hard to follow at times, particularly since the farther back in time (and memory) Sebastian went, the more Scottish his accent became. It was almost as if he was reverting back to his childhood days. He cried and cursed and yelled out loud, which made all of them cringe since the scream was loud enough to have been heard onshore. He explained.

Obsessed with antiquities, the Nazis arrived in Puerto Morelos in 1939, looking for the legend of Lafitte's treasure. What they hadn't expected to find was Lafitte, himself. This discovery, of course, put a whole new spin on their collective curiosity and, like Nazis were prone to do back then, they started accusing the local fishing community of hiding the immortal and his secrets from them. They'd decided to make an example out of the uncooperative natives; the first victim had been Sebastian's mother.

Sebastian recounted in child-like detail, what he remembered of that day. He'd only been five at the time so the horror of the event had rooted so harshly that his only memories of his mother were those that included her being whipped while swinging from a chechen negro tree, the black sap oozing down her lashed and opened skin, blistering it further, making it bubble; he recounted how he'd knelt in front of her, praying for his father's return from the sea; he remembered his mother's glistening eyes, staring vacantly at nothing when, finally, her body had given up the fight.

They'd never captured Lafitte in Puerto Morelos, he explained, but instead, had chased him from the Yucatán, through the Gulf and all the way to Texas. Soon afterward, Germany had invaded Poland, starting the Second World War.

When Sebastian finished, Billy said, "You do know that they must have taken the Cubit."

Sebastian just stared at the water.

"I'm sorry for your pain," Billy continued. "If it's any account, the Cubit has been recovered. What we're here to do tonight is make sure it never gets into the hands of such Evil again."

"What if I had actually done it?" Sebastian whispered. He looked at Billy, the boat's running light adding a green hue to the left side of his face, his eyes saddened and deeply hollow from almost eight decades of pent up sorrow. "While I knelt there watchin' my mother slowly die, I held my father's dagger secretly in my hand. I was gonna end her suffering. But that SS Nazi bastard had gotten in the way. He'd stooped down and had looked me right in the eyes and I could see the horrible man that he really was. All I had to do was thrust quickly forward and the magic of the dagger would have ended the war before it ever started. If I had only killed him, he'd of never followed Lafitte and would have never returned to Germany with the Cubit. If only…"

"You can't change the past," Billy offered, patting Sebastian's trembling hand. "And you can't blame yourself for the future. What is… is. All we can do is go forward." Billy's next action was his immediate response to intuition. He reached up and under his T-shirt, drew the Creation of the End dagger from its sheath, and held it tightly so that it would not fall into the water. "Is this it?" he asked Sebastian. "Is this the dagger?"

Sebastian's tears told him the answer.

Such a coincidence would have had Billy's mind swimming for days back when coincidence really mattered to him. That the dagger he now possessed had, at one time, been the property of Sebastian's father, was far from mere happenstance; it had changed hands from Sebastian's father to Lafitte and Lafitte had buried it in the sands of Mustang Island where Billy had recovered it.

A complete circle—earth-bound objects marking time's passage but never really becoming a part of such linear ideology.

Nothing ever dies.

Perhaps that three-word blink of wisdom applied to much more than the flesh of men and dolphins and birds, Billy thought. Perhaps even the inanimate was never truly inanimate. Daggers and boxes and books—all a part of this *Living Planet* that was always long with surprises.

He sat on the foredeck looking up at the stars as he'd been doing the entire night. The solstice officially started at 6:04 a.m. and he guessed that another thirty minutes remained before they would depart. The plan was to scuba from here to the shore so that they would arrive at El Castillo a good half hour ahead of the event. John had figured the whole thing out using Marine savvy to stage the surprise. If they could at least get the jump on Lafitte, perhaps snatching the Book and key away from him, then all bargaining would be in their favor. It really depended on how much Mu'bä muscle or paramilitary force Lafitte had decided to bring with him. It depended on how much of his real-life arrogance and, therefore, self-confidence remained. A pompous attitude would be to their advantage.

The first slivers of twilight snatched an inch of the night sky above the ocean's horizon and turned it dark blue. Behind him, John and Cooper appeared from the cabin below. Sebastian followed a moment later. Billy sat up and Cooper joined him while John and Sebastian prepared the scuba gear.

"You ready for this?" Cooper asked him.

"As I'll ever be." He draped one arm around her. "You know you don't have to go. It'll be safer out here with Sebastian."

Cooper grabbed his hand and massaged the starry scar in its palm. "You have the gift of foresight. What do you think I'm going to say to that?"

"Stick it up my ass?"

She grinned. "Well, maybe not in such flowery terms. Who knows? I might be the one that saves *your* life." She reached into her pocket then grabbed Billy's hand and brought it to her lap. "Here," she said. "The woman who sold it to me said it helps energize your nahual." She placed a necklace strung with tiny beads shaped like tiny animal heads into his hand. "Besides, you'll need something to hang your new amulet from."

"Nahual?" Billy asked.

"Your spirit animal. The one that protects you. The one you were born with."

"And which one might that be?"

She rubbed a couple of the beads between her fingers. "I'm only guessing but for you, I suspect…"

"A dolphin?"

"Is that what you think?"

Billy nodded, once.

"Then a dolphin it must be." She took the string of beads and placed it around his neck. "May the force be with you."

Billy's eyebrows rose with surprise.

"Yeah. I know it sounds corny but it's about the only thing I could think of." And then she kissed him for the first time, her lips connecting with his for only a moment, as if she did not want any passion to interfere with the importance of their situation. When she pulled back, Billy stared into her eyes, searching for some truth about her future, prodding for answers about her safety that were not forthcoming. Realizing that this chance for their spiritual bonding might be their last, he pulled her close and kissed her deeply, exchanging a hidden energy that only his soul with hers could provide.

"We're ready," John said.

When he released her, he immediately turned and looked at the shoreline. Twilight had begun its crawl across the land, dimly illuminating the seaside structures. El Castillo's pyramidal outline remained prominent, but it was the building to the right of it that drew Billy's attention. Maybe it was the way the nighttime spotlights were directed at it, but the small building sitting on a hill all by itself like a beacon to the sea, glowed a greenish-blue aura. Cooper and John confirmed the anomaly and Sebastian reminded all of them that this might have been what Samaal had seen while escaping from Tulum.

"Oh my God," Billy suddenly said. He jumped up and ran to his backpack where he'd kept his notebook. "It is. That's it!" All of them gathered around him as he flipped through the pages where he'd recreated the Book of the Djed. "Remember this?" he asked John, showing him the sketches that he'd made.

"Yeah. The fourth location. El Castillo."

"No," Billy said. "This here." He lifted the notebook and pointed it toward the shoreline. The haggard sketch and the view of the ruins matched almost precisely. "It's not in the pyramid," Billy said. "The fourth location is in that building." He pointed at the sketch then at the same building glowing above the beach. "The one where Samaal must have kept the Cubit. The one that still has its residual spiritual aura."

"Temple of the Wind God," Sebastian clarified.

"If you're right," Cooper added, "then Lafitte will be looking in the wrong place."

John smiled. "Advantage, good guys," he said and started gearing up. "Come on. Winter's almost here."

666
2008

Evan didn't trust cubits and he never would. How could the dead be trusted? All you had to do was consider Richard Manson. He was a multi-billionaire because he couldn't be trusted. But dealing with just one power-tripping cubit was one thing; Manson, at least, had some appeal to him, some savvy, some moxie, some real cojones. But these others… especially Lafitte and his goonball helpers Manuel and Strykor. He couldn't wait until Manson gave him the word.

Under the early twilight, his iPhone screen illuminated one side of his face as he texted a reply to Manson who was incessantly demanding updates. It had been easy for Evan to ignore his boss's micromanagement tendencies while in the jungle—he'd legitimately used the "I'm losing your signal" excuse just about every time he'd had the chance—but here, standing atop the tallest structure for dozens of miles, he could not.

His stomach ached. He hadn't eaten a decently prepared meal in days. The crap these cubits consumed was too close to rotten for him to stand so he'd had to fend for himself, often snatching quick bites from roadside stands as the "strike force" (Lafitte's terminology) moved quickly from location to location. If it wasn't for the BETH pills that he popped at a rate that was thrice the recommendation, his body would have certainly retaliated in more extreme ways than simple stomach cramps.

He typed "Not here yet" on the iPhone and the response was almost immediate.

Hes got 2 B there. Time is wasting.

"Yeah. Yeah." Evan whispered to the phone.

"What-th that?" the Strykor cubit asked. It and the Manuel cubit stood too close to him on the top platform of El Castillo.

"Fuck off," Evan growled. "And pay attention. They should be here any minute."

"Evan!" It was Lafitte's voice bellowing once again from inside the pyramid's chamber.

Evan reluctantly followed the voice into the chamber for the third time in ten minutes. This second-hand man shit wasn't all it was cracked up to be. "Lafitte," he said.

"Don't mock me piss ant. You haven't let the whores get passed you have you?"

Evan stifled a laugh. "You serious? How the hell are three people whose destination is this very chamber, gonna get passed three guards on the top of the tallest building that has absolutely no other access to it than a bunch of stone steps that provide no cover?"

"A dumbshit human like you is bound to make it happen. After all, you *did* lose their tail yesterday, did you not?" Lafitte stooped against the empty chamber's far wall, looking out a small rectangular opening, the Book of the Djed with the key sticking out of it held in one hand. He didn't wait for an answer. "Winter will be rising any minute. If he isn't here by then, Captain Teigas is going to make a filet out of you and feed it to his men."

"He'll be here."

"Goddammit! Get out of my face."

Evan returned to the top of the pyramid and looked out across the shadowy ruins. Beyond the city's sixteen-foot-high perimeter stone wall patrolled the Los Zetas. Several were stationed at the two watchtowers. Lafitte had asked for their assistance and Captain Teigas had agreed on the condition that Cooper would not be harmed and that she would be his after all was said and done.

Behind Evan, offshore, a channel of blue cut by the ancients slashed the dark reef that was becoming increasingly visible below the water. A boat sat at the distant horizon and as daybreak continued its ascent, the boat's comforting shadow set against a cobalt blue background made the insanity of his current company even more detestable. Thankfully, he'd have to suffer them for just a few minutes longer.

Unknown to Lafitte and his "strike force," the harbinger of their demise already awaited its final orders. It hunkered in the shadows just inside the doorway of the building next to them: in the Temple of the Descending God. Manson had ordered Evan to release Billy's cubit from the well of the Caracol and Evan had stuck it in the trunk of the stolen Cavalier. For Evan, the funniest part about it all was the idea that Lafitte had been driving around for the past six days, acting the part of the big honcho, obsessed with the idea that he would soon rule the world, thinking that after two hundred years his search for immortality was only days from reality, while all along, in the trunk, smoldered the rotten stink of the freshly born dead, a scent that his own inhuman cubited senses had never detected. No one had ever thought of looking in the trunk… why would they? Once they'd arrived at Tulum, Evan had simply let it out. Now, all it had to do was follow its own destiny. All it had to do was compete the circle, kill the Daykeeper and take his place in the world. The part about ripping Lafitte to shreds was just an added bonus, offered as an incentive by the true ruler of the world, by the cubited monster that had manipulated everything just to see fate turn in his favor.

Evan smiled as his phone rang. It was Manson. Unfortunately, Evan had no new information to calm his boss's increasing rage.

Billy surfaced just north of his intended destination. He was alone. The scuba tank weighted him uncomfortably as he removed his flippers and crawled from the surf to the jungle perimeter, scuttling quickly to avoid detection. He sat in the tall, wet grass, the tank behind him, and slipped it off his shoulders. Sporadic breaths seemed impossible to control but he took a moment to concentrate, to breathe, to absorb the good air and expel the bad.

Before dropping into the water, Sebastian had offered him a handgun but Billy had refused. Billy had told him that guns would not help him fulfill his duties. He had the dagger, he'd said. He had himself. He had fate on his side. Sebastian had simply grunted, his intimate personal knowledge of Nazi psychosis evident in that single, brash response. Now sitting below a cliff of limestone, alone and uncertain of his own faith, Billy wondered if he should have accepted it. A Creation Dagger could do a world of damage at close range but a gun…he might not be able to kill them with it but he certainly could have backed them off.

His breathing exercise was subsided by the rising twilight. He had less than twenty minutes, tops. Cooper and John had agreed to run the distraction, acting as if the true fourth location *was* the pyramid. They were to obtain the Book and the key and bring them to Billy in the Temple of the Wind God before the winter solstice arrived. How they would attain this goal was unknown but John and Cooper had both sworn on their lives that Billy would have what he needed in time.

Billy put on his Keds and took off up a path carved into the cliff, keeping low, using the sparse, waist-high grass as camouflage until he reached a broken section of limestone wall, a remnant of one of the city's buildings that had been decimated long ago. To his left, the center of the ruins appeared as scattered dark outlines except for the Castillo which remained illuminated by the spotlights around it. Closer to him,

and sitting all by itself, was the Temple of the Wind God. It still pulsed
with an aura that continued to fade as daybreak neared. To his right,
three shadowed outlines of paramilitary guards sat inside the defense
wall watchtower; a match was lit and a cigarette was shared as the men
talked. Billy scanned the landscape one more time before running quickly
through the fading darkness.

The hill on which the temple sat was made of solid, uneven shelves
of limestone and as Billy shuffled up its short slope, he slipped twice,
his rubber-soled Keds finding no traction against the early morning
ocean spray moisture. Pebbles skittered down the limestone shelving and
Billy fell flat on his stomach, the dagger strapped to his chest pressing
uncomfortably into his flesh. He remained motionless for a full minute,
listening for the guards, before continuing across the limestone and into
the small temple structure.

It was cramped and dark inside, the entire chamber no more than
twenty feet squared. A single window pointed east, in the precise location
where the sun would soon rise. Billy guessed that the temple had been
built for that very purpose: to mark and honor the beginning of winter.
Below the window was the dark outline of a stone pedestal into which
must have been etched the markings associated with the Cubit's throne
though he could not see them.

He stood, staring out the small window, the invisible ocean mist
filling his deep breaths with salty sea, the sun creeping higher to where
Sebastian's boat waited, wondering what he was supposed to do next.
Time was running out.

Rocks skittered outside and Billy quickly turned around. "John," he
whispered. "Hurry. The sun is almost at the horizon."

But it wasn't John. And it wasn't a soldier. And it wasn't anything
that Billy had expected. He could smell it before it entered the chamber.

"Hi," Billy's cubit slurred.

Evan was never going to allow Lafitte to take the Djed. His orders
were to get the amulet and bring it back with him to Mérida. When
Billy's cubit took off in the direction of the Temple of the Wind God,
Evan reacted. He'd already seen John and Cooper surface in scuba gear

along the public beach just to the right of the Castillo. He'd watched them
dodge in and out of the thin tree line just below the pyramid. With every
move they'd made, Evan had distracted the Manuel and Strykor cubits so
that they would not see what Evan was allowing to happen. When the two
intruders started up the pyramid steps, Evan smiled. He would now have
self-gratification. It was time for a little payback.

He casually walked around to the back side of the Castillo platform
where the two cubits stood looking at the brightening horizon. Evan
pointed. "What's that? Down there!" Both cubits leaned forward and with
two swift kicks, Evan sent both of them off the platform and down the
jagged east face of El Castillo. Both bodies tore into scattered chunks as
they continued down the ocean cliff wall before splashing as pieces into
the white foam surf. He then ran into the Castillo chamber where Lafitte
paced back and forth and told him that they were coming up the face of
the pyramid.

"Something ain't right," John told Cooper. "This is too easy."

"Maybe you're just too good," Cooper responded, following him up
the steps of the pyramid. "Wait! Did you hear that?"

"Sounded like something falling off the top of this thing." He didn't
stop his ascent. "Come on. We don't have much time."

Billy had not accepted Sebastian's offer of a handgun but Cooper
had eagerly taken it. She now held the 9mm Beretta in front of her, a
loaded clip of ten shots ready for action. John had told her that bullets
couldn't kill these things but the handgun made her feel safe nonetheless.
She kept an eye on their flanks as John concentrated on their ascent. In the
dark twilight, many soldiers paced aimlessly beyond the perimeter wall,
but none paid them, or anything else inside the ruins, any attention.

At the top of the pyramid, they stepped carefully to the rear of the
platform where Cooper saw Sebastian's boat set against the rising sun,
a postcard perfect picture of man and sea combined. Down below, she
saw what looked like human body parts bouncing against the watery
cliff face. She was pretty certain that one piece, a head, looked a lot like
the Mexican that had tried to rape her. "Poonta that," she said with a
hushed breath that John, with hand signals, told her to quiet. She plucked

Manuel's earlobe from her pocket and threw it at the floating, thrashing body parts. The Wayeb earring twinkled dim reflections before joining Manuel's head under the sea.

John led her back around to the front of the pyramid's chamber and, together, they walked inside. Cooper had the Beretta clenched between both hands in her best police woman pose and when she saw Lafitte, she aimed the pistol at his head. Lafitte was standing on a stone pedestal that, in shape and size, looked a lot like one of the Cubit's thrones except that there were no markings on any side of it. A rectangular window was above the pedestal and Lafitte's arm rested inside its recess. He held the Book of the Djed in one hand. To the left of him, standing in the shadows, was the real human who called himself Evan.

"I have been waiting almost two centuries for this day," Lafitte said. "It has been my life's pursuit."

"But you're dead," John said.

"It's all a matter of perspective, or haven't either of figured that part out yet?"

Cooper stepped forward, the gun heavy.

"I'll throw it into the surf," Lafitte warned, the Book inching closer to the window opening.

"Where's Billy?" Evan asked.

"He's right outside," John lied, thumbing at the doorway behind him.

"Bring him in or the Book is gone," Lafitte demanded.

John reached over and gently pushed Cooper's gun-clenching arms down. "Let's be reasonable here," he said. "We only have a few minutes remaining and then no one will have a Djed with which to do anything."

"Evan," Lafitte said. "Go get our boy." He stepped down from the window and set the Book on the pedestal. The light in the window continued to brighten. "Hurry up!" he yelled.

Evan left, then reappeared moments later. "He's not here," he said. "They lied."

Suddenly, John bolted forward as Lafitte grabbed the Book and tried to throw it through the window. John's shoulder connected with Lafitte's rib cage and the Book careened off the edge of the window, flipped across the pedestal, opened up enough for the key to flutter free, and landed on the floor, face down. Though Lafitte's cubit was half John's size its strength was at least double. It pushed John to the floor and grabbed the

Book as Cooper aimed the pistol at its head. In one quick snap of the wrist, Lafitte threw the Book at Cooper, knocking the gun from her grip. Cooper grabbed the Book and yelled, "I got it!"

Lafitte backed up and stepped on the pedestal. "And I've got the key," he said, raising the page from the Book toward the window. "Now let's try this one more time. Where the fuck is Bill—"

Four quick claps of gunfire erupted from behind them. Evan held Cooper's gun in both hands. The first bullet missed, but the next three struck Lafitte in the face, piercing both cheeks and his forehead. Lafitte toppled from the pedestal and his head cracked against the stone floor.

"Hurry," Evan urged. "Time's almost up."

Billy had nowhere to run. His cubit cornered him. He drew the dagger from its sheath and held it defensively in front of him.

"Gooood," his cubit moaned, its eyes blazing crimson with silver swirls twisting at their centers. "We need that."

"We don't need anything. You need to die."

"Come on, little brother. You've already seen what is about to happen." The cubit sounded nothing like him. The cubit sounded exactly the same as Pedro's cubit had sounded in the Caracol's well. "You give me the dagger and I rip you to pieces."

Billy blinked and so did the cubit, then he stepped up onto the pedestal, and the cubit stepped forward.

"You really don't think I'm going to let you stab me in the back of the head again, do you?"

"Again?" Billy asked.

"Dammit, boy. You sure don't learn easily?"

"Who are you?"

"I'm you, of course."

"I don't believe it."

"Doesn't much matter what the fuck you believe." The sun was moments from appearing above the horizon. The window behind Billy's head began to glow with the same crimson aura that now emitted from the dagger in his hand. "We'll raise the Djed together then I'm going to eat you...alive if possible...dead if necessary. Doesn't really matter. What matters is that you'll be gone, the prophecy will turn in my favor, and the world as you know it will come to a screeching halt in four years. That's what should be believed. That's what reality really is. Thanks to you… and me."

Evan ran in front of them as a dozen soldiers appeared through openings in the city's walls. "I don't trust him," Cooper whispered to John. "I don't care that he shot Lafitte. Just watch him." John nodded and followed Evan into the Temple of the Wind God. Captain Teigas shouted orders, demanding that his men not shoot and to remain at a distance from the temple.

Inside, two Billys stared at her. One held a glowing dagger; the other had glowing eyes. The small window behind them blazed in the same crimson color. "Hurry," Evan said. "Give him the Book."

Cooper walked quickly to the pedestal and gave Billy the Book and key page then stepped back to stand beside John who stood beside Evan.

"Go ahead Presser," Billy's cubit said. "Do your thing."

Billy fumbled with the Book in one hand and the key and dagger in the other. It was evident he hadn't the slightest idea what he was supposed to do.

"Just like Alax did in the Great Hall," Cooper offered.

Billy looked at her, at all of them, as crimson infiltrated the entire chamber. He set the Book of the Djed atop the stone pedestal and immediately, the star at its top edge lit up. Below the star, only the three-dimensional image of a Djed was etched into the stone; there were no daggers. Billy opened the Book to the center page and gasped. Cooper shuffled forward but remained two steps behind him. She had to see it. She had to know what God had written there since the last time she'd looked.

The three sixes and three nines had morphed into five of each number. The phoenix above the numbers was now drawn with fiery bold reds and oranges and yellows. Below the sixes and nines, a third symbol appeared at that very moment; as she stared at the parchment brown vacant space, the outline of a Djed was drawn there, the spiritual lead creating the outline, in one long stroke that took a full minute to complete. Billy held the key but he was unable to turn from the center page to reposition it in its proper place. Instead, he handed the key back to Cooper then grasped the Creation Dagger in his right hand, making sure the star in its haft and the one burned into his hand were properly aligned. He jammed the seven inch blade into the pedestal star at exactly the same moment the crimson red ball of the sun appeared in the small window. His teeth clenched so tightly that Cooper thought the incisors would snap in two. He seemed to want to scream but his jaw would not open. He stared straight ahead, his eyes glued to the crimson ball of solar divinity. And Cooper looked down.

The Djed that had been etched into the pedestal stone popped up and out. It didn't fall to the floor, but instead stuck to the stone surface as a ghostly, holographic image, and began crawling up the face in concert with the rising sun. Up the pedestal it rose, passed right through the implanted dagger and Billy's hand, and flopped on top of the pedestal. As the sun consumed the entire breadth of the window, the holographic Djed positioned itself over the drawing in the Book. The sun's red blaze combined with the Djed's green glow and morphed the hologram into a solid sacred amulet. Then, all at once, as the sun rose above the window opening and its spectral light diminished, all of the occupants within the temple rushed for the Djed amulet in a twisted heap of living and dead flesh. Evan punched Cooper and she fell backward, the key still grasped firmly in her hand. She watched as Billy grabbed the amulet, pulled the dagger from the stone and haphazardly slashed out. The blade sliced a thin, long incision into Evan's cheek, continued onward in a sweeping arc, and planted in the back of the neck of Billy's cubit. Billy released the dagger and his cubit fell to the floor, writhing and grasping at the back of its head, trying to pull the dagger out. It kicked and moaned and molted, its red eyes blinking out as it quickly turned to ash and bone. The dagger rolled from the desecrated mound and Evan snatched it. He still had Cooper's gun and he now waved both of them at John who stood just within his reach.

"It's over," he growled, blood gushing from the slash in his face. "You've done your duty for your Godless country. Give it to me now." He didn't wait for Billy's response as he planted the dagger into John's shoulder. "Don't think. Just do it. Do it now!"

At that moment, Lafitte appeared in the temple's doorway. The three bullet holes in its face oozed a red that was darker than rust. Flesh that had exploded outward from the bullets' impacts with cheeks and forehead flapped against its blazing crimson eyes as it tried to speak. Every word was followed by the whistle of escaping air through the torn cheek holes.

"Yhoo whooren't going to keep it fooor yhooself, Efoon."

Cooper had fallen to the left of the doorway and she kicked Lafitte's knees as John punched Evan in the face with his elbow. Evan flailed backward, his nose busted, and the gun fired, nipping Billy's earlobe. In the same motion, John pulled the dagger from his shoulder and flicked it at Lafitte but missed the falling body. The dagger fell to Cooper's side and she used it to stab Lafitte in the leg.

Suddenly, outside, automatic gunfire erupted all around them. John grabbed Billy who grabbed the Book and both of them swept Cooper from the floor, jumped over Lafitte's body and ran out of the temple. Los Zeta soldiers were firing at something that was returning their gunfire to the right. Down the slippery limestone shelf all three fled. The soldiers saw them and repositioned their guns. Chips of limestone erupted at their feet. When the triumvirate got to the bottom of the temple hill, they saw Sebastian who was crouched behind the chunk of wall that Billy had used for cover on his way into the ruins. Sebastian fired a quick blast from his automatic and two soldiers fell from their positions.

"Come on, dammit!" Sebastian yelled. "You Nazi bastards ain't gonna kill her this time."

Cooper took the lead, running onto the sandy beachhead where Sebastian had anchored his boat just offshore. She rolled the key and stuck it under her shirt then dove into the water with the dagger in one hand. She waded there, watching as bullets erupted in multiple sand explosions all around Billy who fell; John scooped him up and continued running toward the water, the blood from the dagger strike to his shoulder smearing Billy's face which he closely coddled. Several soldiers appeared on the knoll and Sebastian took out two of them before diving into the water to help John with Billy's limp body.

Cooper pulled herself up onto the boat then helped John as he wrestled with Billy's body in the water. Together, they rolled Billy onto the boat's rear platform where Cooper saw three blood spots from the bullets in his chest. As soon as Sebastian was aboard, he turned the boat toward the channel in the reef and throttled forward. Behind them, Captain Teigas stood on the beach, firing his gun angrily in rapid succession over his head.

Richard Manson stood in his fortieth-story office looking out the window but not seeing anything except Evan who lay sprawled on the floor in front of him. His vision was partially blocked by the pieces of flesh that flapped around his eyes.

"You failed, Evan," he said trying not to whistle but unable to control the results of Evan's gunshots to his face. Evan pleaded for his life but Manson, through the eyes of Lafitte, was having none of it. He yanked the gun from Evan's grasp and placed the barrel against the forehead of the human who used to be his assistant. "Your footage of our jump last week absolutely sucked and Jobs hated it," he added, then emptied the clip into Evan's brain.

A minute later, Captain Teigas appeared in the temple doorway. Manson watched as Teigas walked forward, almost robotically, and stepped around the sunshine that infiltrated the room through the small window. Teigas lifted his automatic weapon and hesitated for a moment before pulling the trigger.

Manson's vision of the temple room vanished. In his hand was an iPhone that presented a digital slider which he now turned off. His anger was immense, the Djed was gone, but he still had alternatives. He always had alternatives.

And four more years.

He dropped the iPhone onto his desk and looked down upon the people who littered the Phoenix Tower plaza below.

"Soon," he said.

Below deck, Billy woke to the friendly smiles of three friends. He immediately placed his hand on his chest and Cooper grabbed it, patting the knuckles. "Blood," he said.

He tried to sit up but was unable without the help of John. "We thought we lost you but we forgot," Cooper said.

"Forgot?" Billy whispered. She patted his chest and Billy grabbed her hand. At that moment he felt the beads around his neck and the weight of the Djed amulet hanging from the necklace. He lifted his shirt and saw three scars where the bullets had entered his body. The Djed amulet hung centered between them.

"Immortal," John's deep voice verified. "The bullets just squirted right out."

"The Book," Billy said. "And the key and the dagger?"

"Right here," John offered. He pointed to the foot of the bed.

Billy leaned forward, grimacing. The Book was intact as was the key page. The seawater had not affected either.

He picked up the key page and examined it; he'd always assumed it was necessary for raising the Djed but it had not been. The small glyph of a Creation Dagger and the glyph of the Wayeb had not changed since the day he first saw them sticking out of Albert Stine's briefcase. The key's purpose, he thought, was for something else yet to be discovered.

He opened the Book to the place where the key had been removed and stuck the page against the bound serrated edge. It quickly stitched itself together. He then flipped the pages backward to the center spread to examine the three symbols now drawn there: the colorful bird of fire at the top of the page, the new Djed addition in the middle of the page, and the bold and heavy imprints of sixes and nines between them.

"There's five of each now," Cooper said. "What does it mean?"

"Locate a Mayan date converter and I think we'll find out."

Finally, the Daykeeper opened the Book to its second half and stared with his friends at the story of the fourth creation.

The Creation of the Antichrist.

0-TIME: PUSH*, THE 2012 TRILOGY III
AVAILABLE DECEMBER 21, 2010
VISIT: WWW.0-TIME.COM